RONAH

Book One of the Lissae Series

R. Lennard

Ronah

First published in 2018 by R. Lennard

Second edition published in 2019 by R. Lennard

Copyright © Rebecca Lennard, 2018

Cover Design © Vanesa Garkova, 2019

Printed and bound by Blurb, Inc, San Francisco, USA

Edited by Penmanship Editing

www.PenmanshipEditing.com

Published by Rebecca Lennard

www.lissae.com

 A catalogue record for this book is available from the National Library of Australia

To Danny, for helping make Shari come to life,
and for endless hours discussing Lissae.

CONTENTS

PROLOGUE

Summer 4045

It all started with a trip to the museum and a charging Minotaur.

Shari Dawn was three and a half years old when her dad had left Ronah to go on a rare visit to his family on one of the other Shifting Islands. On a balmy summer day, her mum had given into her incessant pleading and taken her to the museum. The big, white stone building had intrigued Shari for as long as she could remember. She'd always felt a pull to it, but it hadn't been until that afternoon that she'd been able to figure out why.

"Well met!" Anna Warfield, the museum curator, called out as Shari and her mum, Arilla, slipped out of the heat and into the cool shade of the museum. Shari smiled and waved a chubby hand at the curator. Anna wandered over, bringing with her the scent of parchment, dust and something spicy that tickled Shari's nose and made her sneeze. "There are a few new things in the artefact room, Shari. I wonder if you can find them?"

Shari squirmed out of her mum's arms and started to toddle determinedly towards the artefact room, right at the back of the museum.

"Hold on, young lady!" her mum said, grabbing her hand and holding it tight.

Shari sighed but relinquished her freedom when Anna winked at her.

Walking through the spacious rooms filled with treasures and trinkets of times long gone, Arilla tried to dawdle in the Innarn room, where there were all sorts of displays of elemental magic from all over the Realms. Everyone knew that the elemental magic from Lissae was the best. It had to be, it had the best name – Innarn. Her mum didn't use Innarn, but her dad was an incredibly powerful Innarnian who could tap into the elements and wield Innarn.

Shari kept tugging on her mum's arm until she gave in and led her into a room that she just couldn't get enough of. Filled with clear crystal cases containing the ancient objects from all across the Realms, a sense of mystery intermingled with the polished stones, musty books and foreign idols. On the far side or the room, a set of double doors made of wood with an inlaid pattern of seven coloured arrows around a silver ring called to Shari as soon as she spied them.

"Don't wander far, Shari," her mum said.

Shari nodded and kept an eye on her mum, who wandered over to the displays on different books from around the Realms. Sneaking a look and seeing Arilla bent over the books, Shari skipped over to the doors long enough to lay a single, chubby hand on them.

In that instant, her life changed.

The doors flung apart, and falling backwards was the only thing that saved her. A massive bull-headed man stomped through the open doors, bellowing so loudly, the ancient artefacts rattled in their cases. With wide eyes, his huge, pounding steps carried him closer to Arilla, who frantically looked around, more concerned about spotting Shari than getting out of the Minotaur's way.

Shari did what any three-year-old would do when something scary happened. She screamed.

The Minotaur stopped and snorted, throwing a huge, muscled arm out as he turned, sending her mother flying, his hot breath sending clouds of steam into the air as he took in the toddler screaming at him.

When the big, bull-headed being charged at her, Shari screamed again and threw her hands into the air to fend him off. A glowing purple Innarn shield crackled like lightning as it sprang from her fingertips, covering the space in front of her.

The Minotaur bounced off the shield and slammed backwards into a glass case. He'd landed with a crunch, the object from the case destroyed beneath his bulk. Shari, her chubby three-year-old legs trembling, walked up to the giant being and beat her fists ineffectively on his chest as clouds of his breath danced over her head.

Dazed, he looked at his diminutive attacker from his prone position, eyebrows drawing together as he struggled to make sense of this tiny being hammering on his chest.

"You go now," Shari told him fiercely. His dark eyes peered down at her as she scowled up at him. "Now!" she demanded, stamping her tiny foot on the ground.

Rising on shaking legs, he stumbled back through the double doors, glancing over his shoulder at the tiny warrior who glared fiercely at him before the doors shut behind his hulking form.

Arilla's eyes fluttered open as the door clicked closed, and she staggered to her feet, rushing to wrap Shari up in the tightest hug, saying her daughter's name over and over again into Shari's hair.

Shari had a feeling it would be a long time before they could revisit the museum.

"What happened?" Anna called as she came to a shuddering halt in the gateway of the room.

"There was a Minotaur," Arilla said. "It charged at me, I went flying, and when I woke up…"

"Shari?" Anna's hand fluttered up against her throat, and Shari poked her head out of her mum's hair. "Oh, child. What happened?"

The doors behind Shari and Arilla opened, and a small cloaked figure poked a hooded head through. It seemed to pass a message on to Anna, despite its face being hidden beneath the hood.

"Oh, thank goodness. Thank you," Anna said. "Maybe it's time to go home now, Arilla. You take Shari and stay safe, ok?"

"Yes… yes. Thanks, Anna." Distracted, Arilla got to her feet, cradling Shari close to her, trembling all the way home.

Calem Dawn arrived home the next afternoon, his wings beating a gentle down-draft as he landed in the garden, arms outstretched to gather Shari and Arilla into a warm hug. He smelled of sea air and Innarn. One arm around each of them, he led them inside, his wings disappearing as he sunk into a kitchen chair.

After a blissful snack of rutenberry cookies, her mum sent Shari outside to play in the garden. Sitting on the cool grass under the shade cast from their bereni tree home and idly turning the soil over with a tiny shovel, Shari could hear the fear in her mum's voice as she told her dad, Calem, about the charging Minotaur who disappeared. Calem tried to reassure Arilla, reminding her of the beings who guarded the gateways into Lissae.

Who would guard a gateway? That'd be boring, Shari thought, shaking her head.

'*The Ducibus guard my gateways,*' a voice that definitely was not her own spoke inside Shari's mind.

Dropping the shovel that she'd been holding, Shari frowned. "Who're you?" she demanded.

'*Hush, child. Use your mind to talk to me,*' the voice admonished gently.

'*Fine,*' Shari grumped in the way only a three-year-old can. '*Who are you, mind voice?*'

'*I am Lissae.*'

Shari's eyebrows shot up. '*You're a Realm!*'

'*No, dear–heart. I'm the Realm.*'

'*But... but...*' Shari's thoughts stuttered, and she dug her fingers into the soil, trying to hold tight to the voice in her head.

'*And you, you are my little Altoriae,*' Lissae crooned to her.

'*What's that?*'

'*Altoriae? It is a name for my fiercest protector. She is the one who stops the beings who want to take me over. The one who makes sure that all of those who call me home are safe.*'

Mind flicking back to the museum, her mother's fallen form, and the hot, harsh breaths of the Minotaur, Shari nodded resolutely. '*I want to do that.*'

'*You agree, little one? You will be my protector? It is hard work,*' Lissae cautioned.

'*I don't want people to get hurt,*' Shari sent back, her face a fierce scowl.

'You can't tell anyone, little Altoriae, or they will be in danger. There is a curse, a test, which you must take to prove that you are the next Altoriae.' Images followed the words, of bad things happening to the people who had known about past Altoriaes before they had been announced.

Shari shivered. The images were blurry, but the feelings in them scared her, feelings of pain, fear and apologies sent but never received.

Her resolution wavered for a moment, but she peered over her shoulder to see her mum smiling at her from the window. What if someone else lost their mum because she said no? What would she do without a mum to give her hugs after a scary day?

'I'm good at keeping secrets,' Shari said, picking her shovel back up and stabbing it into the ground determinedly. Realising that she might have hurt her new friend, she hastily pulled the shovel out and tossed it aside, gently patting the earth smooth.

The Realm rumbled, and Shari felt as if she was sitting by the fire under a blanket on a cold night. Warm light surrounded her, making her tingle pleasantly as it sank into her skin.

'My Altoriae,' Lissae sighed, and Shari felt the presence withdraw from her mind.

CHAPTER ONE

Winter 4047

Shari's dreams changed after her talk with Lissae. They became more about learning how to shield so she wouldn't be discovered, and how to defend herself from eminent attacks on both her person and her Realm. Summer gave way to winter, and her night time training was done in such a way that Shari herself remained mostly unaware of what was going on, until the day she stepped into the colourful Town Square, eager to play with some of the other five-year-olds.

One of the adults had conjured a ball of water, and the kids were laughing and shrieking as they threw it to each other. One of the kids with fiery red hair threw it to Shari so she could join in the game, and the ball vanished.

"Boo!" the kids called, jeering at her as one broke away from the crowd and stomped over to glare at Shari.

"How'd you do that?" the girl in the flowery dress asked.

'Her name is Anika Thorne,' Lissae supplied.

7

"I don't know." Shari shrugged.

"Give it back!" Anika demanded, stamping her foot.

A tall man with dark hair and Anika's eyes strolled over to see what had upset his daughter. His face seemed to freeze slightly when he looked at Arilla, and his smile appeared decidedly strained when he looked down and saw Shari.

"What's the matter, Anika?" he asked.

"Daddy, she has the ball! She won't give it back!" Anika's lower lip stuck out and wobbled, and she plopped to the ground, fingers skittering over the pavers until she found a rock and started passing it from one hand to the other.

Shari tilted her head. Surely five had to be too old for the tantrum Anika was considering?

"I'll make another one," he said. Glancing at Shari, he added, "Maybe it would be best if you played with something else?"

"Yeah," Anika taunted as she got back on her feet, "like this!"

The rock from her hands zoomed towards Shari, who reached out and plucked it from the air before it could connect with her face. Some of the kids Anika had been playing with fell silent as they realised that something terrible had happened. The adults around her seemed to stop for a moment, and Shari clenched her fist around the rock, the sharp edges cutting into her palm.

As blood dripped down her fingers, the adults sprung into action, and Anika's father bent to scold the scowling girl. Arilla scooped Shari up and held her tight. Sniffling, Shari buried her head in Arilla's hair as Anika's father grabbed his daughter's hand and marched her away.

Twisting her head, Anika glared at Shari over her shoulder and stuck her tongue out. The other kids were hauled away as well, and Shari let the tears she'd been holding in drip down her nose and into her mum's hair as Arilla whisked her away to safety.

That night, in her bed, Shari sat with her head resting on her bent knees, the blankets hiding her from sight as she examined her injured hand.

'*Why are kids so mean?*' she whispered to Lissae.

'*Because they know you are different, and they are scared of different,*' Lissae answered.

'*Don't they know I want to protect them?*' Shari's throat felt thick with unshed tears, and she wiped a sniffle away.

'*No, they don't. And they can't, not just yet.*'

'*How can I make them like me?*'

'*Be the best you that you can be. My people will revere you one day, fawning over you and lauding your deeds to all who will listen.*'

'*I don't want that,*' Shari scoffed and sniffled. '*I want friends.*'

'*I will be your friend, Shari Dawn,*' Lissae said.

'*No one else wants to be,*' Shari sent, bitterness seeping into her heart.

A complete silence settled in her mind, and Shari rubbed at her tired eyes, trying not to let the tears flow when Lissae didn't answer for an age.

'*Shari, I have a new friend for you. One you've known your whole life. You've walked on her soil and sleep on the bed she made just for you. Shari, meet Ronah,*' Lissae sent.

'*Oh. Oh, well met, Shari! I'm Ronah! You might know me by looking out your window,*' a new cheery voice in her mind said.

Scrambling upright, Shari rubbed her eyes again, tears and sleep making way for amazement. "Ronah?" Ronah was the Island she lived on. Could she talk too?

'*Look outside!*' the new voice giggled in her mind, and Shari felt like her insides were filled with happy bubbles. Laughing with delight, she kicked free of her blankets and peered out her window.

The flowers that her mother so carefully tended had moved, and now spelled *well met*, their petals glowing in the lights of the two moons.

Shari laughed and clapped her hands. In the back of her mind, she felt a pleased rumble from Lissae as she chatted to the Island she'd known her whole life.

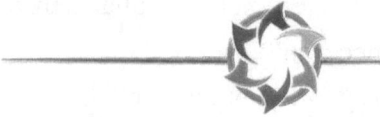

When Shari woke up the next morning, she found that she had a greater appreciation for all sorts of things. As she took her shower, Ronah whispered in her mind about the hot springs that the hot taps on the Island were connected to, and the way the water from the salty oceans became drinkable through all sorts of special filters to make it nice and clean as Ronah moved through the waves towards their next destination.

Sitting down at the table, Shari watched as her mum came in through the back door, the basket on her hip filled with yellow tomatoes, soola – the horrid green leafy thing that Shari kept practising her vanishing on – and the blue shelled eggs from their neighbours' chickens. Her dad set up the pan for the eggs, and as he flicked out a hand, a tiny flame launching from his fingertips, he heated up the flat crystal disc on the cooker so her mum could make scrambled eggs while he cut up the vegetables.

The Dawn's friendly kitchen acted as a focal point in their home. Bright and cheerful, the rose-coloured wood grain walls of their bereni tree home brightened the room. The counter, table, and cupboards were one seamlessly flowing part of the tree. Even the cold storage and oven were panelled in the same reddish wood. The bright-yellow kitchen chairs stood out against all the red. Matching yellow curtains were lying limp from the lack of breeze against glassless windows. Paintings of clouded skies sat alongside depictions of rainforests and waterfalls. A fruit bowl sat on the end of the counter, next to a cooling cake.

'The tomatoes came from a different Realm,' Ronah whispered in Shari's mind. 'They grow here quite well, and I make sure that they don't get too out of hand by limiting the number of seedlings that can live.'

'How can a plant get out of hand?' Shari asked.

'Plants can take over. And the other Shifting Islands and I have to be careful not to let too many foreign species spread to the other parts of Lissae.'

'Wait, there are other Shifting Islands?' Shari asked, sitting up straight and banging her knee on the table.

"Eager for breakfast, hey?" Her dad laughed. "You can have some more soola if you like?" Shari wrinkled her nose, watching her dad load her plate up with the dreaded green leaves before putting it on the table. When he turned back to the cooker, the leaves sparkled for just a moment, and Shari's eyes widened.

'Try now,' Ronah sent, and Shari felt the happy, bubbly feeling again.

Tentatively, Shari bit into her breakfast, her nose wrinkled in anticipation, but the flavour that exploded over her tongue resembled nothing like the ordinarily musty soola leaves. Instead, it tasted deep, rich and earthy, reminding her of time spent basking in the sun with fingers buried in the ground, making new things grow, the tang of sea air searing her nostrils. Shari chewed and sighed in bliss.

Her parents grinned at each other as they joined her at the table.

"We have a busy day at the tavern today, Shari," her dad said.

"Edward and Harmony Thorne are going to look after you while we're there, ok?" her mum added.

Shari's blissful expression turned into a scowl. She had been looking forward to a morning spent discovering how Ronah did things. She didn't want to be stuck away in someone else's house all day.

"Don't want to. I can stay here?" Shari asked hopefully.

Her parents laughed. "You're only little, Shari, you need to be with an adult."

Opening her mouth to tell them that she'd be safe with Lissae and Ronah to look after her, Shari felt the rumbled warning from Lissae in the back of her mind. Pouting, she shoved some more of the suddenly tasty soola into her mouth, chewing with a scowl on her face.

After washing up from breakfast, Shari and her mum set out down the street. In no mood to take in the sights, Shari had left home scowling, but with Ronah's constant commentary, it was hard to maintain her frown.

'Where's your favourite place to go?' Ronah asked.

'I like the museum, but I don't think I can go back,' Shari sent sadly. Her feet dragged, and Arilla laughed, scooping her up. Sighing mournfully, Shari explained to Ronah how they hadn't been back since the Minotaur.

"It won't be that bad!" Arilla said.

'It's hard having two conversations at once!' Shari grumbled at Ronah.

'You'll get used to it. Oh, you'll love visiting Edward and Harmony's house! I made it for them.'

'You make houses?' Shari asked the Island.

'Houses, buildings, furniture, gardens, crystals, clean water and anything else my residents need,' Ronah said proudly. Her tone reminded Shari of a bird puffing out its chest.

As Arilla entered a yard full of beautiful flowers and glossy green leaves, Shari twisted in her arms to see the rezem, a house of hardened earth, the wooden door covered in metalwork that mimicked the creeping vines in the garden. Shari scrambled out of her mum's arms as Arilla knocked.

The door opened, and Shari looked up – and up – into a broad, smiling face.

"Well met! You must be Shari!" the man grinned, and crouched down to look her in the eyes. "I'm Edward, and Harmony is around the back picking carrots." He poked his tongue out and wrinkled his nose, his eyes shining bright in his lined face.

"I like carrots." Shari giggled.

"I get carrot stew twice a week because Harmony just loves growing them. If you want, I'll share some of my stew with you, so long as you don't tell her," he whispered.

"Tell who?" a lady asked, coming around the side of the house.

"Tell you how beautiful you are!" Edward said, sweeping Harmony into his arms and jostling the basket on her hip. "Oops, the secret's out." He winked at Shari.

"Oh, you!" Harmony laughed. "Well met, Shari. She'll be fine with us, Arilla. You go on now; you have a lot of cooking to do for the meeting!"

"Are you sure?" Arilla wrung her hands, eyes fixed on Shari's face.

"I'm good, Mum. I'm going to learn how to grow carrots!" Shari said. Edward's groan was muffled by Harmony's laugh.

"Okay, Shari. Be good. I'll come and get you after the meeting." Arilla gathered Shari in her arms and squeezed her tight.

"Here Edward, you take this inside, and I'll show Shari the garden." Handing over the basket, Harmony smiled at Shari and beckoned her forward. "Make sure you don't eat them all!"

Grumbling under his breath, Edward winked at Shari and disappeared inside the house. Giggling, Shari skipped after Harmony, staring at the bright flowers braided into her white hair.

"I suppose you help out with your mum's garden all the time?" Harmony said as she rounded the corner of the house. Shari came to a stop behind Harmony, her jaw dropping.

Shari felt as if she had stepped into a storybook garden. There were plants everywhere. Flowers bloomed in a riot of colours, and glossy green leaves of all types where everywhere. Flat crystals were set into the ground as stepping stones, and Harmony led the way deeper into the garden. Entranced, Shari followed her past the nodding flowers and thick hedge to the vegetable patch that was just as crowded with plant life. There were raised vegetable beds just like at home, but they had creeping green vines growing on the walls that waved in Shari's direction.

Harmony stopped at one of the beds and beckoned Shari over. "This is where I grow my carrots. Every season, I change over which bed they're in and rotate all the crops. The toulana keeps pests and birds away, although it can get awfully friendly," she said as she patted one of the tendrils the green vine sent out towards her.

"How come you have so many plants?" Shari asked.

"Edward and I are both earth Innarnians. One of the best ways for us to relax is to use our Innarn to shape the earth and make things grow," Harmony said, bending to pick some more carrots.

"You must relax a lot." Shari looked around with wide eyes.

Laughing, Harmony put the carrots to the side and plucked something from the pocket of her apron. "Hold out your hand."

Obediently, Shari thrust her hand out. Harmony placed a seed on Shari's palm, allowing her a glimpse before covering it with her own hand. Shari shivered as a warm tingle filled her hand, a deep-green glow pulsing out from between their joined hands. She could feel something pushing at her hand, and Harmony moved away, allowing a blooming flower to spring towards the sky.

With eyes so wide Shari wondered if they'd fall out of her head, she took in the roots twisting on her palm, and reached out a finger to gently stroke along the stem of the plant.

Smiling indulgently, Harmony beckoned her over to one of the garden beds. "Here, put your plant in this spot."

Gently placing the roots in the hole, Shari took care to pat down the earth firmly. Standing up, she gave a leaf one last gentle pat, and giggled when a tiny vine snaked out and wrapped around Shari's wrist – a leaf patting her hand just as she'd done before.

After a guided tour through the rest of the garden, which neared overflowing with more plants than Shari could ever hope to name, they headed inside, following their noses to the kitchen where a delicious herby smell made Shari's mouth water.

"I started the stew, hope you don't mind," Edward said.

Harmony peered in the bubbling pot and tutted. "You forgot the carrots!"

A chubby, six-legged furry creature wandered in and plopped down beside Shari, leaning up against her and pushing her into the doorframe, its head almost at the same level as hers.

"Oh! Well met," Shari said, not sure what to do. Limpid eyes begged her for something, and she glanced at the adults who had their heads together, bent over the pot.

'He *wants a pat*,' Ronah offered.

Hesitantly, Shari stroked the top of the creature's head, and he grinned up at her, his long thin tongue lolling out of his mouth. More confident, she buried her hands in the soft fur and rubbed him behind the ears, causing a low rumbling noise from the creature.

"Ah, I see you've met Tibon. He's a sucker for pats." Edward knelt down and scratched the creature under the chin. A back leg thumped in delight.

"Tibon?" Shari said. "What is he?"

"He's a palon. They're descended from the wolves of old, but they've evolved to have six legs and a long tongue, perfect for scooping up insects."

Shari wrinkled her nose.

"That's their favourite meal!" Edward laughed. "He helps to keep the garden pest free, although that does mean more carrots for me. Come on, you can play with Tibon while Harmony puts the finishing touches on lunch!" Edward said, groaning as he got to his feet and straightened his back.

Racing the palon outside, Shari whiled away the time until Harmony called them in for lunch.

"Did you know that Tibon can catch? And when you throw a branch, he brings it back! He can stand on his back legs and dance with me and..." Shari chatted her way through lunch, pausing only when Edward scooped some more of the carrot stew onto her plate.

Afterwards, she could barely keep her eyes open, and Shari laid down next to Tibon and dozed on the lounge while Edward and Harmony puttered around the house.

As the sun set, Shari blinked open sleepy eyes as Edward started setting up a board on a small table across the room.

"What's that?" she asked.

"This is an old board game. It's called Sennet. Would you like to play?"

"'Kay," Shari said and gave the still sleeping Tibon a pat before toddling over to the table and clambering into a seat.

Arilla found Shari intently studying the board when she arrived, giving her a distracted wave as she contemplated her next move.

"She's quite a child, isn't she?" Harmony said fondly.

"She really is," Arilla sighed. "She's often out in the garden, but she doesn't seem to have any friends to play with. I don't want her to be lonely, but..."

"Don't worry, dear, I have an idea."

CHAPTER TWO

Spring 4047

Shari spent more and more time out in the garden, digging or gathering fallen leaves aimlessly while she and Lissae mentally chatted. Lissae would often explain to her how to do different things with her Innarn, and at night, while her body rested, Lissae gathered her mind and showed her how to put the theory into practice.

One day, when she had a bundle of leaves gathered in the folds of her skirt, Shari heard a small yipping sound behind her. Slowly, she turned around, arms and jaw dropping, the leaves scattering in the gentle breeze.

Her dad stood just outside the backdoor, a tiny black fuzzy creature cradled in his arms and a dopy grin on his face.

"What do you have?" Shari asked, barely daring to breathe.

"Well, he doesn't have a name yet," Calem said, gently jostling the creature, who yipped again, a long yellow tongue slipping out to lick Calem's face.

"Is it?"

"A palon? Yes," Calem said, settling the creature carefully on the ground.

"Oh." Shari dropped to her knees, and the tiny palon churned his little legs and sped towards Shari. Front paws on her knees, the palon licked Shari's face as she buried her fingers in his soft fur. His two back legs gave way, and his little butt plonked to the ground, even as one of his middle legs came up to scratch at a spot behind his floppy ear. Laughing as tears of delight slipped down her cheeks, Shari gathered the little palon up in her arms.

"How old is he?" Shari asked, tilting her head up so she didn't get a tongue in her eye.

"He's only a pup. About two months old," Calem said. "One of the Thorne clan's had a litter, and Harmony thought you might like someone to play with."

Shari held the little palon tight for a moment but gentled as soon as the creature squirmed. "I love him. Thank you."

"What do you think his name should be?"

Studying the little creature, his bright-green eyes twinkling up at him, Shari sifted through different names before nodding decisively. "Zoomer."

"Really?"

"He's fast, and his eyes are like the brightest leaves from the Earth God, Zoemer. Yes. Zoomer is a good name." Shari buried her face in the soft fur of Zoomer's tummy, and the palon wriggled before sticking his tongue in her ear. Squealing, she put Zoomer gently down, then started racing around the yard, the excited palon galloping after her, paws too big for his legs making him run comically.

Arilla stepped out and cuddled up to Calem's side, watching as Shari ran around like other kids her age, happily playing with her new pet.

When Arilla finally called Shari and Zoomer in for dinner, neither of them could keep their eyes open for very long. Still, Shari made sure she brushed Zoomer and got him ready to sleep, even making a little nest for him at the end of her bed.

For the first time since she'd spoken to Lissae in her yard, Shari let her mind rest, content with knowing when she woke up, she had a day full of play with Zoomer to look forward to.

Waking the next morning to a tongue bathing her face, Shari couldn't help but laugh.

"Are you hungry?" she giggled, slipping out of bed and heading towards to kitchen. Zoomer bounded along at her feet, occasionally jumping up to get a pat.

Laughing, she put out a plate of insects which Zoomer slurped up happily. Scoffing her breakfast while an indulgent Arilla watched, Shari got ready for the day in record time so she and Zoomer could head outside and play.

Shari and the palon spent a blissful half hour in the garden before her parents were ready for work. Arilla took the morning shift, but Calem needed her to bring in the produce from their garden, and Shari danced, giddy with the thought of getting to walk Zoomer and show him just how fantastic it was to live on Ronah.

Skipping along, she laughed as Zoomer yipped and pounced on falling leaves, and cooed when he sneezed into a flower. Calem grinned down at her, making sure to keep one eye on the delivery floating along behind him and the other on Shari.

After they dropped Arilla off at the tavern, Shari, Zoomer and Calem stopped at the Town Square to rest for a moment. Shari made palon eyes at Calem, and he laughed at her, before ducking back to the tavern to get Shari a rutenberry shake.

"That's my palon," a snide voice said as soon as Calem reached the edge of the square, safely out of earshot.

"No, he's mine." Gathering Zoomer up in her arms, Shari looked at Anika, her eyebrows drawn and lips pursed.

"My uncle promised I could have him!" Anika's foot stomped, and Zoomer opened one green eye to regard her sleepily before snuggling his head against Shari's chest.

"Don't palons choose their owners?" another girl, Elizabeth, asked, stepping up to Shari's shoulder.

"Well, he picked me first!" Anika fumed.

Looking down at the sleepy, content palon, Elizabeth shrugged. "Looks like he had second thoughts. Hey, can I pat him?"

Shari eyed Elizabeth for a moment but then nodded. "Sure. His name's Zoomer."

"Zoomer. What a stupid name," Anika snorted.

Elizabeth and Shari ignored her, and Shari's new friend stroked Zoomer's silky ear. "Ooohhh, he's so soft!" she cooed.

Annoyed at being ignored, Anika stomped once more and stormed off, no doubt to complain to someone.

"He really is," Shari said, eyeing Anika's retreating form. Before long, her gaze settled back on Zoomer, who opened his eyes and yawned, flashing his tiny flat teeth and curling yellow tongue. Both girls melted, and Shari felt tears in her eyes as Zoomer caught her gaze and solemnly put a paw on her chest.

"He loves you already," Elizabeth marvelled. "And I think Zoomer is a great name! Is he fast?"

"When he's not half asleep he is!" Shari grinned.

Calem came back, two tall drinks in his hand. He quietly offered one to Elizabeth, and she and Shari happily slurped their drinks and chatted about Zoomer, and what they thought school would be like next year, and how much fun it would be when spring finally came and the flowers burst into bloom.

Finally, Calem and Arilla swapped shifts, and Elizabeth reluctantly went home with her parents, promises to visit spilling from both girls as they parted.

Shari's afternoon with Zoomer was perfect. The sun shone brightly in the crisp blue sky, and she spent hours scooping up leaves in her yard to throw for Zoomer to pounce on, the laughter falling from her lips contagious to anyone who heard it.

As the sky darkened, Shari slipped inside with Zoomer on her heels. She slipped him morsels from her plate while her parents pretended not to notice. Getting ready for bed, she read Zoomer a story before sliding under the covers. Shari twined her fingers in Zoomer's fur, thinking she'd never had such a brilliant day.

After checking on Zoomer a final time, Shari drifted off to sleep, her body resting as her mind slipped away to train with Lissae. The Realm seemed distracted tonight, and in pain. Shari was confused. How could a Realm feel pain? Lissae seemed to speed through her training on how to manipulate earth to create defensive barriers.

Shari felt uneasy. As if someone was watching her. As if from a long way away, she heard a frightened *yip*, and Lissae gasped before shoving Shari's mind back into her body.

Just in time for her to see a long, rope-like tentacle wrap around Zoomer's neck. There was an ominous *crack* as the tentacle pulled violently to the side.

Shari screamed, and the tentacle slithered out her window. Lights flew on, and feet pounded towards her room as Shari crawled out of her blankets and towards the window, trying to see where the tentacle had gone. It was impossible to spot anything in the pitch black of the yard beyond her window.

Turning back to Zoomer, she gathered the lifeless palon in her arms, sobbing into his fur as her parents burst into her room.

Instantly on alert, Calem asked, "What happened?" as he crossed to the window. Shari wondered if he could feel the slimy Innarn signature from the tentacle creature.

"I was asleep, and then this thing, and Zoomer…" Shari burst into unintelligible tears.

Calem shot out the window, wings shimmering into view as Arilla gathered Shari into her arms, tears streaming down both their faces, Zoomer's tiny form cradled between them.

The next morning, Shari woke up subdued, cradled in Arilla's arms as her mum dozed in Shari's bed. Zoomer was nowhere to be seen, and for a moment, Shari panicked, before she remembered what had happened.

"Oh, Shari," Arilla whispered as she buried her head and wept anew in Arilla's arms.

The door gently slipped open, and Shari jolted awake again. She must have fallen asleep again. A bundle of black fur greeted her, and Shari felt her heart leap until she looked into the palon's yellow eyes.

"No."

"Shari, I told…" Calem started.

"No."

"Don't you want to say hello?" Arilla wheedled.

Shari turned and stared at her parents, and the temperature in the room dropped. The palon whimpered.

"No."

Calem gathered the palon up, and Shari's heart ached. She turned and looked out the window, feeling like a chunk of ice inhabited her chest instead of her heart. She went through the motions of getting ready for the day, and her parents guided her to Ronah's cemetery, where they laid Zoomer to rest. Her dad held the earth ready to cover Zoomer's tiny body with, and Shari felt sick. When it was Shari's turn to speak, she found she didn't have the right words, and instead, merely bowed her head, the tears making tracks down her face which felt like they would be etched there forever.

As her dad lowered the earth over Zoomer's body, Shari vowed she would catch the thing that killed Zoomer if it was the last thing she did.

'Lissae,' Shari sent out, '*I need to train more.*'

Winter came and went, and Shari grew stronger, even as she hid her Innarn from everyone. Lissae taught her how to disguise her Innarn with a shield so she wouldn't be found out, and Shari practiced every second she could. Slowly she added to her arsenal of Innarn, learning how to manipulate plasma and fire so it could dance from her fingertips and scorch her attackers.

Spirit and air sighed over her skin and created traps which she could push out at a moment's notice. Water lapped at her feet and dew dotted her skin as she learned how to draw it from the environment around her.

For all her training and hard work, working with earth escaped her. She no longer spent time idling away in the garden. Instead, she would lock herself in her room and practice until her parents called her for meals.

She successfully ignored their worry, focusing instead on learning as much Innarn as she could, until the night her dad kissed her mum at the table and said, "Well, I'm off."

"Off to where?" Shari asked, frowning.

"I'm patrolling tonight. Don't worry, I'll see you in the morning." Calem dropped a kiss on her head as he strode out the door.

"Patrolling?" she asked her mum.

"The Innarnian help the Guardian to make sure Lissae is safe," Arilla said as she gathered the dishes from the table.

Shari longed to tell her mum that keeping the Realm safe was her responsibility, but she stopped just in time. "What's the Guardian?" Shari asked instead.

"Jonathan Buan," Arilla answered. "He's quite good at his job, if not a bit stuffy. He runs Books 'n' More as well."

"Not who, what?" Shari asked. "What does a Guardian do?"

Arilla blinked. "The Guardian looks after the Altoriae. He trains her and keeps her safe so she can protect Lissae."

Shari grumbled in her head. She didn't need anyone other than Lissae training her, and she had her parents to keep her safe. There was no way she was going anywhere near this Jonathan Buan if she could help it.

Still, the thought of seeing what the patrols were all about had her hurrying to get ready for bed.

Tucked in tight, with a goodnight kiss lingering on her forehead, Shari let her mind slip away to find her dad, only to discover she couldn't find him anywhere on Ronah.

'Ronah, where do the patrols go?' Shari sent out.

'They go off-Realm. The patrols check on the gateways which lead to Lissae. I have the most gateways, so there are regular patrols that check the gateways each night. Each Innarnian is called in around once a month to do a patrol, but it depends on how many times there is an attempted gateway breach.'

'Could I go on patrol?'

25

'You could, but there's a good chance you'll be caught by the patrol group, if no one else,' Ronah cautioned.

'How can I not get caught?'

'Well, if you turn your current shield into a mirror, you might be able to trick anyone into thinking you are just part of the scenery,' Ronah mused.

'Can you teach me?' Shari asked.

'It's easy. You know what a mirror looks like?'

'Crystal?' Shari asked.

'Yes, it's made of clear crystal, but it has a layer of silver behind it.'

'So, if I create a spirit shield, and an air shield over the top...' Shari thought. Slipping back into her body, she sat up in bed and raised her standard air shield, testing its strength before lowering it again.

'That's not quite what I meant,' Ronah said, but Shari ignored the Island, knowing what she was attempting would work.

Lissae had taught her early on to never tap into her own spirit, or she'd drain herself too quickly. Shari had a bunch of friendly spirits from the other side of Lissae who would happily lend her their aide, and she called on them now, using their energy to create a spirit shield, before drawing her air shield around the outside, creating a double shield which had both Ronah and Lissae frantically calling out to her.

"I'm here!" Shari said aloud and giggled. 'I haven't gone anywhere,' she sent, dropping the shield to the relieved rumblings of both Realm and Island. 'How about this?' Shari asked, and pulled up her double shield again, but sent out a tentative link, which she saw as a silver thread connecting her to Ronah.

Both Realm and Island seemed to release a breath Shari hadn't even been aware they could hold. Grinning, Shari went to slip out of bed but found her legs were wobbly when she stood.

'Back to your rest, little Altoriae,' Lissae scolded. 'You've pushed your limits for tonight.'

Shari made to grumble, but Ronah added, 'There will be another patrol tomorrow.'

Back under the covers, Shari struggled to keep her eyes open. Even that was too much effort. As she slipped into sleep, Shari could have sworn she heard both her Realm and Island chuckling fondly at her.

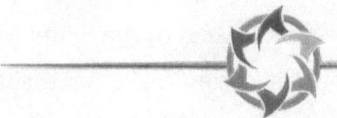

It took a week of practice, but Shari could successfully shield her Innarn from others. She'd been practicing her shield slowly through the week, drawing on different strengths of spirit and air to make it seem like she wasn't physically present, or to make it feel like she was a Blank. That night, as soon as her parents wished her a safe sleep and closed her bedroom door, she slipped to her feet and leaped out the window before they were downstairs.

Her new shield at the ready, Shari easily scaled down the outside of the bereni tree and slipped through the shadows towards the museum, her legs moving fast as she struggled to get there before the patrollers did. As she drew closer, she saw a figure up ahead.

'Shield!' Lissae commanded.

Shari's shields tightened as the lanky figure turned around. Light glinted off his glasses, and she sucked in a breath as she took in the Guardian. He searched the night but turned and shrugged, as if dismissing his concern. If the tense set of his shoulders didn't give away his state of mind, the crossbow appearing in his hand from nowhere, bolts loaded and ready to go would have.

Carefully, Shari crept after the Guardian, making sure she didn't step on any twigs as she went. He made his way towards the museum, clearly on alert, but between Shari's shields and Lissae's intervention, the Guardian wasn't able to figure out the source of his unease.

Shari waited outside as the nights' patrollers gathered, the usual jovial adults were serious, stretching their legs in envious ground-eating strides. Once the final patrol member strode inside, Shari counted to twenty and made her way silently through the front doors.

The museum at night was eerie. Most of the lights were out, and the cases glowed blues and yellows, showing there were active force-fields around them. A few were black behind the glow, and as much as Shari wondered why, she made herself concentrate on her objective.

She came closer and closer to the double doors the Minotaur had burst through, and slowed down, sending out her Innarn to sense where the patrol group had gone, only to find herself drawn back into her body and facing down a cloak-wearing figure whose face was obscured by a hood. She wasn't concerned about the features she couldn't see, but more the pointy end of the pole axe aimed her way. The being stood slightly taller than Shari, and she could feel the absolute intensity of the gaze remained out of her view.

'*Drop your shield, just for a moment,*' Lissae sent to her.

Tempted to cross her arms, Shari shook her head, knowing somehow, Lissae would see.

'*Now, little Altoriae.*'

'*Are you mad?*' Shari sent back.

'*Now!*'

Reluctantly, Shari lowered her shield, and the hooded being stepped closer to her, the point on the top of the pole glinting in the low light. Shari took two shallow breaths, but the feeling of being exposed without her shield made her unintentionally raise it again.

The hooded being lowered the axe, and Shari could feel the gaze under the hood had changed. Slowly, a hand rose, and hesitated at the edge of the hood before grasping the rough material and slowly drawing it back.

Underneath, the being looked a bit like a nut. Silver eyes peered out from wizened, brown skin. A tiny slash for a mouth opened slightly, corners turning up in what Shari recognised as a smile.

"Oh!" Shari breathed out, and the being closed one eye before pulling ze's hood up. "Who are you?"

'I am Pala, the Ducibus who guards the gateway into Lissae here on Ronah. And you are the Altoriae.'

Staring at the tiny being, Shari found she didn't know what to say. She didn't realise one being could send to another, and she found it slightly surprising that a being only a head taller than her guarded the gateways of Lissae.

'Isn't it boring?' Shari finally blurted.

Pala laughed at her, ze's shoulders shaking under the cloak. 'It may have been, for a time, but no longer. Many beings are trying to come to Lissae now.'

'Are they friendly?' Shari sent back, frowning.

'Not all of them, no,' Pala sent.

'And the patrols stop the nasty beings?'

'These beings aren't always nasty. Some are desperate, some are helpful, some are looking for somewhere safe.'

'Are they allowed on Lissae?'

'It can be hard to tell, but we have a special place on Lissae to check if the beings coming through are friendly to us,' Pala sent back.

Shari could feel the secrets the Ducibus intended to hold, but she decided to focus on her mission for tonight. 'Can you show me where the patrol is going tonight?'

'I can't accompany you on patrol, Altoriae, but I can lead you to the gateway they are going through,' Pala sent back.

'I don't understand how the gateways work,' Shari grumbled.

Laughing again, Pala turned and walked back through the double doors, and Shari hesitantly followed zir in.

She didn't know what she was expecting, but the stark grey corridors were not it. Looking down the left hand side, she saw a bright white wall at the far end. A wall deeper than the darkest night was at the opposite end, with shades of darkening grey in between the two.

'What is this place?' she thought.

'There are three levels to each of the Light, Grey and Dark Realms, and each level is represented as a corridor. Behind each door is the entrance to a Realm. Not all Realms are compatible to the beings of Lissae, just as Lissae is not compatible to all beings.'

Shari itched with questions, but caught them behind her teeth, determined to learn all she could and not be overwhelmed.

'The patrols usually focus on the Realms closest to Lissae, and tonight, they have gone to Gerhar, a Grey Realm just a bit lighter than Lissae. Others are talking of a Grey Army patrolling, and the Guardian wants to make sure their intentions are honourable,' Pala sent as he led her down the next corridor on the left, which seemed to stretch on endlessly.

'Can I follow them?' Shari asked.

'You may, but the Ducibus can't help you if you are out of range of the gateways,' Pala warned.

'How far do the gateways extend?'

The corridor was filled with doorways of all types. Shari barely had a chance to take them in as she scurried to keep up with Pala.

'Around fifty clicks from the entrance, or at least, that's what it is for Gerhar.' Pala grinned down their connection.

'Is each Realm different?' Shari asked.

'Yes. But, no more questions. Dillon will guide you through.' Pala nodded to another cloaked figure, who gave Shari a little wave. Dillon's cloak was a lighter shade of grey compared to Pala's, and ze seemed to have a younger energy.

'I will guide you out, Altoriae, and make sure you are hidden from the remaining patrols. Dillon will wait to bring you back through the gateway and safely home.' Pala bowed at her and hurried back the way ze had come.

Dillon didn't seem to want to talk or send to her, and merely extended a grey-gloved hand which Shari carefully took. Turning, the Ducibus tugged her through the now open gateway to... somewhere else.

'So, I guess this means we aren't on Lissae anymore.' Shari gulped.

When she'd left Lissae, it'd been in the deep of night. On Gerhar, twin suns shone down, the harsh heat broken by the dense coverage of orange foliage from yellow-trunked trees which ringed the gateway.

Except on this side of the gateway, there wasn't a door. From Gerhar, the gateway to Lissae was merely a space between two intertwined trees. Dillon closed the door behind zir, and the grey corridor leading back to Ronah disappeared.

'Send out your Innarn, Altoriae, and try to find the patrol group,' Dillon sent to her.

Shari looked for the Ducibus, but found Dillon had disappeared. Sending out the tiniest tendril of her Innarn, Shari found zir standing in the dappled shade by the intertwined trees. Pushing her Innarn out farther, Shari could feel the pattering of little heartbeats from forest creatures she had no chance of naming. Questing farther, Shari stumbled across someone who felt like home. Smiling, she went further afield, wondering what else there might be to discover.

The smile dropped from her face as she felt a swirling mass near the Lissaen patrollers. Opening her mouth to warn them, Shari let out a whimper when she realised she had no way to get the message to them in time.

Even as she whimpered, she felt the Guardian's Innarn uncurling into a shield around his patrol group, dense enough that Shari's gentle questing got brushed aside.

'Are they safe?' Shari sent to Dillon.

'The patrol groups are as safe as they can be when the Guardian leads them.'

Sinking to the ground and crossing her legs, Shari concentrated on making sure to strengthen her shield to go unnoticed. Under the blistering sun, she shifted restlessly, the dry heat so unlike Ronah's her eyelids grew heavy and she rested against the trunk of the tree on the opposite side of Dillon, who projected amusement towards her.

Dillon's gentle teasing fell away, and Shari sensed him straightening in anticipation. Scrambling to her feet, she flicked her hands as she looked around the little clearing.

And froze.

In front of her loomed a beast easily three times her size, its head raised, nostrils flaring, slitted eyes and ropey whiskers quivering, the sides of its vast, bronze-scaled hide heaving in time with its nostrils.

'What is that?' Shari sent as softly as she could.

'A sareglui,' Dillon replied. 'They can't see, but their sense of smell is unparalleled.'

Shari gulped, and the sareglui's head spun to face her, its maw opening to display broad, flat teeth as its sinuous body moved closer to where Shari stood.

'Their hearing is pretty good too,' Dillon sent, and Shari tried her best not to whimper again. The sareglui twisted closer to her and pressed up against her like a massive, scaley cat, its head raised to pull down the orange leaves above her. 'Good thing they're herbivores.'

Looking over the sareglui's back at Dillon, Shari shook her head. He probably could have led with that.

'*The only threat from the sareglui are the vitampit which follow them around.*'

'What's a...?' Shari broke off and slapped at a small insect which landed on her arm. Another one alighted, and she hit it too. Looking over at Dillon, she could barely see him for the cloud of tiny black insects crowding the air around them. A sudden gust of wind blew the insects away from Shari, as she scratched idly at a bite while watching the writhing cloud struggle against the air buffer Dillon had created.

'Were you bitten?' Dillon asked, appearing next to her.

'It's only a bite,' Shari said, shrugging. Sandfly bites hurt worse.

'*A bite from a vitampit is a dangerous thing. They have a taste for your blood now,*' Dillon said, his hooded face hovering above her arm.

'Isn't that what insects do? Bite?'

'*They bite, but the vitampit are a hive mind. What one knows, the others know. Once they taste your blood, they'll want the rest of it as well. It's time for you to return to Lissae, Altoriae,*' Dillon used ze's air Innarn to push her past the sareglui and towards the opening between the trees. '*I will make sure the patrol gets back. Ask Lissae to heal you.*' And he pushed her through the opening, straight into the grey hallway.

"Wha...?" Shari said.

Pala stood, arms folded, across from her. '*Dillon said you were in need of aide,*' the Ducibus sent.

'It's just a little bite.' Shari wasn't sure how she knew, but Pala gave the impression of going pale beneath ze's voluminous hood.

'From?'

'A *vitampit.*'

Pala held out ze's hand, and Shari rolled her eyes but held out her bitten arm all the same. The bite had swollen and the skin around it looked angry. Sighing, Pala took hold of her arm and gripped tightly for a moment. The bite glowed a bright green, stinging like she'd bathed it in the ocean. When the glow faded, Shari's arm looked as good as new.

'When you are travelling the Realms, through our gateways or on your own, you must always heal yourself, and remove any unwanted creatures which may have travelled back with you.' Dropping her arm, Pala turned and started walking back towards the entrance to the museum. *'The gateway into Lissae will scrub you clean of any lingering creatures, no matter how small. Until you learn how to do this yourself, you must shift off-Realm from within the Ducibus' domain.'*

Shari's head spun with unanswered questions. *'How do I heal? How do I scrub the creatures away? Can't I just bathe? What's shifting?'*

Giving her one last gentle push through the double doors, Pala shook his head. *'You must return home. Your parents are about to check on you.'*

'But...'

'Go!' Pala's send was so forceful, Shari found her feet moving before she even realised they were doing it.

Shari scrambled out of the museum, feet moving faster than her body could keep up with. *I wish there was a way to be at home already!* she thought.

The world compressed around her, darkness overtaking her vision. She tried to gasp, but there wasn't any air to breath. Then, she found herself lying in her bed, tucked in tight under her covers.

Bolting upright, tears streaming down her face, Shari looked at her parents as they cracked her door open. As they rushed into her room and gathered her in their arms, soothing her and holding her close, Lissae's voice trickled into her overwrought mind.

'Zhahyeem, little Altoriae. Zhahyeem. I shifted you from the museum to your bed so your parents wouldn't see you were missing.'

'Zhahyeem?' Shari sent as she sniffed, wiping her nose on her sleeve.

'Be calm. Zhahyeem.'

'Can you warn me if you shift me again?' Shari pleaded, fresh tears coming to her eyes at the thought of the all encompassing darkness.

'I can teach you how to do it, and you won't have to be warned.'

Nodding her head, Shari snuggled farther into her parent's arms, content to stay without any more lessons from Lissae or the Ducibus for the night.

CHAPTER THREE

Summer 4049

While other kids her age were chatting about school and just what they thought they'd be learning, and who their friends would be, Shari spent the day waiting for night to fall. She had no illusions the others would want to be friends with her, and after what had happened to Zoomer, she didn't dare risk getting close to anyone else. After another solitary day spent practicing, Shari slipped into bed. Her parents tucked her in, kissed her on the head and tiptoed out of her room.

'So, *how do I shift?*' Shari sent to Lissae as she sat up in bed.

The Realm seemed to sigh. *'Little Altoriae, you had a scare last night. Mortals generally need a break after a scare.'*

'*Don't need a break,*' Shari sent, crossing her arms and frowning. '*Please teach me.*'

'*Little Altoriae, you worry me. It is best I teach you, however, so you don't try and figure it out yourself.*' Lissae sighed again. '*When you start* to shift, you must concentrate on the place where you want to be, think of what it looks like, what it feels like, the sounds, smells and tastes that you think of. When you can hold the feeling in your mind, then you can picture yourself standing in the right place. Gather your Innarn, and pull it into your body while you focus on the place you want to be.'

Shari pictured the double doors of the museum, and the grey corridor beyond it. She tried to see herself in the picture and wrinkled her nose. Her red pyjamas would be ridiculously easy to spot. Screwing her eyes up and focusing, Shari imagined them as dark as the night sky. Opening one eye, she peeked at her shirt and nodded in satisfaction.

Wriggling out of her covers, she closed her eyes tight as she remembered the cold floor, the grey walls and the smell of ozone and spring flowers in the long corridors, and pictured herself standing just in front of the double doors. Hands grabbed her arm and pulled her to the side, and Shari opened her eyes in time to see the Guardian guiding a patrol group into the hall from behind a Ducibus.

'Well met, Guardian,' Pala broadcasted. Shrinking down behind Pala, Shari focused on her shields.

'Well met, Pala,' the Guardian sent back, and Shari could hear his smile.

'There has been some disturbance at Lefo's door,' Pala sent.

'Then we'll head there tonight. My thanks, Pala.' The Guardian motioned to the patrol group, and they started heading towards the darker corridors.

Shari went to slip out from behind Pala, but ze blocked her way.

The Guardian turned back. 'Pala, have any beings crossed over to Ronah lately?'

Shari barely dared to breathe. With each exhale, she concentrated on adding to the strength of the shield protecting her from the Guardian's detection.

'There have been no unauthorised beings on Ronah,' Pala replied. Shari could feel the weight of ze's regard, even though the opening of his hood faced the Guardian.

'Thank you. Please let me know if anything changes,' the Guardian said before heading off after the patrol group, loading his crossbow as he went.

'You'd better hurry, Altoriae,' Pala sent to her.

Taking a breath and checking her shield, Shari scurried after her Guardian. Mentally scoffing at the idea of such a scrawny adult protecting her, Shari slid through the door after him, careful not to brush against him.

The Ducibus guarding the door to Lefo was not Dillon, but ze still nodded to Shari. Giving a little wave, Shari retreated to behind one of the standing stones, her back up against the rough rock as she watched the patrol group organise themselves. Out of the ten beings, there were two teenagers, one of whom Shari recognised as Reanna McMullin, who'd often give her rides on one of Ronah's horses. Reanna flicked the ear of the other teen, who laughed, high-pitched and strained, hands gesturing uncertainly as she shifted her weight from one foot to another.

As Shari struggled to name the other teen, the Guardian clapped the nervous teen on the shoulder. A few quiet words and – Uista Zeypher – smiled, hands settling by her sides, looking more comfortable in her own skin. Reanna and Uista followed the Guardian with stars in their eyes, and Shari tried not to gag. She knew that look. They wanted to kiss him. That's what happened when her parents looked at each other the same way. The Guardian seemed to either be oblivious to their gazes, or focused on ignoring what they were after, and he sent Uista with a patrol group led by Edward Thorne, while Reanna joined the Guardian's group.

Spreading out from the circle of standing stones, the two groups started the long trek to the tree line in the far distance. Shari wondered why they didn't just use their Innarn to travel there, but hastily ran to join the Guardian's group.

The hot sun burned a path across the rocky landscape. Canyons higher than the tallest adult in the group stretched either side of the narrow walkways, making footing precarious as they followed the maze through to the tree line.

The group carried a variety of weapons, which Shari found fascinating, and, as they trudged along, Shari practiced creating them in her size. Reanna carried a rope she twirled in a circle by her side as she walked. Shari tried, and tangled her feet in the rope, almost tripping and giving herself away.

Sebastian Silverstone, his black hair soaked in sweat and limp against his forehead, carried a longsword in a sheath on his belt. Zodian Doonavan, striding along behind Sebastian, seemed to prefer short blades, and used the back of a dagger to swipe away a bead of sweat.

The flash of the blade intrigued Shari, who conjured a dagger with a blade as long as a butter knife, and waved it around experimentally.

Octavia Young wiped her brow and stumbled when she thumped her staff down too close to the edge of their precarious path and it crumbled away, saved only by the Guardian who grabbed her by the elbow until she had her feet under her again. Smiling back over her shoulder at him, two bright spots of colour on her pale face, Octavia seemed more flustered than when she'd almost fell. Sebastian and Zodian sniggered, and she shot them a glare, and resolutely kept her eyes forward.

The rope had been enough to trip her up, and she didn't have a watchful Guardian to grab her from the deep canyons if she slipped, so Shari skipped the staff. She did see the Guardian shake his head slightly as he strode after the others, one hand gripping his crossbow the whole time. She tried to use her Innarn to create a crossbow and found she couldn't hold it at the same time as the dagger.

They reached the tree line without any more stumbles. Shari noted a glint of metal just after the Guardian, but only as the rest of the patrol group threw themselves to the ground did Shari understand what was going on, and she flopped ungracefully to her belly just as a warning shot skimmed through the air where her head had been a moment before.

As Sebastian and Zodian lost their smirks and crawled on their bellies towards the tree line, weapons out, Shari realised she could sense someone hiding in the trees.

The two Lissaens came within reach of striking, and the Guardian stood. Shari almost gave herself away when she went to reach forward and grab him by the belt buckle to pull him to safety, but she managed to catch herself in time.

"Well met! We are from Lissae. We mean you no harm!" the Guardian said.

"Go away!" a trembling voice said. Shari caught a glimpse of a dirty face with big eyes and dark hair peeking out from behind a scrawny tree. He was her age!

"I won't hurt you, I just want to know why you're shooting at us," the Guardian said soothingly.

This time, they shot first. Shari threw her hand with the dagger up, and it flew out of her grip. She scowled at the blade laying on the ground out of reach, as the projectile hit the Guardian's shield.

Still scowling at the discarded dagger, Shari realised she missed something the Guardian sent to his patrol group as they begrudgingly put away their weapons. His crossbow disappeared, and he held his hands up.

"Our weapons are away. We're here to help, not to hurt."

"Go! They'll be back soon." A choked sob and the child trailed off.

Shari felt goose bumps break out on her arms. She rolled over and saw a dust cloud in the distance which seemed to spread from horizon to horizon.

"Save yourself!" the scruffy child said, then bolted from the cover of the trees and started stumbling away from the standing.

Shari watched in horror as the dust cloud descended on the child. Time seemed to stand still as the cloud lifted, and clean, white bones fell carelessly to the ground.

Mouth falling open, Shari realised she'd just watch a child her age die. Tears sprung to her eyes as the dust cloud settled and a being in a long jacket highly unsuited to the climate appeared.

"Hello, morsels," the being said, emerald eyes lighting up in his scaled face.

"Well met, stranger," the Guardian said. Shari couldn't help but feel relieved when she saw his crossbow back in his hand. The others in the patrol group had their weapons out again as they rose to their feet.

"I find I'm still hungry. Who shall I eat first?" the being said.

"Actually, we'd prefer you find something else to snack on."

"I am Yakel of the Q'Aralide. I decide who I snack on, mortal." Green sparks seemed to come from the being's eyes.

Quivering, Shari slowly rose to her feet. She had a feeling this being didn't like to argue, especially when the Guardian gulped. When he squared his shoulders and stepped towards the front of the patrol group, Shari's mouth opened again.

"Yakel of the Q'Aralide, I am the Guardian of Lissae." Thumping his hand over his heart, the Guardian continued, "Am I to understand you are hunting?"

"Yes. I'm one of the Q'Aralide's top hunters," Yakel preened, flicking a grain of sand from his sleeve.

"It might interest you to know that Amaer has an infestation of pteradiles at the moment. I believe that they are a delicacy in the Darker Realms?"

"Do they?" Yakel stepped closer, a black forked tongue coming out to lick his lips. "And if you're wrong?"

Jonathan shrugged a shoulder. "Then you can eat me."

Yakel's eyes flashed again. "Oh, that'd be easy, wouldn't it?" A tail Shari hadn't noticed whipped out and wrapped around Reanna's waist, pulling her towards the Q'Aralide. An undignified shriek left her lips, but the rest of the group weren't mocking her now. Knuckles went white, and weapons rose.

"How about I just check out this 'infestation' with this morsel," Yakel's tongue flicked out and licked a stripe on the side of Reanna's cheek. It smoked and bubbled, and Shari felt her stomach lurch. "We'll be right back. And if you're wrong, I'll make my meal here."

Before anyone could move, a sound like ripping fabric split the air, and Yakel and Reanna disappeared, Reanna's pale face and her desperate, reaching hand the last thing Shari saw.

"Is there an infestation?" Zodian asked, dagger in one hand and a longer blade in the other.

"There is, actually. But whether or not Yakel will live up to his word..." the Guardian trailed off, and Shari felt a lump of tears threatening to clog her throat. "Head back to the gateway. There's no point in all of us being at risk."

"No. There's not. So you go, and we'll stay," Sebastian said.

The Guardian opened his mouth to retaliate, only to be drowned out by the sound of ripping again.

Right behind Shari.

"Well, you were right," said Yakel's deep voice, from right near Shari's ear. There was a chittering, groaning noise, and by the looks on the faces in front of her, Shari didn't want to see just how close the Q'Aralide was behind her. Or what he had brought with him. "Lucky, Guardian, my nest will not go hungry this night."

There was a grunt, and Reanna stumbled past her, close enough to touch. Zodian and Sebastian caught her before she fell, helping her to stand and face her captor.

"Well met, Lissaens. Be thankful the pteradiles are tastier than you are." Another ripping sound, and the patrol group sagged.

"Move. Everyone. Back to the gateway. *Now!*" the Guardian said, and picking up a swaying Reanna, he started running towards the gateway.

The other patrol group apparently got the message too, and they met right at the gateway. The Guardian ushered them through swiftly. No one spoke as they obeyed his order to hurry, and Shari realised if Lissae, Ronah and the Ducibus could send to her, then they were likely sending to each other.

When they were through the gateway, the Guardian gave the Ducibus orders to seal it for the moment.

"What happened?" Edward asked. Gone was the man who'd scraped carrot stew onto her plate.

"We met a Q'Aralide. Amaer is closed until we can confirm they've lost interest in the Realm," the Guardian said, striding down the hall, Reanna still cradled in his arms.

"I've called the Healers," Anna said as she met them on the other side of the double doors.

Shari nodded. It would be handy to be able to send to lots of other people, but it would kind of give away her secret. She watched as the healers came and took Reanna away, whisking her back to the hospital in the beat of a heart.

The others in the patrol group seemed to mill around for a bit, but the Guardian sent them home with smiles and words of how well they'd done.

Only when he thought everyone had gone did the Guardian slump. Running a hand over his face to try and erase the lines between his eyebrows, he sucked in a breath and blew it out again.

He looked over at a statue of a regal-looking woman who held a ball of gently spinning plasma. "I thought I felt her, Kay'imi. When the Q'Aralide returned, for a moment, I thought I felt the Altoriae. I was warned my soul would ache for her, but I didn't know I would feel a phantom Innarnian and think they were her. I wish..." he sighed and shook his head. "I suppose I'm just glad she didn't meet the Q'Aralide tonight."

Taking a moment to compose himself, the Guardian straightened his shoulders, striding out of the museum and into the night.

Shari plonked onto the cold floor of the museum, hugging her knees to her chest. From just one patrol she had learned so much, but the Guardian had almost caught her. Clearly, she needed to be even more careful, and she'd have to come up with a weapon that wasn't too big for her, or easy to lose in a fight – or a fright.

Every night from then on, Shari would follow the patrols out. Over the course of the year, she saw so many Realms and so many beings from a distance as she followed whichever group didn't contain the Guardian. She found herself fascinated by the different weapons the adults wielded, and tried many of them before settling on a glove with twin blades protruding from the knuckles, and a short sword on her hip which she used more for helping to send her Innarn long distances than for slicing and stabbing.

Shari felt happy with how much she was learning, although she found the wounds the others suffered sent tingling green sparks to her fingers which made her flinch when she remembered the Q'Aralide's flashing eyes.

Or it did until the night when she saw the Guardian's intestines spilling out over his grasping hands, his face bloodless and wracked in pain.

The patrol group acted quickly, breaking the Guardian's unspoken rule on no shifting off-Realm, and got him back to Lissae rapidly so that Shari dithered for a moment before shifting directly to the double doors of the museum, in time to see the Healers bursting through.

Distractedly, Shari felt Pala's Innarn cleansing her of any unwelcome creatures. Her whole focus closed in on the Guardian, who became paler by the second.

"What happened?" the Healer snapped.

"Trip wire," Terrance Thorne said, lips in a tight, thin line. "I almost walked into it, but he..."

The Healer rolled her eyes and sighed. "Honestly, half the injuries we heal when you lot get back is from not looking. Now, Jonathan, hold still." The Healer held out her hands, and they glowed a gentle green which reminded Shari of the sweet summer grass on Ronah's tallest hill.

"Is he?" one of the patrol members asked.

"He's taken a lot of damage. We'll need to get him back to the..." the Healer started to say. The Guardian's eyes rolled back, and his head lolled to the side.

The adults went into a panic.

'*Lissae! What can I do?*' Shari sent, eyes wide, thoughts frantic.

'*Heal him, little Altoriae. I will guide you.*'

Strengthening her shield, Shari stepped up beside the Healer and held her hands out. She felt Lissae joining her mind, and saw how to knit together the muscle and skin, how to encourage the blood to grow quicker and flow to the right places, how to clean the wound of the poison which must have coated the wire and how to bring the Guardian back from the dark place his soul had slipped to.

'*Well done,*' Lissae sent to her, almost purring.

So tired, she was tripping over her feet, Shari slipped away as the adults in the room marvelled at the Guardian's sudden recovery.

Caught up in the thought she almost lost her Guardian before he even knew her, Shari missed his frantic scanning of the room before Lissae shifted her straight into her bed.

'*I can't lose him, Lissae.*'

'*I know, little Altoriae.*'

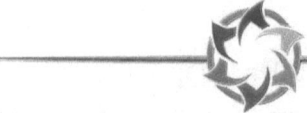

Shari started her first year of school the next day. The Headmaster, a kindly old man called Lawrence Anderson, greeted each student at the gate by name. Hanging back with her dad, she clung to his hand. Apparently stuffing intestines back into a person was a deed easier than approaching the place where the majority of her education was meant to happen.

Then she spotted the Guardian moving carefully, hands resting protectively over his stomach, but smiling just as easily as he always did. When he looked her way, she slipped her hand out of Calem's, careful not to meet the Guardian's eyes.

"Watch where you're going, you Blank," Anika sneered at her, pushing past and bumping shoulders in a way that would have sent Shari staggering if not for Calem's hand on her arm to steady her.

Tears of frustration burned in Shari's eyes as she tried to ignore Anika, and she fought to remember how the sun had seemed a bit brighter when she'd seen the Guardian up and about. She couldn't say how glad she felt, knowing that her healing had helped, and made a note to practice it more.

For now, she smiled bravely up at her dad and trudged into Ridden Hall, the nine massive bereni trees which made up the school towering over her.

As soon as she passed through the crystal gateway, Shari felt like she could breathe again, but a skitter of Innarn against her skin had her shields climbing back up.

"Well met!" the jovial Headmaster said, his balding head glinting with sweat in the last of the summer days.

Shari bowed slightly as her father returned the greeting.

"You must be Shari," the Headmaster beamed at her. "I hear you're an old hand at sennet. Perhaps you'd care to give me a game in one of your lunch breaks?"

Blushing, Shari nodded.

"Excellent! Go join your classmates! We've got a special visit from the Guardian today for our first years before class starts. It's all so inspiring!" Bouncing on the balls of his feet, hands in his pockets, the Headmaster reminded Shari a little of Edward Thorne. He had the same joyous energy that made you glad to be around him.

Giving him a shy smile, Shari walked into the school, looking for someone to talk to from the safety of her father's shadow. Calem flexed his wings, making his shadow bigger.

"Wow! Can you fly?" a boy around Shari's age gaped at him.

"Of course," Calem grinned. "All Ilutri can fly."

"What's an Ilutri?" the boy asked, wrinkling his nose.

"An Ilutri is a winged being from Lissae. We live on one of the other Shifting Islands, and we're really good at air Innarn," Calem said. The Ilutri were winged humanoids able to fly and pretty much had Innarn oozing from their pores. Calem was no exception. He was extraordinarily talented in air Innarn, and held the honour of being one of the youngest High Priests the Ilutri had ever had. He would occasionally fly to Rakemyst, the home of the Ilutri and another of the Shifting Islands, to perform special ceremonies for them. Having an Ilutri father meant that most people held back on saying the insults that popped into their heads about her or her mum being a Blank, although most of the time they were thinking so hard, Shari heard them anyway.

"Wow," the boy repeated again before shifting his attention to Shari. "Can you fly?"

Shari shook her head, startled by the sudden attention.

"Most Ilutri don't get their wing buds until they're fifteen," Calem answered for her. "Shari's still got a bit of time yet."

"Oh." The boy lost interest and ran over to his friends.

Shari slumped, feeling both relieved and disappointed at the same time.

"I'm sure you'll make friends in no time," Calem said softly to her. Kneeling down, he folded his wings back, and they disappeared from view. He often complained they got in the way when moving around on Ronah, as she wasn't designed for winged beings like his home, Rakemyst. "I have to get to the tavern, but we'll both be here in the afternoon to pick you up, okay?"

Nodding, Shari wondered if somehow her voice had escaped her.

"Alrighty. Remember to breathe when it's time to do your test. See you later." Standing, Calem kissed her forehead and left, leaving Shari standing by herself.

It wasn't too long before a noise like tinkling bells sounded, and the older kids started heading towards the largest of the trees.

"Come on then," said an older boy as he passed by her. "We've got to get to the hall."

Mutely, Shari followed along. The hall swarmed with kids who laughed and jostled each other as they sought to find a seat with their friends.

Shari hung back, hugging the smooth round wall until she got to the front of the room. She slipped into the end seat just as the Headmaster stepped onto the stage.

"Well met students! We start another year in our beautiful school!" The Headmaster said, clapping his hands together. "To our new students, stay in your seats. Other students may find the head of their year, who will direct them to their first class of the day. As usual, no Innarn may be used in the hallways or between classes."

The older students filed out, chattering about their summer break as if they hadn't all caught up just the day before.

Fidgeting in her seat, Shari looked at Elizabeth Ribeck, who seemed just as nervous as she was, wriggling in her chair. Shari watched as one after another, her new classmates walked across the stage to where the Guardian waited on the other side. As soon as they stepped up to the stage, a whirling disc of light popped into being, colours appearing in various stages of brightness above their heads as they went.

"What's going on?" Shari whispered to Elizabeth.

"They're testing our Innarn," Elizabeth whispered back, bouncing her legs as she sat. She evidently couldn't wait for her turn.

"How are we being tested?"

"My parents told me that Lissae scans your Innarn potential. Each colour represents a different type of Innarn, and the strength of the colour says how strong you could be! By the time you reach the Guardian, Lissae has figured out your potential, and a bracelet appears on your wrist with beads which show which Innarn you can tap into. You show the Guardian and the Headmaster, and they figure out what classes you should take."

Shari gulped. Lissae had said no one was to know. What could she do? In gloomy silence, Shari sank deeper into her seat as she watched the other kids walk across the stage, the colours spinning around them varying with intensity. Everyone got at least one colour, even if some were dull compared to others.

Then, standing on shaky legs, Shari rose from her seat to take her turn.

'Lissae?' she sent as she slowly made her way to the stage.

'Not now, little Altoriae. I'm a bit busy,' the Realm sent back.

'I know. You're about to scan me for Innarn potential,' Shari sent back as she reached the first step.

'Oh! Oh. Let me see—'

Nervously, Shari climbed the steps as slowly as she could. A blinding burst of light bloomed above her head as soon as her foot touched the edge of the stage. Gasps echoed in her ears as the glowing lights swirled around her head and winked out of existence.

Utter silence filled the hall as Shari released a shaky breath and made her way across the stage, feeling a heavy weight on her wrist as she got half way across.

'Don't meet his eyes,' Lissae warned.

The squeak of her shoes on the polished wooden floor rang out in the silence. Finally, she reached the other side and held out her wrist for the Guardian to inspect, her eyes locked on the pure white bracelet.

Both the Guardian and the Headmaster were silent for a moment. Shari dared not meet their eyes and found she had to blink away tears.

"You don't need to cry," the Guardian said gently. "There are many amazing Blanks in our Realm, and I believe your mother is one of them."

Shari nodded and gulped down the sudden lump in her throat. She'd seen the man's insides, but didn't dare meet his gaze. Hastily moving off the stage, Shari returned to her seat, thumb idly rubbing over the beads of the bracelet.

The other kids chatted excitedly to each other as they examined their bracelets, *oohing* and *ahhhing* over those with the brighter coloured beads.

'*What does mine really look like?*' Shari sent to Lissae.

'*I will show you later, little Altoriae. I have many others to scan today. It is the first day of school for half the Realm.*'

Sighing, Shari slumped in her seat, listening half-heartedly to the Headmaster's speech about their lessons.

Language, maths, science, arts, lore, combat, sports, agriculture and Innarn lessons would fill up her week, with the occasional special class, like the one the Guardian would hold once a month.

Soon enough they had to go to their first lesson, and Shari found she'd been secretly looking forward to school, but the thought of being the only supposed Blank in her year wrecked any chance of making friends. Dragging her feet, she followed the others out, pasting a smile on whenever someone looked her way.

Their first class of the day was Innarn lessons with the Guardian, who smiled at them as they filed into the classroom.

"Well met all," he said as they took their seats and gazed up at him in awe. Shari kept her eyes on the poster of Kay'imi over his left shoulder so she wouldn't make eye contact. "Mr Anderson has decided to start

51

you off with an easy lesson today, so you just get to listen to me rambling about Innarn for a bit."

Shari slumped in her seat and wished she could make the floor open up. Could she make the floor do that?

Before she could try, the Guardian burst into tiny bits of light. Slamming upright and banging into her desk, Shari looked around frantically as her classmates *ooohed* and *ahhhed* over the display.

The Guardian spoke, his voice seeming to come from all around the room. "Innarn requires more than just a connection with the Elements. You need to be able to concentrate, sometimes focusing on different things at the same time." The lights split apart, swirling in beautiful galaxies overhead. "You also need to be able to see the end result you desire as accurately as possible, and maintain that image while you are gathering and shaping your Innarn." The galaxies exploded like fireworks, and rushed together at the front of the room, revealing the Guardian leaning up against the teachers' desk.

"Now, who wants to try and create a ball of light like this?" he asked, extending his hand where a perfect sphere of light balanced a few inches away from his palm.

Hands thrust into the air, and Shari slumped down in her seat. She desperately wanted to practice, but she didn't dare try. Glumly, she watched her classmates clumsy attempts, then she had an idea.

Sitting up in her seat, she peered over the shoulder of the girl in front of her. Anika Thorne turned and scowled at her for a moment, but Shari spotted her bracelet, bursting with colour despite not even a flicker of light on her palm.

Concentrating, Shari envisioned a glowing white ball on Anika's outstretched palm, and was almost blinded. Cries of alarm sounded, and Shari dialled down the brightness of the ball, grinning as the Guardian praised Anika for such a marvellous light.

CHAPTER FOUR

Winter 4053

Each day of school seemed to last a lifetime. Now in her fifth year of school, Shari struggled through her days, eager for the sun to set when she was free to be herself. The only way she'd managed to get through the Innarn lessons at school was by practicing on someone else. The regular classes were alright, and she was better with a blade than anyone else in her class.

Still, waking to another day of school made her groan, even as the first fat flakes of snow drifted past her window. Grumbling to herself, she stumbled out of bed and into the kitchen.

"Can you get the bread down, sleepy head?" her mum asked, trying to tease a smile out of her.

Without thinking, Shari stretched up to reach the bread on a high shelf. Her mum gasped.

"Shari! What's that?" she asked, eyes wide and frantic as she reached to pull at Shari's PJ top.

"What? Nothing," Shari said. *'Lissae! Help!'*

Arilla wouldn't be dissuaded, and lifted Shari's shirt to show her smooth side. "I thought I saw…"

"Saw what?" Calem asked, flicking a flame at the topmost piece of bread and lifting the perfectly toasted slice from the box.

"I thought I saw a great big scar on Shari's side." Arilla's frown hadn't left her face.

"Musta been a trick of the light," Shari yawned. "Dad, could you?" Shari held out a piece of bread, and her dad flicked another flame out, toasting it while it was in Shari's hand. "Thanks."

She forwent her usual slathering of jam and grabbed a solfruit instead.

"Eat at the table, Shari," Calem said idly as he slathered his toast with citrus butter.

Grumbling, Shari slumped into her seat and chewed under the watchful eyes of her mum, who frowned, eyes flicking over Shari, as if to discover any other scars she might be hiding.

'Thanks, Lissae,' Shari said. The ropey scar on her side was, just like the others she bore, a reminder that she'd successfully saved the Realm, and she'd managed to do it over and over again. Lissae might have helped her this time, but now she had to think of a way to hide the scars so her mum wouldn't worry about her.

On an isolated, icy Realm, Shari sat on a boulder and drew her knees to her chest, musing over the last few years as the cold seeped into her bones.

After seeing the Guardian almost die, Shari determined that she would not grow closer to him, and took up her own patrol. Pala had strict orders to send to her the instant a patrol member came back injured. Only last week had she successfully mastered the art of scrubbing the unwanted creatures away on her return, and Pala had granted her the ability to shift directly to wherever she needed to be, and leave or return from patrol anywhere on Lissae.

Lissae had moved on to teaching Shari to project her soul to protect all sorts of dreamscapes, as the longer winter nights meant dreams were more likely to become nightmares for Ronah's residents. Beings from different Realms sought new ways to enter Lissae without having to go through the gateways, and dreamscapes were a perfect opportunity.

Quite often, Shari found herself patrolling the dreams of Ronah's residents rather than leaving her bed. It made her job easier, as her body remained present, although she often had to heal herself from the battle wounds when she woke.

Holding out her hand, she twisted it this way and that, taking in the size and shape of it, the colour, and all of the tiny little marks she'd gathered from all over the Realms. The thin white line along her thumb was from a thorny vine on Mafay, where she'd run from fire-breathing dragons. Ropy, red-puckered flesh ran from her wrist almost up to her elbow, a reminder that it was best to stay away from fiery blades. It matched one from a year ago which decorated her thigh, although that one had only been a glancing blow.

Concentrating on the small patch of smooth skin, Shari pushed her Innarn to make the illusion that all of her skin was just as smooth and scar-free.

Just when she nodded, satisfied with her efforts, the crunch of compacting snow sounded behind her, and a sudden, sharp burst of pain bloomed alongside her spine. Her Innarn burst out of her in a solid red ball, yielding in a yelp and a thud behind her.

The wound on Shari's back screamed at her as she turned and saw a being with four arms lying dazed against the rough ground which had been exposed by her fireball. Rising on shaking feet, Shari shifted to her bedroom, staggering slightly, and wincing as she felt around behind her, sticky wetness coating her hand.

"Erugh." Trying to get her hand in between her shoulder blades to the top of the wound proved to be impossible. Tears burning her eyes and the injury throbbing in time with her heart, she huffed, and swayed on her feet, blood pooling on the polished wooden floor.

'Lissae?' Shari asked.

'Lissae is tired, Shari. I'm just... wait, left. More left. Oops! Reef...' Ronah trailed off, and Shari felt the first tear fall.

Staggering to the door, she reached out a hand to open it, only to stop as a drop of blood fell to the floor. How could she possibly explain this to her parents? Her mum couldn't heal, and tonight her dad would be at the Tavern. She could go to the Healers, but then she'd have to explain to them, and they'd tell her parents anyway.

That left only one choice.

To a ten-year-old girl, the Guardian of the Altoriae made an intimidating figure. He seemed to tower over her, even more than the other adults did. She could not fathom if it were because he towered over even the adults of Ronah, or because his Innarn coiled so tightly around him that it made him seem more formidable than his physical form suggested. Despite the blood trickling down her back from the deep gouge which acted as a painfully distracting reminder of why she had finally sought out the Guardian, she hesitated. She'd spent seven long years learning, fighting and protecting Lissae by herself, and knocking on his door meant she would have to talk to, and rely, on someone else to help her. She didn't know if she was ready for that.

Rolling her shoulders back and catching a hiss of pain between her teeth, she raised her hand and knocked. It wasn't like she had a choice.

The Guardian answered after a long minute, during which time the young girl fought hard not to squirm, nor give any indication of the dripping gash on her back bothering her. When he opened the door, it took him a moment to look down, and when he did, their eyes met for the first time.

His indrawn breath brought her back into the moment. Instinctively, he started to kneel before her.

"No, get up!" she hissed, more from pain than anger. Something in her tone, or maybe the expression on her face, indicated the seriousness of her words. He stepped back from the door, wordlessly inviting her in, so surprised by her presence on his doorstep that he missed the trail of blood she left.

Silently, he led her through to a cramped room where books and scrolls piled high, the occasional odd object whizzing and buzzing above their heads before darting out of the room, and a jade-green jug which rotated while humming a pleasant tune.

The Guardian pointed to a space in the middle of the floor, and the girl nodded before moving to stand there, feet shoulder-width apart, and trying hard not to bleed on the beautiful rugs covering the stone floor.

Arms wide, Jonathan released his Innarn in the form of a mirror shield. It pushed past the girl, making her sway on her feet, before enclosing the two of them in an invisible bubble. A slight buzzing in the air around them told her no one would be able to hear what they said on the inside. The girl raised an eyebrow. The wordless creation of such a shield showed just how powerful the Guardian could be.

"Altoriae, I see you," Jonathan said, kneeling in front of the last person he ever thought he would say those words to.

Memories that weren't hers had the words pouring from Shari's mouth before she could censor them. "Guardian, I see you."

"Altoriae, I am here to serve you."

"I am here to serve Lissae. Will you guide me in my task?" she asked.

"I am yours to command." The words the Guardian spoke were almost reverent, and Shari suppressed a shiver, knowing it would not be a good idea to open up her back even more. She felt the end of the compulsion to speak and sighed softly, causing the Guardian to raise his bowed head.

"Thank you, Guardian. I..." despite her young age, the next words felt bitter on her tongue, and she had to force them out, "I require your help."

Eyebrows raised, the Guardian made no move. "How can I help, Altoriae?"

"I require healing." The words were difficult for her to say, and for the first time that night, the excitement of finally finding his charge faded and he could see the pain and feel the disturbance in her Innarn where she had been injured.

"Of course," Jonathan stood and motioned for the girl to turn around. She did so warily. He bit down hard on his tongue to keep from gasping when he saw the darker patch where the blood had soaked into her shirt. Feeling with his Innarn, he could make out the edges of the wound and lightly placed his hand on her back. She flinched and glanced over her shoulder. He could feel her, ready to attack at the slightest sign.

"I will heal you, Altoriae," he said gently.

She nodded but did not turn her head away. Jonathan sighed and sent out a green pulse of healing towards her injury. She flinched at the tingling it produced and groaned as the pain disappeared. "Thank you, Guardian." Shari turned and nodded at him before shifting away without another word, her courage failing her now he had healed her back.

Jonathan remained in the middle of his lounge room, stunned. In all the times he had wondered what meeting his charge would be like, none had come close to how it had played out. The girl was so young. He knew her face, she'd been born on Ronah, and he couldn't recall seeing her since the start of her schooling. How had she avoided locking eyes with him, the one way for a Guardian and their Altoriae to connect with each other, for an entire decade?

When the Elders had come to him two years before to ask for information, he'd given them none. Not because he had been, as they assumed, protecting the girl, but because he had none to give.

And now, the one child on Ronah who had consistently shown no signs of Innarn had arrived on his doorstep in need of healing. He had no doubt if the wound had not been in a place where she could not have reached, he would still have no idea of the identity of the Altoriae.

Now he had to convince Shari Dawn to talk to him again. If that weren't going to be as challenging as mining ziom with his bare hands, he'd eat his books for breakfast.

Spring 4053

It took four months before he could track down the Altoriae and talk to her again. Shari had avoided him at every opportunity, going so far as to melt into the walls of the school when he visited. He had to admit that he found himself reluctantly impressed by the feat, more because no one else had noticed she had gone missing than because she figured out how to merge her particles with others to move through obstacles at such a young age.

When he finally caught up with her, she stood in the pleasantly cool museum, studying a statue of the first Altoriae. "She seems rather aloof," Shari said as Jonathan shifted in behind her.

"Does she?" he asked, head tilted in her direction, eyebrow raised.

Shari hummed, ignoring his insinuation. Not saying any more for a long moment. Jonathan used this time to reach out and check his young charge for injuries. He could feel nothing. Eyes widening in panic, he reached out again. Where she stood was a void. Most Innarnians could be felt from a distance as if they had a mild current under their skin which made the hair on your arms stand pleasantly on end. Most Blanks felt like a dense void, as if they were made of unresponsive ziom. But with Shari, he couldn't sense a thing, almost like she wasn't there at all.

"Stop doing that," Shari muttered out of the corner of her mouth, eyes firmly fixed on the statue.

"I must talk to you." He prodded at the shield around her, not able to take his eyes off the remarkable young girl.

"It looks odd for you to take an interest in me. Stop following me around."

"I am sworn to protect you and guide you. I need to find out how much you know already so we can start on your training," Jonathan replied.

Shari turned to face him, slowly, green eyes flashing purple. "I do not require training. I have done fine on my own for the last seven years. Stop following me around!" she ground out before she shifted away.

Jonathan remained before the statue of Kay'imi, wondering if the first Altoriae had been half as stubborn as the girl who currently held the mantle.

Winter 4054

After another eight months of playing cat and mouse with her, Jonathan decided to do something he normally wouldn't have considered. Directly after lunch one day, when he knew Shari would be in school, he stalked into The Quiver and Quill Tavern, the storm clouds brewing outside matching his mood perfectly.

Glancing around, he wondered why he didn't come here more often. The tavern also acted as the Island's library. You were able to get a drink, or a meal, and read until your stomach and mind were full. The decorations were decidedly military, and he knew as well as any of the other adults that the bows on the wall and hanging behind the seats of each booth were all highly functional and kept in good condition by Arilla Dawn, Shari's mother. Her father, Calem, kept track of the books and ensured there was something for everyone to read.

As Jonathan tried to figure out the best way to attract the attention of Shari's parents, Calem walked over to him, dishcloth wiping suds from his hands.

"Well met, Guardian Buan!" Calem said, smiling.

"Well met, Mister Dawn. Do you have a moment so we can talk in private?" Jonathan asked.

"For you, Guardian, always." Shari's father stuffed the dishcloth into his back pocket and led the way to the office. He straddled a chair, arms crossed over the back, and smiled up at Arilla as she slid through the door to join them.

An hour later, Calem wasn't smiling any more.

Shari beamed when she swung through the backdoor of the tavern after school. She opened her mouth to greet her parents when she noticed the other person in the room.

Jonathan sat on one side of the desk Shari's father kept in the back room for bookkeeping. Calem Dawn sat on the other side, with her mother hovering uncertainly over his shoulder, wringing her hands as fresh tears streamed down her face.

"But, she can't be..." Arilla Dawn said again.

Before Jonathan could answer, he felt Shari's presence and stood, turning to face her. "Altoriae," he said, bowing.

The rage she never allowed herself to feel on the battlefield surfaced, and the scowl on her young face was enough to make the bravest men cower. Only centuries of memories which were not her own, but were still an integral part of her, stopped her from lashing out at the Guardian. She couldn't prevent her anger from escaping. Papers whipped around the room and a case of bottles exploded, showering the room with glass. Jonathan calmly raised a shield around the inhabitants, the glass bouncing off it harmlessly.

Shari knew what he wanted, but it hadn't stopped her avoiding him. She didn't want to advertise her title; she just wanted to do her job and get on with her life. She hadn't even told her parents for fear of harm coming to them. Her father could protect himself, but her mother... Her beautiful, kind, peaceful mother was a Blank, and had no hope of surviving even the mildest of Innarn attacks that Shari knew she had to defend Lissae from all the time.

'*You told my parents,*' Shari sent to the Guardian, furious.

"I was unaware they didn't know. You have my apologies, Altoriae. It is unheard of for one so young to carry the burden of protecting Lissae alone," Jonathan said aloud, bowing his head.

"Well, why don't we just tell everyone then?" Shari threw her hands up into the air, ignoring the disapproving looks her parents were giving her.

"There is a test which every Altoriae must take to prove they are worthy of taking up the mantle of Lissae's fiercest defender. I need time to find out more information on what your test could be, or it could have devastating consequences." Jon picked up his glass from the desk and took a sip, his eyes refusing to meet hers.

Tentatively, Shari reached out and felt the overwhelming sadness enveloping the Guardian. "Just how much devastation are we talking about?" she asked.

"Do you know the population of Ronah?" he asked instead.

"Seven-hundred-and-eighty-two," Shari frowned at him. What did that have to do with this 'test'?

"What about the population of Akoren?" he asked.

"No one lives on Akoren, it's been uninhabited for a millennia." Shari shook her head. What was he getting at?

"Do you know, in 1026, it had a population of over eight-thousand Innarnian?" Jon finally met her eyes again, and Shari could almost see the battle play out. The deaths and devastation caused by an Altoriae announced before she had trained enough to protect her Realm.

Goosebumps erupted over her limbs, and Shari sunk back into her seat, silenced. No way was she going to say a word of her status as Altoriae if she could help it. Shari felt like breaking something. Had she not proven she could take care of Lissae on her own? She snarled and turned away, struggling to get her temper under control as the memory of the Guardian healing her back played out in her mind's eye. Bottles filled with expensive liquids shuddered on the shelves behind the desk, before settling. "I accept your apology and offer my own. I should not have been avoiding you," Shari said through gritted teeth without turning around.

"Does this mean you are ready to start your training now, Altoriae?" Jonathan asked.

"Stop calling me that. My name is Shari." Clipped words escaped from between clenched teeth.

"I apologise, Shari," Jonathan said.

Something in his apology loosened the tense line of her shoulders. It took a long minute before she spoke again. "I will train with you once a week," she said through gritted teeth.

"Five times a week," Jonathan countered.

"Twice," she shot back.

"Four times," he said.

"Three times and no more," Shari said, finally turning to face him.

"Agreed," Jonathan said, holding his hand out for her to shake. "I will make it so you will be able to train and still go to school, so as not to raise suspicion."

"How will you do that?"

"Time Innarn," Calem whistled, eyebrows raised. "I didn't know you were a Time Innarnian, Guardian."

"I'm a man of many talents," Jonathan said with a twist to his lips as he laid a hand on the door. "I look forward to training with you, Shari."

After Jonathan's exit, Arilla rushed to gather Shari in her arms, and her parents shared a look, wondering just how they would manage with the Altoriae as their daughter.

CHAPTER FIVE

Spring 4054

The next week, Shari reported to the Guardian's house for training, shifting into his lounge room to avoid being seen by the neighbours.

A sickly blue bolt surged towards her.

Scrambling to get her shields up, Shari threw purple flames from her fingertips as she searched out Jonathan's Innarn signature to see if he needed help before she finished off his attacker. When he stepped into the gateway and bowed at her, brushing off a smouldering piece of his jacket, she scowled. "What are you doing?" she demanded, dropping her shield.

"I did tell you I must test you to see where your weaknesses lie," he said before shooting a flurry of the blue bolts towards her again and raising a glowing purple shield.

Shari rolled her eyes as she brought her shield back up. She pulled her Innarn around her and seemed to vanish, leaving Jonathan standing in the room alone. He hadn't felt her shift away, so he knew she had to be somewhere close by. He strengthened his shield and sent his Innarn out, questing for her location.

Time seemed to slow to a halt, but a rapid fire of yellow Innarnian darts swarmed around him, trying to get through any cracks in his shield. He took a step forward, towards where he thought Shari had hidden, and his boot sunk into the normally sturdy floor. He whipped around in time to dodge the blade that *whooshed* past his left arm but ran into a trip wire on the next step. An avalanche of creepy crawlies fell onto his head, and he did what any self-respecting person would do: hopped around like crazy trying to brush them off.

He did manage to retain a scrap of dignity by not screeching, but it was a close call.

When he finally got the last bug off him, a grinning Altoriae stood before him, the tip of her blade barely touching his Adam's apple. He sent his Innarn on a stealthy attack, conjuring up a battle axe with a blunted edge behind her back. He aimed for the spot where she'd been injured when she'd first come to him, and struck just as she nudged him with the point. He swept her arm out so she wouldn't cut him, and caught her as she fell.

"That's cheating," she muttered, scrambling away from him. "I had you."

"The beings you fight are not going to play fair, Alto— Shari. You need to be ready for anything." He helped her to her feet before stepping back a pace and regarding her. The axe hadn't cut through her armour — it hadn't meant to. But a strike, even from a dulled weapon, should not have managed to get through her shields.

"Your shielding is weak at the back. We will need to work on that," Jonathan said. "Before we do, I need you to answer a question for me."

Shari nodded, watching him warily as she dismissed her blade.

"How come I couldn't sense you that day, in the museum?" he asked.

"I shield so my Innarn can't it be sensed by others. Kind of like your mirror shield, except it mirrors my Innarn back to me. It's handy when patrolling because no one knows you're there." She smirked up at him.

"And you use this often?" he asked, curious.

"Every day." Shari shrugged as if it were nothing. In the back of her mind, she wondered if she should mention the first time she'd used her shield to spy on his patrol.

Jonathan raised his eyebrows. Apparently, his young charge did know how to shield correctly. "Why don't you adapt the format of that shield to a defensive one?"

"I've tried, but it takes more concentration than the shield I'm using now," she admitted, gazing at a point over his shoulder.

Tilting his head, he said, "Clearly the shield you are using now isn't as effective as it should be. I think it's time you tried something new." He could see the retort rising by the look in her eyes, but before she could give it voice, he commanded, "Again!" and sent a volley of red sparks her way.

After the initial session, Jonathan mercilessly went after Shari's weakest skills, forcing her to deflect and defend until she felt ready to drop from exhaustion. He focused on the gap in the back of her shield, delighting in driving all manner of weapons through until she had managed to perfect her shielding, and held it for an entire month. Such an exercise would have exhausted an adult, yet Shari handled it without complaint, and without her Innarn attacks weakening in the slightest.

At the end of her first year of training, the Elders had a meeting with Jonathan, ordering him to open the role of Apprentice Guardian up, despite Shari's grumblings.

Shari had sat in on the meeting, hidden from sight, and glaring at the Elders in their robes coloured for their main Innarn, the high collars thankfully blocking Jonathan's view as she mocked them mercilessly.

After an eight month search, Jonathan settled on a teen from Ronah, by the name of Mitchel Hoffman who, despite not being the strongest Innarnian, possessed an unending loyalty to Lissae. Once Jonathan started training with the Altoriae, as well as Mitchel, Shari expected to see his stress level increase with his workload, but he seemed to be content and more inclined to smile.

Spring 4055

During her second year of training with the Guardian, they focused on her range and healing, meeting every night in secret to train. Shari would shift into Jonathans' home every evening and back to her room when they were done. She insisted that she didn't feel ready to reveal herself yet, and would refuse to speak to Jonathan whenever anyone other than her parents were around.

While Shari was concentrating on healing Jonathan's arm from a gash he'd received during patrol one night, he casually said, "I think it would be a good idea to tell Mitchel about you."

Rearing back, but keeping her hands in place, Shari shook her head. Healing seemed to come naturally to her. She had a sneaking suspicion that because she'd seen the insides of so many beings, she could easily picture the way that everything fit together and force her Innarn to make it so. Jonathan had her concentrating on the little details, like growing hair back and making sure tans matched, as well as the big things like putting clean blood back where it belonged, rebuilding muscles and knitting organs back together.

"No way," Shari answered only after she'd safely removed her hands.

"He is my apprentice. He's bound to find out some time." Jon rubbed his healed arm.

"I won't have anyone else at risk. I didn't even want you to know!"

"Are you not glad that you came to me?"

Shari stood, her Innarn bristling out, making the fine hairs on their arms stand on end. "I'm thankful that you healed me, and for everything you've taught me, but so long as you're thinking of telling someone else, I won't come back."

"If I could train you both at the same time, Mitchel will get up to speed quicker," Jon coaxed.

"No," Shari glared at him. "While he's getting up to speed, he's at risk, and the rest of Lissae would be too."

"Shari..."

Turning, she shifted away from him, going so far as to use a burst of air Innarn to make the door slam, marking her displeasure.

Sighing, Jonathan ran a hand over his face. Just how was he going to get her to work with Mitchel?

A month later, and he was no closer to the answer, but was sporting a rather nasty gash in his calf from a runaway Kemmae, which was slowly eating away his flesh.

'*Altoriae. Forgive me?*' Jonathan sent, '*I will not tell Mitchel.*'

There was a sigh down their mental link. '*Forgiven. I suppose you want me to start training again, then?*'

'*Yes. You could start with healing a wound from a Kemmae.*'

'*Who got wounded?*'

'I *did*,' he admitted.

Another sigh, and then Jonathan felt the rush of air moving over him as Shari shifted into the museum. '*Really, Jon? You just want me to heal you*,' she grumbled at him. Hands over his wound, she started the painstaking process of removing the poison eating away at his flesh.

'*I expect a reduction in my training after this, you know*,' she sent as she moved on to knitting his muscle back together.

Gritting his teeth against the pain, he nodded in mute agreement.

'*So, four times a week?*'

'*Five*,' he countered, trying not to curse as she regrew his skin.

'*Done*.' Shari removed her hands and nodded. She'd even gotten the hairs on his legs the right colour. Five was more than agreeable, and she could spend the other two nights secretly patrolling on Realms far away from wherever Jonathan happened to be.

Spring 4056

When Shari stumbled back from patrol one night, blood seeping through the fingers of the hand clamped to her ribs, Jon was waiting for her with crossed arms and a scowl firmly in place.

'*You do realise that I know what you've been doing?*' he asked, healing her with a swift, sharp jab of Innarn that hurt almost as much as the arrow had.

'*Who, me?*'

Unceremoniously grabbing her, Jon shifted with her, and Shari felt like she'd moved sideways into a blank grey space.

'*Where are we?*' Shari asked.

'*This will be your sanctuary. Since you insist on patrolling, but don't want to worry your parents. Here is where you'll come to recover from battle, or when you need a break. You just need to picture a place that makes you feel rested and relaxed.*'

Eyebrows raised, Shari turned to regard the blank greyness that spread out before her. Taking a moment to think about what she wanted, she closed her eyes and pushed her Innarn out.

The greyness changed, and ground appeared under their feet, covered in lush green grass. Trees sprung from the earth and grew to towering heights in a matter of moments. Bushes and shrubs appeared with all sorts of edible fruit, including the frosted purple rutenberries that Shari so loved to snack on.

Straining her ears, she listened for the stream that ran over mossy rocks that she wanted on the other side of the trees, making ferns and fungi safe to consume come to life on the bank. A tree wider than all the rest, and suspiciously resembling her home, grew out of the ground around them, leaving them standing in an empty wooden room.

That changed in the next moment, colourful rugs softening the floor, squishy armchairs appearing, and haphazard stacks of books littering every surface. Broad windows appeared in the walls, showcasing the magnificent view beyond.

Jon marvelled at the sanctuary Shari created. In a short amount of time, she'd put a lot of thought into it.

'*You can change things whenever you feel like it,*' he sent. '*But for now, I think it's beautiful.*'

Blushing, Shari avoided his eyes and looked out the window to where a flock of pink butterflies sprang into the air and fluttered into the trees.

'I have a welcoming gift for you,' he sent, handing her a large black tome with silver writing and Lissae's symbol of seven coloured spikes on a silver ring embossed on the cover.

'A book. How could I not have expected this,' Shari asked drily.

'Not just any book. This is your copy of the Altoriae's Handbook. Mine's at the shop. Anything I write in my copy will appear in yours, and vice versa. This book contains the writings of knowledge of all of the Altoriaes and their Guardians that have come before us.'

He was right. This was far more precious than an average book. 'Thank you,' she sent, hugging it to her chest.

From then on, when she had a rare quiet night, Shari would pour over the information her predecessors had recorded in the Handbook, reading Jon snippets aloud of bits she found particularly interesting. He did his best to encourage habits which taught her things other than how to attack and defend.

Jon still insisted on using her sanctuary for some of their more peaceful training, and in the eighth month of her third year of training, Guardian and Altoriae spent one particularly enjoyable week learning the Veti Cant, which the U'sala used when they couldn't send or talk to each other but were still in sight.

Autumn 4057

As Jonathan deemed her capable, there were more joint forays into the Realms, both extreme ends of the Dark and Light Realms. Nine months into her third year of training with Jonathan, Mitchel burst into Jonathan's house to warn the Guardian of an upcoming attack and saw her dressed in the leathers she wore when protecting the Realm, sans mask in the relative safety of Jonathan's lounge room.

Mitch had seen the Altoriae from a distance before, but never as close as this. He had a brief flash of green eyes before her hand shot out and purple flames seared his eyebrows, sending him stumbling backwards, his eyes closing instinctively, a hand going to his face to beat out the fire.

Before he could smack himself in the face, Jonathan pulled the flames away with a negligent wave of his hand, a gesture he'd apparently made many times before.

Mitch recovered himself, blinking a few times before his eyes locked onto the Altoriaes. "Sorry for interrupting your training, Guardian," Mitch said, never taking his eyes off Shari. "There's a sizable disturbance on Neharn. A Dark Army is massing there."

Shari looked at him, her expression unreadable. She nodded slightly, and Mitch succumbed to the urge to kneel before his Altoriae.

Jonathan shifted out, leaving the two of them in uncomfortable silence.

"So, you're..." Mitch started.

"I am," she said in a clipped voice.

"I guess you don't want anyone to know yet, right?" Mitch asked, tipping his head.

"Right," Shari bit out, twisting the handle of her blade through nimble fingers.

Minutes passed, and the tension became too much for Mitch. "You know, my shem'ar talks more than you," he said with a goofy grin, looking up at her from his spot on the floor.

"You have a shem'ar?" Shari asked, eager for a change in subject.

"Yeah, dad got him to help keep us kids in line when we were little, but we converted him, and now he guards us against dad instead.

Although he doesn't eat dad's cooking – can't say I blame him, though," Mitch said easily, curling his long limbs into a more comfortable position.

"What's his name?" Shari asked.

He rubbed his hand on the back of his neck sheepishly. "Peanut," he said. "One of my sisters was going through a phase where all she'd eat was peanuts, and the name kinda stuck. He's bronze, but you wouldn't know it. He spends most of the time covered in dirt. He can do all sorts of tricks – handy for sending messages, although he's always stopping off at the store, looking for treats. Gotta watch it when he's had carrots, he flies in circles."

"Carrots? I thought they were meat eaters?" she said, wrinkling her nose.

"Just 'cause shem'ar look like mini furry dragons doesn't mean they are. They're omnivores, and Peanut will eat pretty much anything. Even some of the stuff he's not meant to." Mitch shook his head ruefully.

"Can you send to him?" Shari asked.

"Yeah, but most of his thoughts revolve around food and scents. He responds better to my eldest sister, cause she grew up with him. Plus, she sneaks him treats," he added, rolling his eyes.

"Sounds about right," she said with a laugh.

"Don't think I don't know what you're doing, changing the subject. I'm the master of sidestepping conversations I don't want to have," Mitch said, as easily as if he were still talking about Peanut.

"I guess I'm not used to talking to anyone but Jonathan about this." Shari narrowed her eyes at him.

"You can talk to me too. I won't tell anyone." Mitch looked at her out of the corner of his eye as he fiddled with a frayed thread on the bottom of his shirt.

"I might take you up on that," she said with a small smile.

Mitch smiled back and started to say something when Jonathan shifted back in.

"They're massing alright. Shari, with me. Mitchel, stay here and make sure nothing gets past Lissae's Wards. Get the Elders if you must," Jonathan ordered, and just like that, the Guardian and the Altoriae were gone, off to defend the Realm.

Mitch took in the silence of the room. He had never felt quite so insignificant, being left behind while a younger person went off to save them all. He took a moment longer to centre himself before checking on Lissae's Wards.

The Elders would have to be called in, he realised. Mitch sat down and took a breath, taking care to lock away his knowledge of the Altoriae to a place where no one could see it if they scanned his mind. He may have only just found out, but he would not be the one to release her secret.

CHAPTER SIX

Closing her eyes, she concentrated on the Realm of Neharn. The colours of Innarn flowed past her in spiralling multi-coloured streamers, showing up brightly in the desert. Before her eyes, the remnants of Innarn colours faded into the dry orange sand, which coated her mouth and settled on her boots as she walked towards the large rocky outcrop. Jonathan spared her a brief glance, but immediately turned his concentration back to the army the Dark entities of the Realms were gathering on the plane below them.

Safe for the moment on the semi-protected rise, she took a moment to look out at the swarming army restlessly shifting on the superheated ground.

The Dark Army had chosen Neharn to ambush the Altoriae, as the Grey Realms were comfortable for most beings and creatures, no matter their Realm of origin. Only the genuinely Dark or truly Light beings found it painful to be out of their part of the Realms for extended periods of time. Shari knew it meant the attack would begin soon. Now, she just had to wait.

Taking careful note of the placement of the troops, she marvelled at the simplicity of Jonathan's plan. She had worked hard, sending out specialist Innarn traps.

Beings from all over the Dark Realms made up the writhing mass of troops below. Xanterians, a race that used fire Innarn and the Korvie, who primarily used water Innarn and some air Innarnian, served well as frontline troops, their eager cries echoing in the barren plain. Their generals were four of the Q'Aralide. The vicious race would do nigh on the impossible to obtain control of Lissae. They were master wielders of spirit, earth, plasma and air Innarn. With the Xanterians and the Korvie intermingled and backed up by the Q'Aralide, even the crack troops of Lissae would not have much of a chance without the Altoriae and her Guardian.

Shari set about weaving her net of Innarn defence as, unknown to both herself and Jonathan, on the plane right behind them Lissaen troops were preparing for battle behind an Innarn shield which obscured them from outside view. The Elders had nodded wisely when Mitchel had told them about the army massing on Neharn, and thanked him for his message. They didn't inform him their troops were already there, ready to defend the Realm, and now hoping to catch sight of the Altoriae.

When dusk finally fell on the Realm where the battle for Lissae's freedom was to take place, Shari rose from her crouched position. She had done all she could. Her Innarn defences should be enough.

Shaking off the fatigue from casting her defences, she strode to the top of the bluff. The raucous noise from below her died down as the Dark Realm's Army noticed the lone warrior silhouetted on top of the cliff.

She could hear taunts flung at her in multiple languages until the jeering slowed and an uneasy muttering swelled. Finally, silence fell.

Within the eerie quiet, Neharne's second sun slipped below the horizon, and a silent command saw the Dark Army snap to full readiness. After a moment, the white Q'Aralide Elder gave the word, and the entire front half of the Dark Army charged at Shari.

The Korvie sent jets of water pulsing out and threatened to drown her, but they fell just short of her position. Tongues of flame spread amongst the ranks of the Xanterians until they gathered it and shot a vast super-heated cannonball at the warrior on the bluff. Not one of the superheated balls touched her, despite their best sharpshooter's work.

The white Q'Aralide Elder finally released her brethren, turning to imperiously demand her Priest to set the battle wards, only he wasn't there. How, in the name of all the Realms, could a thirty-foot long golden Q'Aralide vanish?

The missing Q'Aralide Priest turned the battle. As Jonathan distracted the golden priest, Shari dropped her defensive net on the Dark Army with a spectacular show of colour. Blue jets of water slammed into the Xanter, quenching their flames and driving them to the ground. Dirt rained down to mix with the water, trapping the Korvie into mud-caked mounds. Before they could remove the mud, purple plasma exploded from under their feet, baking them in place with incredible speed.

Tormented screams rose from below, sweeping up the bluff as plasma continued to cook the mud, searing the flesh of those trapped inside it.

The three remaining Q'Aralide looked at their swiftly-decimating army and roared their wrath, their poisonous breath ending the suffering of many as it washed over the ranks. Shari sent streaks of water and fire rushing towards the Q'Aralide, who turned tail and fled Neharn before it could reach them.

Some of the Korvie managed to regain their senses, and the mud fell away from them. The few troops that were left scattered, feeling scared, hurt and disheartened. Most of them were too unnerved to go on without the sudden defection of their seemingly untouchable Priest and the exodus of their Generals.

The Lissaen army on the other side of the bluff saw everything, thanks to some unnoticed advance scouts. They saw the Innarn Net drop on the Dark Army, and they knew the lone warrior atop the hill had cast it. The Elders amongst them were astounded. The astounding mental control and tenacity it would have taken to construct a defensive net of such a large size left the Elders speechless. As the Dark Army left Neharn, beaten but not vanquished, the Lissaen Elders surged forward, intent on questioning the lone warrior.

Before they had even reached the base of the bluff, however, she turned and sighted them. In addition to her black leathers, the young woman on the knoll wore a black mask. Her facial features obscured, the Elders rushed forward, eager to identify her. She took four steps and vanished before they could reach her.

The Elders froze, stunned. They had just seen Lissae's Altoriae, and she had disappeared before their eyes. Even though they had witnessed her in action, not one of the Elders could put a name to the Altoriae. Her unique fighting style should have made it easier to narrow down her name, but the Elders found that they were no closer to discovering the name of Lissae's protector.

Many months of debating began as soon as the Elders of Lissae were home. After concluding they had no way of knowing who the Altoriae was without further information, the Elders sent their spies out to see what they could discover.

The reports that came back were sketchy and full of missing details. Not a single one gave them any further clue as to who the latest Altoriae of Lissae could be. On Summer's Eve, the Elders sent an emissary to the Guardian of the Altoriae – the man in charge of teaching the Altoriae everything she knew. Again, the Guardian refused to name her.

When the Elders requested to know the Altoriae's location, he finally admitted that she was under his tutelage on Ronah. The Elders, pleased as they were with this crumb of knowledge, refused to leave until they at least had an age. When the Guardian admitted his ward was sixteen-years-old, a few of the Elders refused to believe him. Sixteen? Moreover, she had beaten back the horde which had been intent on destroying them with an ease that many of them secretly envied.

Suspending their disbelief, they issued an order which went out immediately, stating every sixteen-year-old female on the Shifting Island of Ronah would be watched for any sign which indicated she may be the Altoriae. Even the Guardian's movements became more closely monitored. The people of Lissae needed hope in these dark days, with their Realm under constant attack, and the Elders felt their only hope bore the title of Altoriae. The one who discovered her identity would be coveted until the end of their days.

Despite sending their best spies, it was not to be. Six months and still the Elders were no closer to determining the identity of Lissae's Altoriae.

CHAPTER SEVEN

Spring 4058

The thump of drums and squeals of laughter coming from the Spring Festival swelled through the streets of Ronah, drawing Jonathan and Shari away from training and towards the Town Square. Izzy and Xavier Silverstone stood at the closest entrance to the Town Square, dressed as the God of Fire, Adeon, and his husband Ke'ra, God of Plasma. The two greeted Jonathan and, when the other festival attendants heard the Guardian had arrived, Jonathan was immediately surrounded by a joyous crowd of people wishing him a happy festival and begging him to join their party.

Shari smiled at Jonathan through the crowd which had formed around him and nodded, before walking off to enjoy the festival in peace. As she wandered around the inside perimeter, she suppressed a snigger at the look of terror on Jonathan's face before the crowd had consumed him with their good wishes. With so many people around in costume, Jonathan had made her scan the area as they'd walked over. There were only those friendly to Lissae here tonight.

Rasshnae, Goddess of Water, and her husband, Zoemer, God of Earth were standing guard at another entrance. Through their costumes and the fantastical displays of spinning globes of dirt and surprising fountains of water, Shari could see the eyes of Saul and Erica – another couple from the Silverstone Clan. Heading straight for the last entrance of the Town Square, Shari found herself unsurprised to see Desta and Michelle Silverstone, looking unerringly like Vebnah, Goddess of Air and Na'reh, Goddess of Spirit.

Weaving her way through the crowds, Shari felt a tug on her pant leg.

"Ree! Ree!" a little voice shrilled.

Looking down, Shari laughed and scooped up Eric Shansky. "Hello, Eric, did you run off again?" At barley a year old, Eric continually evaded his parents, and many on Ronah had become used to having the bubbly boy around for part of the day. Shari was one of his favourite people to hide with, and he loved patting her father's wings.

Louise broke through the crowds as people pointed her towards her wayward son. "Oh Shari, thank you! I could just see him getting tangled up in one of the displays!" Louise laughed easily as Shari swung the little boy back into his mother's arms.

"It's no problem. Did you still want me over tomorrow night?" Shari asked with a grin.

"Oh, yes please! Andrew and I are so looking forward to having a night out and not having to constantly wonder where our little escape artist has vanished to." She nuzzled Eric's cheek, then with a cheery wave, she disappeared into the crowd. "See you then!"

She pulled faces at Eric, making him giggle as he disappeared back into the crowd before heading back into the middle of the Square, which felt like a pleasant attack on her olfactory senses. New flowers were in bloom everywhere, but as strong as their scent was, it brought back memories of Spring Festivals when life wasn't so hectic, and reminded her of times when her Realm was safer.

A shoulder bumped into hers and brought Shari to a jarring halt. She looked up into the eyes of Rany Thorne, Anika's father.

"Well met, Rany," she chirped.

When Rany saw who he'd bumped, his eyes narrowed, and he wiped at his shoulder, sparks flying from his flicking fingers. "Please watch where you are going, Miss Dawn," he said stiffly.

"Of course, I'm sorry, I was just thinking..." she started.

"If thinking distracts you from your surroundings, perhaps you should do it in a less populated place," Rany chastised, lips curling as if he'd smelt something terrible. He dared not be rude to her, not with her father hovering nearby, but could barely contain his evident disquiet at having come into close contact with a Blank.

Apologising again, Shari moved on, fighting to suppress a sigh. How much longer would she have to hide? In no mood to enjoy the festivities anymore, she started to send a message to Jonathan, but before making it to the edge of the Town Square, she saw Jonathan talking rather intently to someone wrapped in a brown cloak.

Looking up, he caught her eye. 'Meet me at the shop,' he sent, the sharp burst of thought making her feet move before she engaged her brain.

Moving quickly, Shari made her way silently out of the Square and down the street towards Jonathan's shop, Books 'n' More. Just before the festival was out of sight, she turned back for one last glimpse. Brightly coloured costumes twirled on the makeshift dance floor. Someone dressed in fiery red pants dipped a woman dressed in the blues and greens of the sea. Laughter and happy shrieks of children filled the air. The festival seemed Realms away from where she stood.

Squaring her shoulders, Shari turned back to the shop, curious as to what Jonathan had discovered that required such immediate attention. Almost as soon as she entered, Jonathan pulled her down to the end room and shielded it so they could talk freely.

"We need to move, now," he said urgently. "The Army for the Light Realms is amassing on Mid Canak. It's only a matter of hours before they attack."

"What? Why haven't we've heard of this before? I thought you had people out there finding out things like attack plans?" Shari said, startled.

"Yes, well, at least we found out now and not when they began invading," Jonathan groused. "I'm none too pleased with it either, but we take what we can get. We need to leave now, Shari."

"Where about on Mid Canak are they?" she asked.

"Right near Azmine's Ridge," he said, shifting into his armour and urging her to do the same.

Shari felt a shiver tingle along her spine. The gateway for Azmine's Ridge was only a step away from Lissae.

The beauty of the starry night above the blue grassy field was lost in the sounds of a battle which had been going on for close to three hours. Shari could feel herself beginning to tire. Sporting a deep gash on her left leg just above the top of her boot, and a scrape on her right arm from the path of an arrow, Shari did her best to ignore the blood dripping down her brow and into her eye. Thankfully, it didn't belong to her, but she dared not take the time to wipe it away with the ferocity and frequency of the attacks from the Light army.

She took a step back and the platoon in front of her advanced. Another step and more swelled their ranks. One more and another fifty soldiers joined the hundred-strong platoon as they took a collective step forward, the latest troops pouring down over one of the ridges that ringed the perfectly square battlefield.

If Shari had the time, she'd have wondered what sort of Innarnian had created such a beautifully symmetrical Realm. The mountains surrounding the massive field meant that Shari could see how many troops were scrambling down the steep sides, ready to swell the ranks of the Light Army. Their numbers were dwindling now, with only the occasional platoon rushing in to meet their doom.

Another step backwards, and the platoon moved forward as one.

The screams which arose from the throats of 150 of her foes did nothing to improve her mood, although it did allow her the precious seconds she needed to wipe the purple blood from her brow. She spared no time to watch the Light Army soldiers as the air trap flayed the flesh from their bodies, but turned to join the battle raging behind her in earnest.

Three warriors broke away from their platoon and the carnage Jon had wrought came charging at her, and she dispatched one quickly with a surge of water that blasted him right into the side of the mountainous ridge, breaking his bones into more pieces than should be possible. The one to her left had lost his red helmet somewhere along the way and proudly sneered at her, showing off the gaping hole where his nose used to be. He shot a bolt of fire at her, which she effortlessly deflected towards the last yellow-scaled armour warrior wearer on her right. She didn't realise her mistake till it was too late, as he sent the fire bolt at her ten times bigger and infinitely hotter.

Yellow armour – air warrior – Concentrate! she scolded herself.

Scooping up the fire bolt, she lobbed it over their heads. It landed somewhere amongst the screaming masses before her. Noseless threw another flash of fire at her, assuming she'd do the same thing. Instead, she gathered it and pushed it back at him in the form of a lightning strike that emerged from her left hand. A rather distressing whistling noise came from where his nose should have been before he imploded.

The air Warrior sneered at her as he thrust a swirling tempest at her. Stronger than she expected, it momentarily lifted Shari off her feet, before she wrangled control of the tempest and found her footing. Shari parried with a shot of water, but he ducked, and it did no more injury than that of a spring shower. He went to return fire, but she was quicker.

Time froze for an instant and the moment became etched into her memory. Blue fire streamed from her fingers, arching along the air currents before hitting the yellow-scaled armour of her opponent. The look of terror and hatred in their brown eyes as the fire caught their chest.

As time snapped back into focus, Shari watched with detached horror as her opponent became engulfed in blue flames. Air – the Innarn Element they'd fought with – fuelled the fire while the water Element she added virtually suffocated them.

It was with no pleasure that Shari watched her opponent crumble into a pile of viscous ash. Once the last flake of her latest opponent fell to the ground, she allowed her shoulders to slump and released a sigh. Thankful the fight had ended, she turned her back, shoulders squaring again, seeking to aid Jonathan.

Suddenly, a cry of, "Detain her!" sounded from the top of the range.

Shari whirled, surprised. Satyrian troops from Lissae started for her. Without having to look, Shari knew Jonathan was engaged in his own final battle, only a few lengths from where she stood. Refusing to swear, Shari instead sent out a bolt of yellow from her fingertips. The bolt flew from her hand, twisting and spiralling in on itself before expanding into a gale force wind. The wind swept along the battlefield between Shari and the Satyrs, and picked up the viscous, ashen puddles of her fallen opponents to fling them into the faces of the Satyrs' intent on capturing the Altoriae.

Shari used the distraction to shift to Jonathan's side. Another blast of yellow left her hand, fuelling the flames of her Guardian's opponent well beyond the ability of control. A shuddering scream became the last noise on the battlefield for almost a half-minute.

The Satyrian troops stood beside the Ilutri's best archers. Shari desperately wanted to see if her father stood amongst the Ilutri's forces, but refused to look away from the Elders of Lissae who moved to stand in a line at the front of the Lissaen soldiers.

Every single one of the Lissaen Elders had their eyes fixed on her, and Shari knew it was only by the grace of the mask she wore that her Grandfather, SilverCloud Dawn, the Ilutri Elder, didn't recognise her.

Edward Thorne, who she'd seen laughing and dancing only a short time before, looked at her with eyes of steel. He had a slowly smouldering hole in the shoulder of his armour, the stump that had once held his arm dripping blood at a steady rate. Instinct sent a rush of healing power straight to her hands, which flared green for a moment. Jon tapped her on the back, and she shook the green energy away. Even though she desperately wanted to heal her long-time friend, to do so now would give away more than either she or Jon wanted.

Still, the green glow caused many mutterings and surprised exclamations amongst the Lissaen troops, a few of who broke rank to determine if there were still green sparks lingering near her hands. An Altoriae who had the power to heal had not been seen since Kay'imi, who'd passed into the Spirit Realm some thousand odd years before.

A wordless command saw the troops spreading out behind the Elders. Jonathan and Shari found themselves surrounded. Jonathan could feel the tension oozing from Shari's back as they stood, him facing the Elders and her keeping an eye on the troops behind him. Innarn faintly crackled in the air, and he knew it would only take a spark to set off this powder keg of a meeting.

Silence claimed them all. Not even the sound of creaking armour broke it. At last, when it was clear the Guardian and the Altoriae were going to remain silent, the Elder of the Satyrs stepped forward, the traditional greeting tripping readily off his tongue, "Well met, Altoriae."

Shari did not blink, nor did she turn to face him. She continued staring at the troops, none of who would meet her eyes.

"Well met, Elder Zizar," Jonathan replied after a pause.

Although the frustration of Jonathan answering instead of the Altoriae was evident on Zizar's face, he did not betray it in his voice. "We wish to thank you, Altoriae, for your help in defeating the Light Army." He grinned and while, some of the troops smiled with him – a few going so far as to cheer – most looked put out by his wording.

Shari snorted but dared not say or send anything for fear of her identity being discovered. 'The hide of them, though, acting as if they did anything other than stand on the sidelines watching,' she sent to Jonathan.

Jonathan felt invisible fissures of energy running up and down Shari's skin. Her Innarn practically crawled out of her, ready to attack, and he knew he had to diffuse the situation quickly, for the benefit of the Altoriae, rather than the Elders. She needed to know he would be on her side in all things, even against the Elders. "Yes, Elder, your troops did an admirable job at containing the Light Army so the Altoriae and I could finish them off for you," Jonathan said smartly.

He felt Shari's approval humming down their mental link.

Two spots of blotchy colour appeared on Zizar's cheeks. However, he recovered enough to say, "Will the Altoriae not reveal herself to us now? We have fought on the same battlefield, after all," he said, sweeping his hands in a grand gesture and smiling graciously. Jonathan noted the tightening of the skin near his eyes. Zizar clearly did not like lacking knowledge or being upstaged.

"And yet I see your blade is clean, Elder," Jonathan said lightly as he reached back through the link and did the mental equivalent of tapping Shari's arm gently in warning.

Edward Thorne moved then, placing a hand on Zizar's shoulder to calm the Elder as he stepped forward, "Greetings, Guardian Buan."

"Well met, Elder Thorne," Jonathan acknowledged, bowing slightly.

Shari nudged Jonathan slightly so she could see Edward out of the corner of her eye while still making sure there were no hostile movements from the troops behind him.

"Guardian, you and, no doubt your ward, know these last few years have been difficult. The rate of attacks has been increasing, and many lives have been lost. People are losing heart, Guardian. Perhaps it is time to show Lissae the face of our Altoriae," Edward coaxed gently.

His charcoal eyes were so kind Shari could no longer hold back. She stepped around, Jonathan moving with her so he could keep a lookout behind them. Facing Edward, she raised her hand, palm out, and pointed directly towards him. A green light shot out, crossed the thirty odd feet between them and enveloped him.

Exclamations of surprise shot up between the soldiers, who looked on as he shot into the air. Some raised their weapons, trying to figure out if they should attack or not, but the shield Jonathan threw around them would prevent anything from getting through. The green light, now pulsing in time with Edward's heartbeat, poured into his open mouth.

With a flash of light that caused more than a few blasphemous utterings, Edward returned to the ground, stumbling slightly as he found his feet.

Kay'imi was reputed as an amazing Healer. She'd been able to heal horrific injuries in moments, when other Innarn Healers would need days. However, even Kay'imi couldn't perform such demanding healing from a distance.

Edward Thorne looked down and saw his left arm – something he hadn't been expecting to become reacquainted with. Wriggling his fingers and pinching his regrown arm painfully, he muttered "Adeon's fire!" Raising his head, words of thanks ready to trip off his tongue, he paused.

The Altoriae and her Guardian were gone.

Later, during a regular debriefing, not one of the soldiers could lay claim to seeing the Altoriae depart. None, of course, dared debrief the Elders, even if SilverCloud Dawn looked particularly smug about something.

CHAPTER EIGHT

Winter 4059

A piercing, repetitive beeping sounded next to Shari's ear, startling her into consciousness. A curved dagger appeared in one hand, while her other hand formed a fist and slammed into the racket. Wincing at the sound the two made when they connected, Shari opened her eyes to find she had smashed the crystal which served as her alarm clock.

Again.

"Oops." Her eyes adjusted to the Realm of the waking to find her mother standing in the relative safety of her gateway.

"There's really no guess as to what you were doing last night," Arilla commented. She looked at her still half-asleep daughter. Where she had grown up, mothers didn't have to worry while their children were sleeping. Arilla frowned and chewed on her lip. There was no way she could imagine what Shari went through every night.

Calem had tried to explain it to her one night, telling her that while Shari's body stayed safe in bed, her mind was free to travel the Realms. Most Innarnian used the time to catch up with friends or family that they couldn't see through the day, but Shari and Jonathan were, more often than not, protecting Lissae.

"At least the Crystal Guild will love you," Shari muttered, standing and shrugging into her robe. Arilla had been getting Shari replacement crystals from the Crystal Guild for quite a while. At times it could be quite fun trying to come up with new reasons as to why this one had shattered.

"Come on, sleepy head. Go have a shower, and I'll get you breakfast."

"Thanks, Mum," Shari said, yawning.

"You're welcome. Now to the shower with you! I'll see you downstairs."

Wishing she could go up to the terrace, she instead stumbled to the shower, hating the thought of morning. Last night had worn her out. In her sleep, she had been fighting the creature that had injured Jonathan, slashing him across the ribs. She finally managed to destroy it towards the end of the night.

Not a great way to start her first day back at school.

"Lissae is what the Weavers call a 'Mother Realm.' Some even say that Lissae is *the* Mother Realm. Of course, it means our Realm is one of the most important Realms, and anything of importance means it is worth fighting for." Lissae's Lore Teller paused to run his eyes over his attentive class. "Fighting means we need soldiers, and soldiers need a General. Lissae's General has a special name – it is a Rank and Title like no other. She has a life like no other, and although her time is often cut short upon our fair Realm, she always comes back to protect us. She is the Altoriae," the Lore Teller raised his hand dramatically over his heart, eyes closed in reverence.

There were the appropriately awed whispers from the gathered students.

Refraining from rolling her eyes became more and more difficult as the years went by. Once each term, Shari and the other students of Ridden Hall were forced to sit and listen to a day's worth of classes on the Altoriaes past and all of the duties the people of Lissae, and especially those of the Shifting Islands. Finding it a colossal waste of time, Shari often tried to subtly do her daily Innarn exercises during the lessons. Usually, she added to the wards protecting the school as well as those on Ronah.

"Lissae is one of only a handful of sentient Realms. She is able to produce sentient islands as well. The Seven Shifting Islands – of which Ronah is one – are the only sentient landmasses on Lissae at the moment. As you all know, Ronah was chosen to house the Altoriae, as when the Seven Shifting Islands come together, Ronah is the most protected. Who can name the other Shifting Islands and the Races which inhabit them?"

A hand shot into the air. The Lore Teller pointed at Carly Thorne, who giggled with her friends and fanned herself. Placing her hands on her lap and sitting up primly, she recited, "Rakemyst, the Island inhabited by the Ilutri."

Shari did her best not to snort at the superior look on the girl's face. Everyone knew about Rakemyst because of her father who grew up there before moving to Ronah. Plus, his Ilutri heritage was a little hard to ignore. Having someone with a wingspan of over twenty-two feet swooping over you at dusk is not something you could easily forget.

"That is correct. Is there anyone else who cares to answer?" the Lore Teller asked, with a satisfied nod in Carly's direction.

"Cantash is the Shifting Island that is home to the Daens," said Lee O'Doherty.

The Daens were a short, fierce race who prided themselves on their loyalty. Their incredible control over the fire Element meant they were able to produce embers or walls of flame at their whim. Shari had seen the Daen troops practising, and couldn't wait to work with them if she ever got the chance.

"Ginorti is the fourth Shifting Island we'll join with," said Diana Winter.

Not entirely accurate, thought Shari. When the Islands converged, it was usually predictable, but occasionally they entered into alignment out of the supposed 'order' of things.

"He's home to the Satyrs," Niketta Thorne murmured.

'He' being Ginorti. Each Island had developed its own personality and preferred pronouns over the years. The Satyrs of Ginorti trained some of the best rapid response troops on Lissae. Heavy hitting earth elementals, their forces topped Lissae's first line of defence, and often left the Realm to flesh out the armies in other Grey Realms.

"The only Shifting Island to start with an all Human population was Talhan," said Rea Flint.

"But," interrupted Lucy Boyce, "in 3026, only sixty years after Talhan was formed, they accepted immigrants from all the races on Lissae."

"Very true, Lucy, but please wait to be called upon. Anyone else?" the Lore Teller lightly scolded.

Oh, ouch, Shari thought, *the poor Innarnian children mustn't suffer being told off.* Rolling her eyes, she struggled to keep her thoughts from her face and concentrated instead on sending trickles of Innarn through the heels of her feet to add to the wards around the school without getting caught.

"Akoren housed the Deities. Now he is inhabited by a few select representatives of the races that came from the other Shifting Islands," Herbet Thorne remarked.

The six Deities of Lissae had left long ago. In the last ten years, their former homes on Akoren had become the central hub for new developments and technologies which would lead Lissae into the future. Shari hoped to get a glimpse of their ancient home mingled with the latest technology one day.

"The Weavers live on Vannali," Ira Ribeck commented.

The Weavers were a somewhat mysterious race who tended towards seclusion. Little was known about them by Lissae's general populace, but as four of the past Altoriaes had been full-blooded Weavers, Shari had a wealth of information about the secretive race at her fingertips, she just had to check the Altoriae's Handbook.

"Aren't we forgetting something?" the Lore Teller hinted.

"The Wisara. They travel between the Islands and provide merchant services to the Islands as they shift around," said Cassie Hudson.

"That is correct. Thank you, class. Our lesson is complete today. I bid thee well," the Lore Teller smiled at them, and Shari gratefully rose to her feet, happy to be able to escape to a lesson where she might actually *learn* something.

"I bid thee well," the students repeated back before noisily gathering their belongings and chattering as they left the room. Shari hung back, disliking the crush which happened between classes. There was something entirely disconcerting when you were pressed against the invisible barrier on the wide, flat tree branch walkways while you were three stories up.

As she dawdled, she noticed the Lore Teller sending to someone outside the school. Without entirely intending to, Shari widened her range a bit and listened in.

'*Do you think you found her?*' a deep voice asked.

'No,' the Lore Teller sent back. '*There is not nearly enough time to discover anything of importance.*'

'*Ridden Hall's Wards were added to through your lesson,*' the voice commented.

Shari knew that voice.

'*That proves nothing at all. There were so many different lessons going on at once. You cannot tell me that you think she is still a student. Surely she must be older?*' the Lore Teller replied.

Shari left the room, wondering at the conversation she'd overheard between the Lore Teller and the Mayor of Ronah. Who could they be talking about? Classes lately had been odd. She had been catching reports from the teachers to the Mayor and occasionally to the Elders of the Island. However, precisely what they were reporting about, she wasn't sure, and whenever she mentioned it to Jonathan, he would remark that it was nothing of consequence and that she should concentrate on her training.

Sighing as she arrived at her next class, Shari tried to look as enthralled as the others did when a different Lore Teller began to tell more of Lissae's tales to the students.

"As Kay'imi raised her hands, the winds rose up to meet them. The three-thousand Ahana Warriors took no notice as they charged towards her on their terrifying steeds, never stopping, never faltering, even as Kay'imi stretched her Innarn to the limit to rain fire down amongst their ranks. Too soon the fearsome Warriors reached the brave Altoriae, and she was overcome by the Ahana ranks. In her last battle, Kay'imi managed to decimate the Ahana Warriors to just a third of their forces before she fell. And thus, ended the life of Lissae's first Altoriae, Kay'imi," the Lore Teller paused, sadness evident on her lined face.

Scoffing inwardly, Shari sent her thoughts out to her Guardian, '*Are you kidding me? Kay'imi was ambushed by the Ahana and taken down by a lone Innarnian Archer. Please, Jonathan, tell me I don't have to listen to any more of this,*' she begged.

'*Shari! Behave,*' Jonathan admonished as he sent his thoughts back to her. '*You must listen. You know that. You must act as enthralled by the Tales of the Altoriaes as all of the other girls in your class are.*'

'*I detest this. Why can't I just skip this class and look up the real facts in the Handbook?*' she grumbled back.

'*We've been over this, Shari. You need to know how the rest of Ronah's residents view the Altoriae,*' Jonathan said, his tone heading towards lecture mode.

'*Fine. But don't think I like it!*' Shari grumbled.

"Shari!" hissed Cassie Hudson, nudging her in the ribs.

"Huh?" Shari asked. She'd entirely tuned the lesson out.

"Miss Dawn? Back with us then?" the Lore Teller asked, eyebrow raised and lips pursed. The other girls in the class giggled. Cassie gave her a sympathetic look.

"Yes, Lore Teller," Shari said, trying to appear contrite.

"Good. Perhaps you'd like to tell us how old Kay'imi was when she died then. I know it's not essential to a Blank, but it is still required learning on Ronah," the Lore Teller said snidely.

The superior look and condescending tone of the Lore Teller made Shari shift in her seat and concentrate on her breathing to remain calm.

When she looked up to answer, Anika Thorne smirked at her from across the open air room, and Shari found it too much to ignore. "Kay'imi was 1217 when she died," Shari answered clearly, meeting the Lore Teller's eyes.

The Lore Teller blinked in surprise. "Well, yes, she was." Her gaze hardened. "But that knowledge does not give you the right to daydream in this class, or in any other."

Shari lowered her eyes and cursed inwardly. "Sorry, Lore Teller." Despite her downcast eyes, she did not miss the smug look Anika gave her, nor did she miss the titters and whispers of the others.

Cassie nudged her shoulder, and she briefly looked up to smile at her. Cassie was one of few people who didn't seem to worry she might be contaminated by the touch of a Blank. In another lifetime, one where Shari wasn't the Altoriae, she and Cassie would have been friends.

There were days like today when she wondered if her secret was really worth this much hassle.

CHAPTER NINE

Spring 4059

Shari flopped onto her bed, exhausted. Ronah and her residents had spent the last week filled with frenetic energy, preparing for the arrival of Ridden Hall's new Headmaster. Every surface had been scrubbed and cleaned, gardens blooming and shops ready to serve. Forced by the watching eyes of others to do every little thing as a Blank, Shari fell gladly into her bed at the end of each day. After the long, stressful week, Shari fell asleep, dreaming of a peaceful glade.

Relaxing into the dream, she unintentionally shifted into the glade and sighed as she lay back on the sweet-smelling grass. Quiet times, whether awake or asleep, were so seldom, she almost wasn't sure what she should do. Closing her eyes and smiling softly, Shari settled back and listened to the gentle chittering of insects.

Drifting off for a moment, Shari wriggled awake at the feeling of wrongness. Frowning as she tried to place it, she was grateful for the complete silence which let her sift through her thoughts in peace. Total silence. Where were the insects? Something must have disturbed them.

Shari rolled into a crouch, a gleaming silver sword appearing in one hand, and her preferred weapon, the black glove with two wicked, razor-sharp blades extending out over her knuckles was ready on her other hand. Her clothing morphed into black leathers without her even realising it, as a deep velvety voice laughed at her from within the mist that started rolling in.

Senses on high alert, Shari remained in the centre of the glade, weapons at the ready. Out of the swirling mist came a speeding dart, so quick and small most beings wouldn't have noticed it. She raised her blade and brushed it away before it could be embedded in her neck.

A veritable storm of the tiny missiles rained down on her as she twisted and turned. Concentrating on slashing the tiny darts out of the air would have been easy if they were just coming from one direction, but Shari persevered. Using air Innarn to disturb the path of the darts, her blades to stop the ones which managed to make it through, and maintaining the shield that hovered just above her skin as her last resort in escaping the indubitably poisoned tips.

After five minutes of twisting and turning, and one particularly impressive back flip, Shari wondered if her attackers had unlimited ammunition. After ten minutes, Shari could feel her concentration slipping, and tried to use her Innarn to pull a boulder from the ground, but try as she might, she couldn't get it to budge from the earth.

Cursing, she pivoted, pushing a great wave of air Innarn down her blade and out, forcing her hidden opponents back. Crashes and breaking branches told of her success. Shari crouched, preparing for the retaliation and drawing in heaving breaths. She had been in enough battles to know this was just a short reprieve.

Then the being with the deep, velvety voice called out a sharp command in a language that caused Shari to relax. She knew those words.

Heavy footsteps alerted her to someone approaching. A broadsword and a dart blower were thrown at her feet. It was a mark of Jon's training that she didn't flinch. Mentally checking her mask was still in place; she put her blade in her thigh sheath and lowered her gloved hand, although she left the claws extended.

"Who are you that dare to enter our glade?" the deep voice demanded.

"Someone in much need of rest," Shari replied smoothly.

The muffled noise of grumbles and stamps surrounded her as the owner of the voice stepped out of the mist. He was gorgeous. Flowing silvery-blond hair fell to his waist, his dark eyes almost identical in colour to the black fur of his legs. His hooves stamped, causing Shari to raise her eyes back up to his. Belatedly, she realised who stood before her.

The head of Lissae's Satyr army.

He must have seen the recognition in her eyes, for he inclined his head to her, although his eyes never left hers.

"I asked not why, but who you are," he spoke again, startling her out of her thoughts, although she betrayed no physical sign of it.

Again, Shari reached out, hoping to discern where on the Realms she had been resting. She almost laughed when the answer came to her. "Forgive me, General Morrow, I was unaware of where I rested."

The Satyr blinked at the mention of his name. His shrewd eyes held hers, and although she knew he couldn't get past her mental shields, she felt a tingle of his Innarn brush up against her. Abruptly the mist cleared, showing the previously empty clearing that held a dozen or so of the Satyrs best ambush troops surrounding her.

"You are of Lissae, but how do you know me?" the General asked, curious.

Shari smiled at him, noting in her peripheral vision the other Satyrs had not lowered their weapons. "We are from the same Realm General, how could I not know you?"

The General looked her over, and this time she felt him probing at her mind. She wasn't quite quick enough to stop the General from discovering her secret. The hardened warrior swallowed audibly and backed out of her mind.

To the surprise of his troops, he dropped to one knee before her, "Forgive me, Altoriae, I did not realise you were..." he broke off, not sure how to continue. Around them, weapons were hastily lowered, and Shari could feel the muttering more than she could hear it.

"There is nothing to forgive, General. It is heartening to see that you and your troops are so vigilant." She could feel the General's relief rolling off him in waves which were almost visible to her.

'Is it true you're residing on Ronah, Altoriae?' he sent to her. Clearly, this was something he didn't want his troops to hear.

Shari sent to him, 'Yes, why do you ask?'

'My daughter and her family should be arriving there tomorrow.' He paused as if he was unsure how much to reveal. 'Please take care of them for me.'

Shari nodded and sent back to him, 'I will do my best.'

'Your best, Altoriae, is almost more than I dare ask for.' The General smiled.

The troops surrounding the two shifted uneasily as the General's weapons levitated off the ground and floated back into his hands. "My thanks, Altoriae," he said out loud. She knew he referred to the silent conversation – which had passed so quickly it was barely noticeable – as much as her audible praise of him and his troops.

"Continue your vigilance, General Morrow. I fear the beings on the other Realms have been growing more restless of late," she said.

The General nodded, and as Shari went to shift away, he said, "It is comforting to know Lissae is once again protected from our foes on the other Realms, but Altoriae, I beg of you, your name, please? Let all Lissaens celebrate your return."

"General Morrow, now is not the time..."

"Altoriae, we have so little to celebrate nowadays. Please," he begged.

"I cannot. I am... forbidden." The General's face fell, and in a move she would no doubt regret, she added, "I can tell you I am SilverCloud's granddaughter."

"You are the Granddaughter of an Elder?" he asked, surprised.

"Yes, General." Before the stunned satyr could ask any more difficult questions, Shari said hastily, "I bid thee well."

As Shari disappeared from their sight, she saw the General turn to his troops and pumping his fist in the air, he declared, "We have discovered the Altoriae!"

Shari groaned as she shifted back into her room. Jonathan was not going to be happy about this.

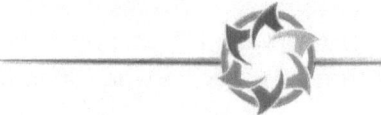

Jonathan Buan scuffed his boots across the rocky ground. He was out patrolling the Realms with Mitchel, and sixteen-year-old Cassandra Hudson, a promising animal trainer from Ronah. The others in the group had split up, and they were doing their level best to rid Amaer of its latest threat.

Finally free of the Q'Aralide's interest, the Grey Desert Realm had been experiencing some trouble with a group of Kemmae – a race of malicious mischief makers who delight in moulding the earth of the

Realm they inhabit to make it inhospitable to others. The Kemmae were a crab-like race who stood between two and four feet tall and between six and eight feet across; their pincers have a toxic coating which eats away at the flesh of humanoids. Not a race you want to run into.

Despite the protective gear he had on and the repeating crossbow he held in front of himself, Jonathan felt his apprehension building. Uncomfortable, he stretched his shoulders and scanned the area. His Innarn failed to sense anything, again.

Jonathan stirred the air around them to create a slight breeze. He was working up a sweat in this dry, desolate Realm. Mentally nudging his glasses back to where they were meant to be, his head tilted slightly to the side as he caught the sound of a faint click of claws behind the mass of boulders which made up the left-hand path they were following.

Motioning to his companions, Jonathan sent to them, 'Ready?' They nodded, and although Cassandra seemed somewhat nervous, Jonathan could see she wanted to show him what she could do.

He counted them down, and on one Cassandra focused her Innarn on the boulders and pushed them out of the way. Mitchel and Jonathan combined their Innarn to shift the Kemmae back to their home Realm of Bantaris.

Cassandra sighed with nervous relief when Jonathan motioned to her that the last of the Kemmae had been relocated. She gave him a tentative grin, which Jonathan returned.

"Pretty good for your first time out on patrol," Mitchel said to her.

Giving him a blinding smile, she laughed. "I can't believe I haven't patrolled before. It feels like every other Innarnian has been out except me!"

"Cassandra, can you move the boulders back..." Jonathan trailed off. Something niggled at him. The fine hair on the back of his neck stood on end as adrenaline began pumping through his body. Breathing deeply,

Jonathan sent his senses out and saw something too big and too dark for the younger ones to handle.

It felt evil and intent, and massive, like the Realm wasn't big enough to contain it.

He'd felt something like this before...

'Jonathan, look out!' Mitchel's warning echoed in his skull seconds before a large, golden shadow flew overhead. Its three eyes peered down at the trio, spotting an easy snack, the claws on the ends of its massive wings flexing menacingly. Its breath hissed out in a giant deadly cloud.

Jonathan stood his ground, thumb and forefinger curled to make a circle, his other fingers in the air as Mitchel threw up a shield over the three of them while Cassandra used her Innarn to lift a boulder, hurling it at the creature.

The enormous creature soared out of the path of the boulder effortlessly, flying a short distance away and breathing out another deadly cloud. Mitchel trembled under the effort of keeping his shield solid enough to ensure the gas stayed away from them.

Cassandra, her breathing ragged and streams of sweat running into her eyes, lifted another boulder despite the effort it cost her. Taking quick note of her actions, Jonathan came to the conclusion she was running on instinct by this stage.

Jonathan shouted a hoarse, "No!" at Cassandra, who dropped the boulder just as the creature flew overhead. Its eyes scanned the two teens, making them tremble before its golden eyes locked onto Jonathan's brown ones.

'Q'Aralide konraei!' Jonathan sent at it. The creature reared back in shock, then it seemed to double in on itself before disappearing, leaving a deafening sonic boom in its wake. The Realm shook. The three humans lost their balance and fell onto the unforgiving ground. Slowly the Realm steadied, although the ringing in their ears remained.

"Jonathan?" Mitchel asked. The student stood beside his mentor, a steady hand held out should he need it, despite the quiver in his voice.

"By the Life of Lissae," Cassandra breathed. "What was that?"

Jonathan grasped Mitchel's hand, and his Apprentice promptly pulled him to his feet. He shook his head as Mitchel looked him over for injuries. It would take more than a fall to hurt him. The pact he had called upon had been the only way to stop the deadly being about to attack them, and let him know just who he was up against at the same time. It was something he'd hoped he would never have to use. He couldn't change what had happened, but now all he could do was make sure Shari and Lissae were as safe as possible.

"It's time to go back. The Altoriae is in more danger than we feared," Jonathan said. Swearing under his breath, he closed his eyes. Darkness surrounded them as they traversed the Realms back to Lissae at a dizzying speed.

Shari relaxed back against the squishy cushions of the couch, spending a rare night lounging with her parents and watching a Silverstone Clan drama on the Crystal Video Screen. She wanted to savour the time she had between now and the morning when all and sundry would find out who bore the title of Altoriae. She had tried contacting Jonathan when she'd returned from the glade, but he'd been out on patrol.

Arilla nudged her as she laughed over something on the screen. Shari grinned and rubbed at her tired eyes. It appeared she'd dozed off.

"Can you hear them? The spirits are close tonight. They don't come for me yet. Wonder if I'll ever see Immosa?" one of the characters intoned dramatically, arm thrown over their eyes for good measure.

Immosa, Shari idly thought, *the final resting place for the souls of Warriors who left Lissae.*

Arilla giggled at the overacting, and Calem hugged her tighter to his side, dropping a kiss onto his wife's head.

'. . . *ri!*' Jonathan's shout penetrated her mind.

'*Jonathan? What's wrong?*' Shari sent back, eyes wide as sleep became the farthest thing from her mind.

'*Shield yourself!*' Jonathan sent, the panic colouring his words spurring her into action. Her training had her reacting before she even thought. Shari immediately shielded herself, and then the rest of Ronah, as Lissae seemed to tip onto her side. She heard her parents gasp even as she caught all of those on the Island who were tossed out of their beds, and laid them back there gently.

She set Jonathan and Mitch back on their feet and found herself glad she'd been lying back on the couch. The power sucked out of all the crystals, only to return in a rush three times as powerful, and there was only Shari to prevent everything from exploding.

'*Jonathan?*' she asked, trembling at the amount of power she held.

Lissae slowly returned to normal. Finally, Mitch contacted her, '*Shari? Are you all right?*'

'*Where's Jonathan? Where's your third patroller?*' Shari sent back, feeling frantic for the safety of her Guardian and buzzed from the amount of pure Innarn running through her system.

'*Jonathan's on the floor curled into a ball. He shifted Cassie home. What's going on?*' Concern for both friend and mentor overcame him, causing a noticeable waver in his thought patterns.

'*Something crossed over. Something big,*' Shari sent before she slumped back into the couch, her exhausted mind ignoring her aching body, already flying out to help Jonathan, Innarn at the ready.

CHAPTER TEN

T he next day Shari lay atop a bluff, watching the waves dance towards Ronah's shore as the wind ruffled her hair. Last night had been frustrating. The breeze teasing her hair went a good way towards blowing her frustrations out of her mind before they consumed her. They had no other sightings of the being who had crossed over. In between searching for it, tending to Jonathan, and her nightly patrol, Shari was exhausted. It was a lovely reprieve to lay on the sandy bluff, with the sun shining on her and the waves kicking up the sea salt so she could taste it.

Below, a rowboat gently nudged alongside the dock. Seven people disembarked. The man in the rowboat waved jauntily, and used his air Innarn to lift their bags and cases onto the dock. Once the last case was out of the rowboat, he turned and headed back to the ship anchored just out of Ronah's perceptive range. General Morrow's daughter had to be one of the seven heaving their bags as they took in Ronah's beach. Gently, she scanned their minds and found herself up against seven brick walls. Either they had natural shielding, or they weren't ready to release their Innarn yet. For most of them, Shari bet on the former, but for two of the younger ones, it may be the latter. Time would tell.

On the bluff, she couldn't be seen. Shari easily slid into Alan Pratt's mind as he greeted the newcomers. Through his eyes, she saw the seven newest arrivals on their Island step unsteadily onto the sandy beach. She felt him reach out and solidify the sand so the family could have a more dignified entrance.

"Welcome to Ronah!" Alan said, a smile flashing in greeting. The tall Mayor had charcoal eyes, straight ebony hair, and light tan made him a shining example of one of Ronah's finest citizens.

"Thank you," said a slim man, his blue eyes piercing Alan's charcoal ones in a way that no one with Innarn would dare. "I'm Jordan, and this is Liza."

'Are they Innarnian, Ronah?' Alan sent to the Island.

'If they are, they are not active at the moment,' Ronah replied. The term active was used to describe a person's Innarn when it manifested, and they became aware of it.

"My name is Alan Pratt, I'm the Mayor of Ronah. I hope you enjoy living here as much as the rest of us do," Alan said out loud.

"Thank you, Alan," a woman said. Slender and medium height, Alan found he couldn't get a good look at her face as she had a hood pulled up and her face hidden in its shadow. "These are our children: Caleb, Christopher, Alistair, Tania, and Jessica."

Shari tuned out after that. She had found out what she needed to know. The woman, Liza, was the one General Morrow had been talking about.

If Shari had been aware that she was going to replace Mr. Anderson as the Principal at Ridden Hall, her answer may have been different.

Laurence Anderson was a name she never wanted to hear again. It made her eyes well up with suppressed frustration, knowing that she'd so badly failed the kindly headmaster. After going on out patrol last year, he'd been replaced with a creature from Vennph, a particularly Dark Realm which is home to the tripodic Wikkur, as well as the Eni. The Eni were malicious shape-shifters, able to permanently assume the form of influential figures to summon others of their kind to possess the subjects they gain. Seriously Dark beings, the Eni are not often seen out of the Dark Realms, but when they were, the aftermath they leave is devastating and generally long lasting.

The one who'd taken over Laurence Anderson had done so when the man had been out on patrol with Jonathan. It had only taken a few months before Eni Anderson had called upon his brethren to take over the bodies of the students.

Fortunately, Shari and Jon had managed to stop the attack before any more lives had been lost, but it still burned Shari's conscious to know she hadn't been able to stop his senseless death.

Although Shari knew Ridden Hall needed a new Headmaster, she deeply regretted the circumstances that caused Laurence Anderson to rest amongst the spirits in the graveyard. The attack by the Eni had been the first she'd faced on Lissaen soil since she'd taken up the mantle of Altoriae, and it was still a bitter blow.

Rising from her post, she turned back to the town. Shari had the feeling that she'd have to work double-time to protect the new Headmaster. As she slipped into the shade of the tree-lined path into town, she realised she hadn't told Jonathan about being found out by General Morrow yet. They'd been so busy last night dealing with the fallout from the creature crossing over. She guessed the creature had to be either really Dark or really Light from the way Lissae rocked on its arrival.

Still, she hoped her Guardian wouldn't begrudge her this one last morning of freedom. She didn't know how Ronah's townsfolk would react to her secret. She was dreading their reactions. After a lifetime of thinking she was one thing, finding out she was the direct opposite would be quite a shock for a lot of people.

Heading back into town, her heart felt like it had sunk to her boots. She stumbled on the path her feet knew so well, and drew the attention of the Mayor and the Hollingsworths.

"Ah, Shari, just the person I hoped we'd meet! I wonder if you could show our new residents around. They need to know how to use things the way you do." Alan smiled at her.

Shari mentally snorted. The 'way you do' meant the Blank way. "Sure, Mayor Pratt, I can do that." She squared her shoulders and plastered on a smile.

"Thanks, Shari. I knew I could count on you!" the Mayor said, beaming at her. Turning to Ronah's newest residents, Alan said, "I'll make sure your luggage gets to your new home. They have number two Arrow Street, Shari. Don't make the tour too long; Ronah can be a bit overwhelming."

"I won't scare them off," Shari said. She turned to the Hollingsworth family and introduced herself.

The father shook her hand and presented his family. Having heard it before, Shari used the moment to look over Ronah's latest residents, doing her best to commit them to memory in the shortest possible time. Jordan and Liza appeared to be close to their forties, and while Jordan stood a head taller than his wife, Liza was of average height, with a lock of silver hair peeking out from her hood.

Caleb, the eldest boy, had to be in his late teens and his short, spiky silver hair gave him away as Liza's son. He towered over the rest of his family, and Shari had to kink her neck to look up at him. Alistair, Christopher, and Jessica all had blue eyes and copper hair, which made Shari think they were Jordan's children. Jessica must be the youngest of the group at nine-years-old.

Alistair was about fifteen, his large eyes straining to take everything in. Christopher, folding his arms in sullen silence, had to be around twelve. Then Shari's gaze fell on Tania. Standing shyly to one side, watching everything with wide, grey-green eyes, her slender form hidden by a loose white shirt and brown knee-length skirt. Her long silver hair done up in an intricate braided. She looked so innocent.

Shari's vision shifted for a moment, and she saw Tania with a sword in her hand, running backwards into a Hantra who had just managed to haul itself from the ground. Standing in front of the first Hantra, Mitch laughed at the expression on her face. Tania turned, saw the Hantra, and scowled. She severed its head and arms as if she had been doing it all her life.

An innocent no longer. Shari blinked and looked up, the family clearly waiting for her to say something. "Pleased to meet you all. I was told you'll be our new Headmaster, Mrs. Hollingsworth?" she said, hoping they didn't notice the tremor in her voice. Who would raise the Hantra on Ronah? Just what did this new family bring with them?

"Yes, that's right. And Jordan will be the new Vice Principal," Liza replied. She took the errant strand of her silver hair and tucked it back under her hood.

Deciding to take a bit of a gamble, Shari said, "One of the things you should know about Ronah and her residents is that you don't have to hide who you are or where you come from here. Feel free to let your hair down, so to speak," she said as she flashed an easy smile, deciding she'd just have to put what she'd seen out of her mind and get on with the tour.

Liza's startled gaze met hers. "What are you talking about?" she asked, her voice shaking.

"It doesn't matter here if you're a Satyr's daughter or an Ilutri's niece or a Wisaran young. Actually, my father is an Ilutri. We're a rather mixed bag here, and no one needs to hide." Shari took Liza's piercing gaze in stride. She'd been under far more intimidating gazes before.

"I'll take that into consideration," Liza said stiffly.

Shari nodded. Jonathan had told her that persecution was common off the Shifting Islands, so it might take a little time for the Hollingsworths to get used to not being judged. "Now, what would you like to see first? Your new home, the school or the main street?" she asked, leading the way up the path towards the town.

"I think the school first, please Shari. Then perhaps our new house?" Jordan said, slipping an arm around Liza. "We might wander around the main street tomorrow if you could point us in the right direction."

Nodding again, Shari said, "Sure. If you see anything you don't understand, please let me know. Ronah is very... different to a lot of other places, or so I've heard." So she'd seen as well, but she wasn't meant to mention that. Soon enough, the charade would be over. She sent a message to Jonathan saying she needed to talk to him after she had finished showing the new family around. She'd been found out, and couldn't keep the person tasked with protecting her out of the loop any longer.

As Shari guided the Hollingsworth family towards Ridden Hall, Jordan asked her about the duties they had been told about in the letter they'd received inviting them to the Island.

"The duties are something each new resident to Ronah must agree to. Otherwise, you need to find somewhere else to live."

Caleb stopped in his tracks. "Are you serious? You mean if we don't agree to these duties, we have to leave? We just got here!" Incredulity dripped from his voice.

"Yes, I'm afraid so. The duties bring a common goal to all of Ronah's residents. Some of us feel we don't have much in common with the others." Shari's mouth twisted into an ironic grin. How true!

"Can you at least tell us what the duties are?" Caleb stubbornly asked. Shari didn't have to be an Innarnian to feel him balking at the thought of having to leave Ronah so soon after they'd arrived.

Shari shrugged. "Sure. They all pertain to the Altoriae. First and—"

"The Altoriae? I thought she was a myth!" Alistair exclaimed, cutting Shari off.

"No, the Altoriae is very real."

"Who is she?" Alistair asked.

Shari bit down on the inside of her cheek before she could speak. "The Elders haven't said." There, she told the truth, as the Elders of the town really didn't have any idea she was the Altoriae. They thought of her as a Blank.

"But if the Elders don't know who the Altoriae is, how can we do our duty to her?" Jessica asked, nose scrunched up and lip curled as she tried to process the idea.

"Ronah is never without an Altoriae for long." Shari smiled patiently.

"But if the myths are true," Tania said, "then there hasn't been an Altoriae for over sixty years."

"If the Elders do not discover who the Altoriae is, the duties the residents of Ronah swear to default to the Guardian."

"I've never heard of the Guardian," Jordan said with a frown.

"The Guardian is the one who trains the Altoriae," Liza said before Shari could respond. Her children and husband looked at her in surprise.

"What?" she asked. "My father told me the stories in great detail when I was younger."

"So, what are these duties we're meant to swear to anyway?" Jordan asked.

"Protect the Altoriae at all costs, assist her, answer her call, ensure a safe place for her to train and help to maintain peace amongst Ronah's residents," Shari said.

"That doesn't sound too bad," Caleb admitted.

An uncomfortable silence descended on the group for a moment as everyone tried to digest what Shari had said as they followed along behind her.

"How far until we get to the school?" Tania asked, fiddling with the cuff of her sleeve.

"Just around the next bend," Shari replied. The group walked to the corner of the road and turned. As one, the Hollingsworth's let out a gasp.

Nine massive bereni trees stood in a ring. Each tree had four levels before the thick green leafy canopy. Wide, flat-topped branches on all bar the ground level acted as either outdoor classrooms or walkways to the other trees, with purpose crafted classrooms on each level, created straight out of the trunks of the trees themselves. Around the outside were smaller shrubs, helping to divide the area into places to eat and play. Although they could only glimpse it, there was a huge area in the middle of the trees which acted as a sports field.

"That's the *school*?" Jordan asked in amazement.

Looking fondly at the school, Shari announced, "Welcome to Ridden Hall!" Turning to face her companions, she saw their expressions ranged from awe to excitement.

"We're going to school here?" Jessica shrieked, practically jumping up and down on the spot, her eyes shining.

"Yes. This is where we go to school," Shari confirmed with a smile.

Christopher let out a low whistle. "If this is the school, I can't wait to see what our new house is like!"

Shari had to laugh at that. "Ronah is just putting the finishing touches on it. It should be ready by the time we get there. We can go the long way, or take a shortcut through the main street," Shari said.

"The short way, please," Jordan said faintly, looking back over his shoulder at the school and shaking his head in amazement.

"How can an island possibly do that?" Caleb scoffed, arms folded.

"Ronah isn't just any Island," Shari said easily. It wouldn't do to put a block on any Innarn they had due to misunderstanding or fear. They walked for a bit in silence, the family waiting to see if she'd elaborate.

"What are all these crystals?" Alistair asked when it became apparent she wasn't going to say anymore. The crystals were everywhere and in all different shades.

"The crystals are what gives us the power to turn things on. Each colour has a different purpose. Each crystal has only so much power to give, so they're often installed in clusters. The more in a group, the more power the crystals can gain and the longer they'll last. The main ones you'll use are the white ones which are used for communication, the black ones which gather power and the orange ones which are fences."

"Fences? But they're just pillars?" Caleb asked, narrowing his eyes.

Pointing to a spot between two of the orange Crystal pillars, Shari said, "Try and walk through there."

Caleb walked up to the spot and inspected it before turning to look back at them. "There's nothing to stop me," he scoffed. Shari started to notice that it had to be his default way of dealing with new or uncomfortable situations.

By his words and actions so far, Shari guessed that even if Caleb weren't Active now, he never would be. There had to be a certain level of acceptance for him to become Active, and it seemed he'd spent too much time on the mainland, where Innarnians were not always accepted.

"Go on then!" Christopher goaded him.

The others watched as Caleb tried to walk forward, before bouncing off the field between the two pillars. Not willing to give up, he put his hands out and pushed as hard as he could, still trying to walk.

"It feels like I'm walking against a cushioned wall!" he exclaimed.

"Between the pillars runs a type of gentle current. By using these instead of the kind of fences you may be used to, we don't have to worry about cluttering up the space we live in, but we can keep animals from the crops and in special yards instead."

"But we've been walking between these pillars since we arrived on Ronah," Liza said, frowning in confusion.

"Only some of the Crystals are linked, just like only certain fences meet up. When we get to your house, you'll receive a Crystal like this." Shari pulled hers from a long chain around her neck. Opaque and oval, all young children and Blanks had one, so she wore it to keep up appearances. "This will allow you to get through the fences without being stopped. Unless someone has keyed the fence for privacy, in which case a chime will sound inside the house you are seeking enter. You can also use it to command other Crystals, but you'll be told more about that later."

Liza and Jordan exchanged a look.

"Life here is going to take a bit of getting used to," Liza murmured.

"Ronah is very different to anywhere else. But it's a good sort of different, or at least I think so. Now, here's Barkley Street, the main street in town. All of the shops are on this street, and if a town meeting is called, it'll be held in the square, which is a bit farther along," Shari smiled.

Silence fell as they walked along, and Shari let them take note of the different shops. The opaque walls of The Top Cat Café caught their eyes. A two-story structure, the walls were transparent in places, allowing them to see the chairs and tables set within. A few shops past the café and they came to the Town Square. When they'd reached it, Tania let out a gasp.

Peering into the other girl's thoughts, Shari smiled.

Tania could quite clearly remember the Town Square of her father's town, where she'd lived until her mother had moved them away. Dingy cracked pavers even the weeds had given up on. Dirty grey seats no one used, not for fear of hygiene, but because they were so neglected they might break if sat on. It was yet another example of the stark difference between where she had grown up and where she would spend the rest of her life.

The lush emerald lawn, just tall enough to wave gently in the breeze, looked so soft and inviting, it made her want to scrunch her bare toes in it. In the very centre stood a stone well, but the brightly coloured stones were like nothing she'd seen before – they were pulsing gently in the morning sunlight. Royal purple flowers that crackled like lightning next to delicate sunny yellow buds, bright-orange leaves waving cheerfully as ruby-red flowers sparked. The vibrant emerald-green lawn led to a bright stone fountain with the clearest sapphire-blue water. Sparkling stones of silver which seemed to flash every now and then dotted the square and drawing her eyes to new and wonderful things.

People were in the square, sitting quietly or talking and laughing with friends. A large hexagonal gazebo rose out of the ground towards one end of the park. The flowers and plants were like nothing she'd ever seen before, and she desperately wanted to learn more about them; like the stones that made the walls of the well, they were in vibrant colours, and they bordered the Square in a way that did not make you feel fenced in, merely surrounded by colour.

Although bright, it wasn't ostentatious. It seemed the rest of the world would be dull compared to Ronah though. Tania thought there was no place quite like this.

Shari slipped out of Tania's thoughts, knowing from her brief trips to the mainland, and endless pouring over the Handbook, that there really was no place quite like Ronah. As they walked on, the incredible mishmash of Elemental Homes had the Hollingsworth's struggling to keep their mouths closed. Domes of water stood next to crackling, purple-flamed walls of the house next door. Alongside stood a moss-covered hill, another version of a rezem, with a door peeking out from behind a creeping vine and open windows made of solidified air. A seemingly frozen yellow twister of air created the house next to it.

Caleb stopped by the air house and pointed to its neighbour. "What is *that*?"

"A house made of plasma," Shari said as she stared at the shimmering, silvery dome-shaped goo.

"Plasma?" Liza asked, and flinched as the sound of muted thunder announced the arrival of a bolt of lightning in the wall of the plasma house.

"Yep. You know about the Elements, right?" Shari walked as she talked, drawing them further down the street.

"Yes," Jessica said, impatient. "There are four. Earth, air, fire and water."

"Close. There are actually six. The four you mentioned as well as plasma and spirit," Shari said.

"Plasma and spirit?" Liza asked weakly.

"See the purple-flamed house?" Shari asked. The family turned and looked behind them, nodding. "It was made by a spirit Innarnian and a fire Innarnian."

Sounds of understanding were made, and Liza asked, "That isn't *our* house, is it?"

"No, you have the one next to it," Shari replied. Their gazes were drawn to the next house. They all gasped while Shari leant back against an orange Crystal pillar and watched.

Ronah was indeed putting the final additions to the Hollingsworth's new residence. The limbs of a bereni tree were twisting and flattening out before their eyes, creating a balcony on the second story. They watched in awe as another thinner limb sprouted and grew, twining its way along to form a guardrail on the outside of the balcony. Vines sprouted from the rail and grew downwards, connecting with the floor of the balcony, creating a strong barrier to ward against falls. A gentle chime sounded from the depths of the house, and Shari pushed herself away from the pillar. Time to show them the new house.

"Is it safe?" Jordan asked as Shari made her way to the front door.

"Yes. That's what the chime was for. Come in. There are a few more things I need to show you before I'll leave you to get settled." Shari walked through the front door, the others following her slowly.

Making her way to the living room, Shari pointed to a large oval of white Crystal once they were inside. "Here is your CVS or Crystal Video Screen. Once you have your crystal, you can use voice commands to operate it, like this. On!"

The Screen slowly came to life, showing a replay of a performance the Silverstone Clan had done a few months ago.

"The other commands are written on a sheet for you. It'll be with your Crystals. Also, I have to show you the CS&SC."

"What's that?" Alistair asked.

"Crystal See and Speak Communications. One of the Guardians came up with it—she was sick of people trying to send to her in the middle of the night, so she came up with a way to 'screen it,' so to speak. Usually, we just call it a Crystal Send."

"Send?" Jordan asked.

"Innarnian telepaths can 'send' their thoughts to other people," Shari explained.

"Ah. So, this will allow us to communicate with telepaths?" Jordan poked at the screen, pressing different buttons to see what they did.

"Yes, as well as anyone else who has one," Shari said.

"How does it work?" Christopher asked, looking around in awe.

Shari moved to stand in front of the small oval-shaped white Crystal portal in the hallway. "Send to Arilla Dawn." Over her shoulder, she added, "She's my mum."

Arilla's face appeared on the Crystal. "I'm sorry, we're out at the moment. If you wish to speak to Calem or me, we can be found at The Quiver and Quill Tavern on Ronah, where for this week only, you can get two main meals for the price of one! Thank you for your send!" her smiling face faded from the Screen.

"Hi mum, just a test run to show the newest family to Ronah how the Crystal Send works." Shari took a breath. "Screen off. My mum and dad own the tavern in town."

"Oh." Liza looked a bit frazzled.

"Why don't I leave you to get settled in? Did you want me to come back and show you to the school tomorrow?"

"No, no, that's ok. I'm sure we can find it again," Liza said.

Shari could sense how overwhelmed the new Headmaster felt. "If you get lost, hold your crystal up to one of the orange pillars and say, 'Guide me to Ridden Hall' and then follow the lit up pillars."

"Thanks for the tour, Shari. We might see you tomorrow," Jordan said, holding out his hand.

Shari made sure her shields were firmly in place before she took his offered hand and shook it. "Probably. If you need anything, I'm only a Crystal Send away." Amidst the thanks of the others, Shari left the house, wondering just how many of the Hollingsworth Clan would turn out to be Innarnian. As it was, she didn't have time to wonder long, as Jonathan's voice sounded in her head.

'Shari, come to the shop when you're ready to talk. We have to work on the wards for the Wisara arrival too,' Jonathan sent her.

Ahhh, her work was never done. 'On my way.' She couldn't fault his timing though.

CHAPTER ELEVEN

 n her way to the shop, Shari ran into Cassie.

"Shari! Did you hear?" Cassie said.

"Hear what?" Shari asked.

"I patrolled the Realms last night with the Guardian for the first time, and..." Cassie was bouncing on her toes, hands clenched together in front on her chest.

Shari hated that the residents of Ronah needed to patrol the Realms with Jonathan. They were doing something she considered to be one of her tasks, and she dreaded hearing – or worse, seeing – when things went wrong. Shari unobtrusively checked to make sure Cassie had all her limbs intact.

"And?" Shari prompted.

"I can't believe it! It was so exciting!" Cassie squealed, jumping on her toes. "The only thing that would be better is if I could go on the Altoriae's patrol!"

Shari clenched her jaw and then forced herself to relax. If she had her say, no one would ever go on patrol with her – it was far too dangerous. "Even if the Altoriae was Anika?" she said, one corner of her mouth quirking up.

"Hmmm, maybe not. I'm sure she'd find a way to get me shovelling the dung of some unspeakable creature," Cassie snorted.

Laughing, Shari said, "That would be typical Anika, wouldn't it? What made your patrol with Jonathan so exciting?"

"Jonathan? How can you call him that? I could barely talk to him last night! The Guardian is the single most important person on Ronah until the Altoriae reveals herself! Even the Mayor has to defer to him," Cassie said, eyes wide as she tried to rationalise Shari's audacity.

"I work at his store. When he hired me, he said I could call him Jonathan," she said with a shrug. They'd been using a job as a cover story to explain why she went in and out of the store so much. Not that Shari ended up doing much work in the bookshop. Most of her time was spent training in the backroom, which she and Jon had expanded and linked to her sanctuary years ago.

"I forgot you work there. You're so lucky." Cassie sighed. She shook her head, and continued her tale. "Well, we were on Amaer, a Grey Realm. We were meant to be relocating some Kemmae, and just as we'd finished when something..." Cassie lowered her voice and leant closer to Shari, "something *crossed over*."

"Really? What?" Shari feigned excited terror. A dread settled deep in her gut just at the thought. Jonathan still hadn't figured out what the being was, and the Ducibus had been surprisingly unhelpful. They really needed to find out exactly who or what had come into Lissae.

"Jonathan!"

The cry from the front of the shop sounded loud enough to startle Jonathan – not the best thing when he had crawled under his desk to find his favourite pen in amongst the haphazardly placed stacks of books.

"Jonathan!"

Ah, the dulcet tones of his Altoriae. The call came closer this time, and Jonathan knew if he didn't move now, Shari was more than capable of using her Innarn to drag him out from under his desk. Even though he managed to get out without banging his head, he still ended up sprawled on the floor in front of his charge.

Rolling her eyes, Shari helped him to his feet. When the door swung closed behind her, she gathered her courage.

Taking a deep breath, she finally submitted to her fate. Already, she'd held off on telling Jonathan for far too long. "General Morrow knows who I am," she said, squinting as if preparing for a blow.

Jonathan closed his eyes and took a breath. "When did he find out?" Shari could almost see his mind racing through plans and contingencies.

Shari winced and admitted, "Last night."

"Last night? What made you think it would be alright to wait this long until telling me? You should have told me as soon as I got back from patrol." His words came out clipped and harsh. He put a hand over his face as if he wanted to hide.

"We did have a few things to take care of last night," Shari said evenly, refusing to take all the blame, even though she did feel slightly guilty. She should have known better than to rest in an unfamiliar place on Lissae. Maybe she'd subconsciously chosen that particular glade because she felt sick of hiding.

"We'll have to inform the Elders," Jonathan sighed and pinched the bridge of his nose. He'd wondered for a while now if Shari would be able to continue to hide her identity. Apparently, his instincts had been correct again. Sometimes, he really hated when he was right.

"When do we have to do it?" Shari asked, startled. Even though she may have wanted someone to know *she* kept the Realm safe, it didn't mean she was ready to face the consequences.

"As soon as possible," he said, sitting down heavily in his chair.

"But..." The look Jonathan gave her stopped her protest before it could start. Shoulders slumping, she nodded once. "Just let me know when." It was her own fault. She didn't have to give General Morrow the scrap of information which would lead to her discovery. Whatever her motivation had been, she'd deal with the fallout as best as she could. To be identified by a well-respected General? They had some serious damage control to do. Now the General and his troops had found out, she and Jonathan had to inform the Elders quickly before they ended up neck-deep in political palon dung.

She cleared her throat. "We can't forget about the being that crossed over either. Any ideas yet?"

"Not really," Jonathan said. "I'm still searching, but I'm having trouble locating the information I need." His face went back behind his hands.

Shari tilted her head, curious as to why he was hiding. After last night, she decided not to push it. "Anyway, can I help?" she asked.

"Unfortunately, no. It's just a matter of sifting through far too much material to determine exactly what sort of being crossed over," Jonathan said, rubbing his temples.

Shari sighed. She couldn't protect the Realm if she didn't know anything about the threat – if the being was even a threat. Mitch seemed to think so, and his word was enough to put her on edge. If they couldn't identify the being that had crossed over, then they'd have to inform the Elders soon. Shari wrinkled her nose, her entire body tensing up. Announcing such a failure just as she was about to publicly take up the mantle of Altoriae had not been in her plans.

The townsfolk already thought of her as a Blank, and she most definitely did not want to give them the idea she was in any way incompetent. A significant deal of pressure fell on her to prevent beings from other Realms crossing over into Lissae, and the pressure came to a head when she didn't know who or what she should even be looking for.

The torch lights in the back room flickered, several of the flames changing colour while others leaped higher and threatened to scorch the roof.

Silently, Jonathan raised an eyebrow at her as he added to the Wards around the room that prevented the roof from being set alight.

Releasing the breath she had been holding, Shari slumped. "Sorry, Jonathan," she murmured.

"Believe it or not, I do understand. However, you must keep your thoughts centred and controlled, especially now," he chided gently.

"I know. I'm working on it," Shari replied. "How long until we have to tell the Elders?"

"Don't worry about reporting it. This one's on my head, seeing as I led the patrol," Jonathan said, brushing away her concern and rising to his feet.

Shari relaxed, letting go of some more of the tension she'd been carrying on her shoulders. Heading for the door, she turned back and watched as Jonathan brushed off the cobwebs he'd collected when he'd been searching under his desk. He flinched as he dusted off his torso, and Shari remembered the slash he'd received a few nights ago.

"Ribs still hurting?" she asked.

"Like Adeon's own," he scowled.

"Here," Shari said. She took a few steps forward and held out her hand a fingers' length away from Jonathan's ribs. A green glow poured from it as her brows drew together in a fierce frown. He'd been more seriously hurt than she'd realised. Healing complete, Shari stepped back and shook the green glow from her hand. It vanished in a shower of sparks.

"Thank you," Jonathan sighed. Breathing was so much easier now his ribs no longer had the persistent ache. He must have broken one without realising.

Shari nodded and gave him a small smile before she quietly left the backroom of his store. Looking back over her shoulder, the weight of her gaze said how upset she felt.

He rubbed a hand over his face and sighed. Both he and Shari needed to work on not keeping secrets from each other. Adeon knew they kept enough from everyone else.

CHAPTER TWELVE

ania woke up the day after arriving on Ronah feeling confused. Her dreams had been really strange. She had all kinds of weird things running through them, and she swore she'd seen Shari chasing the things down in a rather odd costume. Well, school started today, and that would be sure to take her mind off her dreams.

Looking around her room still startled her. She wasn't used to such a vibrantly colourful place. Long, sheer-red curtains fluttered in a soft breeze, flowing over her desk with the sunlight, where her school bag waited for her, packed and ready to go. A painting her grandmother had given her for her last birthday had pride of place above her desk. It depicted a satyr standing in a soft green field, his silver hair flowing out behind him as he looked off into the world. It was a picture of her grandfather as a youth, the first time her grandmother had seen him. He'd been staring off into the forest when her grandmother had stumbled up the hill, bloodied and bruised by the beating the townsfolk had given her when they had discovered she was an Innarnian. The painting symbolised new starts, as well as the love her grandparents shared. Today marked a new start for Tania, but if she didn't get out of bed, the day would start without her.

After her usual wake-up ritual, Tania wandered down the hall to the kitchen. It appeared her mother and stepfather had already gone, but they'd left out a breakfast of fresh fruit and bread which smelled like it had just come out of the oven.

Looking around the warm, inviting kitchen, she couldn't believe how different this house was compared to the one she'd grown up in. The old house was dank and dark, reeking of mouldy tobacco and fear. This house was bright and airy. The kitchen, like the rest of the house, was done in bright, earthen colours. Rich red walls framed by pale-green curtains fluttered in a glassless window. The elements and bugs were kept out by an invisible force-field thingy. Tania and Jessica had watched, entranced when the force-field had activated.

Turning away from the window, she faced the table. Made out of one solid piece of wood, its base was a round pedestal, before curving in and then out again to form the tabletop. Tania loved just running her hands over the table to feel the grain of the wood and wonder what artisan was so skilled to make something so beautiful. The other furniture in the house was the same kind of thing: solid pieces of timber carved into benches or desks or cupboards so skilfully it looked as if the tree had grown that way. Come to think of it, from what they had seen yesterday, they probably had been.

Lost in the beauty of their new home, Tania settled down at the table. As she made herself comfortable, she felt a rush of air and managed to grab hold of the smooth table edge just as her stepbrothers, Alistair and Christopher, burst into the room, followed shortly by Jessica and her oldest brother, Caleb. A slight frown marred her features as she wondered what kind of breakfast her younger brother and sister would be having back on the mainland. Not one as good as this, she decided, biting into an orange slice.

"The first day of school on this weird island," Chris mumbled around a slice of bread smothered with honey. "Wonder what the other kids will be like?"

"Creepy, I bet. They're so quiet!" Jessica, the youngest at the table, shuddered dramatically. The others nodded.

"Has anyone else been having weird dreams?" asked Caleb. Tania looked at him in shock. Her moody older brother was usually the last one to contribute anything to a family conversation. Or any conversation.

Again, they all nodded. Looking at one another, Tania thought none of them really knew quite how to feel about it. Silence descended swiftly over the table as they continued with breakfast.

Alistair broke the tension by saying, "Probably just because of the new house."

Relieved to have someone explain it, they all nodded and noisily agreed as they tidied away. Privately, Tania thought it was usually old houses that contained ghosts and bad dreams, not new ones, but she didn't say anything to the others as they finished tidying and left for school.

As they were walking, Jessica exclaimed in delight as the sun caught a cluster of black crystals in a windowsill as they passed by.

"Remember, they're what give us power," Alistair said. He meant well, but occasionally he came across as a complete know-it-all.

"That doesn't stop them from being beautiful!" Jessica huffed and heaved her heavy school bag up more firmly on her shoulder.

Looking around, Tania couldn't help but agree with her. The crystals were beautiful. Laughing softly, she smiled brightly and caught the gaze of a couple as they walked past her. They smiled back at her, causing her to do a double take. People did *not* smile at each other in her birth father's town. To see someone smiling and free of the heavy burden she had always believed adulthood to be was a welcome change.

With a skip in her step, she walked further down the main street. Ronah was truly a town like no other. Her stepsister had been unable to keep her mouth closed when Shari had been showing them around, and Tania could understand why.

The boys were teasing Jessica again, but once they reached the massive bereni trees, they forgot their teasing and raced ahead to the field in the middle. Jessica wandered off in search of other girls her age, and Tania stood just outside the gate, wringing her hands. She had been standing silently for a while, watching the other students walk into the school, letting their happy chatter wash over her when a group of girls approached her.

"I'm Anika," one girl announced as if Tania should have already known her. "And you are?"

Mayor Pratt cleared his throat, and the students of Ridden Hall settled back into their seats. "As many of you know, we are here today to welcome Ridden Hall's newest Headmaster. Please welcome to our hallowed halls, Liza Hollingsworth."

As Alan spoke out loud, he also included a send. *'There are to be no significant uses of Innarn without great reason as our newest residents have yet to have their Innarn abilities tested. This goes for everyone on the Island, young and old. Any crafting must be shielded. Thank you.'*

Liza stood, smoothed out her grey skirt, and rose to stand next to Alan on the broad branch which formed the stage of Ridden Hall's assembly area as the students applauded.

"Thank you. Although my family and I are new to Ronah, I have great plans for our school. Ronah, as one of Lissae's most famous Islands, is to me, the pinnacle of racial acceptance. No matter what race, creed or Innarn ability, everyone from our Realm, and a few from other Realms, are all welcome on this Shifting Island. This is the ideal I wish to embrace here at Ridden Hall. Over the coming weeks, I hope to meet all of you personally and discover your strengths and weaknesses, as well as your ideas to make Ridden Hall a truly remarkable school," Liza said, her voice strong and friendly, carrying easily through the crowd of students.

Some of the parents who were standing at the back nodded to each other as cheers arose from the gathered students as Headmaster Hollingsworth took her seat.

Mayor Pratt rose and indicated Ridden Hall's newest Headmaster again. The resounding applause made more than one pair of ears ring.

A break was called directly after the assembly, and Shari retreated to one of the semi-secluded courtyards surrounding the bases of Ridden Hall's bereni trees. Just as she settled in, Shari felt a group of people approaching her from behind.

"What do you think you're doing here?" said a snide voice from behind her. It was only because she'd heard the girl approaching – and knowing Jonathan had put in specialised wards at the school which prevented any dangerous beings within them after the fate of the last Headmaster – that Shari didn't react.

"Eating," Shari replied without turning around. She knew it would annoy the girl behind her to no end.

Muttering started up behind her, which grew in volume when it became apparent she wasn't going to turn around. A stampede of pointy heels sounded on the cobblestone path until the group stood in front of her. It seemed Anika Thorne was born for popularity. Her groupies were standing together, off to one side and behind her. *Typical*, Shari thought. She had never seen any of them walk *next* to Anika. They were always one step behind.

Today they were dressed in bright, clinging tops and short black skirts. Shari looked the group over. Anika was making the most of her slim build, wearing a red top with an odd, chunky ruby pendant.

"This isn't your area. Freaks like you aren't welcome here," Anika sneered at her, flicking her blonde hair impatiently as she waited for Shari's response.

Shari bit the inside of her cheek and started reciting the names of the Altoriaes who had preceded her to stop from lashing out at the girl. Liz Ribeck, who had been quietly talking to her boyfriend in the corner, took Shari's angry silence for embarrassment and stood, crossing to Shari's side.

Being familiar at recognising the different signs of Innarn in use, Shari could tell Liz was trying to send to Anika. After several tense seconds in which Anika and her cronies eyed Shari and Liz, Liz evenly said, "Lower your shields, Anika. I know your parents taught you better manners than that."

Tossing her long hair, Anika shot back, "Whatever trivial thing you want to say to me can be said in front of... *her*." She made the word sound dirty.

"You know as well as I that the doors and grounds of Ridden Hall are open to anyone regardless of Race, Creed or Innarn ability. Headmaster Hollingsworth just announced as much this morning. Is your memory really that bad?" Liz said, meeting Anika's sneer with a fierce glare of her own.

As Anika opened her mouth to retort, Aram Thorne cleared his throat from the other side of the courtyard. "Anika, your attempt at levitation this morning was really subpar, so I don't think you're in any position to criticise or demand anyone goes anywhere," he said, shaking his head.

All colour drained from Anika's face before it rushed back in an angry flush. "Oh, you think so, do you? Well, levitation isn't really my thing anyway," she said snidely, flicking her hair behind her shoulder. With an undignified huff, she stormed off, her cohorts trailing behind her in a flurry of sniffs, and muttering unflattering things about Aram and Shari as they went.

"Everyone is entitled to an off day," Carly Thorne said snidely as she turned to follow her cousin.

"It's a shame Anika seems to have more off days than on," Aram said with a friendly wink to Shari.

Shari mumbled affirmative from around a mouthful of food. Idly, she wondered if she had really been a Blank, would Aram comparing her to Anika offend her or not? Before she had time to dwell on the thought, she realised Liz had been talking to her.

". . . Can you believe the Elders think that she's the next Altoriae? I mean really, that just doesn't ring true to me."

Swallowing with great difficulty, Shari sent her thoughts out to Jonathan again. 'Do the Elders think Anika is the next Altoriae?'

'Well... yes, most of them do. Anika is the right age, and in the Annual Tests she is one of the highest,' Jonathan sent back.

Shari did some mental calculations. Did she call Jon out on the Elders knowing her age? Did it really matter? They'd be revealing her name any moment now. She contented in grumbling to herself and closed the connection with Jon. If he could hide the Elders knowing her age, what else was her Guardian keeping from her?

Shari blinked as she came back to her conversation with Liz and Aram. The good thing about instantaneous mental communication was that you lost no time. Which meant no one knew you'd talked to anyone else, but also made for confusing conversation leaps at the best of times.

"So who do you think is the Altoriae?" Liz asked smoothly as Aram stepped up to her side.

"It could be anyone," Shari idly replied. Liz listened, too enthralled with Aram as he rattled off a list of people who would do a better job as Altoriae than Anika to notice Shari's fleeting smile.

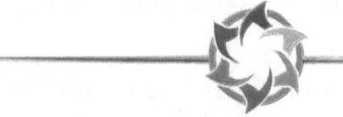

Mitch looked up as the bell over the front door rang, smiling as Jonathan stepped into the shop.

"Hello Mitchel, has it been busy this morning?" the Guardian asked as he hung his hat on the coat rack just inside the glass-panelled door.

Stifling a laugh at Jonathan's ever-formal manner, he replied, "Oh, not at all, good sir. Although," he added, dropping his officious tone, "Isobelle Thorne asked if you could give her a call. She wants to order a particular book – apparently, it's very rare."

"No problem, I'll call her after our lesson," Jonathan said, heading towards the back room. '*Your shields are getting stronger,*' he sent, as he said, "I almost didn't catch the 'ever-formal' crack."

You were meant to hear it! Mitch sent back, laughing out loud.

'*You know it is part of –*'

'*Your training. I know, I know! I should be eternally thankful you aren't forcing me to change my way of thinking into the out-dated, over-formalised way you were taught. I am grateful, and I appreciate how much your teaching method varies from the way you were taught,*' Mitch sent, even as he wiped the dust rag over the shelves.

Pausing at the gateway of the backroom, Jonathan smiled at him and sent, '*Ok, you've got me there.*' Out loud he added, "I have a new shipment coming any moment now, so can you empty out the receiving room?"

"Already done. Although I don't know why you get me to do all the grunt work when you could do it in two seconds flat!" Mitch said

"Builds character," Jonathan replied as he stepped into the backroom.

"Builds muscles is more like it," Mitch muttered in response. Shifting had to be the one Innarn skill he wished for. To be able to move things with his mind would make life so much easier. However, it would also give Jonathan the opportunity to take him through more torturous lessons. Each day during the quiet period before lunch, Jonathan would tutor him in either Innarnian skills or Guardian duties. He wondered what method of torture Jonathan would invoke on him today.

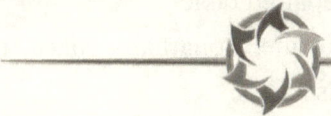

'*Again!*'

The command thundered through Mitch's shields, threatening to break his concentration as he tried to shrink the pile of books on the table in front of him. So far, he'd managed to do the backdoor, Jonathan's glasses, and for some bizarre reason, he'd turned a tool set into a vase complete with flowers.

'*Again!*' came the command.

Concentrating with all his might, Mitch blocked Jonathan's voice from his mind and closed his eyes. In his mind's eye, he pictured the books shrinking. Opening his eyes, he focused on the books, just as the ring of the bell over the front door sounded. His gaze shifted and he watched, horrified, as the table underneath the books shrank to the size of a matchbox before he heard a tiny splintering sound as it was crushed by the pile of books.

"I take it you can fix it?" Jonathan asked kindly.

Mitch nodded. Fixing was something he excelled at. He should be, Adeon knew he had enough practice at it. Jonathan gave him a small smile and went to see who had rung the bell. Crossing to the mess, Mitch moved the books, flipped the miniature onto its back before melding the broken legs back into their rightful spots by pushing the particles of wood back together with his Innarn. Flipping it back on its feet, he returned it to full size with ease. If only Jonathan's lesson were on enlarging things instead of shrinking them, he'd have it mastered in no time!

"Right," Jonathan said, re-entering the room, "where were we?"

"Testing the table's strength," Mitch muttered as he lifted the pile of books back onto the newly repaired table.

"Looks strong enough to me," Jonathan replied, not glancing up from the flier he carried in his hands.

"What's that?" Mitch asked, curious. Not much could distract Jonathan from a lesson.

Clearly startled, Jonathan looked up. "This? It's nothing. Now," Mitch sat down with a thump as the chair Jonathan had shifted behind him collided with the backs of his knees, '*again!*'

Another half hour later and both Mitch and Jonathan felt confident he had mastered the transmutational earth shrinking skill. By the end of the lesson, Mitch had been able to shrink down the new shipment when it had arrived and put it all out on the shelves without breaking into a sweat, and without misplacing a single book – which was quite a feat for him, no matter what size the books were.

"If you are feeling more confident now, I will give Isobelle a call," Jonathan said. More to himself than Mitch, he added, "I wonder what book she's after this time?"

As Jonathan sat down in front of the smooth white Crystal Send to call Isobelle, Mitch picked up the flier which had distracted Jonathan during the lesson. It was one of the Wisara fliers, he noted with surprise. As usual, it depicted everyone who travelled with the troupe, from the performers to the merchants and their families. Amongst the various people who were moving around in the black and white photo, a cocky man came to the front for a moment. He faced the camera squarely and winked at it before another man pushed him aside, his eyes flashing gold. Mitch blinked and watched the scene repeat itself again. However, before the golden-eyed man came to the front again, Jonathan's voice distracted him.

"*Which* book?" he was saying. Pretending to search for a book behind Jonathan, Mitch crept around so he could see into the crystal without being seen.

Isobelle Thorne, looking as serene as always, calmly smoothed her deep red hair. "The *Hekkor Mafae*."

Jonathan turned pale, "Isobelle, I don't think it is a book you should be looking into," he said cautiously. "I don't mean to offend but..."

"Don't worry Jonathan, it's not for me. It's for my father-in-law. He's fascinated with the Dark Ones, and a book about their council would be perfect for him," Isobelle soothed even as she looked slightly down her nose at him. Clearly, she wasn't going to take no for an answer.

"Still, I don't think that..." seeing Isobelle's look, Jonathan paused, "I'll see what I can do, Isobelle, but no promises. I know Benjamyn would not do anything silly with it, but even knowing it was in Lissae is enough to bother me."

Bother him? *If he were any more bothered by it*, Mitch thought, *he'd have to change his pants.*

Jonathan's lips thinned, and he shot Mitch a disapproving look out of the corner of his eye. Hiding a grin, Mitch picked a book from the bottom of the stack and held it up as if to say he'd found what he had been looking for. Out of range of the Send's view, Jonathan motioned to the front of the shop. Mitch wasted no time in taking the hint.

As he passed by the door, his eyes fell on the Wisara flier again. He couldn't help but wonder what had gotten Jonathan so spooked by it. Usually, his tutor carried himself with an enviable calm, but he seemed extraordinarily jumpy since the being had crossed over. It wasn't like Jonathan to take so long to identify a being, nor to make plans and contingencies for when it appeared on their doorstep. So far, he hadn't heard so much as a whisper of thought that Jonathan was working on finding and sending this being back to where it came from. He made a note to talk to Shari about it just as the bell signalled another customer.

CHAPTER THIRTEEN

Walking to school the next day, Shari found herself dawdling. Jonathan had requested to meet her there this morning to make it look like they were just crossing paths, and she knew he would want to talk about meeting the Elders, something which she wasn't looking forward to. Eventually, she came within sight of Ridden Hall and sure enough, Jonathan stood patiently near a Crystal Pillar, casually greeting people as they went in – which caused the older half of the female students to swoon.

Rolling her eyes, Shari walked up to him.

"Well met, Jonathan," Shari said, jostling him lightly with her shoulder.

"Shari! Well met. I wonder if I could talk to you for a moment, please," he said pleasantly.

"Of course," she said easily.

'*I've arranged for us to speak to the Elders and the Mayor before school today,*' Jonathan sent to her.

'*Before school? The Wisara are arriving today. Won't they be too busy?*' Shari sent, eyes flicking over the students as they poured through the gates, looking curiously at the Guardian.

'*Shari, the Wisara will bring word from General Morrow and the other Elders,*' Jonathan reminded her.

Sighing, and muttering something about the talk lasting the rest of her life, she sent her agreement. She bowed her head like a good little Guardian groupie and moved away from Jonathan. His celebrity status meant he was always highly sought after, much to her amusement. She leant against a tree to watch his groupies swarm towards him when she felt a group of people approaching her. Sensing no threat, she paid them no mind.

"Oh, your outfit is so tacky!" a voice said from behind Shari.

"Anika. How nice to see you again," Shari drawled, her tone saying quite the opposite. Shari turned around to see Anika standing in front of her groupies. Rea Flint, Carly, and Rhianna Thorne were intently looking at Maeve Riley, who was showing the group her new gold tongue ring. Erica Ribeck loudly exclaiming that she would be the next to get her tongue pierced.

While the others giggled, gossiped and exclaimed over Maeve's tongue ring, or peered with ill-disguised longing at Jonathan, Anika sauntered over and stood in front of Shari, a smirk on her face. Jonathan moved subtly closer to her, mentally reaching out to let her know he was there.

"I figured you might want to meet Tania. Her mother is Mrs. Hollingsworth, our *new* Headmaster." Anika delivered the last with a decided increase in her smirk factor. "Tania, this is," Anika's gaze condescendingly wandered over Shari, "no one of any real importance." Anika walked past Shari to talk to Jonathan, bumping her shoulder into Shari as she did so. Shari rolled her eyes, used to Anika's posturing.

"You really should meet the Guardian, though. He's even more important than the Mayor!" Anika gushed as she boldly grabbed hold of Jonathan's arm.

Jonathan stiffened slightly, and Anika's groupies looked on, stunned. No one touched an Innarnian of Jonathan's level without permission. Even Anika should know that.

With all the stunned faces gaping at her, Anika seemed to realise she may have overstepped her bounds. She patted Jonathan's arm fondly and beckoned Tania over. Tania stubbornly stayed still, looking at Shari curiously. Rolling her eyes, Anika started blathering to Jonathan, who did an excellent job at covering up his uneasiness at being so unceremoniously grabbed.

"Sorry about Anika, we don't get on very well." Shari gave Tania a half smile. "Did you get a chance to use the Screen yet?"

"Yeah, it's the *best*! Is there something that will tell us what will be playing when?" Tania grinned.

"Yeah, our newspaper, the *Shifting Island Sentinel* does. It should be delivered tomorrow," Shari replied.

Anika seemed to realise Tania was actually conversing with Shari. "You know her?" Anika asked condescendingly. She clearly thought Shari wasn't worthy of anyone's time.

"Yes, Shari showed us around town when we arrived," Tania said.

"You *would* be the one chosen to show the newbie's around," Anika said, returning to them, a sneer marring her features. "No Innarn to speak of."

Shari didn't glance at Jonathan, but she mentally asked him, '*Can I tell them now?*'

'*We don't know what your task is, Shari, and we really shouldn't tell them before we tell the Elders,*' Jon sent, subtly stepping away from Anika so she wouldn't grab him again.

Each Altoriae had a particular task to do once she announced herself to the rest of the Realm. Their individual tests varying, but all were deadly to the people around the Altoriae. There were no records of the test – or curse – ever being found before the new Altoriae was announced. The idea stemmed from a slew of false people claiming to be the Altoriae, and the real one would complete the test to prove to the townsfolk that she was actually the Altoriae and not a phoney. Jonathan had tirelessly been searching his records for any hint of what they might be facing for years, but had yet to turn up anything.

'*You know you aren't going to find it before the meeting, so why not?*' Shari wheedled.

She caught sight of the grin forming on his face. '*Alright, you may as well,*' he sent back. He crossed his arms and leant back against the Crystal Pillar behind him, taking in the faces of the students around them.

"I have more Innarn than you could ever imagine," Shari said evenly. It wouldn't do to appear snide and condescending in the history books.

"You're lying! Everyone knows you're a Blank!" Anika scoffed, rolling her eyes and looking at her groupies for backup. They were shaking their heads and laughing.

A blade appeared in Shari's hand, her glove on the other and her pants and shirt morphing into her black leathers. "I have been honing my Innarn skills since three years of age. I know of more ways to protect Lissae and her residents than you could ever hope to imagine. While you sleep peacefully at night, I am out defending our Realm against threats too horrific to mention. While your biggest daily problem is what to wear, mine is whether I'll get enough time to clean my weapons between each bout of fighting," Shari said in a low voice, war leathers morphing back into her regular clothes, her weapons disappearing with a sharp snap that made the closest people jump.

Shari had the satisfaction of watching Anika's mouth drop open as she turned away from the crowd and headed towards Ridden Hall. She could hear the murmurs swelling behind her. No doubt they were trying to figure out how she – supposedly a Blank – had managed such a feat.

Tania, walking to the front of the swelling crowd of school students stopped and called out to Shari, "Wait! Who *are* you?"

Shari looked over her shoulder, grinned and said the answer the students of Ronah had already guessed. "I'm the Altoriae," she shrugged, as if to say, *who else?*

Shari could feel the shock rolling off the crowd, and although she could feel Jonathan's silent support, she used her long legs to advantage and paced away from the crowd as fast as she could without drawing attention to herself.

She stopped on the far side of the closest bereni tree, away from the prying eyes of the other students. By mid-morning, everyone in the school would know what she had declared, and by lunchtime, the entire Island would know. News would reach the rest of Lissae before nightfall, if it hadn't already. Her peaceful world had just ended.

Liz Ribeck caught up to her, only the slightest bit out of breath. "Shari?" she asked quietly.

'Yes?' Shari sent back.

Liz flinched, clearly not having expected Shari to send to her. Shari's eyes hardened at the tiny movement, but she waited to see what Liz would say.

'Is *it true?*' Liz sent.

'It *is.*' Shari didn't pretend to not know what Liz was asking.

"You aren't joking, are you?" Liz asked softly.

"No, I'm not," Shari said, a tiny laugh at the idea escaping before she could censor herself.

Aram, out of breath, rounded the corner and spotted his girlfriend. "Liz! I've been looking for you," he said, crossing to her side, before noticing Shari. "Hey Shari, I just heard, and I wanted to say…"

Liz suddenly became fascinated by a piece of lint on her shirt. She didn't look directly at Shari or Aram, but Shari could tell she was listening intently.

"Yes?" Shari asked, warily.

"I just wanted to say… I just want you to know I'm glad – we're glad," Aram amended when Liz gave him a nudge, "to know you're… well, that you're you," he said clumsily.

Shari just stood there for a moment, stunned. Somehow, she hadn't expected any indication that people were happy she was the Altoriae without some sort of political gain for their involvement. "Oh, I… thanks. That means a lot."

Bowing their heads slightly in deference, Liz and Aram said their goodbyes, not quite meeting her eyes, but sending rapidly to each other as they walked away.

CHAPTER FOURTEEN

few minutes before the first bell to signal the start of lessons, Shari got the send she'd been dreading.

'Shari, it's time.'

Shari sent an acknowledgement to Jon and took a breath. Shifting in public for the first time, she reached out, pulling Jonathan and Mitch with her to the Mayor's waiting room. She had to stifle a giggle as she saw Mitch only had a towel wrapped around himself. Jonathan, as always, looked calm and put together.

"You're meant to at least warn us first," Mitch grumbled as his clothes arrived.

Shari grinned, before looking away. "I love your towel," she muttered to Mitch, "it's very suave."

Mitch glared at her, grumbling under his breath. Shari had to bite her lip before laughter burst from her. Jonathan looked the other way, a smile tugging at the corner of his lips briefly. As Shari hastily shifted Mitch out of the room, Alan Pratt came out of his office.

Genially, he greeted Jonathan before turning and nervously smoothing his hair down and turning to Shari and bowing his head to her.

"Well met, Altoriae. Are we ready to start the meeting?" he asked.

"Just waiting on my apprentice. Mitchel will be along in a minute," Jonathan said easily, while mentally nudging Shari.

They both tried to smother their laughter but failed when Shari shifted Mitch into the centre of the room, his pants inside out and his shirt back to front. Alan stared at him, and when Mitch looked down and cursed, Shari shifted him out again.

When he reappeared again, clothes worn the right way, it was to a room full of laughter, and he had to join in too.

"I think," he said when they had stopped long enough to draw breath, "this is as good as you're going to get me."

Alan nodded. "If you'll follow me?" He motioned them into his office, and they went in.

Tania walked into the Mayor's office. Her feet had led her there from the school. No doubt her mum would be upset she'd missed out on her first classes, but she felt right down to her bones that she had to swear to the duties Shari had mentioned. Looking around the room she was in, Tania couldn't help but admire the elegance and simplicity of the furnishings. *There I go again,* she thought, *sounding like Dad.*

'*I do not think you sound at all like your father,*' said a soft voice. '*I think you sounded like yourself, although I must admit, I have not heard your natural father speak, so I have nothing to compare.*'

Looking warily around the room, Tania tried to spot the speaker and failed. She couldn't see anyone or anything to hide behind. "Hello?"

'Yes, hello. Could you explain why you have a different surname to your mother?' the voice said, a touch impatiently.

Standing abruptly, Tania raced to the potted jade plant and peered behind it. She was definitely the only one in the room. Confused, she slowly returned to her seat. There were no other living souls around.

'Well! Excuse me! I am most definitely living, thank you very much!' the voice sounded insulted, but Tania couldn't even see the owner of the voice.

"Maybe if you told me where you were..." Tania began.

'I am under you,' the voice said impatiently.

Once again, Tania leaped to her feet, sending the chair skittering to one side. She eyed it warily, half-expecting fangs and eyes to appear at any time. She could almost see the owner of the voice rolling its eyes.

'I do not have eyes to roll, and I did not mean directly under you. I am Ronah,' the voice was gentler this time, as if soothing a frightened creature. To be fair, that was pretty much how Tania felt at the moment.

"You're... you're the Island?" Her eyes widening, Tania tried to stifle a gasp.

'Yes. Didn't anyone tell your family about me? You have been the only one I can talk to,' Ronah said, curiosity clear in her tone. Her tone? His tone? Ze's tone? Did Island's have genders?

"No, they didn't," Tania eyed the floor warily. "How can you speak anyway? You don't have a mouth, do you?"

'No, I don't have a mouth.' Tania swore she heard the Island chuckling. 'I send my thoughts to you – I'm a telepath – and you can do the same to me. The rest of your family may not be able to. Or they may just choose not to use their abilities.'

"How do you know I can send?" Tania asked, looking at the ground.

'Try talking in your mind,' Ronah coaxed.

Tania rolled the thought around in her head. Her birth father was rather closed-minded when it came to the elemental magic many people of Lissae had inherited. However, her mother and new stepfather weren't. She wondered if she could...'Do you mean like this?' she sent.

'That's it! A bit louder, maybe, but then, you have a soft speaking voice to start with,' Ronah practically trilled.

'So, what's this then? My thinking voice?' Tania asked, one side of her mouth quirking up in a half smile.

Ronah chuckled. Waves lapped against the beaches. The experienced residents grabbed onto something, almost unconsciously, leaving the newer residents and guests struggling to keep their feet on the rocking isle.

'Thank you, friend Tania,' Ronah sent when she could think clearly again. 'It has been a long time since someone has made me laugh like that. But now,' her voice turned pleading, 'would you answer my earlier question? I fear I will never understand the intricacies of human relationships.'

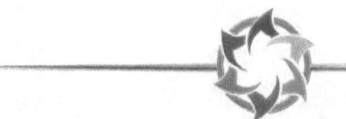

"So, now we're all here," Alan said, clearing his throat and looking distinctly nervous. In his whole time as Mayor, he'd never had to deal with or answer to an Altoriae, and now, one sat on the other side of his desk. Shari could see that in the Mayor's mind, she was coloured differently. No longer was she the sweet little girl he could relax around. Now he saw her as a warrior, a fighter, and possibly a threat to his position as Mayor. More than one previous Mayor had been kicked out of office by an Altoriae, after all.

"Now we're all here," Shari said, picking up where he left off, "you can relax. I'm not going to kick you out of office. I think you're doing a fantastic job," Shari said. She felt Jonathan's approval as well as the lessening of tension in Alan.

"Well, thank you," he said jovially, sitting down in his chair behind his desk, "but I do have a few questions for you, and I'm afraid they can't be put off any longer."

"Ask away," Shari replied.

"First – and traditionally, I suppose – your duties as Altoriae." He held up his hand when she opened her mouth to speak. "I know you most likely know what they are already, but as part of the tradition, I have to tell them to you again." Taking a deep breath, Alan began, his eyes sliding down the sheet of paper in his hand as he read out loud: "The Altoriae's duties include first and foremost protecting the Realm, protecting Ronah and its residents, calling Ronah's residents to arms in times of need, teaching Ronah's residents, maintaining peace on Ronah, and ensuring Ronah's young remember their Elders pledges to the Altoriae."

"You missed one." Shari looked up from studying her chipped nails.

Alan, apparently about to continue, paused with his mouth open and frowned. Snapping his jaw shut, he looked down at the notes on his desk. "I did?"

Shari received the Innarn version of a kick under the table. Smiling brightly, she said, "Nope. Just testing." To Jonathan, she sent '*What about the seventh duty? The one you keep saying I neglect?*'

'*That is between the Altoriae and her Guardian. It is not for outsiders to know the Altoriae has a Handbook. Can you imagine what would happen if the information fell into the wrong hands?*' Jonathan sent back.

'*Yeah yeah, alright. Keep your shirt on!*' As Shari tuned back in, it appeared the Mayor had been reciting Ronah's duties to her as well.

"Guiding and Guarding the Altoriae when no Guardian is available," Alan's voice came back into focus. The Mayor met the steely look in Jonathan's eyes, which was intended for Shari, if she'd just turn around.

The Mayor gulped noisily. "Not to say you won't be around, Jonathan. It's just... uh..."

"Tradition," Jonathan supplied. "It's tradition for you to read the duties out."

Smiling, relieved, Alan nodded. "That's right. Um, there are a few things about your duties we need to discuss, Shari," he said, referring down to his notes again. "Your fourth duty – teaching – we should get you started as soon as possible."

"I'd prefer to start after the test is done."

"Of course," Alan said, nodding his head. "You can start teaching after you finish the task. We'll discuss what lessons you want to take over then." Seeing Shari nod, he gratefully continued, "You have a safe place to train?"

Shari nodded again and felt a shift in the wards and a tickling in the back of her mind as someone tried to send to her. She blocked it with an ease borne of long practice.

"Altoriae or not," said a voice behind her, "it is rude to block out your Elders."

Turning, Shari saw Edward Thorne and smiled, until she glimpsed the other Elders from Ronah crowded around him.

He smiled back at her and glanced down at his left hand as his fingers flexed unconsciously. "I never got a chance to thank you properly for this."

"No problem, Elder Thorne. You wouldn't be the same with only one arm." Shari tried to make her voice light but feared she had failed.

"So, it is true," he said softly.

"I have never lied to you, Elder," said Shari, "maybe misled..." she paused, awkward at having finally admitted her deceit by omission.

His gaze hardened. "Then say it."

Shari sighed, right from the tips of her toes. "I, Shari Sky Dawn, do swear to you, Elder Thorne, that I am Lissae's thirteenth Altoriae," she said, with her fist over her heart.

Edward looked at her for a long moment. "I, Elder Thorne, accept your vow as Truth, Altoriae Shari Dawn," he said, smiling at her through the tears which were threatening to fall. The other Elders sucked in a breath. Clearly, Edward had spoken out of turn.

"Care to explain why we should take you at your word as well?" Elder Silverstone said, looking down at her.

Jonathan and Mitch stood as she did. She morphed into her leathers again, feeling somewhat more exposed this time. The blades on her glove glinted in the sunlight bathing the room, and she took a tiny moment to breathe.

"I've fought for you for longer than you've realised. I fought for you when the Eni tried to take over Ronah's young. I've fought so many battles I can't remember them all, but perhaps, for those of you who were there, you'd remember the battle of Neharn or the fight at Azmine's Ridge? Those are but a few examples, but if you want I can give you more." her eyes locked with Elder Silverstone, who peered down his nose at her.

"I thought you'd be older," he murmured, "or wiser, maybe. Certainly not the sort of person who would talk to an Elder this way." His lip twisted with disdain as he sized her up and found her lacking.

"Are you serious? You want someone passive as the person who's protecting your Realm?" Shari raised her brows. The blades of her glove trembled in their casing for a moment, but she managed to keep them sheathed.

"Not passive, merely more respectful," he sniffed.

"I'll respect you more when we've fought side by side," she snorted. She crossed her arms, the bladed glove disappearing.

153

"Okay," Alan interrupted with forced cheerfulness, "I think that should do us for today. Let me know when you've discovered what your test is. I need to know when to let the town know. I'll let Ridden Hall know you'll be in contact."

"Sure thing," Shari said moving towards the door. Jonathan and Mitch followed silently, eyes locked onto the Elders.

"You're the first Altoriae Ronah has seen in over sixty years," Alan said, "I know you'll do us proud."

"I intend to," Shari replied, meeting his eyes.

Alan gave a solemn nod as Edward Thorne moved to open the door for them.

"Thank you, Elder Thorne," Shari said, dipping her head. She could feel Elder Silverstone bristling.

"No, thank you, Shari. It is gratifying to have a name to our Realm's protector now. I wish you the best of health, although I can't help it if I'd hoped..." Shari's eyes hardened for a moment, and he raised a hand against her assumptions. "I have all the faith in the Realm in you, Shari. I just wish you, of all our young people, didn't have to carry the burden of your title. Who is going to help me eat all of Harmony's carrot stew when you're out fighting now?" he said, his eyes downcast.

"Edward..." she said, trying not to laugh.

"Now, now. Don't mind this old man. Shari, I..." his eyes lowered, and the fingers of his left hand flexed again, "I bid thee well, Altoriae."

"I bid thee well, friend," Shari said. Looking up at her sharply, his eyes glistening suspiciously, he nodded as Shari, Jonathan and Mitch slipped out of the office.

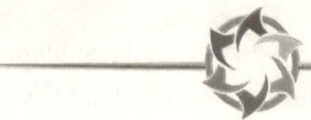

When they stepped out of the Mayor's office, they found Tania, still in the waiting room, with a look of intense concentration on her face. Shari, curious, tried to tap into her conversation but received the equivalent of a mental slap on the wrist from Jonathan, and a mortified '*Shari!*' from Ronah. This seemed to break Tania's concentration, and she looked up at the group.

"Can anyone think of a way to explain the joys of marriage?"

"Who are you trying to enlighten?" Jonathan looked amused. Tania looked him straight in the eye, unaware yet just how unusual it was for him. Most people tried to show the Guardian deference by not meeting his gaze for too long.

"Ronah," Tania said simply.

Mitch was about to lean against the doorframe and missed, having to mentally catch himself before he fell. Jonathan stood there slack-jawed. Shari seemed to be the only one who wasn't surprised.

"Anyone?" Tania asked, looking at the trio hopefully.

"I guess," Shari said, "you would have to get someone who is married to answer such a personal question." '*Ronah, why don't you ask Shelley Ribeck? She'll tell you.*'

"Thanks, Shari. I honestly don't know what Mum would have said if I'd asked her!" Tania said, sighing in relief.

Shari turned her piercing gaze on Tania. '*How did you know I was talking to Ronah?*'

"What?" Mitch asked, lost.

Tania looked at Shari, '*I have no idea,*' she sent, shrugging her shoulders.

Shari could see the honesty colouring her thoughts.

"Am I the only one who missed something here?" asked Mitch.

'*Tania and I are Linked,*' Ronah informed Shari and Jonathan.

"Yep," Mitch continued, seeing no one was answering him. "I'm the only one here who has no clue."

'*What do you mean?*' Tania and Shari both sent to Ronah.

The Isle merely replied, '*Ask Jonathan.*'

"Shari, you should know this," Jonathan chided gently. Shari took a moment to think, then her eyes widened with the implications.

Before she had time to dwell on it anymore, Alan's door opened and he said, "Miss Bryant, I believe you wanted to see me?" He indicated to his office.

"I do, thank you," Tania replied. The others had time to watch her rise, take a breath, and then they were out on the sidewalk.

Mitch shot Shari a look, and she shrugged. Time to get to work.

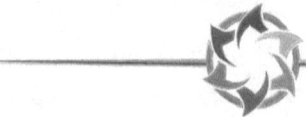

Tania looked around the Mayor's office, surprised. It was decorated in an eclectic elemental fashion. Bookcases of air twisters, a desk of water with shots of Flame curling through the top, chairs of earth and pictures of all the Elements at their most powerful adorned his walls. His desk was bare apart from a folder, a fountain pen and a name plaque which read: *Mayor: A. Pratt.*

She started to chuckle before thinking it might not be such a good idea and choked on it halfway, ending up coughing.

The Mayor looked at her and laughed. "My parents thought it would be funny too. I have to check after every meeting to make sure it doesn't read 'Our Mayor is A Pratt'."

Laughing freely now, Tania smiled at him warmly.

"Do you know," he said after he conjured up a glass of water for her, "today is an excellent day for our Realm."

"Why?" Tania asked, head tilted to the side.

"Because today, Lissae has found Her Altoriae, and Ronah has linked with another," the Mayor said back, smiling so wide Tania thought it must hurt.

"And that's a good thing?" she asked, wrinkling her nose.

"Yes, it is. Ronah hasn't linked with another in over fifty years. Basically, it means when Ronah wants a spokesperson, you're it," he beamed at her.

"But I just got here!" Tania protested.

"That actually makes you perfect for the job. You aren't jaded by living on a Shifting Island the way the rest of us are," he said kindly. The Mayor seemed at ease with having both a newcomer and a teenager as the voice of a sentient Island older than her entire family combined.

"But I'm not even an Innarnian!" Tania protested, her knuckles going white as she gripped the glass in her hand tightly.

The Mayor caught her gaze, and Tania found herself mesmerised by his gaze, unable to look away. "Listen to me, Tania Bryant," he said, leaning forward in his chair, "and answer me truly. Can you hear Ronah?"

"Yes," she said, eyes wide, the words pulled from her mouth before she could stop them.

"Has Ronah told you that you are linked?" the Mayor asked.

"Yes." No matter how hard she tried, Tania found herself unable to look away from him.

"Your past may contain horrific things, Tania, but your future here on Ronah is guaranteed to provide outstanding undertakings." He sat back in his chair and looked away from her.

Tania, free of his gaze, blinked and shook her head. "How did you do that?" she whispered, shaken.

"I specialise in a spirit Innarn which encourages others to tell the truth," he replied.

'He means *you can't lie,*' Ronah interpreted. Like an impatient child, Ronah grumbled at the Mayor, '*You are supposed to be telling Tania about the Innarn testing, not divulging all of my secrets.*'

The Mayor chuckled. "Sorry, Ronah. Now, the testing. It is something all of our new residents undertake, whether they have had it done before or not. It is a series of mild probes initiated by the Elders of the town. If it is discovered you are an Innarnian, you will undertake extra lessons at the school. And no doubt Ronah will be giving you extra lessons as well," he added.

"So, I have to tell my family?" Tania asked, fidgeting in her seat.

"Yes, but you don't have to tell them about your link with Ronah until you are ready to," he said gently.

"Uh, Mayor Pratt," she stifled her automatic snigger. "Can I swear to the duties and do the testing now?" Tania said, slightly breathless.

"Now?" he asked, eyebrows raised.

"Yes, please," she said, straightening her spine and shifting forward in her seat.

"Let me check with the Elders." He was silent for a moment, resting his chin on steepled hands. "They agree. They can test you now, but the rest of your family will have to ask when they are ready. Usually, the testing happens when you first start school, but Lissae..." A shadow crossed the Mayor's face. "Well. No need for you to worry about that. All right. I need you to sit back and relax. Six of our Elders will gently test your Innarn strength and we'll see how you fair. Then, if you're still up to it, you can swear to the duties."

"Okay," Tania said. Carefully placing the cup on the desk, she clenched her hands tightly in her lap.

Alan smiled at her. "Sometimes it's easier if you close your eyes."

Giving a tiny nod, Tania scrunched her eyes up tight.

"Relax, Miss Bryant. Just breathe." The Mayor's voice washed over her and Tania forced herself to take a deep breath, and then another, and before she knew it, her muscles had unlocked and she relaxed back into the chair.

A bright yellow light flashed inside her eyes, spinning like a top. Tania tried to keep track of it, but it seemed to be dancing all around her insides before it faded away.

Another bright light, this one red, flicked to life and seemed to burst inside her, burning her insides. She cried out in pain, and it vanished, soothed by a blue light that washed over her like a wave.

A purple light flickered and spluttered, dying out before it could grow. It was followed by a green light that seemed to grow a tangle of roots that tickled her insides.

Giggling, she sighed in disappointment when the green light disappeared. She didn't have time to feel sad, as silver fireworks went off behind her eyelids. Laughing with delight, Tania opened her eyes to see the fireworks were actually filling the Mayor's office.

Yellow, blue, green and silver, with the occasional dash of red burst around her in a spectacular light show. The colours flashing faster and faster, getting smaller each time, until with a last zoom around the room, they settled in the form of beads on a bracelet on her wrist.

"Well," the Mayor said softly. "That was quite impressive." He glanced at her bracelet and nodded to himself. "Not a plasma Innarnian, but that's to be expected. All right, time to stand up then," the Mayor said as he got to his feet.

"But what does this mean?" Tania asked.

"Each Innarn is represented by a colour. On Lissae, there are seven main types of Elemental Innarn, which is what the Elders just tested you for. Purple is plasma, and the last person Ronah was linked to was a high-level plasma Innarnian. You will be able to work with plasma because of

159

that, but if you had a purple bead on your bracelet, you would most likely burn out."

"Oh." Tania felt like she'd failed before she'd even started.

"Yellow is air, blue is water, green is earth and silver is spirit. You're very strong in four Innarn disciplines, which is quite unusual. You can also use fire, which is red, but see how the colour isn't as vibrant? You'll find it harder to master fire Innarn, but you'll get there if you work on it."

Tania ran her finger over the beads. "That's only six types though. What's the seventh?"

"Technology Innarn. It combines fire, air and spirit, so quite often it isn't tested for on Ronah. We currently don't have a high-level tech Innarn to test you."

"Oh," Tania said. She was feeling slightly overwhelmed.

"Do you still want to swear to the duties now?"

"Of course!"

"Very well. Hand on heart, and mean it with all of your spirit, Miss Bryant."

Solemnly, Tania swore to the duties she would perform as a resident of Ronah, smiling the whole time. She couldn't believe her luck to be living in such an amazing place.

CHAPTER FIFTEEN

hari shifted Jon and Mitch with her into the back of the bookstore.
"Anyone want a drink?" Jonathan asked.

"Some rutenberry tea would be great," Shari said with a sigh.
The hot, rich drink was just what she needed after their meeting with
the mayor.

"Any chance of something a bit stronger?" Mitch asked. Jonathan
raised an eyebrow at him. "Tea would be great, thanks Jonathan." Mitch
grinned back unrepentantly.

Jonathan nodded and walked into the tearoom, and Shari followed
Mitch at silent request into the store, just beyond the door to the back
room.

"Do you know what crossed over? It seems to be getting to
Jonathan," said Mitch as he stepped away from the door.

"If only I did. Maybe everything else would make sense if we knew,
and maybe Jonathan wouldn't be so tense." Shari couldn't help but sigh.
Even more than her huge announcement and the different looks, ranging
from disbelief to scorn, that was exactly what had been plaguing her all
day.

"We'll figure it out." Mitch gave Shari's shoulder a supportive squeeze.

"I just hope we're not too late," she murmured, slipping out from under his touch.

"We won't be," he said. Certainty may have coloured his words, but Shari could feel the edge of fear he was determined not to show.

"What did it look like?" Shari asked him. "Jonathan said he wanted to search by himself, but if I knew, I might be able to help."

"I'm not sure, to be honest," Mitch replied. "It happened so quickly. I just caught a glimpse. It was big, and it had wings, but that's about all I remember."

"It's a start, but there are a lot of big winged creatures in the Realms." Shari sighed.

"Jonathan said I should close up for a while. We all need to talk," said Mitch.

"Let me speak to him first. I want to find out what's going on," Shari said.

"Not a worry," Mitch said, smiling that easy smile of his and dipping his head as he slipped through the shelves into the front of the store. Who would have guessed a brooder lived under his laidback attitude? Even though she had known Mitch her whole life, he continually surprised her.

Walking into the backroom again, Shari found Jonathan poring over his personal journals, three steaming cups of tea perched precariously on piles of books. "Hoping to find the cure for all life's ills in there?" she said lightly.

"I wish it were that simple," he muttered, gently closing the book. "Is Mitchel joining us?"

"I told him I need you to help me figure something out first," Shari said, picking up a cup.

"Oh. Figure out what?" Jonathan blinked up at her.

"What to do about this." Shari showed him her vision of Tania. He saw it as she had, and a great shudder seemed to rip through his body. Hastily, he backed out of her mind.

Opening her eyes to find Jonathan slumped in his chair, sweat pouring off his body, Shari instinctively rose to stand guard. The fine hairs on the back of her neck pricked to attention as she became aware that something was watching them. She whirled to face the doorway and found Mitch standing there. Her eyes slipped past him and landed on three points of golden light which flashed before fading away.

Shari narrowed her gaze as she sent out a net, hoping to entrap the being whose eyes she'd glimpsed. Minutes passed; all three of them tense as they searched.

'Who are you?' She sent out, frustrated at her lack of success in tracking the being. A smug chuckle rumbled back at her, just enough to tempt her, but not enough for her to pinpoint its location.

"Zoemer's Rocks!" Shari cursed. It originated on Ronah!

As suddenly as the trail the being had left behind started, it ended. The three looked around for precious minutes more before silently pulling back to the bookstore.

Breathing hard, they took a moment, before Shari shrugged off their failure. They had been alerted now and would be on the lookout for the mysterious being with enough Innarn to break through their Wards.

"Jonathan, do you have any ideas on what crossed over?" Shari asked.

"Don't look at me for answers, I haven't got anything as solid as ziom to go on!" he said, holding up his hands.

"I'd take something as substantial as air at the moment, although something as solid as ziom would be a big help!" Mitch muttered.

"I wish I could have stopped it," Shari grumbled, staring dismally out of the single window. The room with its tawny walls, beige bookcases, and cream desks seemed to be closing in on her.

"Big things like this are going to happen, Shari. You can't stop them any more than you can change them," Mitch said kindly.

Shaking her head, Shari said, "I'm meant to change them. I'm Lissae's message to the bad guys, remember? I have to deal with them."

"Shari, it's what you do *after* they've been dealt with that counts. That's the part which tells you who you really are," Jonathan added softly.

"I already know who I am. I'm the Altoriae. And I have a job to do." She looked at both the men, then stood. "We should open the store," she said to Mitch as the outside bell chimed.

Mitch nodded, and they both left the room. Shari, determined to do her duty, and Mitch, wondering how on Lissae he was going to be able to help his friend this time.

"Remember, you have classes today," Jonathan called out futilely as Shari waved him off.

A shape detached itself from the shadows and strolled over, standing directly behind Jonathan. "That one's gonna have it tough. She's just a hatchling. And the Realms are full of things worse than me."

"No. You have it wrong. None are quite as bad as your kind," Jonathan told him without looking around.

"I'm going to take that as a compliment." A deep chuckle filled the room.

"Take it any way you want, just get out of here before Shari comes back." Jonathan shrugged.

"Protective now, aren't you? Aren't you glad to see me?" For an instant, the being's hand hovered above Jonathan's shoulder. Finally, he laid it on the back of the chair, barely a hairsbreadth away from the mortal's form.

Despite his resolve to remain unaffected by the one behind him, Jonathan could not prevent the shudder skittering down his spine. A deep, raspy chuckle sounded close to his ear, and Jonathan wondered how many creatures heard the very same noise right before they died.

"I haven't seen you yet," Jonathan replied tightly, his Innarn almost snapping in the air around him. "Let's keep it that way."

Another raspy chuckle filled the room, then the backdoor opened and closed softly, and Jonathan was alone.

He slumped in relief, holding his head in his hands. "Dear Na'reh," he murmured, burying his head in his hands, "what have I done?"

He took a moment to gather himself before he joined Shari and Mitch out the front of the store, too wary to work out the back by himself at the moment. If he kept the teens busy out the front for a while, they didn't think much of it.

CHAPTER SIXTEEN

L ate in the afternoon, Shari, Mitch, and Jonathan wandered through the main street towards the Wisara, who'd made camp on the beach. Wisara were primarily ocean-dwelling beings whose bodies, although humanoid, looked like the tangled roots of lotus flowers. Their 'hair' looked like the leaves of the lotus, and the flowers acted as adornments. The Wisara could change form to a more traditional humanoid shape with eyes and skin and such, and they could inhabit land areas in either form. Mostly, though, they moved around as traders between the continents and Islands of Lissae by walking the ocean beds. They were the perfect merchants, as the violent storms of Lissae's oceans have almost no effect on them.

They strolled along in silence, lost in their own thoughts, until Jonathan cleared his throat. "Did I tell you I hired Tania Bryant?" he asked.

"No," Shari and Mitch chorused.

"Well, I did. As of now, Tania is the only staff member of Books 'n' More who doesn't have to work at protecting Lissae as well." Jonathan sighed and rubbed the bridge of his nose. "Na'reh help me if the end of the Realm comes anytime soon."

"With Shari on the case, I doubt that'll happen!" Mitch laughed.

Shari bit her lip in an effort not to remind Jonathan of what she had seen. His eyes caught hers before she could look away, and she realised he hadn't forgotten, he just hadn't told Mitch yet.

"Let's go see the Wisara," Jonathan said, leading the two subdued teens onwards.

Arriving at the beach, Shari, Jonathan and the rest mingled amongst the other townsfolk who were waiting for the Wisara to arrive. People stared and moved out of Shari's way as she passed through the crowds. It didn't really feel much different to how things were before her announcement, but the whispers were new.

"Did you hear...?"

"Where were you when...?"

"Can you believe...?"

"Surely she can't be...?"

Shari shut her ears to the whispers and moved through the crowd, trying to look like she had a purpose. She made some serious headway until Reanna McMullin saw her and called her name.

"Shari!" Reanna called again and swept Shari into an exuberant hug. There were quiet gasps around them as the people were amazed by Reanna's audacity.

"Well met, Shari! I am so excited! The Wisara are meant to bring in some Sephina silk to trade. I'm hoping to get some so I can make new blankets for the horses."

"Excuse a male's ignorance, but what is so special about safena silk?" asked Mitch, sliding casually to Shari's left side to try and block a portion of the crowd from the exchange between the two women. Jonathan stood silently on Shari's right, his presence detracting some of the naysayers and lending credence, as well as volume, to the rumours going around.

Reanna replied, "Se–fine–a silk is collected from silk worms which feast on the Darfionious Oak tree, which is only found in the Sephina Ranges. It's the warmest, softest, strongest fabric on Lissae, and there's just something about it that makes it immune to fire and water Innarn."

"Really?" Mitch asked, surprised, "Why aren't your leathers made of the stuff, Shari?"

"What leathers?" Reanna asked, tilting her head to the side.

"Shari's leather armour," Mitch replied.

"Why would you need armour, Shari?" Reanna asked with a confused expression.

An awkward silence crept up on the group, and they all gave each other incredulous looks before Mitch asked, "You haven't heard?"

"Heard what?" Reanna asked, scrunching her nose up.

Jonathan glanced at Shari before looking at Reanna. "The news about Shari?" he queried softly. Shari tried not to squirm under Reanna's gaze, as she looked at Shari, concerned.

"No, I haven't... Guardian Buan! I, ah, didn't notice you before. Well met," she trailed off blushing.

"Have you looked at your Crystal Send today, Reanna?"

"No, Guardian. I haven't had the time, Jasper injured his leg and–"

"I released the identity of the Altoriae today," Jonathan broke in gently.

It took about a half a minute for Reanna to connect the dots. "Are you telling me that... Shari?" Reanna asked, trailing off as she searched Shari's face.

"I'm the Altoriae." Shari nodded and sought to resist the urge to duck her head and hide as Reanna's jaw tried to meet the ground. Shari wondered how sick she would be of saying that by the week's end.

"Really?" Reanna squeaked. Shari nodded again. "Wow, I... wow. Does this mean you won't have time to visit me anymore? I really enjoy it when you help at the stables," she said mournfully.

"I'll still come by as much as I can," Shari said with a smile.

"Good," Reanna said, flashing them a cheeky smile. "I always need a hand mucking out! I bid thee well," she added as the crowd pressed around them and swallowed her from view.

Shari had a moment's peace before a deep voice to her right said, "Well, well, Shari Dawn."

"Well met, Elder Silverstone," Shari said smoothly, even as she swallowed a groan.

"Seems our humble isle is prone to more drama than we had previously thought," he said, his booming voice carrying amongst the chattering crowd.

Shari tried to smile, though she feared it came out as more of a grimace. She sent Jonathan a mental kick in the shins to stop him from grinding his teeth together as he stood beside her. There was no love lost between Jonathan and the Silverstone Clan. They were always pushing him for more information than he thought they had the right to know.

"At long last, Lissae can put a name to her saviour again!" Sampson fell back, placing his hand over his heart dramatically. "I do hope you shall last longer than our tenth Altoriae," he said, his insincere tone grating on Shari's nerves.

Beside her, Jonathan bristled, but it was Mitch who spoke up. "While Jali Thorne was a great Altoriae, she only survived three years under the title. Shari has been defending Our Realm since before she started school. However secretive her name may have been, she has flourished under the title of Altoriae for over fourteen years, Elder." The last word of Mitch's tirade bordered on disrespect, and by the silvery flash in the Elders eyes, his tone had not gone unnoticed.

"I was not trying to cast dispersions on Shari's proficiency as Altoriae, I was merely trying to display my concern for her welfare," Elder Silverstone said smoothly, brushing off the invisible dust from his coat.

"My thanks for your concern, Elder, but both my health and my proficiency as Altoriae is as good as ever. I bid thee well," Shari said, voice as hard as ziom.

Elder Silverstone sniffed derisively, peering down his nose at them before nodding and swaggering off into the crowd.

Shari and Jonathan had not taken two steps forward when Becky Ribeck, an exuberant thirteen-year-old, raced up and embraced Shari around her waist, sending, '*I'm glad it's you!*' before racing away again.

Blinking in surprise, Shari laughed, a tad uncomfortable.

Mitch laughed at Shari's expression before taking pity on her. "I heard the Wisara have shem'ar with them," he said as he nudged her.

"Really? I haven't seen a shem'ar in..." Shari grinned at her friend. A tingle raised the fine hairs on the back of her neck. The golden-eyed being was somewhere near them.

Shari's head flew up. '*Where are you, coward?*' The same smug chuckle answered her. He was close! Her mind reached out through the crowd, only to return to her body, enabling her to see someone slide swiftly out of the side of one of the ancient caravans. She would never catch him now; he was lost in the crowd. Damn it, he wasn't going to ruin this as well! Forcing herself to relax, Shari applauded as a passing troupe finished their song.

Jonathan politely offered them their choice of some small crystals held in the palm of his hand. The leader of the troop dithered before he chose four small blue ones and bowed. Shari and her companions moved onwards in search of the shem'ar.

"Well, well, if it isn't our *saviour*," drawled a smug voice. Shari turned around, unsurprised to find Anika Thorne hanging off one of the Wisara men. This one wore a human form and had golden hair, a golden tan and the deepest black eyes Shari had ever seen. He was dressed all in black, right up to the stone gleaming in his ear. He gave Shari a smug grin as he looked her up and down. Anika pulled on his arm, and he smiled down at her. Anika had changed into a white top and a deep-blue sarong. She wore ridiculously high, pointy heeled shoes and the ruby pendant.

"These people are your friends?" he asked Anika while looking straight at Shari.

"Oh no! I only talk to the Guardian," Anika purred and clung tighter to the guy's arm.

"You don't want to claim to know Lissae's latest Altoriae?" the Wisara prodded.

"Oh, I doubt it's *her*. She hasn't passed the test yet, at any rate," Anika said dismissively.

Baring her teeth in a grin, Shari declared, "Don't worry Anika, my task will be easy after listening to your witticisms."

The guy on Anika's arm chuckled, and Shari looked at him, her eyes narrowing. "I don't believe I caught your name."

"No," he said, grinning, "I don't believe you did."

Out of the people milling around, Liz and Aram appeared next to Shari.

"Are you enjoying the festivities, Anika?" Liz said pointedly. Even after Shari's announcement, it seemed a lifetime of running interference between Shari and Anika's taunting was still at the forefront of Liz's mind.

"Yeah, have you seen the jugglers yet?" Aram asked. "They are amazing! They were tossing fish in bubbles of water without a drop being spilt!" he enthused, teeth flashing white against his light tan skin as he stood beside Liz, the two subtly guiding Anika and her partner away from Shari.

Shari sighed quietly in relief as Anika's entire group followed her away.

Once the crowd around them had dispersed, Mitch asked, "How was your first 'official' day as Altoriae?"

"Could be worse," Shari answered with a shrug. After so many years of secrecy and so much speculation and anticipation, announcing she was the Altoriae had actually been rather more peaceful than she had anticipated. Very few people had approached her all day, and the stares and silent treatment from years of others thinking she was a Blank seemed normal, even if the reason was different.

"I hope your test is going to be easier than Jonathan thinks it'll be," Mitch said as they strolled along.

Shari found herself wishing the same thing. The test was simply to prove to the Elders she was truly the Altoriae. The element of suffering contained in the tasks was a way to help stop those who falsely claimed the title. Why anyone would want to do that was beyond Shari. Being the Altoriae was *hard*.

The crowd continued to swell and pass Mitch and Shari by. Occasionally, Shari felt like she drifted along, alone at sea in crowds like this. Few were game to come near her, even now it seemed. Mitch, however, stood steadfastly by her side – never wavering, never faltering in his belief in her. He knew with Shari around, everything would turn out okay in the end.

"Where'd Jonathan go?" Shari asked Mitch.

"He slipped away when Anika showed up with her latest boy-toy," Mitch tried to say, but he was drowned out by the Wisara starting another song, the cheery melody echoing throughout their campsite.

"Come join us at our fire, and listen to our tales true, for what we have to share, are true stories just for you." A Wisara minstrel walked past, strumming a lute as he sang his song repeatedly.

Other musicians joined him, and the townsfolk of Ronah found themselves helpless against the compelling music. As Shari's feet carried her towards the bonfire in the middle of the Wisara camp, she wondered just how strong the spirit Innarnian had to be to compel such a large group of people. Pretty much all Ronah's residents were here tonight.

The townsfolk of Ronah crowded around, and in a custom older than anyone could remember, they offered the Wisara meat, bread, and other items to restock their larder with. As payment, the Wisara would tell the Tales of Lore and bring them news from the Mainland. Only the Eldest of the Wisara was given the title of 'Lore Keeper', although anyone could tell one of the tales.

Tradition meant that Brayden, the leader of the Wisara, wore his natural form. Tiny white roots intertwined to make his body. The leaves of his 'hair' were slightly spiked at the edges, which seemed to be the fashion at the moment. Dark eyes which appeared to dance with mirth shone clearly in the light of the bonfire. He wore pants of seaweed and shredded lotus leaves but had not bothered to fashion himself a top. The women around him wore simple seaweed dresses, and most of the men wore open tunics over their pants. Only a few were still in 'human' form, including, Shari noted, Anika's latest boy-toy. Her attention turned to where Brayden stood as he cleared his throat.

"My good friends, I have heard tell that exciting news came your way this morning!" Brayden called as silence fell.

The silence didn't last long as murmurs overtook the crowd. Everyone knew what Brayden meant. Shari slumped slightly, wishing she could disappear as she'd been able to do before the big announcement, but eyes were turning her way. She straightened her shoulders and smiled, feeling Jonathan's mental nudge, reminding her that she was not alone.

"Will you share your good news with us, my friends?" Brayden bade them, his arms outstretched and a beguiling smile on his handsome face.

The murmurs rose to a crescendo, which almost matched the one in Shari's head. Over to one side, someone rose. For a moment, she was relieved to see he was one of Ronah's Elders, but when she saw who it was, she had to suppress a groan.

"Well met, visiting friends! I am Sampson, Elder of the Silverstone Clan. And I do indeed have a tale to tell." His strong voice carried easily over the crowd.

The noise around the bonfire died until just the cracking of the burning logs could be heard. Most of Ronah's townsfolk felt that if anyone could do justice to the tale of their newest Altoriae, it would be a Silverstone.

"My story starts eighteen years ago, when an Ilutri Priest and his new bride landed on our shores," Sampson started.

Shari could still see her father's blush, even from the other side of the bonfire. Ilutri Priest or not, he did not like drawing attention to himself.

"Although an accomplished Priest and one in much demand, the young Ilutri decided that he and his bride would make their home on Ronah, as our own Isle was better equipped to handle the needs of his Blank bride than that of his native Rakemyst," Sampson carried on.

Shari didn't need an ounce of her Innarn to feel her mother bristling. Arilla worked hard to prove that she was just as useful as anyone with

Innarn, and disliked attention drawn to the fact that she had none. So far, Sampson was doing a bang-up job with his backhanded compliments.

"A year after joining us, the happy couple introduced us to their new-born daughter. They named her Shari Sky Aonarach Mair Dawn," Sampson said with a flourish in her direction.

Those who hadn't heard were now looking at Shari in astonishment. She clenched her jaw and kept her gaze fixed on Sampson, wondering what he would say next.

"It had seemed to us that Shari had inherited her mother's lack of Innarn, but this morning we were proven wrong. Shari Dawn is Lissae's next Altoriae!" Sampson finished with a wave of his hands and a bow.

There were cheers from the residents of Ronah, loudest from those who'd seen her in her leathers out the front of the school. The Wisara sat with their arms crossed over their chests, distinctly unimpressed.

Brayden stood once more. "What? No tales of daring-do? Just the word of a teenage girl? Where is this Shari Dawn?" he asked, voice rumbling in discontent.

"Hiding in the back, sulking, no doubt," a velvety voice from the front of the crowd said.

Seeking out the speaker, Shari was unsurprised to see the guy Anika had wrapped herself around. Straightening her spine and rising to her feet, Shari used her Innarn to create a dramatic flurry of leaves and sparks around herself. The crowd parted around her, leaving a path for her to walk to Brayden's side, her head held high despite feeling like she was walking to her doom. She half-wished a battle would start up somewhere and she'd have to be called away.

The townsfolk were bristling with anger as Brayden's words planted little niggles of doubt in the minds of the people she worked so hard to protect.

When she reached Brayden, his shoulders were shaking with suppressed mirth. "You don't give the impression of being the Altoriae, Shari Dawn," he murmured to her. This close, she could smell the lingering salt of the sea on him.

She flushed but held her head high. She had gone through more than this man could even dream of – she had nothing to fear from him.

Brayden tilted his head to the side, listening to someone sending to him. A devious smile lit up his face, making his eyes twinkle. "We of the Wisara have a test for you, Shari Dawn. Hard times are about to stretch before us, and we of the Lore need to know our Altoriae is strong. Do you accept our test?" he asked, his dark eyes searching hers.

Shari looked at him and raised an eyebrow. Surely he knew of the test she was about to undergo. His eyes took on a steely flatness which practically dared her to say no. In the back of her mind, she could feel Jonathan telling her to be cautious.

"I accept," she replied, steel in her voice. Holding her identity secret had left people doubting her, which was one of the many scenarios she and Jonathan had discussed when talking about possible reactions people may have about her identity.

"Very well," Brayden turned and went to walk away.

"What is the test?" someone in the crowd cried out. Shari refrained from rolling her eyes. The Wisara were testing her, not giving her a lesson where the answers were obvious.

"That is up to your Altoriae to discover." Brayden turned back to them, the thick white roots which acted as his teeth were gleaming in a parody of a smile.

A whispered word later and all the Wisara vanished into their caravans – a place none of the townsfolk could enter without invitation. They were so heavily warded Shari didn't bother trying to get in. The Wisara had set their test, now she just had to pass it.

The crowd slowly dispersed, discontented murmurs at the shortness of the night and the lack of news spreading through the throng. Shari could feel the constant press of people trying to send to her, but she blocked them out. It wasn't really the best time for small talk.

Jonathan and Mitch came up to her. "What do we do now?" Mitch asked, wringing his hands.

"How about we look for the shem'ar while we're waiting?" Shari asked, trying to keep the mood light. If they searched the camp, she might get an idea of what the Wisara were planning for this test of theirs. She sent her father a quick message to let him know she'd be out late.

"Good idea," Jonathan said. Mitch agreed, and although they spent the next hour searching the Wisara camp for the elusive shem'ar, it seemed they'd been sequestered in the caravans along with their owners. They didn't find a single clue about the test either.

"Let's call it a night," Shari said. She held a hand up when the others started to protest. "I'll call you if something happens."

After their goodnights, Shari saw them off out of the boundaries of the Wisara camp. She remained behind for a while, gazing at the ocean lapping at Ronah's shore.

"My people are unsure you are the Altoriae, Shari Dawn," said a voice behind her.

"What do you think, Leader Brayden?" Shari asked softly.

"I believe there to be none truer," he admitted. "I am one of the few of my kind who has seen you fight for Lissae."

Closing her eyes, she nodded, grateful that at least one of the Wisara believed her.

"There are some on the Island you should be wary of, Shari Dawn. There is one who..." Brayden trailed off, and Shari turned to face him fully.

177

"Yes?" she prompted.

The leader of the Wisara could not meet her eyes. "I cannot say."

"Cannot or will not?" Shari asked, frowning.

He raised a leafy eyebrow. '*Cannot,*' he sent in a short, sharp burst as the leaves of a tree rustled behind her. Shari nodded her head in understanding.

'*Get some sleep, little Altoriae. Our test will be tomorrow night. If you survive, we shall grant you a boon,*' Brayden grinned, teeth gleaming white in the darkness.

'*Why would you grant me a boon?*' Shari asked.

'*Because that is our way, little Altoriae. Sleep now, you will need it,*' he insisted, and disappeared with a flick.

As Shari shifted to her front yard, she felt Brayden's chuckle vibrating around in her mind. Tomorrow would be interesting.

CHAPTER SEVENTEEN

Shari walked through the kitchen door and greeted her mother, who stood at the kitchen counter cutting vegetables for a late dinner.

"So, how did your shem'ar hunt go?" Arilla asked Shari as her knife flashed over the carrots and buta sprouts. Next to the fruit bowl sat a cooling cake.

As Arilla moved from the carrots to the potatoes, Shari grabbed a knife from the block and began to slice the cake as she answered. "It didn't. It seems the Wisara took the shem'ar into the caravans with them," Shari grumbled.

"Don't worry, maybe you can see them tomorrow," Arilla said to console her daughter.

Shari shook her head. "I don't think I'll be able to see them tomorrow, Mum. I need to find out what the test will be."

"Maybe there will be time afterwards," Arilla said consolingly.

"Maybe. How's the Tavern going?" Shari asked, desperate for a change of subject.

"We had a pretty quiet day. Everyone was preparing for the Wisara. We did get a few regulars in for lunch, though."

"Thank Nar'eh for the regulars." Shari kissed her mother on the cheek. "I've got to go talk to Jonathan. I'll be back in time for tea."

Not turning around, Arilla asked, "Okay, but why do you need to...?" she began to ask, and then she closed her mouth with a snap when she heard the door slam shut. No one ever said it was easy being the mother of the Altoriae.

"Jonathan!"

Banging his head on the base of one of his numerous hanging plants at the shout inside his home, Jonathan groaned. "I'm outside, Shari," he said calmly. Rubbing his head, he bent down again and then thought better of it. He moved just in time to avoid being hit in the backside by the door being forcefully opened.

"What's wrong?"

Shari sniffed the air. "Peewhew! Whatta reek! What are you doing out here? Starting your own fertiliser plant?"

Jonathan grinned. For all the respect Shari had for nature, she still couldn't fathom gardening. "I'm preparing the ground for planting."

"If you say so. Can we get out of this stench?" Looking down at his filthy hands, she added, "And can you wash your hands?"

Opening his mouth to say something, Jonathan stopped when Shari levelled her most charming smile on him. It faded too quickly, leaving a concerned frown to take its place. "We have to talk, and I won't be able to concentrate if you smell like a dung heap."

"Charmed, I'm sure," he muttered, nudging the backdoor open with his foot.

Following him inside, Shari moved restlessly around the kitchen as he took his time washing up. Jonathan marvelled at each bead of water as it ran over his hands, taking the earth and fertilizer with it. He focused on the soothing properties of the water until he felt ready enough to turn and watch Shari pace the room.

Picking up a curved shell he'd been gifted from the Wisara on a previous visit, she ran her hands over it before putting it down and moving on to a yellow flower in a green vase. The petals flickered in and out of sight and Shari sighed before turning around and catching him watching her.

"Can we sit somewhere?" she asked.

He indicated to the chairs around the kitchen table. "What's wrong?" he asked again.

Shari's frown deepened. "Brayden talked to me after everyone left. The test they're giving me will be tomorrow night."

"Do you believe him?" Jonathan asked softly.

Shari clenched her hands together. "No."

"Then why don't we do a check and see what's going on?"

Giving him a brilliant smile, Shari nodded. Checking Ronah's borders was one of her favourite tasks.

Shari soared above the fields of Ronah.

She and Jonathan had combined their minds, and although their bodies lay shielded on his living room floor, their spirits flew above the town of Ronah.

'*Time to narrow it down,*' Jonathan sent to her.

'*Where to?*' Shari sent back.

'*The Wisara camp.*'

'Are you sure it's wise?'

Jonathan's mind laugh was just as husky as his verbal one. 'I *never said this was wise!*'

Shari chuckled. '*True.*'

'*Ready?*' Affirmation. '*Good. On my count, dive. Three, two, one, dive!*'

Their minds plummeted downwards, and Shari took in everything around her: the trees, the houses, the school, the museum she used to drag Mum to when she was little, the stables she'd spent so much time relaxing in, and all the residents whose lives were a part of something greater than they realized. All of this was her duty, her Island. Everything that was rushing up to greet them was hers to protect. Her heart swelled with pride as for the first time in her life, she was happy to acknowledge that she was Lissae's Altoriae.

'*Shield your thoughts!*' Jonathan commanded as Shari's gaze locked onto her house. She could make out her parents dancing to music only they heard. '*I can't shield from you. We're joined, remember?*'

'*If you can't shield, concentrate. Your house is too close to mine. If we get any closer, we'll be drawn back.*'

Mentally chastising herself, Shari forced her concentration away from her house. She didn't even have the excuse of wanting to look for something familiar. All of Ronah was familiar to her. She sent Jonathan a silent apology and focused back on the task at hand.

'*Almost there,*' Jonathan sent. She felt him stiffen and withdraw slightly as they got closer. '*This isn't right.*' Shari could feel Jonathan's frown, even though she couldn't see it. '*Oh Na'reh,*' he breathed, '*Look at the sky!*'

Shari looked up and gasped. The vast blue sky of her Realm was gone. No, not totally, it was being torn away. No! Shari cried inwardly.

"Not to my Realm you don't!" she snarled aloud. She banked upwards, carrying Jonathan with her. '*Go on! Just try to fight me!*' she snarled to the entity ripping the sky apart. It appeared the Wisara had employed a beast to keep people from spying on their camp, no matter what their form.

A giant claw reached out of the sky, trying to catch them. Shari wheeled and banked, weapons appearing instinctively. Summoning the power of the oceans, she threw a shaft of water at the Guardian beast.

The entity's scream as the water hit it sounded like distorted thunder.

Amongst her relief and triumph, she felt Jonathan's soundless scream. Shari froze, torn. Acting quickly, she shielded the Realm and concentrated on their bodies. She screwed up eyes that didn't exist and pictured them in Jonathan's lounge room.

She was slammed back into her body at what felt like sixty clicks an hour. Gasping for breath, she immediately rolled over to check on Jonathan, and froze. Sticking out of his rib cage, buried to the hilt of the short, yellow handle was a blade. On closer inspection, Shari realised it was crafted exactly like one she carried on the Realms. She tried to get a grip on it. Upon wrapping her hands around the handle, her fingers neatly fitting into the grooves, she realised it *was* her knife. The guardian beast they had fought must have summoned it before Shari had withdrawn.

Oh shite, she thought in the privacy of her own mind. The serrated edges of her blade were designed to do maximum damage. Getting it out was going to rip open the wound.

'*Could you give me the good news first?*' Jonathan sent.

Shari burst into action, although her body didn't move so much as a heartbeat. Mentally she took hold of the blade. '*This is going to hurt,*' she sent.

'*You call that good news?*' Jonathan grumbled. Shari twisted the blade up and out. Jonathan's scream had her wishing she had never set eyes on any knife, let alone this one. She flung it at the door and went to work patching up Jonathan's rib cage.

Mitch paused outside Jonathan's front door. Normally, he would have a 'lively discussion' with the Guardian after an event like the Wisara coming to Ronah, but with Shari's announcement, and upcoming test, he wasn't sure if now was the best time. Deciding it could wait at least until after dinner, he turned to walk back down the path.

'Aarrruughhh!'

Mitch froze at the sound of Jonathan's scream. He turned back to the door just as the tip of a blade thunked through the wood inches from his eyes.

Ducking automatically, it took Mitch a few seconds to realise that if he could only see the tip, then the rest of the blade had to be on the other side of the door. He gulped and went pale when it dawned on him – for the knife to be embedded in the door, someone had to have thrown it.

Shari let out a sigh of relief. Jonathan would be all right. He'd be sore for a few days, but it was better than having a permanent gap in his ribs where his Innarn could leak. That's why she'd crafted the knife; it worked on both the physical and the Innarn level of anyone unfortunate enough to be struck with it.

"You ready for the good news yet?"

'You mean there is some?' He gasped.

Shari sighed and started pulling his pain into her, taking it as her own. She knew she had received all of it when a dull ache took up residence in her rib cage. 'Yes, *it's over.*' She leant over and whispered in his ear, "You're safe now."

The door burst open, and Shari threw herself in front of Jonathan's body, blades appearing out of nowhere, moving around them to take defensive positions. It took a few seconds, but she realised Mitch, mentally armed to the teeth, was the one who'd burst into the room. She looked at him and, by unspoken agreement, and not without a bit of nervous laughter, they both dismissed their weapons.

Mitch took one look at Shari crouched in front of Jonathan's body and flicked his gaze to the door and the blade sticking out of it.

A piece of paper sparked into being under the blade, and from her crouched position on the floor, Shari read out loud, "Do not test us, we are the ones testing you."

She watched in a detached manner as Mitch pulled the blade out of the door and handed it to her. As though from far away, she heard him say, "I believe this is yours."

She took the blade from him and studied it, realising with a peculiar sense of detachment that she had never seen it covered in the blood of someone she knew before.

Jonathan broke her inspection when he muttered, "Think I can get off the floor now?" The teens helped him onto the couch, where he looked down at his rug and groaned.

"I don't think blood stains go with your colour scheme," Mitch quipped.

Jonathan groaned again, and Shari patted his arm comfortingly. "Don't worry, I'll get it." Levelling her gaze on the stained rug, they watched as the blood syphoned off, leaving it clean within minutes.

"Anyone want to tell me what happened?" Mitch asked.

Indicating they should all get comfortable, Shari filled them in on the aborted attempt to get info from the Wisara camp. At the end of her tale, a booming knock at the door made them all jump and laugh uncomfortably. Extending her Innarn, Shari nodded to Mitch who rose to answer the door.

"Hello, Mitchel! Is Jonathan or Shari around?"

"Hi, Anna. Um..." Mitch glanced behind him where they were out of sight of the door. "Now really isn't the best time."

"It's important, Mitchel," Anna replied.

Shari could hear the urgency in her voice. 'Let her in, Mitch,' Shari sent to him.

"All right, come on in. They're in the lounge."

Looking up, Shari met the gaze of the thirty-two-year-old wiry Museum Curator. Anna Warfield blinked and looked away before returning her green gaze to Shari. Her charcoal hair glinted in the light, and a red flush crept over her lightly-tanned skin.

"Hi Shari," Anna murmured.

"Hey Anna, long time no see." Shari hadn't been to the museum much after she'd become the Altoriae, the task of saving the Realm overcoming her love of ancient objects. Anna's gaze remained on Shari. She seemed oblivious to Jonathan's prone form on the couch.

"Is it true? Are you," Anna's voice lowered, "the *Altoriae*?"

Shari sighed. *Is everyone going to treat me as if I'm some kind of some sacred relic?* She caught sight of Mitch, who gave a small shake of his head and poked his tongue out at her. Obviously not. "Yes. I'm the Altoriae."

"Then we are in luck." Anna gave her a relieved smile.

"In luck? Why?"

"Do you remember the statue of Kay'imi at the museum? This appeared in her hand today. I had a time of it, trying to get it without damaging the scroll or the statue," Anna said and handed her a parchment scroll.

"What is it?" Jonathan asked, sitting forward on the couch and unsuccessfully hiding a wince.

Even as Mitch moved closer to Jon, ready to help his mentor if he should need it, his eyes remained fixed on Shari and the scroll in her hand. He was kind of hoping that it wasn't what he thought it was.

"A curse. My test," Shari said as she scanned it quickly, then stopped halfway through and read it word for word.

Mentally, Mitch was cursing. He had hoped that thirteen would be a lucky number, and that Shari wouldn't need to prove she was the Altoriae. So much for his luck. Now Shari had two tests and they didn't know what either of them entailed.

Shari rolled up the scroll and went to hand it back to Anna.

The curator shook her head. "You must keep it. If anyone else touches it now, it'll be destroyed."

Sighing again, the Altoriae gave a rueful grin. "The Deities don't make anything easy, do they?"

Anna laughed. "I suppose they want to keep us on our toes."

"That's for sure!" Shari laughed dryly.

Suddenly becoming sombre, Anna murmured, "Good luck. The museum will be open for you at all hours, no matter what."

Shari grabbed her hand. "Thanks, Anna, you're a gem."

"No, but what you're looking for is. I'd translate this fully for you if I could, but the only bit I can get is something about a red jewel. Good luck, Shari." The lean woman stood and walked towards the door. "Take care, Altoriae. This Realm needs you!" She called over her shoulder as she opened the door and left.

Shari looked at the parchment with disgust. "Doesn't it just," she muttered.

"Care to inform me what's happening now?" Jonathan said, standing on shaking legs.

"I can't make all of it out, but there are snatches that seem to make sense. Maybe you can translate more than I can?" Shari asked. Unrolling the scroll, Shari held it open so Jon could read it.

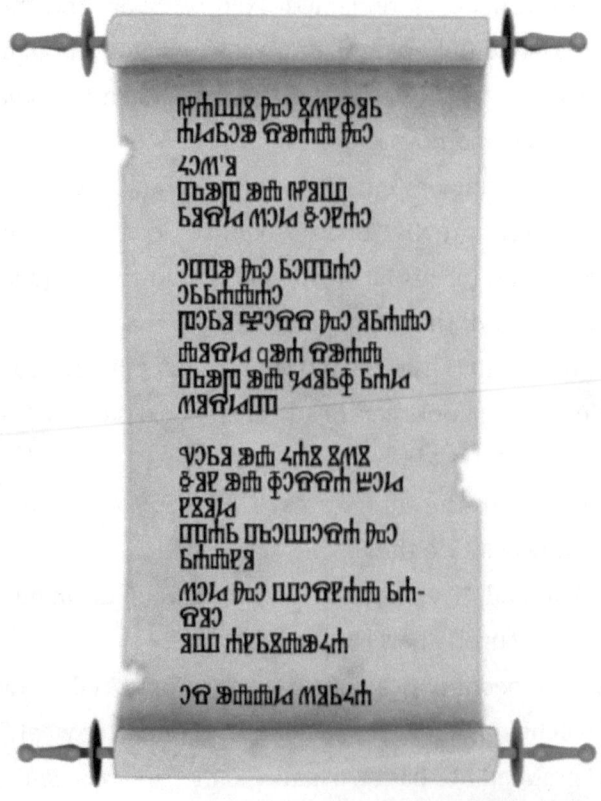

Jonathan blanched. His face slowly went all the way to white. "Anriluka," he muttered. Then he passed out, falling back onto the couch, his head at an uncomfortable angle. This news, on top of his wound, proved to be too much for her Guardian. He'd been under a lot of stress lately, ever since the being crossed over into their Realm. It was strange for Jonathan to take so much time in solving such an important mystery, but at least one mystery had been solved today. Shari had thought he'd been worried it would have something to do with her task, but now she wasn't so sure.

Anriluka, like all of her race, was prone to cruelty, but Shari felt that she would be easy to defeat. The only problem she could see in defeating Anriluka was the lack of time. Of course, time was something that, according to the curse, she didn't have.

Hissing under her breath, she muttered, "Ten days. Vebnah's breath. How in the Nine Hells am I going to succeed this time?"

"With our help," Mitch said firmly, gesturing to Jonathan and himself.

Shari paused for an instant. She met Mitch's eyes. Determination flared out at her. Shari realised that at this moment, she could dismiss the half-baked plan of Jonathan's. More fighters, more patrols, more training, all leading up to an Altoriae Guild. No other Altoriae had needed one before her. However, things were getting harder. There were more attacks, with greater ferocity as well as frequency. Even the Handbook confirmed it. If the number of battles she fought continued increasing as they had been the last few years, she would need the help of more than just Ronah's residents.

Sighing, she nodded slowly. Maybe the Altoriae needed to be part of a group of fighters, rather than a lone assassin amidst hostile masses. "Sounds good to me. Do you have any ideas?"

The tension Mitch carried in his shoulders relaxed as he took in a deep breath. "Why don't we wake sleeping beauty here, then we can get to figuring out what's on the self-destructing parchment."

Jonathan woke with a grumble when they nudged him. "I can't believe you left me here," he muttered, picking himself up and stretching, trying to work the kink out of his neck.

Shari sent a pulse of green light towards him – something that seemed to be a regular occurrence as of late.

Melodious voices filled Shari's head. 'We shall soothe him now,' said the past Altoriaes. 'Watch out for Anriluka. She is unusually cruel,' one voice broke off to say. Shari took a shaky breath and cleared her mind, trying not to show any sign of how talking to the past Altoriaes affected her.

"So, what did it say?" Mitch asked after Jonathan stopped glowing.

It finally clicked for Shari that he didn't understand. "I don't know the exact translation, it's too old. Basically, there's a curse that started when the being crossed over, and I have to find a 'Thorne red jewel' and kill an U'tan called 'Anriluka.' According to an unmentioned tradition, the curse activated the moment I touched the parchment." She took a deep breath as if taking it all in. "What we need now," Shari said, "is an exact translation of this curse. We need to know who and what it will affect. And how to stop it."

Jonathan harrumphed. "I suppose you want me to translate this?" he said, nodding to the parchment.

"Got it in one. I always knew you were smart, Jonathan," Shari murmured, affecting a laugh from Mitch.

"'Smart's right, my head hurts like Adeon's own." He rubbed the back of his skull, and they chuckled ruefully.

"As if anything can hurt that thick skull of yours, Jonathan," Mitch said, laughing.

For an instant in time, the smile froze on Jonathan's face.

"As if anything can penetrate that thick skull of yours, Jonathan Michael Buan. If all of humanity were to die from a head wound, you would be alive long after everybody else was rotting in the ground."

"Quit trying to be charming, Sanithane. Someone will think you're giving me a backhanded compliment."

Sanithane took his words as some kind of permission, and promptly backhanded him, his scaled paw open and his talons extended. His smiling maw opened wide, filled with smooth pointed fangs sharpened down to the last molecule. "Can't have anyone thinking that now, can we?"

"Guess not," Jonathan muttered, his mouth filling with his own blood from the force of the hit. "Promise you'll come when I call you, and I won't tell."

Sanithane let rip with another powerful backhand. "Humans are weak. You will tell."

Jonathan staggered to his feet and envisioned a white cage around the Q'Aralide. He filled it with all the Light Innarn he could summon. Sanithane snarled when one of his golden wing tips touched a bar. It came away smouldering.

"Weak?" Jonathan gasped, forcing a laugh and almost choking on his own blood. "Promise me!"

"Konraei!" Sanithane snarled.

Jonathan laughed and gave him the 'okay' sign. He shifted himself through the Realms and back to his sanctuary before he dissolved the cage.

The Realms filled with Sanithane's furious scream.

Jonathan chuckled, shaking himself out of the memory. "You're right, Mitch. Not much can." *Except for a backhand by a Q'Aralide,* he thought deep in the recesses of his mind. "I'll get to work on translating this. I'll go and visit Martin. He may be able to help."

"Martin? He doesn't speak the Language of the Weavers," Shari said, looking up from studying the parchment.

"But he's the oldest member of the town, I thought he would..."

"Nope. We had a really long discussion on it one day. He can't speak a word of it and has no wish to do so. Cris Vesta might be able to help you. She has an interest in old languages, and last I heard she was working on a program to cross-section modern languages with the old ones."

"How do you know these things?" Mitch asked.

"It's part of the job description," Shari answered tiredly. As she copied down the curse, she said, "the Wisara visit is not meant to be this intensive."

Mitch grinned at her. "It could be worse," he said.

"Don't say that! Never say that. Why would you say that?" Shari glared at him.

"What?" he asked, holding up his hands in mock surrender.

"When someone says 'it could be worse,' things *always* get worse."

"How bad can it be?" Mitch asked.

Shaking her head at him, she turned and handed the copy to Jonathan. She muttered, "Go, do your best."

Jonathan gave her a sickly-sweet smile. "I try to."

"Now," Shari said, turning back to Mitch, "we need to find out more about the Wisara test."

Jonathan knocked on the door of the rezem at twenty-six Ridden Road and tried not to fidget. He absently rubbed his neck where his muscles were still tingling from when he'd been healed. He knocked again and stretched his side gently, trying not to damage Shari's healing.

The door opened, and Jonathan paused in his greeting, stunned.

Cris Vesta was dressed to kill, wearing... well, Jonathan didn't know much about fashion or clothing, but whatever it was, there wasn't much of it. Scraps of silk covered very little of Cris' voluptuous form, held together with bits of translucent lace. Hastily raising his eyes to focus on the bridge of her nose, he gulped, not sure what to say.

In a throaty voice, Cris said, "Well met, Jonathan Buan. How can I... help you?" She lounged against the gateway, lifting a foot up and parting her very, very bare legs, a hand trailing down her throat, across her scantily covered chest and farther south. Jonathan wrenched his gaze upwards, gulping.

The air was rife with innuendo and the smell of heavily scented candles. The initial shock wore off, and Jonathan reverted to the manners the Guardian before had literally pounded into him. "Well met, Ms. Vesta. I was wondering if you could take the time to translate this for me. It is of the utmost urgency."

Disappointment flared behind Cris' heavily made up eyes, but her voice betrayed none of it. "Certainly. Why don't you come inside, Guardian, while I do this for you?"

Cringing at the volume of her voice, he stepped through the gateway, trying and failing to avoid brushing against her. He felt quite like a fly entering the spider's web, and wondered if he'd get out intact.

Two hours later, Jonathan returned to his house where he grasped the scroll with the translation on it, looking more than a little mussed.

"Are you alright, Jon?" Mitch asked, eyes wide in mock innocence.

"Fine, fine. Nothing I'm not accustomed to," Jonathan muttered as he handed the scroll over to Shari.

Laughing at your Guardian does not make for easy training sessions, Shari repeated over and over in her head. Jonathan glared at her as if he'd guessed what she was thinking. Shari unrolled the scroll and read the curse out.

"Start the curse
Through all the True
Come a being
Dark from agony

Under the angry galaxy
Silence fills the night
Slow to all
Come a bright new death

Until an Altoriae
Find a thorn red jewel
And free the cure
From the shining (life force – blood?)
Of Anriluka

Ten by day."

Shari swore.

The entire Island cringed.

Mitch, once his ears had stopped ringing, said, "What is so bad about it? Ten days is a long time to defeat a creature."

"Anriluka is older than Lissae's calendar. Whatever attack she has planned, she has had since Muran Curtis' Guardian locked her away in her own Realm. She's going to cause as much death and devastation as she can." Jonathan took his glasses off and rubbed the bridge of his nose. "Just informing Ronah is enough to panic the Island and unnerve all the rest of us in the process."

"So, the next ten days are going to be..." Mitch started.

"... the most stressful and hectic you'll hopefully ever experience," Shari finished.

"Oh yay," Mitch groaned. He seemed to shrink into himself, hugging his arms around his middle. "What are we going to do?"

"Rest," Jonathan said firmly. When neither teen made a move, he scowled. "Go home, the both of you!" Jonathan said as he shooed them out of his house.

"Will you–"

"Keep you informed of any and all possible facts and finds I may make in your absence? As always, yes." Jonathan smiled at Shari. "Now go before your parents hold me to ransom."

"Can I stay here, Jonathan? Dad's cooking tonight..." Mitch mumbled.

Groaning with sympathy, Jonathan still pushed his apprentice out of the house. "You need rest, and I need to plan. See you in the morning, if not before."

10 days left

Night had descended long ago, and Shari still hadn't calmed down. Why did the ancients have to leave so many damned riddles behind? As if her life wasn't complicated enough already. She couldn't stay still. Not tonight. She felt too restless, too tightly strung to think straight. As she paced, she reached her decision. Gathering up her jacket, she hurried downstairs.

"Where are you going?" Arilla asked.

Looking up in time to catch Arilla's startled look, Shari managed a semblance of a smile. "Need to get some air."

"Be safe," Arilla whispered as the door shut behind her daughter.

Shari paused on the other side of the door, hearing her mother's whisper. She held her hand up against the door as if she could push all her love for her mother through the door to surround her in a beautiful bright light that felt like the warmest of hugs. Then she slipped out into the night to see what mischief the Wisara might be causing while the rest of Ronah's residents slept.

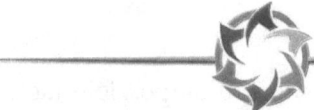

Mitch slid his boots off and slipped in through the back door of his house, in time for his younger brother, Kris to tear past him. Krya and Lyndal, his older sisters, followed close behind.

"Hide," Lyndal hissed, "Dad's *experimenting* again!"

Swearing, he scrambled after his siblings, socked feet skidding on the wooden floor. He slipped through the gateway of the room he and Kris shared to find his brother's foot poking out from under the bed. He kicked it as he went past, aiming for the closet and hoping his father wouldn't check under the mounds of clothes piled up in it.

From the other end of the house, a cheerful voice called out, "Dinner's ready!"

A long-held Hoffman family tradition said that when his dad cooked, everyone hid. It started when Kyra was a toddler, and Dad had tried to feed her liver, buta sprouts, and aniseed pâté. She'd run the other way and hid for the better part of the day. Now, he was a better cook – not like it was hard to top his previous efforts – but everyone still hid. A few years ago, Kyra had tried saying she was too old for the game, and their dad had served up the most disgusting combination any of them ever laid eyes on. Even he hadn't been able to eat it. Ever since then, they played along, not wanting to risk such a revolting meal again.

Heavy footsteps tromped down the hall, followed by a jaunty whistle. "I could have sworn there were some hungry people around here," his dad said as he passed by the bedroom door.

Mitch dared not poke his head out. That's how he'd ended up eating a heaped serving of buta sprouts for a week last time. A few minutes later, Lyndal went skidding past the door, trying to hide again.

"Aha! Saw you, young lady! Off to the table!" said his father. Lyndal groaned, and by the sounds of her dragging feet, she was reluctantly making her way to the dining room.

Heavy footsteps stopped by the closet door, and Mitch found himself holding his breath. The door creaked open, but before he could be discovered, Kris sneezed.

The footsteps stomped over to the bed, and then, "Aha! Off to the table, young man!"

Scrambling out from under the bed, Kris mumbled something before shuffling out of the room.

"Two more empty bellies to fill," his father said. "I wonder if they're both in here?"

He held his breath again. With the cupboard door open, he had no warning. Mitch felt more than a bit childish, but when his job was as stressful as it had been lately, having a bit of fun like this couldn't hurt.

Just as he felt his dad start to reach for the clothes covering him, there was a loud *thump*, followed by a rather concerning groan.

"Aha! Maybe next time you won't hide in the rafters. Off to the table! Your sister can heal you," Dad said cheerfully.

"I'm not hurt dad," Kyra grumbled.

"I know kiddo, but I got to watch out for you, don't I?"

Mitch could almost see his father reaching up to ruffle Kyra's hair. He wondered how different life would be in the Hoffman household if Kyra hadn't hidden all those years ago.

"Come out, Mitch, the others are waiting," his father called.

No way. He was staying put. The clothing igloo he had happening here was quite cosy. His father poked around for a bit before stomping out of the room. Mitch rested his head on his knees, closing his eyes.

An unknown time later, a hand clamped down on his head, "Gotcha!" his father called.

Mitch pushed down the instinct to lash out, thankful that even through the muffled clothing, he'd recognised his father's voice.

"Come on out Mitch, time for dinner! I've got a treat for you tonight!"

Standing upright, he shook the clothes from his hiding place away. "A treat sounds good." Mitch smiled tiredly. He must have fallen asleep while he was in there.

"Thought you might need it. I got take out from the Tavern!" Dad said as they wandered down the hall.

"Really?"

"Yes. Come eat. Arilla Dawn does amazing things with buta sprouts!"

Mitch groaned. "Why do you love buta sprouts so much?"

"They're tasty and full of goodness," he said, ruffling Mitch's hair.

"They're about as tasty as one of Kris' socks. You know, the ones which can stand up by themselves," Mitch grumbled as he slid into his seat.

"Oi!" Kris said around a mouthful of food. "My socks are far tastier!"

The others laughed. "They probably are," Mitch mused as he heaped his plate high.

"You lot just have no taste," their dad said, shaking his head sadly. "No taste at all."

198

They laughed and ate and enjoyed each other's company, occasionally making sure to tease their dad about his cooking. At the end of the meal, Mitch stayed back, rubbing his full belly, content. Moments like this made up for the stuff he had to worry about.

The others cleared the table and wandered off to do their own thing while Mitch sat there, too full to move.

After a while, his dad joined him. "You alright, Mitch?"

"Yeah, Dad," Mitch said with a smile. For the moment, he was. He'd worry about the rest of the Realm tomorrow.

CHAPTER EIGHTEEN

Walking along the streets of Ronah at night was generally not a dangerous practice, but when someone lunged out the shadows and stood in front of her, panting, Shari immediately began to summon a protective shield around herself, her glove morphing onto her hand before she took a good look at the person.

"Reanna?" Shari asked, concern making her voice softer than normal. "Are you all right?"

"Me? Oh, I'm fine. I just wanted to tell you," she bent over, trying to catch her breath. Gasping, she sent, '*The Wisara, they're leaving Ronah. I think the test they set will start soon.*'

Shari started. Apart from Jonathan and Mitch, none of Ronah's residents had sought her out to inform her of a potential threat before. "I..." '*Thank you, Reanna. I'll take a look around.*'

Reanna stood after a moment and gave an awkward bow, mumbling something about animals needing to be fed, before she turned and jogged away.

Shari stood for a moment after Reanna rounded the bend, still slightly stunned. Gathering her wits, she turned to go, but found the path blocked.

"What are you going to do?" asked a male voice from the darkness. "You can't go in there Innarn first."

"What I do is none of your business," Shari replied, brushing past him.

"No," he said, grabbing her arm roughly and pulling her close to him, stepping fully into the light at the same time. He was Anika's latest conquest – the golden-skinned Wisara man. "I think it is my business. Neither you nor your friends know how Wisara think. I do. If you help me, I'll help you. Deal?"

"What's in it for you?" she asked. She moved to step away from him, and for a moment, they paused. His grip tightened to the point where Shari could feel bruises forming. She pulled away from him, and he reluctantly released her. He stepped back into the shadows again. Shari sent a silent command to the nearest orange pillar, and it lit up, casting his face in an eerie glow. In this light, his skin actually shimmered as if it were made of real gold.

Arching an eyebrow, he said, "I help you, you help me. I'm sick of the roving lifestyle," he said, glancing at his nails, the picture of cool, calm and detached, despite the danger lurking underneath. "I want to become more settled. And where else to do it but here?" he added, spreading his arms wide. Although he smiled, Shari detected a hint of a dark smirk hidden in the twist of his lips.

She stared at him for a few moments longer, but she finally said, "Fine, but it's not up to me to decide. If you want, you can come with me to see Jonathan, and we'll talk about it. But every second you hold me up is another second there's a threat loose on Ronah."

"Then let's go get this Jonathan of yours," he replied, taking her arm again, his grip gentler this time.

As Shari reluctantly shifted them to Jonathan's front yard, curiosity overcame her. "Are you going to tell me your name this time?"

"Why?"

"Because I have to introduce you to the others, and it might help if I knew your name. Your *real* one."

"I'm called Samuel Caragnton."

"Sure you are," Shari said flatly.

"Well, I am," he said, shrugging. The corners of his mouth turned up slightly.

"By some," Shari said, finishing the end of his sentence for him.

"By some," he amended.

"You won't give me your real name?"

"Nope."

"Why not?"

"Because there's no need for you to know it. Yet."

"There is a need. It's called curiosity."

"I believe that's what caused my felines to become deceased," he said dryly. Shari found a corner of her mouth twitch upwards in amusement which she quickly stifled as she led him to the door.

She knocked, but no one answered. Reaching out, she realised Jonathan was at the store and not at home. Cursing under her breath, she turned and almost walked into Samuel. She moved to take a step forward, expecting him to move, but he remained still.

Energy crackled around them.

They were standing so close Shari swore she could hear his heart beat as it sped up. Compelled, Shari raised her head to meet his eyes. The energy swirling between them sparked, and his eyes flashed as she became aware of his hand reaching for her arm.

Her breath caught in her chest. There was something 'other' about Samuel.

Without warning, she shifted them to the store. When their feet touched the ground, Samuel held her gaze for a beat before reluctantly stepping back, leaving just enough room for Shari to walk past him and into the store to drag Jonathan from the depths of the backroom.

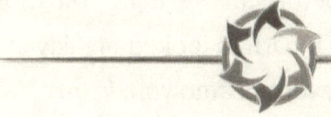

Jonathan slumped over his desk, his head on his arms, fast asleep when they arrived.

"Jonathan?" Shari asked softly.

"Huh? Oh, yes. I'm all right, just... resting," he muttered. "I've been looking for any reference to a red jewel, and I haven't found anything so far. I'm sure I've seen something somewhere, but..."

"Jonathan, you're babbling," Shari said, amused. It was a fairly regular sight for her to see her Guardian slumped over the parchment he'd been studying. He swiped a tired hand over his eyes, and Shari sent a little green burst of light his way. Not for healing, but to help him recover his strength. She had a feeling they wouldn't have time to sleep tonight.

"Okay sleepy head, time to get up. We need to go to the Wisara camp."

"Why? What's going on?" Jonathan rubbed the sleep out of his eyes.

"The Wisara have left their camp, and I want to know why," Shari said.

Jonathan stretched and, despite his bones protesting, he rose from the chair and followed Shari to the front of the store, where they found Mitch standing awkwardly alongside Samuel. "Do you have any idea why they haven't told anyone?"

"They wanted to watch from a distance. Your test has started, Altoriae," a voice drawled.

"It's started? And you wasted all of this time before you said anything?" Shari said, rounding on him.

As Jonathan turned to face Samuel, confusion overcame his refined features and clouded his warm brown eyes. "Who are you?"

Samuel grinned darkly before answering. "You know me, Jonathan. It's Sam. Samuel Caragnton." Jonathan looked blankly at the Wisara man before him. "Playing dumb never became you, *ketarr*."

Jonathan's eyes widened. Tiredness disappeared as he burst out laughing. Still chuckling, he said, "Samuel Caragnton? By the Light of Lissae, San... Sam, I didn't realise you were so funny."

Samuel smiled at his friend's mirth. "Didn't recognise me, did you?"

"I'm afraid I didn't, *dathae*, but," Jonathan sighed, sobering instantly, "reunions can wait until later. Now we have a test to ace. Can you give us any more information?"

"Head for the graveyard," Samuel replied, and then melted into the shadows.

"All right, let's go." Shari and Mitch hung back as Jonathan led the way.

"Do you trust *him*?" Mitch asked her softly, nodding his head in the direction Sam had vanished.

"In this, yes. In anything else? No."

"Why not?"

Sam, who had slid into the shadows instead of leaving, caught their conversation and waited silently, barely containing his curiosity at her answer. It seemed as if a lot of it was going around these days.

During the pause, Shari had gathered her thoughts together. "Call it what you will, but there's something... off about him. About his story. I just don't think it's a coincidence he showed up here after whatever crossed over."

Mitch laughed. "The being who crossed over was huge and felt like the Darkest Innarnian I've ever seen. It couldn't possibly have survived this long on Lissae, our Realm would be far too light for it to survive. He can't be it."

"Why not?"

"It had claws and wings, which this 'Samuel Caragnton' is missing."

"Still, he has a lot to prove before I'd trust him."

He had to give it to the Altoriae. She was quick. Sam wondered to himself what she would do if she discovered his secret.

'Don't you have somewhere you are meant to be?' Jonathan sent to Shari.

Shari let herself glide out of her body, through the roof and into Ronah's sky. She flew over the Wisara camp, and sure enough, the only remains were gently smouldering coals from hastily extinguished fires. She made her way through the town and to the harbour. The Wisara were wading into the water. Shari could see out past the breakers where all the Wisara Elders were gathered. She flew closer, determined to make out the words of their chant.

Hantra zenovar, Hantra venteer, Hantra zenovar, Can den ossh za fear!

Shari paled when she realised what the Wisara were calling up. As they continued to chant the same words over again and again, she translated in her head: *Earth spirit come, earth spirit hear, earth spirit come, and never leave here!*

How could they do something so horrific? She sent a quick message to Jonathan and Mitch, *'We'd better get to the cemetery quick! The Wisara called on the Hantra!'*

The last vestiges of fatigue were dismissed by Shari's frantic call. Jonathan looked at Mitch and saw his apprentice nodding.

"We should warn the residents," Mitch said.

"Right, there's no use in being overrun by the Hantra. Mitch, can you send out the call?"

"No problem."

Jonathan could feel Ronah crying out beneath him, and for once, he didn't know what to do. Ronah knew the Hantra would hurt its inhabitants, but as they were earth spirits, there wasn't a lot the Island could do to help. Ronah fighting the Hantra would be like Jonathan fighting his own arm.

'Why don't you ask Tania to fight for you?' Jonathan sent to the Island in desperation. When he felt Ronah calm down, he shifted to the cemetery to find Shari already fighting the zombie-like creatures.

Tania turned, and Mitch caught sight of her in a white shirt, which was luminous in the yellow light of the second moon.

'Watch out!' he sent frantically as three of the Hantra strove to attack her from behind. He imagined a sword taking shape in her hands and then, thankfully, it was there. He sent her the image of what to do, as another four creatures tried – in vain – to surround him.

He could hear Shari and Jonathan on the other side of the cemetery as he battled his four. One with only a hole for a nose began to clumsily extend clawed fingers at him. Not wasting any time, Mitch elected to chop the offending digits off. No-nose looked startled, and as Mitch separated its head from its body, its eyes blinked. He cut the creature's left arm off just as his second zombie – one without eyes – attacked. It raked a claw-filled hand over Mitch's right arm. He didn't pause to draw breath to scream. He lopped no-nose's right arm off just before it managed to reattach its other arm.

As its warped body crumpled to sludgy grey dust, Mitch raised his broadsword and was able to part his other three Hantra from their heads, all in one go. As they scrambled to retrieve their heads, Mitch managed to rid two of them of their arm, but in the foray, he lost track of the third.

Shari drew in a breath, left arm gone, release breath, the right arm gone, in, head rolling, out, the body was ash.

She and Jonathan fought back to back without breaking a sweat. They had quickly passed through ten score of Hantra.

'It's not the amount but the deed that counts,' Jonathan silently admonished Shari. She snorted, and two more of the Hantra turned to ash. As she drew another breath, they heard a male scream.

"Shari!" Mitch managed, barely, to convert his scream into something understandable.

His last Hantra had displayed more intelligence than most. It had managed to sneak up behind him and scour his back with its claws.

Suddenly, Mitch heard the squelching noise of a Hantra's head being removed, and the claws, still in his back, went limp, dragging through his skin even more before *shniik shniik*, and he flinched as his back was coated in warm, wet mushy ash.

He went to turn, but when he saw the ring of Hantra surrounding them and felt Shari's back against his, he decided against it.

'Don't worry, I've got 'em!'

The intense broadcast almost caused Mitch to lose his newly conjured sword, as he'd lost the old one. Shari and Jonathan winced before putting out a dampener.

'Sorry,' Tania sent out at a more subdued level.

Mitch almost cut his own arm off. '*Tania?*'

'*On my word, everyone duck.*' Tania, from her perch in a tree, visualised a ring of diamond-sharp metal, the blade part at head height with the Hantra group surrounding Shari, Mitch and Jon. Attached to the ring, and at shoulder distance apart, were sword blades, ready to cut off the arms of those... things.

'*All you have to do is see the ring getting smaller,*' Ronah sent to her.

'*Easy for you to say,*' Tania thought back, struggling to keep hold of the image in her head.

'*Ok. Ready and... Now!*'

Shari, Mitch, and Jonathan ducked, barely missing the rapidly contracting ring of metal. The Hantra surrounding them were all taken care of in one fell swoop. The three Innarnians rose to congratulate Tania, who relinquished her tree perch and gracefully dropped to the ground.

"See. I can handle myself fine," Tania said, sauntering over to the group. Out of the earth, a few paces in front of her, suddenly shot the hand of another Hantra. She looked at it dumbstruck. "What the...?"

The hand was followed by an arm, and then a head popped free of the soil.

Tania's eyes widened, and she stumbled backwards, half running until she crashed into a Hantra still shaking the dirt from its limbs. Mitch laughed as Tania turned, face losing all colour as she saw what she'd run into.

She severed its head and arms as if she'd been doing it all her life. "I thought you said this was a friendly cemetery!" she said scathingly as she turned back to Mitch.

"I thought you said you didn't know how to fight!" Mitch shot back.

"I don't!" Tania yelled back at him as she severed another Hantra's head.

"You're doing pretty well then!" he grunted as his Hantra turned to sludge. "I hate these things," he muttered to himself.

"Déjà vu," Shari muttered.

"What?" Jonathan asked as suddenly a whole pile of Hantra appeared.

'To *me!*' Shari cried as she shifted the others to her side. "Here we go. One of them must be hiding. Jonathan, Mitch, see if you can find it. Tania, you're with me. Let's do this!"

Five scores of Hantra descended on the two girls. Tania, buoyed by her previous success, concentrated hard on refining it. In various places around the 'friendly cemetery', she set invisible rows of the contraption, and almost instantly, half the Hantra turned to sludge.

Shari, back to back with Tania, let her mind fill with the up-to-now useless facts Jonathan crammed into her head about the Hantra. Blessing them, she remembered, just made them stronger. The only way to stop them was to find them all and ensure they were ash. Therefore, some of them must be hiding. She sent out Hantra-specific kinetic fireworks. Five went off. She noted the thanks that Jonathan and Mitch sent her as they dispatched the loners.

The battle here, she noted, was rapidly sliding their way. Shari let her mind drift again, and she watched as she and Tania were surrounded by a glowing ring. It was as if the sun had come up.

The Hantra hissed and gurgled, struggling to get away from the sudden light. Half of them stumbled into the contraptions Tania had set up before, and the rest, only a half score, were quickly finished off.

Shari felt Jonathan and Mitch returning to the cemetery just as she finished off the last one. Just slightly out of breath, she noted. Not bad for their first proper battle in *this* Realm.

She noted their various scrapes and sores. Mitch had come off the worst, so she healed him first. Jonathan had a nasty scratch across one cheek, but he was already taking care of it. Turning to inspect Tania's wounds, Shari stopped in shock. Jonathan and Mitch, who had been talking to each other, looked up at Shari's abrupt halt. Then they saw her.

Legs crossed in a meditation position, Tania floated a body-length off the ground. Levitating itself wasn't very remarkable around here. Seeing the girl they barely knew bathed in Ronah's own green light, however, had stunned them into silence.

"I guess she actually is linked to Ronah," Mitch murmured.

Subdued, dirty and tired, Jon told Mitch to head for home as the first rays of morning light filtered through the trees surrounding the cemetery.

Jonathan paused at Shari's shoulder. "Don't wait too long."

Nodding, she continued to study the curious girl in front of her.

Tania willed herself to rise out of her meditation. It felt like she'd been there for eternity, and yet at the same time, only the blink of an eye had passed.

"Refreshed?" asked a voice.

"Mmm, much better," Tania replied, looking around her. Out of the tree she had perched in last night dropped Shari.

"You can get down now."

"What do you...?" Tania said as she looked down. She cried out as she fell, hitting the ground hard. Wincing at her aching joints, her eyes closed tight against a bright green glow. Suddenly, she didn't hurt anymore.

'*Ronah, I think you'd better tell her what being linked to you involves,*' Tania heard Shari send as if she was saying it from a long way away, and Tania suddenly realised Ronah was letting her know what was going on.

'*She needs to be trained in the basics,*' Ronah sent back. '*Can't you train her?*'

'*You are always suggesting better ways for me to do what I do. Tania is a raw talent you can train up to do the best possible job she can do, without all of my irritating little quirks.*'

'*Yes, you do have quite a few of those, don't you Shari?*' Ronah chuckled. '*OK, Tania will be at the caves for the rest of the night.*'

'*Do I get a say in this?*' Tania sent out, her frustration evident.

She looked up as Shari bent over her. "You know the most annoying thing about being someone important?" Shari asked her as she helped her up.

Tania shook her head silently.

"You don't get much of a say in anything."

Tania opened her mouth to object, but she found herself in a cave, ready to argue with a blank wall. She banged on it once, and an image appeared on it. Hastily, she scrambled backwards and promptly tripped over her own feet and landed in a somewhat ungraceful heap on the floor.

'*Hello, Tania.*'

Tania's breath left her body in a rush when she realised the face projected on the rocky wall was the face of Ronah.

Shari watched as Tania disappeared before she shifted herself to the Town Square near the old fountain. It was the only thing that remained of their ancestors. It was a peaceful place, and at one stage or another, everyone in the town was drawn to it. Lizbeth Ribeck, a woman who Shari often chatted with, said it could be because of her blindness, but she could often hear whispered speech near the fountain.

Tonight, however, the Weavers were quiet, and Shari sat on the cool green grass, enjoying the peaceful moment.

CHAPTER NINETEEN

9 days left

Tania sighed in contentment as a pleasant heaviness surrounded her. Hundreds of thoughts, hundreds of questions, comments and queries flew at her every second. The answers were flung back just as quickly. There was a comforting presence of others. The gentle lapping of water was all around her. Single identities did not matter here. The soothing sigh of the wind as it blew past. Ancient. Wise. Mystical. The whole thing felt beyond her comprehension, but she managed to soak up the sensation and could feel understanding seeping into her spirit.

Shyly, Tania reached out, ready to touch the other souls – the ones who resided with her, in the heaviness – not the others who resided on the surface of Ronah.

She reached out, joining the communal flow of thought, marvelling in being a part of something so big. It didn't make her feel insignificant, the way it might have done a month or two ago. Instead, she felt as if a piece of her which had been missing for too long was back where it was meant to be.

As Shari sat on the ground in the middle of the Town Square, she felt the weight of dreams overcome her. Dark, strange shadows swirled around, keeping away from the fountain by the protective enchantments placed upon it long ago.

The shadows swirled closer, but none could touch her. Snippets of dreams and of things that had happened long ago crept into her mind.

Then the Realm went to the Nine Hells.

The earth rocked and shook around her, almost as if the Island was going to tip over. She felt a deep-seated trembling in the ground next to her. She watched in fascination, her spirit hovering a few feet above her body, as Samuel arrived and whisked her out of the way, right before the earth where she sat exploded upwards, and a fountain of water gushed out.

It was one of Ronah's highly unsubtle wake-up calls. As suddenly as the water had jetted out of the earth, it stopped, and the ground was smoothed over as if by an invisible hand. The only remaining sign of the disturbance was Samuel standing in front of her. His shirt soaked through, his fists clenched and breathing haggard.

Shari dared to peek into his mind and found she didn't have to look far. He was making no effort to conceal his surface thoughts.

'You little tu'zar!' he raved. 'You knew that was going to happen! Did you not realise the force of the water jet? It could have killed you!'

Shari watched in amazement. This man who she barely knew was genuinely worried about her. He knew who she was – he'd been there when Brayden had confronted her in front of the whole town. Maybe he didn't know exactly what being the Altoriae meant.

"Samuel?" His mental raving continued. "Sam?" Tongue of a Ne'fora? She had never been called *that* before – she had to give marks to him for originality. '*Hello in there, Samuel Caragnton.*'

Samuel looked down at her, crossing his arms over his broad chest. The shadows seemed to gather around his back, pantomiming wings. She shook her head to clear her vision, and they were gone. Sam didn't say anything, but his mind quietened enough for her to get a word in edgewise.

"Thank you. Now," pausing, Shari wondered how best to tell him, "the water jet would not have hurt me. I am the Altoriae." She shrugged as if that explained it all. When she realised comprehension was far from dawning on his face, she continued. "A force of nature – any force of nature – cannot kill me. I am made from Lissae, and Lissae protects her own."

Sam looked at her, stunned. His mind flashed back to the times where his tribe had tried to kill an Altoriae by throwing a boulder at her, pushing her off a cliff, opening up the ground beneath her feet. Each time, the Warrior would get to her feet, unharmed. '*Shari should be more careful with who she gives sensitive information to,*' he sent to Jonathan on a tight band.

Sam heard Jonathan laugh. '*Sam, haven't you realised yet?*'

Shaking his head, Sam sighed. '*Realised what?*'

Jonathan's laughter trickled through his mind. '*No matter how powerful you are, my friend, you wouldn't be here if you didn't have good intentions.*' Sam grunted. '*Ronah protects her own, just as well as Lissae does.*'

'*Who is Ronah?*' Sam shot back. The ground quivered beneath his feet.

'Ronah is our home. She was created by the Weavers to protect the Altoriae. Ronah is the Island.'

'Are you trying to tell me the Island is alive?' The ground around Sam rocked more violently, and water rushed out at an unnatural angle from the old fountain and soaked him. Sam shot Shari a glare, and when he realised she hadn't done it, he glared at the ground beneath his feet.

'Welcome, Samuel Caragnton. Try not to hurt anyone while you are here. While Lissae may not harm our beloved saviour, she and I certainly can hurt you.'

Shari watched as Sam's eyes went wide and his jaw dropped. He had the look of someone talking to Ronah for the first time. Grinning, Shari opened her mouth to say something, but she caught the flicker of fear he was just a shade too slow to hide. What could he possibly be afraid of?

'Shari Sky Dawn! Get your butt home young lady – you have school tomorrow!'

Sam couldn't help but chuckle at her father's broadcast. It was loud enough so everyone in Shari's vicinity would know she had to go home. "Guess I shouldn't detain you any longer," he muttered, still chuckling.

"Listen, Mr. Mysterious, I..."

'Shari! That means now!'

"Have to go." She scowled at him, before turning to jog home. Why she bothered to walk when she could shift, Sam didn't know.

"Some of us like to keep fit," said a voice from behind him.

Sam turned and studied the man before him. He stood slightly shorter than Sam, but his black eyes equalled Sam's in their barely contained ferocity. Something about the man's jet-black hair and the line of his jaw said he was related to Shari.

"Mr. Dawn?" Sam said.

216

The stranger extended his hand. "Got it in one. Calem Dawn. And you are?"

"A friend of Jonathan's." Samuel's eyes hardened as he took the man's hand.

"Well, any friend of Jonathan's..." Calem paused and withdrew his hand from Sam's grasp. Something was not right with this stranger. "Any friend of Jonathan's would realise how important Shari is to this Island, and to this Realm. And any friend of Jonathan's would know to watch his step around *my* daughter."

Samuel gritted his teeth, but before he could reply, Calem took a step closer to Sam. Glaring up at him, he hissed, "I am not some teenage girl whose thoughts are so clouded with hormones that I cannot see the coincidence between the crossover and your arrival here. Even Ronah is watching you, so you'd better not even *breathe* wrong around Shari."

Looking down at Shari's father, Samuel smiled. "Ronah has offered me hospitality."

Calem reared back, his scowl changing to an expression of shock.

"The reason you didn't see me when the Wisara arrived was due to time spent in one of the caravan's, trying to recover from a bout of sea sickness. I have no respiratory ailment, so it is doubtful I will breathe 'wrong' around anyone. So, fear not, good sir." Samuel gave a mocking bow and stood back. "I would not harm anyone on your Fair Isle." The merriment went out of his eyes as quickly as it had appeared there, his black eyes looking as hard as ziom. "Unless they give me just cause to."

Leaving Calem reeling in shock, Samuel swaggered off into the shadows, noting that he needed to add Calem Dawn's name to his exceedingly long list of people to watch out for.

Sam stood in the shadows, letting the cool night rain pour over him. He found the colour and the light of this Realm too bright, especially compared to his native Realm. The beings of this Realm! He made a noise deep in his throat that resembled the sound a disembowelled camor in its last moments. The beings here touched, poked, questioned and commanded without thought of whom they could be talking too. Never in all his centuries had he come across another Realm where beings were so free with what they said and how they acted. It was enough to drive him to...

"Who are you?" a soft voice called out from his left.

Baring his teeth, Sam let out a soft growl. He was getting sick of the locals and their never-ending questions.

"I mean no disrespect, sir. I cannot see, and you are a stranger to me. Did you come with the Wisara?" A lady walked out of an alcove in the set of shops.

Sam took in her beige clothes and plain shoes. He almost rolled his eyes until he looked at her face. Her eyes were opaque. Once, it seemed, they had been a light blue, but it looked like there was a silvery cloud over them.

"My eyes have always been like this."

"How did you...?"

The strange lady didn't wait for him to finish. "Everyone stares at the unusual."

Looking at her eyes for a moment longer, he shuddered. He had seen wings torn apart, limbs ripped off and skulls shattered. Very few beings with any kind of disability survived in the Dark Realms for long, so it was something he had not encountered before – particularly not blindness. Well, at least, not blindness while the being still had their eyes in its skull.

The lady laughed. "That, friend, is a gruesome thought! And I like my eyes, so if you'll be kind enough to leave them where they are, I would greatly appreciate it."

Sam couldn't help but grin. "I think I might be able to manage that." He paused. Surely he could question this stranger without rebuke? After all, she'd started with a question. Biting his lip, he asked, "Why did you call me friend?"

She laughed again, a merry sound which was not intended to scorn. "Because I know you will be. Care to walk me home?"

"With pleasure."

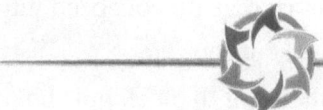

Sam stood outside the charming lady's house. Even though they'd not exchanged names, Sam knew, just as she did, that they would become good friends. He needed one good friend who would know him from now, not like Jon, who knew him from before. He liked this woman, who didn't pull any punches. She told him outright what she thought of what he had been and who she thought he would become. He didn't entirely agree with her, but then, he never fully agreed with anything anyone said.

As he headed back to Jonathan's, he wondered what other surprises Ronah had in store for him. Throughout his walk, Ronah was a gentle voice chattering idly away in the back of his mind. Although far from intrusive, it didn't stop him from feeling thoroughly disconcerted.

Stepping into Jonathan's house, he yelled, "What in the name of the Nine Realms of Hell is going on?"

Jonathan, who had apparently fallen asleep on his couch, let out a particularly loud snore and turned his head away from the source of the noise, which only seemed to infuriate Samuel more.

"The damn Island talks, Jon! It *talks!* Things made of dirt that are filled with worms should not be able to talk." Samuel could hear the condemnation, confusion, and amazement in his voice. Not for the first time, he marvelled at how many emotions human vocal chords could emulate.

Jonathan grunted and muttered, "Tell Lissae that."

"What?" A beat passed as realisation sank in. "You mean the whole *Realm* can talk?" Samuel could hear his voice rising in volume on each word, but paid it no mind. No doubt, Jonathan was used to the tantrums his teenage charge threw. "Unbelievable. Next thing I know you'll be telling me it's sentient." He snorted as he collapsed into a lounge chair, swinging one leg up over the side of the arm.

"She," Jonathan mumbled, trying to block out the noise Samuel was making by throwing his arm over his face. It didn't work.

"She?"

"Lissae isn't an 'it.' Lissae is a She." He opened his eyes blearily. "Are you done with your tantrum yet? And for your information, Shari doesn't throw tantrums... often."

Samuel ignored Jonathan. He'd not heard much after 'Lissae is a she.' "The Realm is sentient?" he whispered. He leaped to his feet. "The *Realm* is sen*tient!*"

"It doesn't matter which words you choose to stress, it still remains a fact."

"The Realm is sentient."

"You are becoming repetitive, old friend."

"But there are only a handful of sentient Realms, and only one of them is Grey..." Samuel trailed off, looking stunned.

"The gaping fish look really suits you, Samuel." Jonathan finally looked at his unexpected houseguest. "I trust you've figured out where you are?"

Samuel nodded. Although the information stunned him, he felt things sliding into place, the pieces of the puzzle finally fitting together.

"Are you planning on hanging around for a while?" Jonathan asked, rubbing his tired eyes.

Smirking at him, Samuel said, "How can I pass up an opportunity like this? I assume you will want to keep an eye on me, to keep your little Altoriae safe."

Jonathan debated whether glaring at him would do any good. Deciding it would only be an exercise in futility, he stood and stretched out the kinks in his back. "You're welcome to stay here. The couch is very comfortable."

Still smirking at him, this time from the doorway, Samuel said, "Glad to hear it. Wouldn't want you to be uncomfortable in your own home." Without another word, he bounded down the hall to Jonathan's bedroom.

Staring after him, Jonathan tried to summon the energy to be outraged and found he couldn't. Lying back down on the couch, he could only come to one conclusion for his current, completely undesirable predicament.

He had to have seriously annoyed one of the Weavers. It was the only reason he could think of for having one of the Realm's deadliest beings as his house guest. Who knew what misdeed was horrible enough to have that tu'zar sleeping in his bed instead of him.

CHAPTER TWENTY

Despite the early hour and a lamented lack of sleep, Shari gave a gentle warning to Mitch, Jonathan, and Tania as the sun appeared on the horizon. Ten minutes later, she shifted them all to the Wisara campsite. It was all but abandoned; only flattened grass and a faint smell of brine gave any indication as to where the camp had been. The Elders of both Ronah and the Wisara stood in a circle, waiting for her. They had landed in the middle of the circle of Elders from both Ronah and the Wisara.

Sensing the tension in the air as they arrived, Shari's instincts kicked into overdrive, she threw up an invisible shield around Mitch and Jonathan. She looked at the Mayor, who stood with Ronah's Elders, and raised an eyebrow.

He dipped his head and opened a connection to her, showing the rather heated discussion the two groups had been having. Ronah's Elders were not happy the Wisara had used the Hantra as a test. Many were furious and had argued that the Wisara should be banned from coming back to the Island for generations to come. The Wisara were unsympathetic. They could not see the issue with using the available spirits as they had different customs for their dead. There was a tense standoff between the two groups, and Alan wasn't sure how far he could push either way without it being a diplomatic failure.

Shari stood tall. "I understand the Wisara needed me to pass a very visible test to ensure that you had more than the word of a teenage girl to go on; however, by using the spirits on Ronah, you were summoning those who we consider our ancestors, and telling them to fight their children. This, I will not condone again. It is like gathering the bones from the seabed and waving it in your faces. The people of Ronah will be devastated when the news breaks. Ronah herself was distraught during the attack. I trust it won't happen again?" Shari said.

The Wisara elders looked to be in various stages of shock and horror when the realisation of what they'd done was pointed out in terms they understood. "We apologise, Altoriae. We will not use the Hantra on Ronah again," one of the Elders murmured.

'Thank you, Shari,' Alan sent to her.

'You're welcome. I truly think they meant to harm. It's not taboo for the Wisara the same way it is for us,' Shari sent back.

'I understand,' Alan replied.

Out loud, Shari said, "So, did I pass your test?"

Brayden stepped forward and shuddered a little as tendrils of her shield brushed against his skin, feeling out his intentions. "Yes, little Altoriae, you did. You did very well, even if your Guild helped you." His eyes slide over the others. "You must learn that they will not always be there to help you."

'Guild members?' she sent to Jonathan, Mitch, and Tania.

'I think he means us,' Mitch replied.

'But I never announced a Guild,' Shari sent, confused.

'In the eyes of the Wisara, we fought by your side and therefore must be members of a fighting Guild. Clearly, they haven't been able to track down any membership for us, so they've assigned what they see as the most appropriate name,' Jonathan sent.

Shari tried not to bristle. She did not want to lead a Guild. She had never even intended to become a member of a Guild. 'How official is this?' Shari muttered.

'Entirely unofficial. We'd not appear on any records, but the Wisara are likely to carry news of the Altoriae Guild everywhere they go. It is a substantial piece of news that they would see bartering value in,' Jonathan sent back, a mild rebuke in his tone. 'You know I've been working towards this anyway.'

'I know. Still, nice to know the on goings of my life have just become bartering chips,' Shari sent, sarcasm evident in her thoughts. She sighed. Guild members. 'By Na'reh, how weird does it sound – I have Guild members.'

'Concentrate, Shari,' Jonathan admonished.

'I am, don't worry.' Shari understood Brayden's warning. By labelling them as 'the Altoriae Guild' the Wisara were, however unintentionally, inviting all sorts of threats on their lives.

"Now, little Altoriae, tell us what boon you would ask of us?"

Although Jonathan did not say a word, she could feel her Guardian's tension as a palpable pressure on the back of her neck, right where his gaze was boring a hole into her.

"The boon I ask of the Wisara is for them to help protect Lissae when the Altoriae or the Guardian calls for your help," Shari said carefully. Wisara were careful in their bargaining, not because they were dishonest, but because the Settled had tried to turn their own words against them too often.

"That is a rather significant boon to be asking," Brayden said, his brow drawing down while the mutterings of shocked Wisara Elders were heard behind them.

Shari could feel Jonathan's indignation as a force rolling up her back. He felt that any and all residents of Lissae should help to protect their Realm when it was needed, but the Wisara were survivors. As a group, they would often avoid conflicts rather than contributing to ending the threats to their Realm. "Not all helping is fighting. Often in a battle, the fighters need healing or feeding so they can continue to keep Lissae safe."

"You wish for us to patch up and feed the fighters for you?" Brayden asked his brow furrowed.

"Yes, I do."

"Garayen, do you agree?" Brayden's eyes didn't leave hers.

An Elder left the circle and stepped up to Brayden's side. "We are not all Healers, Altoriae," Garayen said, his voice melodic and soothing.

"I understand. But those who are not Healers could organise food or supplies, or lend the Healers their strength."

Brayden and Garayen looked at each other for a long minute, and then Garayen nodded and stepped back into the circle.

"Your boon has been granted, Altoriae."

The Wisara Elders bowed before taking a step back from the circle and silently disappearing. Brayden stayed for a moment longer, his eyes catching hers and reminding them of their interrupted conversation. Shari nodded slightly and Brayden bowed before stepping back and sinking into the sea foam.

"Well, Shari Dawn, congratulations are in order. It is no small feat to drive back the Hantra," Alan said.

"Thank you, Mayor. Ronah and Lissae are safe again."

"You have completed your task, Altoriae, now it is time for us to discuss the future. You may dismiss your Guild," said Elder Zephyr, a sneer in his voice and his nose in the air.

Despite keeping her eyes trained on the Elders before her, Shari could feel the members of her fledgling Guild bristling behind her. The superior way Elder Zephyr tried to dismiss them was not in the best of taste.

"Elder Zephyr, we have just fought against the spirits of our fallen, in a battle they had no say in. We are tired, and I have another test to complete. We wish to go home and prepare, but as you have requested a meeting, my Guild and I are most happy to attend."

Stepping forward to stand firmly by Shari's shoulder, Jonathan nodded and went so far as to call up chairs from the ground beneath them. Ronah added her own flair, making the seats look rather more ostentatious than was needed. The Elders settled in with a harrumph and a few grumblings into the lumpy chairs they summoned. Only Elder Thorne's came close to looking anywhere near as fancy as the ones Shari's Guild sat in.

Once everyone was comfortably situated, the Mayor spoke up again. "Altoriae, is it true you've pledged yourself before one of Ronah's Elders?"

"Yes, Mayor. I swore to Elder Thorne that I am the Altoriae."

"Is it true you have agreed to abide by the traditions and duties of the Altoriae of Lissae as I read them out to you previously?"

"Yes, Mayor, I did."

"And have you found the task the Weavers appointed to the thirteenth Altoriae?"

"Yes, Mayor, we did." When she didn't expand on it, Alan gave her a look, and she sighed. "My task is to defeat Anriluka."

As one, the Elders shuddered. Muttering rose up amongst them, and Edward caught her eye. Fear for her was evident in his gaze, and she dared to peek beneath his shields and found it was not a fear of her success or failure, but fear that in the attempt of defeating such a Dark and dangerous creature, she would somehow be injured.

"Elders of Ronah, do you agree to help the Altoriae in this task and any other which may befall her?"

There was a long stretch of silence. Clearly, some of the Elders were still having trouble wrapping their minds around her going from a relatively unthreatening Blank to the Altoriae. Shari started to bristle with annoyance when the required answer was finally voiced, albeit reluctantly in some cases. "We do."

"Very well then. After Anriluka is defeated, we shall converge in the Town Square to recite the vows."

"As you will it, Mayor," the Elders and the Guild intoned.

After an awkward silence, Jonathan mentally nudged Shari, Mitch, and Tania and they rose, their chairs silently slipping back into the earth.

"Thank you, Elders of Ronah. Now we ask our leave of you. We have much to do," Jonathan said, coming to stand beside Shari.

"Of course, Guardian. As you desire. We need you well prepared so you may now defeat Anriluka." A shiver went through the collected Elders as Solomon Silverstone spoke, "We wish you well."

"Thank you, Elders of Ronah," Shari said, dipping her head in a small bow. 'Are things always going to be this formal from now on?' she sent to Jonathan as the Elders shifted home or left the circle by foot.

'Only with the Elders. And those above seventy. The younger generations haven't had the need to practice the formal ways, more's the shame.'

Shari inwardly shuddered. 'Well, I hope they don't start practising on me!' Including Mitch into their conversation, she sent, 'Let's see what else we can find out about the U'tan.'

'Not quite, Shari. I will see what we can find, you need to cover some training with Mitch and Tania,' Jonathan reminded them.

Mitch and Shari both scowled.

'They are both important. We need to be safe on Ronah, and doing two things at once will help us to be safer than we would if we worked on one at a time,' Jonathan admonished them.

'Well, I don't know about you two, but training sounds exciting!' Tania said, almost bouncing on the spot.

Tania screamed as a fireball erupted around her. Smelling burning hair, she started frantically patting her head, until Mitch said, "Don't worry, it's me." Turning, she saw his right eyebrow smouldering. Without thinking, she raised her hand and released a gentle stream of water at it.

Mitch yelped and glared at her, his face dripping. Then something behind Tania caught his attention, making his eyes widen. He threw up his hands, just in time to stop another fireball from connecting. Tania watched, fascinated by the pale-orange, translucent shield appearing in front of him. She watched the fireball rage against it, trying to find a weakness but unable to. It fizzled out slowly. When it was gone, Mitch left the shield up for a few moments before dropping it.

"Are you alright?" he asked. He took a step towards Tania, and the fireball they thought had gone out roared back into being. Startled, he took a step back and threw his shield up again, but not quite quick enough this time. A thread of flame was caught inside the shield, and it shimmered around the shield before turning on Mitch and settling down on his head, setting his hair smouldering. "Shari!" he cried, trying to keep the shield up while batting at his burning hair.

Shari released her control on the fireball, and it faded out for good.

Mitch dropped his shield, and Tania sent a stream of water out to soak him.

"Just when I was drying off," he muttered, disgusted with himself.

"Mitch, you have to concentrate. Fire is something you can see – something you can physically prepare yourself for. Having someone in your head isn't something you can see. You can't go, 'Oh, here comes a person now, better get those shields up!' You have to be prepared *all the time*."

Giving her a funny look, Mitch said, "You're beginning to sound like Jonathan."

"Then I must be doing something right," she said with a quirk of her lips. "Ready to try again?"

Rolling his eyes at Tania, he said, "Ready." He staggered at the sudden onslaught of Shari's Innarn attack. She pounded against his mind like a tsunami taking over a beach. She was everywhere he was, in his every thought, his every action, his every word. It felt as if he was smooshed up against the back of his skull and she wasn't ever going to let him out.

He could feel himself panicking and was on the edge of giving in – and giving in was the one thing Shari always told him not to do. Never give up. Never say die. With a mighty roar – which sounded more like a strangled squeak to Tania – he forged out from the back of his skull and pushed Shari clear out of his mind. Panting from the effort, he dropped to the ground, sweat pouring from his forehead.

Tania was saying something, but her words sounded fuzzy. The whole Realm felt fuzzy. He took a few deep breaths and looked up, to find Tania leaning over the side of the platform. When he pushed Shari out of his mind, he'd also pushed her over the edge of the platform. The innate Innarn surrounding the school had prevented her from falling, but she still had to climb up from where she had landed.

Mitch crawled over to the edge on his hands and knees in time to see Shari levitate up. Sitting cross-legged in mid-air before him, she smiled. "Well done. If you do that every time, those who would wrongfully claim Lissae as theirs will fear your name."

Grinning stupidly, Mitch turned and high-fived Tania.

"I'm done then. Better get back to the shop before Jonathan docks my pay." He grinned and, with a wave, he disappeared, leaving Shari and Tania alone.

"Alright Tania, your turn now," Shari said.

"Now? Don't you have the scary thing to squish?" Tania asked nervously. Shari had some serious firepower, and she really didn't want to be on the receiving end until she had learned how to use her Innarn better.

Shari sighed, her shoulders slumping. "Yes, I do. I suppose training can wait until after we speak to Jonathan."

"You seem to be... annoyed with him a lot," Tania said carefully. She winced when she realised that even despite her care, her words were still quite blunt.

"I suppose I am in a way. I still find it hard to work as part of a team. Guess having a Guild means getting used to it a whole lot quicker!" Shari forced a smile on her face, trying not to think of how much easier everything seemed when she only had to look out for herself on the battlefield. Having to rely on others was something she struggled with. At least if it was just her and something went wrong, she had no one else to blame.

The two girls walked in a strained silence towards the bookstore, Shari lost in her thoughts, and Tania lost in wondering how she could cheer up the person destined to save them all. For all the stories and hype about the Altoriae, she was glad she'd never had to carry the mantle of the Realms' protector. "Can I ask you something?" Tania said suddenly.

Shari looked at her, startled. "Sure."

"Lissae is a pretty big place, right?"

"Right," Shari said, tilting her head, confused as to where this was going.

"Well, if Lissae is so big, wouldn't it make sense to work as part of a team? That way there are more people and less area for one person to cover," Tania reasoned.

"It doesn't quite work that way," Shari said. "Each Realm is like a room. There are only a few entrances. Lissae has all the openings lined up. Most people have to travel to various points on Lissae to cross the Realms, but when Kay'imi was Altoriae, she made them easy for the Altoriae to access. Some nights, patrolling is as easy as walking down a hallway with six doors. There are the Ducibus, of course, who guide the travellers through the gateways of the Realms. I know most of them by sight now, even if they don't know me. But having large landmasses to protect isn't what I do."

"So, what do you actually do?" Tania asked.

If anyone else had asked her the same question, Shari would have been likely to snarl at them, but from Tania, she knew it was genuine, innocent curiosity. "Have your dreams changed since you arrived on Ronah?" she asked.

Tania nodded.

"Ronah is one of the six gateways to the Realms, which means people on or near Ronah are more likely to unconsciously travel across the Realms when they're sleeping. My job is to not only keep malicious intruders on the other side of Lissae's gateways, but to protect the travellers from Lissae, particularly the dreamers. I am the slayer of the monsters and demons you see in your dreams, the ones that would hurt you, or kill you and take over your body to try and enter our Realm."

Tania gasped. "They wouldn't. People don't *do* that."

"We're on a Grey Realm with a very specific moral and legal code. Here, killing another is forbidden, and you'll be punished if you do kill someone. On other Realms, killing is a sport played for fun. The idea of ripping someone into tiny pieces is as normal as deciding what's for dinner."

Tania couldn't help it, her stomach twisted, and she could feel bile working its way up her throat. "That's disgusting," she choked out.

Something in her voice made Shari give her a sharp glance. "You need to remember, I'm here to stop anything like that from happening. So, as long as I'm around, you'll be safe."

Tania didn't know if she should feel grateful or nauseated. She settled on a bit of both as they pushed through the bookshop's door.

Standing on the path just before the bookshop, Samuel smirked as he watched the two girls slip through the doors. The little Altoriae needed to pay more attention to the beings entering her Realm.

While Shari tested Mitchel and Tania's shielding, Jonathan laid out the research he'd found on the U'tan, ready to show his charges after their training. He had one task that chilled him to his core to complete before their training was over, but he wouldn't have handed it to Shari for all the ziom on Lissae.

'And the Realm shall fade away to nothingness once you leave its fleshy grasp.' Jonathan looked away from the tombstone and shuddered. Every single time he read those words, they froze his insides. Knowing what would happen once his soul left his body was one thing, but it didn't mean he wanted to be reminded of it every time he visited his teachers' grave. Yet he knew there was yet another lesson in this too.

Learn to accept the inevitable, he could almost hear Joshua saying.

The old man's spirit appeared, sitting on his headstone, puffing away at a translucent pipe. The smell of Sage, herb of the wise, suddenly hit Jonathan. 'Hello *again, boy. Have you found your Altoriae?*'

"I have," Jonathan replied, smiling.

'*It seems to me that it has been some time since we last conversed,*' he sent. Time in Lissae's Spirit Realm was not like time on Lissae. In the Spirit Realm, you could choose if time went faster or slower than Lissae.

"Yes, sir. It has been quite a while," Jonathan admitted. "I had to check on you. There was a... a disturbance here last night," he finished abruptly, not quite sure how to say what had happened.

Joshua's face grew cloudy. 'Yes, we know. The Wisara raised the Hantra. A most cruel and devastating thing to do.'

Jonathan let his grief and condolences show in his public mind. Joshua bowed his head, silently acknowledging his pupil. "I am here to... to report on who is missing," Jonathan murmured. The spirits of Lissae's deceased usually moved into a Spirit Realm, which co-existed alongside Lissae. The Spirit Realm was like a waiting room. The only possessions in the Spirit Realm were your memories.

Nothing else is necessary, not even flesh. Spirits of the departed can stay in the waiting room for as long as they desired. Once they were ready, they could say goodbye and continue to their next life.

By raising the Hantra, the Wisara called upon any available spirits, including those in the Spirit Realm. The closest spirits were forced to answer – to ignore such a call was unthinkable – and the nearest portal into Lissae's Spirit Realm was Ronah's cemetery. When a Hantra was killed, the spirit residing in the flesh was thrown out of the Spirit Realm, due to one of Lissae's lores, which stated that no spirit could inhabit a second body until *after* they have moved on from the Spirit Realm.

The Hantra, from a spirit's point of view, are dangerous creatures. They are designed to do their caller's bidding and are unresponsive to the commands of the spirit who was called in them. At the same time, they cannot move without a spirit, for to do so would contradict one of Lissae's other lores.

'*May I assume you would like my help?*' Joshua sent.

The student looked at his teacher. "Your help, as always, is greatly appreciated.

"However..." Jonathan paused, and he could feel his mentor and dear friend waiting for him. "However, the main reason I am here..."

Joshua held up an ethereal hand. '*I know why you are here, Jonathan Buan. Do not presume you know all there is to know just yet.*' He paused, taking a draw on his pipe. '*Now then. How about we find out who is... missing?*' Joshua Izzaya Clemise, for all his bustle and pomp, was deeply touched that his star pupil still worried about him. Deep in the back of his mind, he knew he would soon be leaving the Spirit Realm. However, there was no time to think of leaving now, he realised. After all, he had a student to hassle.

Watching the old man float up off his headstone, Jonathan couldn't help but feel relieved. Just knowing his mentor had been spared was...

'*Come on now, boy-o! All your flesh seems to be slowing you down!*' Joshua chortled, hovering a good ten paces in front of him.

. . . Yet another night spent in Adeon's wake! Refraining from rolling his eyes, Jonathan retorted, "Just because you are now made up of refracted light particles does not mean you are quicker than me, old man!"

'*Still depending on schoolboy taunts, eh boy-o?*'

Jonathan just laughed. It was a relief to be working with his mentor again.

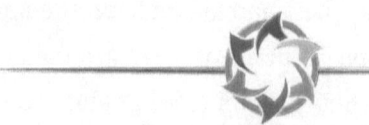

Jonathan sighed. Three-hundred-and-sixty-four spirits destroyed. On a tiny Island with a limited population, that was far too many. He stifled another sigh. Three-hundred-and-sixty-four was too many no matter where you were. He and Joshua had gotten all but two of the names. It had been no small feat to get as many as they had, seeing the remaining spirits had not wanted to communicate with those not in the spirit Realm – including Jonathan.

'So, *boy-o. You have your names. Come to see me when the next disaster strikes!*'

Jonathan regarded his former mentor. "How many are left?" he asked.

Joshua paused, turning his translucent form away from his pupil. Jonathan looked at his teacher, and translucent or not, he could see the new pain etched into the older man's face. "How many are left, Joshua?"

The teacher turned once more to face his student. 'Not *enough.*'

Trying to keep his temper in check, Jonathan waited, and sure enough, Joshua gave him the answer, one which had him gulping and realising he was indeed very fortunate to be talking to his former teacher.

CHAPTER TWENTY-ONE

Shari and Tania greeted Mitch, who groaned at them.

"The task master returns," Mitch said dramatically.

Tania made a show of sniffing the air. "Can you smell burned hair?" she asked.

Shari grinned, and Mitch scowled at her. "Ha ha. You got here rather quick, did Shari take it easy on you, squirt?"

Tania poked her tongue out as Jonathan stepped into the room from the back of the store.

"Good, you're all here." Jonathan smiled. Shari sent him a quick thought. He raised an eyebrow in her direction but nodded minutely. "Tania, can you mind the store while I talk to Shari and Mitch?"

Shari smiled as Tania stammered her reply, "Umm... sure. I don't really know what I'm doing, though."

Mitch threw her a cleaning rag. "Just dust the shelves and send me a thought if a customer comes in. It should be pretty quiet this time of day. If you get all the dusting done, there's a delivery you could start to unpack."

"Okay," Tania said, standing uncertainly in the middle of an isle as the others made their way out the back.

Shari got the impression that Jonathan had arrived not long before she and Tania had. She narrowed her eyes at him but refrained from commenting.

"So, what's the deal with this U'tan?" Shari asked, cutting straight to the heart of the matter.

Jonathan retrieved a book from his cluttered desk and handed it to Shari. She silently looked at the picture of the multi-eyed, tentacle-waving purple... thing.

"No," said Jonathan, noticing her thoughts, "it's not a thing. She is a variant of the beings who feeds off souls, emotions and flesh."

"Weaknesses?" Mitch asked.

"Physically, here," Jonathan pointed to a gill-like membrane under one of the thicker tentacles. "This, it is said, leads directly to what passes for her heart. She, and indeed her whole race, are extraordinarily powerful Innarnians. The U'tan are a race of strategists. As it's been so long since her last attack, I do not doubt she has thought of every contingency. She's almost devoured Ronah's entire population before, and we cannot operate under the assumption that she will fail to make it to our shores. There is no doubt that she will be back."

Shari nodded. The fear Ronah would produce at Anriluka's return would be like a never-ending, all-you-can-devour smorgasbord. She would need to find someone deeply connected with the Island and get them to distract Ronah while she fought the U'tan.

"Tania," she said out loud, "Tania could distract Ronah, but what could she talk about to distract the entire Island?"

"Sex," Mitch said.

Jonathan and Shari glanced at him. "Excuse me?" they said in unison.

"Ronah is very... interested in how people show love and affection for each other," Mitch replied, blushing.

Ronah generally piped up with one or two interesting questions for the residents at least once a week. "But we'll need someone who has actually experienced those things," Shari mused.

"It wouldn't have to be just about sex," Jonathan said.

Mitch nodded his head in agreement. "Ronah hasn't experienced loads of things, like holding someone in her arms. She hasn't experienced kissing, hugging, or holding hands. She may have felt the backlash of the emotional high which comes with intimacy, but not the deed itself, or the feelings that lead up to it," Mitch said.

"When did you get so wise?" Shari teased.

"Hanging around Jonathan too long," he said, grinning. "Ronah is always asking what things like emotions look or feel like. We could just get someone to sit down and answer some of her questions while the creature's here."

Mitch and Jonathan jumped at the slight tap at the door. Shari raised an eyebrow at them. The tap sounded again, and Jonathan bade the person enter.

Tania had tried to dust, but as soon as she'd raised the dusting cloth, a fine layer had risen into the air and swooshed out the front door before she could do anything else. She stared in amazement for a few moments, before shrugging and wandering around the store, trying to get a feel of where everything was. She spent a while idly tidying up the shelves, and mentally noting that she wanted to get a copy of *Guide to the Realms* by *Resa Sunab*, *Cultivating your Island Garden* by *Harmony Thorne* and *Beginners Guide to Innarn* by *Zali Erde*.

After straightening the shelves and taking the time to run her fingers over the spines of the books, there was nothing much else she could do.

Tania decided that if she was going to get paid for working at the store, then she'd better actually work. She decided to brave the backroom to see where the delivery Mitch had mentioned was hiding. Standing in front of the door to the backroom, she took a deep breath and hesitated. She didn't want to interrupt but didn't know what else to do. Taking another deep breath, she tapped lightly on the door.

There was a beat or two, and an amused feeling from Ronah, before Jonathan said, "Come in."

Tania pushed the door open and walked into the backroom. Jonathan, Shari, and Mitch were sitting in various chairs around the office. Jonathan sat in front of his old, dented cream-coloured desk. Shari sat cross-legged in one green plaid armchair, while Mitch seemed happy to lounge in his chair. "Mitch said there was a delivery you wanted me to unpack?"

Jonathan nodded and stood to rummage around in a pile of cardboard boxes, allowing Tania to take the rest of the room in. Done all in light wood, bookcases lined every wall. They even acted as a divider, she saw now, cutting the room in half.

'Unless you are invited,' a deep voice, much like Jonathan's said in her mind, 'You are not to go into the other room.'

Tania nodded. 'Some things are private,' she sent at the voice.

'And some things are privately shared. If you ever do stumble in there, do not touch anything.'

Nodding, Tania realised the stack of boxes Jonathan had been sorting though had halved. "They're out on the carts. Have a look around and see if you can figure out where everything goes. If you can't see an obvious spot, just leave it on the carts for us."

Tania nodded again, slowly backing out of the room. So, Ronah wasn't the only one who could talk — well, talk without saying anything — to her.

Interesting.

Walking back into the front room, she saw a man who looked vaguely familiar browsing the shelves.

"Hello," she said with a smile.

He turned to look at her fully. His eyes raked her, stripping her down to her soul. She shifted uncomfortably on the spot before he seemed to remember his voice.

"Hello," he said. His deep baritone carried the hint of a threat with it.

"Do I know you?" she asked, keeping the smile on her face while she practised the breathing techniques Ronah had shown her last night — *was it just last night?* — for keeping calm.

'*He has my blessing, Tania. He has much to learn here,*' Ronah sent to her, trying to soothe her.

'*He doesn't feel safe at all. Who is he?*' Tania asked plaintively.

'*He arrived with the Wisara. He wants to settle and is staying with the Guardian while his house is being made,*' Ronah sent.

"You might do. We have mutual acquaintances who know each other," he said smoothly.

Tania tried not to snort. "Pretty much everyone knows everyone on Ronah."

He inclined his head to her. "True."

"So, you were travelling with the Wisara?" she asked, a little bell going off in her mind at the word travelling. Something about this man was itching at the edge of her consciousness.

"Yes," he said easily, taking in the girl before him. She surely wouldn't last two seconds away from Lissae, for all the untapped, untrained Innarnian she had at her disposal. He wondered what it would be like to spar with her when she had control of her Innarn. He'd bet she would be a formidable foe.

"What have the Wisara been saying about the Altoriae?" Tania asked, breaking him out of his inspection.

"They are quite impressed by the Altoriae's performance in her test. They are a bit divided however on the Altoriae *Guild*. Some think the Guild points to a long-forgotten Lore, while others believe that Shari is not enough of an Altoriae to handle her responsibilities by herself."

Tania looked at him, astonished he'd divulged so much. The Wisara were notoriously closed-mouthed. "Why are you telling me this?"

He smirked as he said, "Because no matter how much you might want to, there's nothing you can do to change their opinions."

"You're incredibly smug, aren't you?" Tania asked innocently and then winced. One day, she was going to get her foot stuck in her mouth, she was sure of it.

He – '*Samuel*', Ronah informed her – raised an eyebrow. "People are not always what they seem."

"That is fairly obvious. You look like a smooth-talking berk, but you feel like you breathe violence," Tania said.

He moved before she could blink, looming over her with shadows which cloaked his back. His proximity meant that light seemed to be pulled from the shop. She could feel his hot breath on her forehead.

"Just because most of one's species is violently destructive, doesn't mean that all of the species is," he practically snarled at her.

"Well, you're doing a great job of proving your point," she said, false bravado colouring her words as her nerves writhed. Shari's words of beings which delighted in ripping someone into tiny pieces came back to her.

Tania watched in fascination as a look of desolate sadness crossed Sam's features for a brief second. She watched with fascination as a nonchalant mask slipped back in place as he stepped away from her, the shadows retreating and light filling the shop once more.

"I am more than I seem," he said.

Watching as he turned and walked away, Tania's heart thumped so hard against her chest she thought it might break through her ribs. Clearly a man of many contradictions, Samuel seemed so at war with himself that it made her ache.

As his hand reached out to open the door of the shop, he turned his head and looked at her from over his shoulder, "Isn't everyone?"

Finding she couldn't hold his gaze, she looked at the floor, almost ashamed at making such a quick judgement about his character. She vowed not to be so quick to judge next time and to make it up to the man who was cloaked in shadows; she made a silent pact to Ronah to help him, but when she looked up, he was already gone.

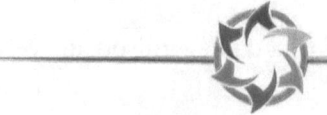

8 days left

After her meeting with Jonathan and Mitch, Shari shifted straight to her bedroom. She was tired right down to her toes. It seemed like every being – both Light and Dark and everything in between – had been out to test her since her name had been revealed.

Needless to say, she hadn't had much rest at all since then. Shari tossed and turned as she lay in bed; strange phrases kept echoing around her head. Jonathan had told her that the Wisara were happy with how she handled her test, despite their abrupt departure. Clearly, they were aware of how upset certain residents of Ronah would be by their choice to raise the Hantra. Idly, she wondered whether her Guild would get a chance to see them again.

Then there was the whole thing with the Weavers test. Anriluka. If she had to pick a being that Ronah feared more than any other, it would be the U'tan. Anriluka had actually 'eaten' the soul of the only male Altoriae, Muran Curtis, in 3739. Although 320 years had passed, Ronah would be unable to clear her mind of the threat Anriluka presented. The demon had decimated the population of the Island back then, and even now there were not as many people living on the Island as before Anriluka's attack, despite the centuries in between.

Wondering the best way to start the search for the 'cure', Shari thought about the curse. She only had eight days left. The bit which had her most concerned was the 'bright new death' that was mentioned. Finding a red jewel didn't seem too hard on the surface of things. Maybe it was a red crystal? Ronah had masses of crystals. No, it had to be something more specific, something from the time of the Weavers. Who would have jewels which had once belonged to the Weavers? Maybe one of the old Clan's would have some.

Her thoughts wandered, and she found herself wondering how Tania was doing. She didn't desire to be Linked with Ronah. The fate and responsibilities of being Altoriae were more than enough for her. She wondered how Tania would take the news. She smiled as she thought back a few days, and remembered seeing Tania in the schoolyard; she'd been hanging out with Anika and her crowd. They had all been wearing their typical short skirts and tight tops. Anika had been wearing red, with a weird ruby pendant.

Until an Altoriae

Find a thorn red jewel

Not thorn like the one on a plant, but Thorne, like the Clan. The Thornes were one of the original Clans who colonised Ronah. There was a possibility the Elders passed on trinkets from their Weaver ancestors to the best of each generation, and Anika did appear to be the best. Maybe the pendant she wore could be the red jewel?

Maybe they'd beat the curse after all. Shari instantly shifted to the bookstore. Even as she arrived, she could sense he wasn't there. "C'mon Jonathan," she whispered, shutting her eyes, "where are you? I've figured it out!"

"Talking to yourself is a sign of madness," a snide voice said.

Shari's eyes flicked open. Carly Thorne was standing in front of her. "Sorry?" Shari asked.

"Look, I don't have all day for your mind games. I have a book on order. It's kind of a rare book, and it's critical to my grandfather, so if you could just..." Carly said nervously. She was clearly in a hurry, but she'd given Shari an idea.

"That's it!" Shari exclaimed.

"Oh, that's so..." Carly Thorne stood in the middle of the store. Alone. Shari had disappeared. If someone had seen her, what would they think? "So unfair!" Stomping her foot so hard she almost unbalanced herself, Carly stormed off. How was she going to get the book now?

Anika counted as she ran the brush through her hair. One hundred strokes exactly. Concentrating, she lifted the lipstick brush with her mind. "Steady!" she muttered. Closing her eyes, she guided the brush to her lips. A cool breeze blew past and, concentration lost, Anika's cheek ended up covered in 'Delight,' the new summer shade.

"Put you off, did I?" asked a velvety voice.

Anika's eyes flew open even as she gasped. "You!" she squealed, even as a whip-thin tentacle took up a surprisingly firm grip on her upper arm.

"Don't even pretend to be surprised," the owner of the tentacle snarled as the two of them disappeared.

"So, Samuel Caragnton, tell me about yourself," Lizbeth said as she gently set down a tray of tea and biscuits on the coffee table in front of him.

He followed her movements, not answering until she'd poured herself a cup of tea and sat in a pale blue armchair.

"Not much to tell, really."

Lizbeth smiled and sipped her tea, waiting.

Samuel sighed as he fixed himself a cup. "It is not something that is talked about."

"By whom?" Lizbeth asked innocently, settling back into her chair.

His teeth clacked shut with an audible snap before the instinctive cutting remark left his lips.

She laughed gently, and he felt his hackles rise, yet he still took a moment to breathe through his ire. After composing himself, he finally answered. "My mother was a much-adored member of the race I call 'family,' my sire... my sire is a late member of his race. One who had not been lamented once since his passing."

"Well, that is sad," Lizbeth said. "His own son does not lament his passing?"

"I did not know my mother or sire – none of my race does. It is our way."

"Yet another sad fact of life."

"Not sad, a necessity," Sam countered with gritted teeth, shifting his back and trying to get comfortable under her unseeing gaze.

"Necessities can be sad too," Lizbeth said mildly as she took a sip from her cup.

Suddenly they both jerked upright, scalding tea spilt unnoticed over shaking hands.

"Did you feel that?" Lizbeth asked, the terror evident in her voice.

"I did." Samuel rubbed the back of his neck as if he were trying to rid himself of an unpleasant sensation. "I've felt it before."

Lizbeth's head snapped up, her sightless eyes meeting his, causing another shiver to run up his spine. "When?"

Tearing his eyes away from hers, he said, "Over four hundred years ago."

Lizbeth's eyebrows rose. "Four hundred years ago? You're older than I credited you for, friend."

Knocking on the door again, Shari wondered why she even bothered. Now she had revealed her true nature, she had the right to enter any premises on the Island. But here she was, waiting. *Old habits die hard,* she thought, resting a hand on her suddenly queasy stomach.

After Shari knocked once more, Rany Thorne finally opened the door. Looking up at him, she said "Hi Rany, how are you?"

Rany's charcoal eyes widened. "Shari!" Brushing his unruly blond hair out of his eyes, he dropped down to one knee and bowed his head. "Altoriae. Clan Thorne is ever at your service."

Shari caught the faintest sign of a blush rising through his angular features. He recalled all the times when he had publicly scorned and privately ridiculed her. She knew the family Thorne had pledged their allegiance to Kay'imi when the first Thornes landed on Ronah. They had sworn to assist any Altoriae however they could, just like the Ribeck Clan had sworn to protect the Altoriae.

Although her training covered this sort of thing, for the life of her, she couldn't remember what to say. She decided to deal with pledges of allegiance and the like later. Now, however, she had a pendant to find.

'*Rany Thorne, I thank you and the rest of Clan Thorne for your pledge of services,*' Shari sent formally. "However, at the moment, I am only after an object I believe your eldest daughter is in possession of."

Rany looked at her, surprised. "Something Anika has?" he asked, standing.

Shari nodded. "I believe Anika has a particular artefact that I require," she said.

Rany stopped, taking a closer look at the girl who stood in front of him. Although he had wished the next Altoriae would turn out to be one of his girls, deep down, he had known that it wouldn't have been Anika. Even though she had proven her abilities repeatedly, Rany was more than doubtful of her skills. And now, Shari Dawn, self-declared Altoriae, wanted something from the daughter he had pushed so hard.

Clearing his throat once, then twice, Rany finally found his voice. "Let me... let me just check to see if..."

Shari met Rany's gaze with her own unblinking stare, unnerving him. Flinching, somehow he knew she had heard his thoughts. His shoulders slumped. "I'll just get her."

As Rany turned back into the house, Shari sighed. It was tiring to constantly have to prove herself. Even though she had known that some parents hoped their child would be the next Altoriae, being faced with it was something else. Suddenly, she was hit with the realisation that by declaring her true nature, she was inadvertently disappointing almost half of Ronah's population. She had been the girl everyone pitied. The girl who'd apparently inherited her mum's lack of Innarn, yet it turned out she was the one everyone had been waiting for. Shari shifted her weight from one foot to the other, uncomfortable with the whole thing.

Staring straight ahead, she could see through to the view offered by a window looking out over the Thornes backyard. Shari, who took delight in everything Ronah had to offer, wasn't watching the view for once. She remembered an entry in Fiona MacAde's journals. Fiona had been her Great-great-aunt, as well as the previous Altoriae. In her journal, she had written about the night in 3981 when she had announced that she, a girl of ten years, was the next Altoriae. She had been showered with gifts, praise, and pledges. Neither she nor the ones before her had mentioned the folk of Ronah being disappointed with their new Altoriae. Shari sighed again. She just hoped the disappointment of some and the doubts of many would ease over time.

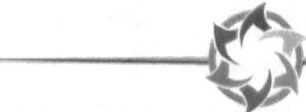

Rany came back down the stairs, running a hand through his hair as he tried to compose himself. This was Ronah. No doubt Anika was just blocking him. He knew she was a very active and private girl. No doubt she was just out making mischief. No doubt. He tugged on the suddenly tight neck of his shirt and took the last few steps to the front door.

It seemed that Shari had not moved an inch. Probably hadn't even blinked. Rany knew the Altoriae was not generally a vengeful being, but he still gulped, knowing he'd failed a relatively straightforward task. Especially when the Altoriae was a girl he had scorned and avoided, going so far as to warn his children away from her and her mother. The Altoriae was far from the simple being she had wanted everyone to believe her to be, much like Anika really. As much as he loved his daughter, he knew that nothing was ever simple when it came to Anika.

"Forgive me, Altoriae," he said, head bowed. For an instant, he had the feeling he had startled her. But Shari was the Altoriae. There was no way *he* could have startled *her*. He decided that worry was making him imagine things. "Anika doesn't appear to be here. I've tried calling her, but she doesn't seem to have heard me."

Rany hoped the Altoriae didn't feel his shiver as she settled her green gaze on him once more. "Anika often appears to have trouble... hearing people."

Rany knew, without a doubt, that Shari had discovered Anika's secret. He could sense Shari casting her mind out in search of his missing daughter. He just hoped, deep inside himself, the Altoriae couldn't sense his sinking heart.

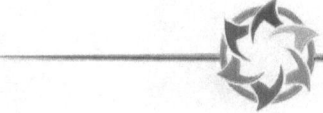

It took Shari a few seconds to centre her mind. She dreaded what she had, or more to the point hadn't found. "Would Anika leave Ronah without telling anyone?" She knew Rany was upset and worried that she had figured Anika out, but she couldn't dwell on anything other than finding the jewel.

"No. Why...?"

"Anika isn't on Ronah. And..." Lightning quick Shari checked with Ronah. "Ronah did not see her leave, but she did hear protests from Anika. Which is unusual."

Rany shot her a horrified look. Shari returned his gaze and lowered her eyes slightly, conveying her silence regarding Anika's 'abilities'. Bitterly, she accepted his shaky nod of thanks. Rany Thorne had never been particularly kind about her lack of Innarn, even when he was hiding his daughters non-existent ability.

"Ronah says she was taken from her room. However, Anika's blocks are preventing Ronah from pinpointing where she was taken to. Did Anika leave a necklace with a red jewel in her room?"

"She always wears that necklace. It was a gift from my grandparents."

Shari looked over his shoulder. Sometimes she forgot that the Edward and Harmony were Anika's grandparents. Taking a deep breath, she locked eyes with Rany once more.

"We will get her back." Shari wasn't sure if the vow was for Rany's peace of mind, or her own. Even as she shifted away from Rany's house, Shari sent out the call. As soon as she arrived at the bookstore, she started shifting the others in.

Before he could argue or wish her good luck, Lissae's newest Altoriae was gone. Rany stared blankly at the spot where she had been.

"Bring her back to me, just please bring my little girl back," he whispered to the empty air, struggling to keep tears from running down his face. In a matter of minutes, he'd failed the Altoriae, his daughter had disappeared, and he'd had his worst fears confirmed.

Not knowing what else to do, Rany leant his back against the hallway wall, and slid slowly down it, thinking of how much he pushed his girl to be something she had no chance of being.

CHAPTER TWENTY-TWO

As Anika struggled back to awareness, she let her body remain slack. The scent of copper filled her nose, and warm, sticky wetness dribbled down her arm. Pain bloomed from wounds she didn't want to see, but as something struck her stomach, she flinched, and her eyes opened to a horror she had not been expecting.

She struggled, cursed, cried and pleaded. None of it mattered. This being, this evil, ugly, foul fiend was not going to let her go.

Something struck her stomach again, and she looked down in shock to see a thin tentacle lying across her belly. It felt like a line of fire emanated from it. A second later she realised it was due to a myriad of tiny barbed hooks digging into her skin. She looked up as Anriluka pulled on the tentacle, and the skin attached to the hooks started to pull away from her stomach, showing the red twitching muscles underneath.

Anika always considered herself to be strong, but as the scream she'd kept trapped behind her teeth escaped, she realised she either wasn't as strong as she'd thought, or she had finally found her breaking point.

She gasped for breath as Anriluka let loose a weird watery chuckle, and she looked around, but the room seemed to be a cave made of dull black rock, bare except for her and the rock column she was tied to. Her hands were tied together in knots so complex she'd need to cut the rope to get out of it. Even so, there was just enough slack in the rope so she could turn around.

Usually, having any sort of movement would allow her to escape. By awkwardly shimmying up the pole, she could get her hands over the top and jump over the rope binding her hands. The pole, she discovered by craning her neck at an awkward angle, was a stalagmite. It rose out of the floor, plunged from the ceiling and met in the middle to form one smooth, strong pillar.

Anika sighed and threw her head back. A dull, echoing sounded around the cavern. When the stars finally cleared from her vision and her thoughts, she muttered a few curses, then said aloud, "Damn stuff's as hard as ziom!" she complained a bit more, then stopped. As hard as Ziom? Ziom was the hardest metal in all the Realms, and one of the reasons Lissae had to be protected. It was only found on Lissae. But that meant... and if she was right, then she was still on...

"Ronah! Lissae! Save me!" she screamed. Her voice echoed around the cave, the sound bouncing around for a moment before the slap of a tentacle joined the echoing chorus of her cry. A few seconds later, Anika released another scream, this one wordless, as a cruel tentacle snapped forward and sucked another strip of flesh from her exposed abdomen.

Shari muttered a curse. She could faintly feel Anika's torture. She took what pain she could, but the other girl was stubborn, and would not allow Shari past the blocks she had in place. To push her way through the mental barriers would end up hurting Anika more than it would help her.

Jonathan could see by the expression Shari wore that it was not good news. He too had reached out and felt Anika's mental blocks. They were strong as a Blank. But that wasn't possible... was it? Anika had tested time and time again as the best Innarnian in her age group. Surely, it couldn't be a lie? Could it?

Shari felt Jonathan's confusion, and she agreed. She had heard of the Rassu – people who claim to be Innarnian, but who use trapdoors, sleight of hand and tricks to reproduce the effects of what a real Innarnian could do.

Talking to Rany Thorne again was now critical.

Rany was levitating, trying to calm his thoughts and alleviate his worry over Anika in an attempt to reassure himself it was needless. He had almost succeeded when a knock sounded at the door of his mind. So startled and unprepared for it, he ended up mentally – and unfortunately physically – reeling away from it. As his mind smooshed up against the back wall of his mental shields, his body crashed into the wall of his retreat, rebounded, and ended up cartwheeling rather ungracefully around the room.

When he opened his eyes, he was sprawled upside down in his office chair with his head inches from the floor and his feet, which were hanging over the back of the seat, were missing the socks he had put on earlier. He had enough time to see one was resting on the windowsill and the other was across the room, hanging haphazardly on a coat hook before the knock sounded inside his head again.

Regaining a little of his composure, he bade the person enter.

'Greetings, Rany Thorne. We (and he understood the powerful voice which had entered his mind was a combination of Shari Dawn's and Jonathan Buan's) have a query about your daughter. The information you give us is private and will not be revealed to any person it does not pertain to. Do you agree to answer our questions?'

Rany sighed. Today was a day he should have stayed in bed, he realised. 'I agree to reply to your questions as best I can, Guardian, Altoriae.'

'Is your daughter, Anika, a Rassu?'

Scrubbing his face with his hand, Rany could no longer deny the inevitable. 'I believe so.'

Jonathan and Shari instinctively drew back as they felt Rany's self-loathing. He blamed himself for his daughter's lack of Innarn. Together, they calmed him. They tried to soothe his battered soul, and as his pain was shared, it diminished, leaving him slightly drained, but feeling better than before they had started talking to him.

Bidding him goodbye, they left him and retreated to their bodies. Shari felt queasy, as if she had eaten something bad while Mitch groaned and looked green. Shari rubbed her own stomach, bile threatening to rise up her throat.

Tania looked at them. "You too, hey?" she muttered, holding her stomach.

Shari looked at Jonathan, who looked just as bad as Tania and Mitch. Realisation dawned. 'Anika is on Lissae!'

Mitch looked at Tania as Shari and Jonathan disappeared from sight. "And here I thought it was just Dad's cooking," he grumbled. Tania's lips quirked upwards in a smile, but her eyes gave away how worried she was.

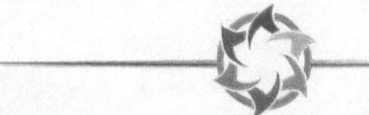

Darkness surrounded them as Jonathan and Shari arrived in Lissae's deepest caves. Made of ziom, they created a labyrinth underneath the mainlands of Lissae and were home to all manner of creatures, but the one they were hunting was not meant to be there.

As their eyes adjusted slowly, Shari pushed a wave of air Innarn into the labyrinth of tunnels to map where they had landed. The wave spluttered out a few lengths into the tunnels leading from the cavern they'd landed in. Shari huffed in aggravation.

Jonathan raised his eyebrows, and Shari rolled her eyes. She knew as well as he did that ziom had a tendency to absorb Innarn, but it had still been worthwhile to try and get a fix on their location.

Shari tried to reach out and sense Anika instead. Down here there was even less signal from Anika than normal.

That meant they had only one choice.

Shari and Jonathan split up, each choosing a direction and hoping against all hope they would be able to find Anika before Anriluka left Lissae with her.

CHAPTER TWENTY-THREE

S hari was trudging through another tunnel, trying to sense what was ahead of her, when she felt a heartbeat. She crept closer to the sound, following the curving wall of the tunnel. Shari followed a glimmer of light as it lit up the wall until it opened out into a massive cavern.

She paused at the lip of the tunnel and looked out to the enormous area. The structures inside the cavern took her breath away – there, carved right out of the ziom itself, was a city full of buildings. Sparse plant life waved in a slight breeze. Soaring blocky buildings towered over low, round buildings. Arched bridges connected the blocky buildings, and a round dome stood in the heart of the cavern. Somewhere below her water softly lapped against intricately painted ziom pools.

Shari stepped forward slowly, weapons drawn but not raised. The heartbeat she'd sensed picked up speed. She tensed slightly as a being came into view.

A humanoid with a lizard-like, flat head ending in a thick snout stepped from behind one of the buildings across the cavern. Amber eyes glared at her beneath deeply ridged brows. He was covered in copper scales, and his pants did nothing to conceal the throwing knives strapped to his thighs.

Shari bowed her head cautiously. He stared at her for a long minute, before dipping his head in return.

"I am Sulak of the Da'mar. What is your purpose here?" he said his voice carrying across the cavern.

"I am Shari Dawn, Altoriae. I come seeking the whereabouts of a resident of Ronah," Shari replied.

"Altoriae?" Sulak asked, his brow ridges rising.

Shari nodded.

"You are the only stranger here," Sulak said. "But there is a feeling of great horror in the tunnels. My people have fled to a different place."

"Why did you not go with them?" Shari asked, curious as to why the lone Da'mar had stood his ground.

"I am here to tell the others what happens to our city, and when it is safe to return."

"You think the great horror will pass?"

Sulak tilted his head to the side. "Of course it will. Otherwise, I would not be here."

"Do you know where the great horror is?"

Shuddering the Da'mar shook his head. "I wish to keep my city and my people safe, not to seek out death."

"Which way would I go if I wanted to find death?" Shari tried again.

"Into the tunnels," Sulak said. He stood there for a moment, regarding her. "You are a great warrior, are you not, Altoriae?"

Shari blinked in surprise. The Da'mar lived by their own warrior code, but little of it was understood by others. "Many think I am."

"And yet many doubt your word," Sulak finished.

Shari nodded. There was no need to try and hide it.

"You are a true warrior. The Da'mar would be honoured to help you, but not for this test," Sulak stated.

"Thank you, Sulak," Shari said, bowing her head. "I must continue my search."

Sulak bowed his head. "I bid thee well, Altoriae."

"I bid thee well, Sulak of the Da'mar," Shari said. She took one more look around the cavern, and at the subtle way Sulak was trying to angle his body. Taking his cue, she chose the tunnel to the left of where she had entered and begun her search anew.

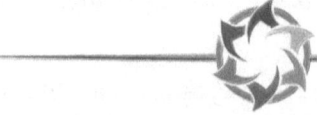

Shari followed the tunnel Sulak indicated until she hit a wall which curved back towards the direction of the cavern she and Jonathan had arrived in. Frustrated, she stopped. There was no other way to go now, but she could feel, somewhere beyond the thick layers of rock before her, Anika's suffering.

She wasn't getting anywhere here, so she headed back to the cavern where they arrived at a jog. Maybe Jonathan had more luck.

Hot, sweaty and exhausted, Jonathan and Shari jogged into the cavern at the same time. There was simply too much ground to cover and not enough time to do it in.

Shari looked at Jonathan. "Maybe we should get everyone from Ronah down here to scour the tunnels?" she offered weakly, knowing it wasn't a good idea.

Jonathan shook his head mutely.

"Maybe Lissae can guide us in the right direction?" she asked.

Tilting his head, Jonathan said, "That might work." Jonathan announced to Lissae, '*We believe you have an unannounced visitor.*'

'*Why would I have a...*' the Realm sounded more strained and tired than Shari had ever heard before. Despite the unaccustomed weariness in Lissae's voice, Shari could feel the formidable concentration scanning the Realm for any being which should not have been there. Jonathan tried to get a message through but was unable, and without warning...

'*I see you!*' Lissae screamed.

At what was essentially the epicentre of the scream, Shari and Jonathan grasped their ears and drew in on themselves reflectively, feeling the scream like a boulder slamming into their solar plexus. Shari could feel an incredible amount of rage directed at the intruder, most of which was coming from the Realm, some of which was Ronah's, but the remainder – not an insignificant part – definitely belonged to her.

'*How dare you enter my Realm?*' Lissae roared at the trespasser.

The Realm's concentration now split between its usual mundane tasks and the trespasser. Shari was finally able to send '*Careful! She has a...*'

Too late.

'*. . . hostage.*'

Lissae and all of the seven Shifting Islands worked together, releasing a massive amount of power into one of Lissae's caves. Jonathan could feel Ronah trying to pull back when she realised Anika was in there with the creature, but Lissae held the younger Island in check. No one trespassed on her and got away with it! Together, Realm and Islands sent the interloper back into the Dark Realms, where she made her home.

Jonathan could feel Ronah trying to reach out and snag Anika. He lent as much of his power to the Island as he dared and he could feel Shari doing the same, but to no avail. Anriluka's home Realm was too dark, draining too much of Ronah's power. Without Lissae's help, there would be no way the Island could get Anika back now.

The townsfolk could feel the Island mourning. For what, they did not know. Silently, as they continued to go about their everyday tasks and chores, they provided Ronah with their support on an almost unconscious level. The entire community experienced the relief when they began to feel her slowly calming. That they were able to help ease and share her grief, whatever the cause, strengthened each person. Such was the way of an Innarnian community.

Lizbeth's teacup clattered to the floor, and Samuel found himself shoving the low table to one side to catch his hostess before she followed suit.

"Oh no, no, no," Lizbeth muttered under her breath.

"What is it?" Sam asked, holding her by her shoulders and unsure of what he was meant to do.

"They've taken someone from Ronah," Lizbeth moaned.

"Who has?"

"Your old acquaintance." Lizbeth rose awkwardly to her feet, her hand lingering on his shoulder as she regained her balance.

"She's taken someone from Ronah?"

"For someone so old and powerful, you can really be clueless, can't you?" From between her tears, Lizbeth laughed softly.

If anyone else had said words like that to him, they probably wouldn't have had the power of speech much longer, but because it was Lizbeth, he gnashed his teeth together and made her laugh again.

"Enlighten me," he tried not to snarl, but from her tinkling laugh, he didn't manage it very well.

"Your acquaintance has taken a girl from Ronah, and the Island *aches*." Tears streamed down her face. "Can you not feel it?"

Closing his eyes, Samuel could feel the oily, acidic scum coating the back of his throat, the same feeling he had last time he'd left Anriluka. He liked the feeling a whole lot less this time around.

Gentle fingers wiped at his cheeks. His eyes snapped open, locking onto Lizbeth's sightless orbs even as his hand automatically grabbed her wrist, squeezing hard. He let go of Lizbeth's wrist slowly when she gasped softly, as if she dared not make a louder sound which might set him off. A large part of him was happy with her reaction, but an ever-growing part of him was disgusted at his behaviour.

He shrugged it off. He had a few lifetimes of bad behaviour to unlearn. There was no sense in beating himself up about it.

"You were crying," she said soothingly. Staring at her fingers, damp with his tears, it took Sam a moment to process it.

What was this Realm doing to him?

He blinked a few times. He nodded his head silently at Lizbeth, and quietly took his leave. He couldn't remember the last time – or the first time, for that matter –he'd cried. He wasn't entirely sure he ever had. He had been on this blasted Realm for such a relatively insignificant span, but it had changed a part of him.

He wasn't sure he liked the change.

Hands shoved in his pockets, he prowled the streets. Even though he doubted Jonathan would want him back at his house at this point in time, he had no doubt he could find something to do instead. Maybe there was someone on this Island who could make him feel a bit more like his old self again. With a feral grin, Samuel strode out, happy to be on the hunt once more.

CHAPTER TWENTY-FOUR

Mitch gave Tania a horrified look. '*Anika's gone,*' he sent to her. They looked at each other, and Tania broke the silence by releasing a shuddering breath. "What do we do now?"

"I guess we'd better try and figure out where Anika is," Mitch said after clearing away the terror clogging his throat.

"Ok, how do we do that?" she asked.

"Maybe Ronah knows where Lissae shifted them?" Mitch replied.

Tania nodded, a glazed look coming over her features for a minute. Ronah was able to pinpoint the Realm Anika had been sent to, but not the exact location – not that it mattered anyway, as Anriluka would have most likely moved them to a different, more secure spot. All of which made their job of tracking the two down rather frustrating.

"So, any ideas?" Mitch asked.

"Ronah said Lissae shifted the trespasser home to Rataeo," Tania said, unable to control the instinctive shiver due to the way Ronah had said the name of the Realm she'd never heard of. Then again, a few weeks ago, she'd never heard of a sentient Island either.

"Well, let's start researching it then," Mitch said, trying to smile but failing. He shivered as they moved into the backroom of the bookstore.

Rataeo. The home of Anriluka.

He never wanted to research anything less than he did at that moment. The home of one of the most feared beings on Ronah was sure to be a place that haunted his nightmares for a while – and having nightmares on Ronah weren't always the safest things, with the gateway between Realms so close to them.

He shot a grin at Tania, trying to cover his unease as he plucked books off the shelf and handed her a stack. Maybe they'd be lucky enough to find something which would help Shari in her search for Anika.

7 days left

The sun was rising when Shari and Jonathan appeared in Jonathan's lounge room. It seemed to have become their unofficial headquarters.

Mitch and Tania didn't waste any time on pleasantries. Mitch kicked a seat towards Jonathan, and Tania conjured one up for Shari. Both eased into their seats with weary sighs as Mitch started the briefing on Rataeo.

"Rataeo is a Dark ice Realm. It's virtually uninhabited, although Anriluka and her tribe are not the only ones who call it home. As far as we know, this Realm isn't sentient, so getting in should not pose a problem. It's time speed is double Lissae's – so two of their days' equals one of ours," Mitch stated. He had seen Anika around Ronah, knew her as a vague memory from school. Of course, he knew her family. You couldn't live on Ronah and not know of the Thornes. Two of the Thornes had even been Altoriaes, but the Clan's primary duties were to assist and protect the Altoriae. Among their numbers were some of the strongest Innarnian on Lissae.

Tania continued with the information they'd gathered. "Most of Rataeo's animals are relatively harmless, except for the Metsari. They're a small, reptilian animal which spits poison to protect their territory. They also have a very eerie call, which sounds like a cross between a high-pitched whistle and a wolf howling. They usually live in packs of ten or more," Tania continued.

"There's one particular 'sacred' area on Rataeo where there's an abundance of Metsari. It's called the Planomest, where sacred rites and rituals used to take place. It has a labyrinth of tunnels and caves and would be the perfect place for Anriluka to hide out," Mitch said.

"The only way to avoid the Metsari is to not touch the ground. Like snakes, they feel vibrations through their bodies, and that's when they spit their poison. Even touching the walls of the caves could cause them to spit. If you do manage to get poison on you, there is only one cure," Tania, who had been looking at the book in her lap, looked up, directly into Shari's eyes.

Shari shuddered. "I get the feeling I'm not going to like this."

Grinning, Tania continued, "You have to lick it off. Once it's inside your system, it cannot hurt the outside – such as your skin. However, it will burn the inside of your mouth and throat because it needs to be metabolised before the 'cure' will be effective. In that time, you can suffer some pretty severe burns, and whatever wounds you suffer from won't magically be fixed by the cure."

"Ugh!" Shari winced. "I was right."

Jonathan looked at his ward and grimaced at her. "Are there any weapons that work better than others on Rataeo?" he asked his pupil.

"Well, Anriluka and the U'tan have always used their natural weapons, whether they are physical or psychic ones. There's no record of carried weapons working on Rataeo. But, at the same time, there's no record of them not working either. It seems that it just isn't done," Mitch replied.

"Which means we could have a big advantage," Shari began.

"Or a great deal of unusable luggage," Jonathan finished.

Sighing, Shari muttered, "Nothing is ever easy, is it?"

"Nothing worth doing, anyway," Mitch replied.

"Do we have any allies there?" Jonathan asked.

Mitch screwed up his nose, looking thoughtful before replying, "One of the U'tan elders helped Shael Robertson, a former Altoriae. But he did so under pressure and vowed never to do it again. So, no, not on Rataeo."

"Alright. Half an hour, our time, get ready. Shari, Mitch and I will do this one. Tania, distract Ronah if Anriluka should come back this way," Jonathan said, and then sighed.

As a group, they hadn't had as much training as he would have liked to go into a situation like this. But it's not as if they could avoid it. "When we get to Rataeo, we'll go straight for Planomest. If Anika is not there, we'll split up. See if you can find any more viable places for Anriluka to hide out."

Speaking up, Shari said, "We want to get Anika out. She has the gem which can stop Anriluka. If we can't get her out then..." Shari didn't have to finish. They knew that if they couldn't stop this being it would come back and drain Ronah until she had no soul left. "We've got seven days left to finish this, and we know where Anriluka is hiding out. We can do this."

The serious looks on the faces of her friends disappeared. This was their first major task together. Shari could tell they were all worried about how they would handle it. She knew they would do fine. She broadcasted the feeling and felt their responses. "C'mon you lot, half an hour isn't long!"

265

They started shifting out, with Jonathan sending to Mitch and Shari, 'We don't need weapons for this one! They may not work, and the lighter we are, the easier it will be!'

'Don't worry Jonathan, we'll be fine!' Shari sent, laughing.

Mitch acknowledged Jonathan's warning, and as he arrived in his room, wondered in his private, innermost thoughts how in the Nine Hells they were going to pull this off.

An hour later, hovering above the ground, Mitch wondered how it was all going to work. Jonathan rounded yet another bend in the complex and confusing ice tunnels. Following him, but lost in his own thoughts, Mitch bumped into Jonathan but had enough presence of mind to grab his mentor before he went careening into a nest of Metsari.

'Dead end,' Jonathan sent back to Shari, who was waiting back where the tunnel split.

Just as Mitch managed to turn around, he felt a familiar tingling envelope his body. Shari had shifted them back to where the tunnel split. From his vantage point, he saw a crack in the cave walls they hadn't noticed before.

'Turn around,' he told the other two. They did so, and he could feel Shari's disgust at herself for not seeing the crack. 'Hey, I was just at the right angle,' he sent to her.

She nodded. Later there would be time for self-recriminations. 'Let's go.'

The trio made their way carefully into the narrow crack. There was just enough clearance so they could fit without having to touch the walls. As they proceeded farther down the tight tunnel, Shari jolted, only just managing to miss the walls.

'Anika's here!'

Mitch strained his senses, and he could feel Jonathan doing the same. They could faintly feel the missing girl's pain, but it was like a faraway echo and not something tangible they could lock onto. Shari, however, didn't seem to have the same issue.

'Come on!'

Anriluka could feel the humans coming. Pathetic, useless beings. They had no subtly. No finesse. They always charged ahead without thinking things through. The U'tan, however, planned every attack out in minute detail, with contingency plans for everything they could think of. Anriluka considered herself the best strategist her race had seen in aeons. She was capable of planning up to eighty detailed attacks and at least fifteen counters and contingencies for each of them for one situation, all of which contained a subtlety that no mere Lissaen would be able to understand.

She thought back to the day when she had first met the pathetic thing in front of her. It had been whining quite loudly how some other kid had gotten the pet it had wanted, and how it just wasn't fair!

Just at the thought of how much their first encounter had annoyed her, Anriluka released a thin feeding tentacle and withdrew a bit of flesh from the creature's back. It cried out in pain and Anriluka, who'd had enough of the creatures snivelling, circled until she stood in front of it, then she slapped it across its face – if you could call *that* a face.

Mind you, the eyeballs did look quite tasty. Anriluka decided she'd save them for later. Perhaps they would be tender after all the horrors they'd witness her inflicting on the pathetic lump of goo and bones before her.

Lifting her feeding tentacle to her maw, she delicately gnawed on the human's flesh. It turned its head away and released another stream of tasty bile. Grinning triumphantly, Anriluka lowered herself over the steaming mess, and her feeding tentacles scooped it into her maw, softening the flesh that remained in there.

She felt the intruding humans coming closer. How were they tracking her? The useless creature she captured sent out nothing and could receive even less. The humans had an unknown advantage on their side. She hated that, hated even the concept of it. Unknown meant she'd have to revise her carefully crafted plans. At the moment, she wasn't going to worry about it. If it meant the humans would walk right into her icy lair, then she would receive even more tasty meals.

Gathering her powers, Anriluka laid a thick primary tentacle on her prisoner. Ignoring the flinch, she wrapped the tentacle tighter around the creature and concentrated.

Grinning, she wondered how the humans would like Yettara. Assuming her weakening hostage would survive the inhospitable Realm, that is.

With a wicked smirk, Anriluka and a whimpering Anika disappeared, Anriluka's tentacles reaching out to stroke a few particular rocks just before they faded from the Realm.

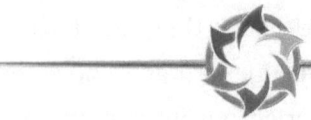

Shari and Jonathan both felt Anriluka leave. Then they felt the tunnel around them start to rumble. '*Time to go!*' Shari sent. Grateful they even had the option of shifting, Shari gathered Mitch and Jonathan and shifted them back to Ronah. Seconds later, boulders clattered down, pounding into the ice where they had just been.

Left alone once more, the Metsari, oblivious to the departure of their unwelcome guests, started spitting at the rocks falling from the roof. Not able to see the danger they were in, the Metsari continued to spit as their home disintegrated around them.

In just under an hour, the sacred site of Planomest, and all the Metsari who dwelt within, were little more than rubble and puddles of gore.

CHAPTER TWENTY-FIVE

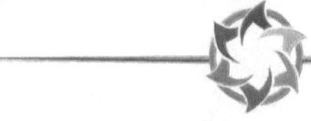

Cursing even as he found his feet, Jonathan hastened to send to Tania, '*Anriluka has taken Anika to Yettara.*'

'*Got it.*'

Jonathan could almost hear the cogs grinding away in Tania's head as she tracked down the information for the Realm of Yettara.

'*It's a Dark Realm, isn't it?*' Tania sent after a quick consult with Ronah. She was having trouble finding it in any of the books.

'*I think so. I can remember Joshua saying something about it, but I can't remember what. Somehow, I can't envisage it was anything good.*'

Tania chuckled. '*I bet you're right. Rest up, I might be a while.*'

'*All right, but don't take too long.*' Jonathan looked around the room. Shari was in the corner, meditating, finding the strength to continue the fight against Anriluka. Mitchel was at the book stacks, rummaging through the various volumes, trying to find some information on the next Realm that the U'tan was leading them to.

He liked Shari's sanctuary, Jonathan thought, leaning back into the reclining chair he conjured up. It was a comfortable, cosy place. How a being designed their sanctuary – their personal safe place on the Realms – was the best way to gauge their personality, and how they kept it was quite often the best way to discover their state of mind. Shari's was simple but elegant. Since first creating it, she had coaxed the tree into making amazing spiral patterns for the archways, and she had somehow managed to get most rooms a deep blue colour. There were books, tomes, and scrolls and letters by former Altoriaes, scattered and stacked around the room. Today, they appeared to be stacked neatly into piles of various subjects.

Jonathan, who had seen the state Shari usually kept her sanctuary in, was a little worried about this. Usually, to find something was impossible. He had to dig and search and have a few days spare. But today, Mitchel appeared to be having no such trouble.

He was flicking through something, and Jonathan could feel him conversing with Tania. Quickly checking with Ronah, he discovered only a few minutes had passed since they arrived in Shari's sanctuary.

'Got it,' Tania sent. Jonathan widened the link to include Shari and Mitchel. *'Yettara is a Dark Realm. It resides in perpetual darkness and is one of the few Realms to have a black sky. Its time speed is five times slower than Lissae's. It's sentient and feeds off any creature from the Light or Grey Realms who come to visit. Apparently, it's a most unpleasant feeling, and one that only the strongest beings from the Light Realms can survive. Also, any Innarn from a being of the Light or Grey Realms which is performed there will not only be severely hampered, but is unlikely to succeed in doing anything but draining said being further.'*

"Oh great," Mitchel muttered.

As if she had heard Mitchel's sentiments, Tania continued, 'It gets better. On the bottom of the page with the info about Yettara, there's a big "Please Note." And... well,'

'What does it say?' Shari sent.

'It says... well, it says that a prolonged stay of a being from the Light or Grey Realms on Yettara is guaranteed to end in death.'

'Exactly how long is a prolonged stay?'

'I would say it depends on the being.'

Jonathan looked at Shari, and then at Mitchel. They both shared his grim expression. 'Anything else we should know?' he sent to Tania.

'The only other info I could find says every being and creature who inhabits Yettara is an enemy. Not very helpful, unfortunately.'

'That's alright. What you've found is very useful,' Jonathan sent.

"So, what do we do?" Shari asked.

"We do nothing," Jonathan said, leaning back even further in his chair with his head resting in his interlaced hands.

Shari looked at him. Did she really have to tell him how much time was of the essence? And of how much danger Anika was in?

Seeing her expression, he leant forward, allowing his arms to drop to his sides. "If any of us go to Yettara, we won't last very long, and any magical defence or attack we raise will only weaken us. So, we send someone who won't be affected by Yettara. Someone who will blend right in. Someone," he said, leaning back in his chair again, "who owes me a favour or two."

"Who?"

The grin on Jonathan's face was so smug that if he didn't have the answer to a critical question, Shari would have smacked it off. "An old friend."

Sam was trying to get used to this hideously light Realm by lying on his stomach in minimal clothing on a 'sun lounge', when he felt a tap on his shoulder. He leaped to his feet and spun around so quickly the being who'd touched him wouldn't have seen him move. His hand reached out to grasp it by the throat, and he found himself holding only air.

"Um, hi."

It was the girl with the wide eyes – the one who looked like she'd never seen Innarn used before.

"Hello." Sam glared down at her, and the girl swallowed nervously. "Do you not know it's bad manners to sneak up on someone who's resting?"

"I... uh... sorry. I didn't mean to... it's just... well, Jonathan sent me to get you, and it's pretty urgent, so I shifted in. I don't really know how to do a noisy shift, but I promise I'll try..." Tania realised she was talking to the air, "next time. Right. Ok." She turned around to see if Sam was behind her. He wasn't. She sat down on the sun lounge and sighed, then jumped up again when Sam reappeared.

"Where is he?" Sam growled.

For someone who seemed so light, he certainly had a Dark aura, Tania mused as she answered the strange man who appeared to become stranger by the second. "He asked if you could just send to him. He said you can't get to where he is at the moment."

"Thank you."

Tania watched as Sam disappeared again, and shook her head. There was something just not *right* about Jonathan's friend.

273

'What *do you want? And where are you?*' Sam sent to Jonathan. He was in Jonathan's house, standing with fists clenched in the study, glaring at the wall. He sensed his current major annoyance appearing behind him, and turned.

'*I need help.*'

'*Why me?*' Sam looked at the information Jonathan sent him. He sympathised with the need, but he couldn't understand it.

'*You help me out, and I'll get you set up on Ronah. I'll even explain why this means so much.*'

'*After I get the girl back.*'

'*Right.*'

'*I should have just eaten you when I had the chance.*' Samuel's thoughts were snarled, coloured a dark-red in Jonathan's mind.

Jonathan laughed. '*You wouldn't want to. These thought patterns,*' he sent, tapping his head, '*are way too stringy for your liking.*'

Sam bared his teeth and gave a parody of a laugh that sent shivers of apprehension skittering down Jonathan's spine. Satisfied he'd put Jonathan in his place again, he shifted out.

Jonathan sat down. He knew he could trust Samuel, but he wondered if Samuel knew. What he had asked Samuel to do was... well, it wasn't just a simple favour. Samuel had to change his appearance to rescue Anika. If she saw him and realised only dark beings could be comfortable on Yettara and put two and two together, well, he doubted she'd get four, but she would be closer to the truth than anyone else on Lissae.

He told the Guild that Samuel knew a few darker beings who could help them out. It had helped to explain why he had turned to Samuel for help. He just hoped his friend could get Anika out of there in one piece.

CHAPTER TWENTY-SIX

After a tense few hours of research in Shari's sanctuary, they shifted back to Jonathan's house to see if they could find any information there.

Before they could even crack open a book, Mitch's belly rumbled loudly.

Shari's head snapped up, her bladed-glove appearing on her hand as the book she'd been holding tumbled to the ground. Mitch held his hands up in surrender.

"Nothing evil here, Shari. At least, not unless you count not being able to remember the last time you ate as being evil," Mitch joked weakly.

Tania, walking past the back of his seat, bopped him on the head with a book. He ducked and grumbled, rubbing his head as Jonathan sighed and got to his feet.

"I'll see what I can rustle up," Jonathan said.

"I'll help!" Tania announced cheerfully, following him into the kitchen. A few minutes later, she brought out a tray of fruit and bread, announcing that Jonathan wouldn't be long and he was bringing out something more substantial.

The trio sat and munched absentmindedly as they flicked through books, more as a way to pass the time while they waited for Samuel to get back.

Jonathan came back into the room with a tray of bowls. Mitch's stomach rumbled at the smell of savoury stew. Shari grinned at him and rolled her sleeves down as Jonathan passed her a bowl.

He saw a hint of darkened skin on her arms and scowled. Raising his eyes to meet hers, he lifted an eyebrow and waited.

"There's nothing to explain," Shari muttered, dropping her eyes and swirling her spoon through the stew.

"You are meant to..."

'Report each and every injury received in battle. Yes, I know Jon. I just...' She trailed off, not knowing how to explain. Absently, he put the tray down on a teetering pile of books. Tania and Mitch grabbed their bowls and made sure Jonathan's meal wouldn't coat the centuries-old tomes it rested on.

He turned back to her and gently took her arm, rolling her sleeve back up. The bruises stood out clearly on her skin. She winced and wished she'd thought to heal them earlier, but she hadn't had the time, and then she'd just forgotten about them.

Jonathan looked at her with raised brows. 'These are finger marks!' he sent.

'Just from a concerned citizen,' she replied, fiddling with her cuff and drawing it down to hide the marks again.

'Who?' his mental voice was coated in so many emotions, it took Shari a moment to sort through them. Anger, definitely, but there was also a deep-seated concern which pulled at her heart a bit more than she expected.

'Your friend, Sam. He thought I would be hurt by a jet of water, and pulled me out of the way. It's just a little bruise.' Shari shrugged. It was nothing to her, she'd received worse in training.

Grumbling under his breath, Jonathan muttered a few choice words before a green glow gently settled around Shari's bruises. It faded, leaving behind unmarred skin.

'Next time, any and all injuries are reported to me. No matter what.' Jonathan turned and picked up his bowl of stew. That his *friend* could so easily hurt the one under his care was more than a little concerning. Considering that Sam was not even in the Realm to question at the moment, there was little Jonathan could do. He grumbled as he ate, and a dark mood seemed to settle over the group.

Mitch and Tania ate in silence, aware of the tension in the room, but not sure what they could do to release it.

Half an hour later, Jonathan found himself pacing alone in the kitchen. He started trying to read half a dozen texts about Anriluka but found himself unable to concentrate. Every minute on Lissae equalled five on Yettara. What could be taking Sam so long?

Almost before he could continue the thought, Sam blinked into existence before him, supporting a being Jonathan hadn't met before.

'He needs help!' Sam sent.

The being had plasma dripping from a nasty wound. Almost all the flesh had been torn off his right side and front. He appeared humanoid but was missing a leg.

'He's *actually missing two. Normally, he's a tripod,*' Sam sent with a tight chuckle.

This must have been an ongoing joke between the two, because the wounded man snarled at Sam, and sent, '*Tripod! Who are you calling tripod, you overgrown golden turkey? Yer mother must have been blind or ugly or both, seeing she didn't kick you out of the nest as soon as you were hatched. You miserable, misbegotten fuluni ass.'*

Jonathan chuckled at the beings' colourful description of Sam as he set about healing him. He noticed the being – 'Jeran,' Sam sent to him – had scales in varying shades of green. If he was right, and Sam silently confirmed he was, Jeran was a Wikkur. A particularly cunning and savagely dark race. That Sam had enlisted Jeran to help him didn't bother Jonathan, but bringing him to Ronah...

'Oi, go a bit easy there, lad. Regrowing things itches just a mite,' Jeran sent to him.

Jonathan grinned. *'This shouldn't take too much longer,'* he replied. Sending only to Sam, he asked, *'What happened to Anriluka?'*

Sam's features tightened. *'She got away. She had the whole damned place booby-trapped. That's why I called in Jeran. He and his crew are the ones to turn to in a delicate situation. Besides, he owed me.'*

'Owed you? How can one as fine as me owe one as despicable as you?' Jeran replied to Sam's taunt. Sam responded by raising a hand, which turned into a claw. Before Jonathan could say a word, he raked the claw across the newly grown skin. Jeran's howl vibrated inside Jonathan's skull and bought Shari rushing into the room. Sam swiftly hid his hand. Mitch and Tania followed Shari and were left standing in the doorway; the kitchen was far too small to be holding them all.

'Do you mind?' Jonathan sent to Sam. *'Healing wounds of this magnitude are hard enough without you adding to them!'*

Sam apologised, but Jonathan heard him chuckle deep in the back of his skull.

With Shari adding her power to his, it only took another few minutes of healing before Jonathan pronounced Jeran done.

Jeran stopped leaning on Sam and looked down at his new legs. *'Ah. They aren't nearly as handsome as the originals, but it's far better than havin' only one. You're a top-notch healer, Jonathan. My thanks to you.'* Sam looked at Jeran for a moment, and when the Wikkur didn't continue, he raised an eyebrow. *'Oh, all right, you basalt-chewing, hemmit-loving buzzard. Me and mine owe you, Jonathan Buan. Name it an' it'll be yours.'*

'Who are you and yours?' Jonathan asked, aiming for a professionally curious tone. Shari, Mitch and Tania stood behind him, Shari practically bouncing with curiosity.

Astounded, Jeran looked at Sam and then looked at Jon. *'He doesn't know who I am? He doesn't know.'* The Wikkur shook his head and sighed. *'I'd be thinking you would know of me, Jonathan Buan. I am Jeran Metasta Voutar. The leader of the U'sala.'*

Jonathan drew a breath between his teeth. He just healed the Leader of the U'sala?

The U'sala were a group of beings from all over the Realms who had banded together to protect the Realms from creatures who wished to change them for their own benefit. Kind of what he and Shari were trying to do, but on a much larger scale. The numbers of the U'sala varied because of the high... turnover rate. He had heard much about them from Joshua, had stumbled across their tracks from time to time, but he had never had the pleasure of meeting a member of the U'sala until now. *'I am impressed. Pleased to meet you, Jeran Metasta Voutar. I have heard much about the U'sala.'*

Shari tried not to gape. She too had come across signs of the U'sala. More than once they'd saved her time on the battlefield, even if they hadn't been aware she'd been there as well.

'No offence lad, but who hasn't? And who might you be, Jonathan Buan? Sanithane here will only tell me you're too tough to eat.'

Jonathan looked at Sam and grinned. 'So, you've finally admitted it!' he sent to Sam. To Jeran, he sent, *'I am Jonathan Buan, Guardian of the Altoriae and of the Realm Lissae.'*

Jeran rocked back on his new legs. *'I wasn't expecting that! And this one here calls you a friend? Well, I'll be a damned fulni-arsed donkey!'*

Jonathan grinned at him, delighted with the thought that while everyone may know who he was on Lissae, there were still people out on the Realms who weren't aware of his identity.

'You're welcome, lad. And thank you for the healing. It's good to be back on three legs again! If you or your Altoriae be needing help, just call, and the U'sala will be there.' Jeran turned to Sam, surprisingly agile for a tripedal being, and sent to him, *'Now, you big bloody bag o' bones, take me back to me ilk!'*

Sam mumbled a few choice words but did as he was asked, sending Jonathan the name of the Realm he believed Anriluka had gone to as he shifted Jeran back to where the U'sala were currently camped.

'Coqi.'

CHAPTER TWENTY-SEVEN

6 days left

Glaring at the books lining the shelves as if they'd personally wronged him, Jonathan ran a hand over his face before turning to the rest of the Guild. "The only information we have on Coqi is that it's a Dark Realm," Jonathan briskly told Mitchel and Shari as soon as they were safely back in Shari's sanctuary. They paced the floor as they absorbed the news.

"Helpful," Shari muttered.

"We'll just have to see what we can find when we get there," Jonathan replied.

"Maybe we should leave this one to the U'sala," Mitchel said, looking at Jonathan.

Jonathan looked at him with a rather blank expression, and then he scrubbed a hand over his face. "I think it would be wiser to save the favour the U'sala have granted us, rather than asking for it straight away."

"Let's get going then," Shari said. Sitting around doing nothing wasn't something she was good at.

"I think this is one for you and me to tackle by ourselves," Jonathan said to Shari.

Mitchel started, and then said, "Great! Gives me a chance to rest up!" He grinned, and Jonathan shared a look with him. Mitchel nodded and left the room.

"What was that all about?" Shari asked.

"Just making sure he'd rest. To Coqi?"

"To Coqi."

Sam paced up and down in Jonathan's study, waiting impatiently for his friend to reappear. He had taken Jeran back to his 'ilk' and was impatient to see what his friend had learnt.

Feeling an impending shift, Sam whirled and was shocked to see Jeran's second in command, Yessna, arriving.

The smell of singed fur overtook the room.

Burnt and bleeding, Yessna held out a paw to him as she collapsed onto the floor. 'Help me..'

They shifted into a Realm of darkness. Jonathan felt as if he was unable to see anything around him. As a Light being, buried deep inside him was an innate fear of pitch-black places – such as the one he and Shari had just found themselves in.

Despite all of his training, a primordial part of his brain took over, and he felt his breathing become frantic and shallow, sounding a hundred times louder in the darkness that was pressing in on him than he would have ever thought possible. Jonathan could feel his heart jumping around inside his ribcage, racing around so fast he was surprised it didn't just jump out of his chest and sprint away.

'Jonathan! *Zhahyeem!*' Shari sent to him. *'You are not alone. We will fight this together.'*

Zhahyeem, be calm, zhahyeem. And finally, he was. Mentally, he reached out to Shari and felt her presence next to him. Her mind was as fiery and intense as ever. She always burned with a passion for protecting her own and to right wrongs; and now more than ever, protecting was foremost in her mind. It also helped that Shari was a Grey being. Neither Light nor Dark, but a combination of both meant that it would take longer for either extreme to affect her – and it prevented her from being scared of the dark.

'Are we going?' she asked.

'Well, I would, but I can't see a thing,' Jonathan grumbled. Being visually impaired in any way worried him – a childhood fear he'd never quite gotten over.

'Oh, for the sake of Na'reh! Don't you remember anything you teach me?' Shari muttered. She snapped her fingers together, and a small globe of dim blue light appeared in her upturned palm. It rose above her hand and drifted out about a foot in front of them.

Hoping it was dim enough to conceal his embarrassment, Jonathan started forward. Shari, still muttering something about lessons taught going unlearnt, followed behind.

With the meagre light in front of him, Jonathan felt his fear subside. He knew firsthand how fragile the mortal soul could be, and had thought he was stronger than the requisite of having light to guide the way. Funny. Take away his light, and he became a blithering mess.

No sooner had the thought crossed his mind than the light flickered out.

'*Jonathan! You should know not to get so close!*' Shari scolded.

About to protest, he was silenced by the click of Shari's fingers. Once again, a dim yellow ball of light appeared in her upturned palm, and once again, unable to help it, Jonathan thought of how easy it was to unsettle him – just take away his light.

This time, the little light globe didn't even get the chance to float off Shari's palm. It just winked out of existence.

Somewhere in the dim mountains ahead, they heard a creature laughing.

'*Anriluka!*' Shari and Jonathan both exclaimed.

'*Be my eyes,*' Jonathan sent to Shari. She didn't argue. She attached an Innarn lead to him and took off at a run for the distant hills. Jonathan, not expecting her to be moving at such a pace, was almost yanked off his feet. He mentally grasped the lead and struggled to keep up, following the map Shari laid out in his mind and being as careful as he could with his footing. He still stumbled a few times, but the feel of the wind hitting his face had a somewhat grounding effect.

Shari was in her element. All the little 'parlour tricks' Jonathan had begrudgingly taught her – the things she had enjoyed learning – were finally of use. The light globe was taught to very young children who were scared of the dark. And the travellers spell she used now helped young children and those who found they could not shift themselves to travel distances quickly. It also helped when you didn't know exactly where you were shifting – that way you wouldn't become a permanent part of a wall. Typically, the travellers spell leashed the child to a parent and slightly levitated them, but seeing Jonathan was taller than her, he'd just have to manage as best he could.

Within a few minutes of the punishing pace Shari had set, they reached the foothills where the laugh had originated from.

'You think I'm easy to catch?' sent a booming voice. 'You'll have to try harder, cestoray maiden!'

Shari had been called a lot of things by some not very nice beings, but being called a cestoray maiden stung her enough to make her stumble. Cestoray implied she was basically as useful as a wet rag in a fight.

Shari snarled. Both Altoriae and Guardian felt Anriluka grab Anika and leave the Realm of Coqi.

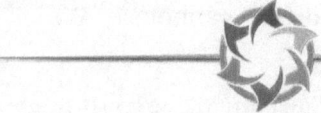

Defeated, Shari slumped before her shoulders drew back and she tossed her hair. Jonathan watched proudly as Shari had managed to, in complete darkness, trace Anriluka to Karara. Deftly, Shari grasped Jonathan's arm and shifted them both to Karara, but Shari couldn't find a trace of Anriluka presently on the Realm.

"Shari, you must stop and think. Why would Anriluka come to this Realm only to leave it so soon?"

Snorting inelegantly, Shari muttered, "To annoy me?"

Torn between laughing and rolling his eyes in exasperation, Jonathan settled for sighing. "Think Shari," he said. What made Karara a stopover Realm for the canny U'tan?

As Jonathan paced, Shari sent her senses out again. Close to the location they'd arrived at, she felt a dense Innarn that felt like the sensation of shifting but wasn't. "Jonathan, what do you think this is?" Shari asked as she walked back over to the area. She stood close enough that Jonathan could identify what she was talking about, but not close enough to be pulled into its field.

Jonathan came closer to the anomaly, and Shari could feel his Innarn spreading out, prodding and poking at the site to determine what was causing the Innarn field.

"Of course!" Jonathan exclaimed after a few minutes. "This is a xarit!"

"A xarit?" Shari asked. She could remember hearing the term in her early training, but couldn't recall what it meant.

"Yes, a xarit. They're special portals which lead to and from neighbouring Realms. There are only a handful of Realms which have xarits leading to them, and Karara is near only one."

"Which one?"

Jonathan's brow furrowed. "I... I cannot say. We will have to go back to Ronah and look it up."

Groaning, Shari asked, "Can't we just step through and find out?"

Holding up a warning hand, Jonathan said, "No! The Realms that xarits lead to are completely neutral. Xarits are the only bit of Innarn which will work on the Realm they connect."

"So, we're looking for a Realm which neighbours Karara?"

"That's right."

"Then let's get going."

"I don't want you exploring a Grey Realm without back up."

"I don't know what the big fuss is all about. I know how to fight with weapons without using my Innarn, so there shouldn't be — hold still! — be a problem. There. Done."

Yessna rubbed her newly healed wounds. Although a healer talented, she had no bedside manner to speak of. "My thanks," Yessna purred. "Might I ask the name of my healer?"

"Ask away," the healer responded before returning to the conversation she was having with her companions. "Really, what's the danger? If it gets too hairy, I can always use a xarit to leave, and once I'm out, I can call you."

A xarit on a Grey Realm? So, they were talking about Xaviour, Yessna mused. She shot a look at 'Sam', who wore a frown. The Great Golden One rarely looked happy, unless he was torturing something. "Well then," Yessna growled softly. As second in command of the U'sala, she was not used to being ignored. "What would your name be?"

The healer blinked. It looked as if she had forgotten Yessna was even there. She still had difficulties reading the body language of humans, so she could be wrong.

"Shari," the healer said, holding out a stiff-fingered, hairless paw. Yessna held out her own paw in a similar fashion, and watched, entranced, as the healer's fingers touched her, before the healer – Shari – bent her fingers and bought the pad of her paw in line with hers and brushed her fingers against the front of Yessna's.

Confused, Yessna looked to Sam for clarification. 'A *traditional greeting from this Realm*,' he sent her. She nodded her understanding. "Well met, Shari. I be Yessna, second in command of the U'sala."

"Well met, Yessna." The healer was most definitely distracted. At least she was mannered enough to respond to common courtesy. "So, there's no argument then. I'll go. And the quicker the better, Xaviour's time runs a lot faster than ours."

"I'd feel better if you had a guide," said the one Samuel had called Jonathan. This human had a wire and glass contraption which he wore on his head. Sam told her it enabled him to see clearer, as his eyesight wasn't good. Yessna couldn't really understand but figured that Sam knew enough about these strange beings not to be wrong.

"You require a guide for Xaviour?" Yessna asked. She couldn't help but let out a small purr of amusement as Samuel's head turned so fast to stare at her it almost snapped off.

Jonathan looked at her, and even she could read the apprehension in his features.

287

Her fourth set of eyelids slipped down to cover her eyes for the briefest moment, allowing her to clearly read his aura. She'd never seen someone so deep down, bone-tired before. Not even Jeran after a huge battle.

"A guide would be... appreciated," Jonathan said at last.

"I can guide your healer. Xaviour is my home Realm." Yessna saw the startled look Samuel and Jonathan shared.

"I didn't realise the Ferah's were native to Xaviour," Jonathan said. A light began to shine in his eyes. Silently, she confirmed with Samuel that it was only curiosity and not something more malicious.

"We aren't."

The others in the room waited for her to expand on her statement. Yessna let out a soft snort and flexed her healed paw. Unlikely.

"Well, we have a guide, and I'm ready to go, so can we do this?" the healer asked.

"There's something you need to know about the U'tan first," Samuel said grudgingly. He looked as if he were storming towards his own death, and he would be if he were about to give away the secrets of another Dark race.

"Well? Do I have to pull it out of your tonsils?" the healer asked impatiently.

Fangs bared at the healer's impertinence, but Yessna found she was unable to attack, held back by no less than three lots of Innarn.

"When you kill the U'tan, do it in an enclosed place. Otherwise, the consequences could be catastrophic."

With a roll of her eyes, the healer muttered, "I'll keep that in mind."

Yessna could sense the thought exchange between the healer and Jonathan, and the far more rapid, much more subtle exchange between Jonathan and Sam.

"If Yessna is agreeable," Jonathan finally said out loud.

"May I have a moment to talk to Yessna?" Sam asked.

"Make it quick," the healer muttered as she and Jonathan left the room.

Yessna tried to contain her shock. Did this human know what Sam was capable of? Did she know *who* he was?

"No and no." Now it was Samuel's turn to chuckle at her rapidly turning to look at him. '*Shari does not and is not to know of my true nature,*' he sent to her.

Yessna could see the danger of Sam's true form lurking just beyond the shadows. She bowed her head, her ears and whiskers twitching.

Sam nodded, understanding her show of compliance.

"Oh, and one other thing you should know," he added. Yessna raised her head. "Shari isn't our healer." Whiskers twitching again, Yessna scented the air. Sam was about to tell her something big. "Shari is the Altoriae."

As her eyes widened, Yessna realised there was no way she could have ever guessed that the diminutive healer was the protector of Lissae.

CHAPTER TWENTY-EIGHT

hari and Yessna were decked out in war leathers, with what seemed like a battalion's worth of weapons arrived at the xarit on Karara, ready to travel to Xaviour.

"Are you ready, Healer Shari?" Yessna asked. The Ferah seemed amused to see a healer dressed as Shari was at the moment.

"As always," Shari replied. She couldn't figure Yessna out. She knew Sam had told her who she was, but Yessna seemed happier to continue referring to her as a healer.

Without saying anything further, Yessna stepped through the xarit, leaving Shari to follow.

Arriving on Xaviour was like nothing she'd ever experienced before. She felt a weight so intense in body and soul that she fell to her knees.

Roughly, Yessna grabbed Shari by her crossbow quiver and dragged her into some nearby bushes. As Yessna looked down at her, probably wondering what in Immosa's name was wrong with her, Shari tried to regain her control and instinctively reached out to Jonathan. She felt a lump of horror form in her stomach when she realised the support she had resented, and perhaps taken for granted for so long, was not available to her here.

Yessna watched Shari carefully. She wouldn't be the first high power who was unable to set foot on Xaviour. Her home Realm had a way of weighing down beings like Shari. Even Jeran could not come here. Privately, she doubted one as powerful as the Altoriae would be able to last very long on Xaviour at all.

Therefore, when Shari straightened, with what Yessna determined to be a look of stubbornness on her face, Yessna could not have been more stunned.

She was not, however, particularly surprised when a whirring sound filled the air. She pulled the Altoriae to one side, and the girl didn't fight her on it. As the whirring sound drew closer, a coarse rope, weighted at each end with heavy balls of metal, came swinging through the air. The meteor hammers slammed towards the xarit but missed by a few feet.

"Welcoming committee?" Shari whispered.

Nodding, Yessna pointed to a clump of trees which served as a screen for their attackers. The little Altoriae nodded her understanding, then dropped to her belly and seemingly disappeared straight into the ground.

Hissing in surprise, the Ferah looked around and was able to see – if she squinted and tilted her head just right – the outline of her companion against the dark soil.

Although she kept one eye on the girl as she moved, Yessna continued to move her head as if she couldn't locate the girl. She watched in amazement as the Altoriae crawled behind the bushes and bound the bandits before they realised anything was amiss.

Muttering fiercely to herself, the Altoriae met Yessna's eyes. "I don't want to leave them here. We need a clear exit."

The Ferah agreed and stepped forward, raking her claws over the throats of the bound bandits. Sucking in a disapproving breath, the Altoriae met her eyes, the censure apparent in them, even to Yessna.

"This will serve as a warning to the other bandits. Now, none will come here for at least the next moon-set."

The Altoriae nodded, her eyes set on the fallen bodies before she resolutely turned her head away and they set off.

During their hunt for Anriluka, Yessna's respect for the one she had thought was 'just' a healer increased exponentially. The way the girl was able to handle herself in a place where almost all of her natural instincts were unusable was admirable. Occasionally, Yessna caught what she couldn't mistake as anything but frustration crossing the young Altoriae's features, but the girl carried on, uncomplaining, regardless of what she was feeling.

One of the things which impressed Yessna the most was when she sensed they were getting closer to their prey, Shari was the one who informed her. Considering Yessna was in her element, and Shari must feel like a Frito out of the air, it was rather astounding.

"I bet Anriluka will have some type of early warning system set up, so as soon as she knows we're close by, then she can run the other way," Shari whispered bitterly. She felt rather than saw Yessna nod her agreement; her eyes were trained ahead, ever searching for more clues as to where their prey had gone.

"Favourite warning systems on this Realm are insects. You can get ones who change their pitch when people approach. It's simple, and beings often don't notice it."

"Do these types of insects gather in one central area? Anriluka is liable to go where most of them are."

"There are many different types. If I were holding a hostage, I would go to the caves where the uallmi live. They are an insect whose noise can burst humanoid ear drums. They can also spit acid if anything but one of their own gets too close."

"Lead the way," Shari motioned, and Yessna, fangs showing as she grinned, began to lead Shari to the caves.

Shari was finding it harder than she ever imagined it to be, being on Xaviour. Not only did she have to find one of the townsfolk who despised her, but she was in a Realm that blocked all her Innarn. *Just another dull day in her increasingly boring life*, she thought with a self-depreciating chuckle. Her life was anything but boring, but if thinking about it that way would allow her to get through this, then she'd do it.

It felt like the air weighed more than it should, and she took in a great gasping breath, finding it hard to fill her lungs. Sensing Yessna's concerned gaze on her, she grinned, shrugged and continued to trudge forward through the endless rolling planes, red grass swishing in their wake.

What seemed like hours later, Yessna held up a warning paw. Shari noted, and not for the first time, just how long her companion's claws were. Four inches long, incredibly clean, and razor sharp. She never wanted to be on the receiving end of those.

Yessna started a series of complicated hand gestures and froze halfway through, an expression of annoyance and frustration crossing her feline features.

'*I understand what you're saying*,' Shari signed back. All the hours Jonathan had spent teaching her the Veti Cant had been worth it. A sign language which used hands and facial expressions to communicate could be quite helpful when overcoming language barriers. There were, of course, variations for beings with more limbs, but the essentials of the Cant remained the same.

'Right. Anriluka's up ahead. See the yellow slime on the rocks there? It's a sign of the uallmi. I know how to get past these insects. It's best if I go in alone.'

Shari didn't even bother to respond to the last comment. She just shook her head.

Yessna began signing a rapid response, but Shari didn't move or respond. She just stood there, staring Yessna right in her eyes, not blinking and not flinching when Yessna snarled softly. Finally, she broke eye contact with a flick of her tail.

'I did not come all this way to be left behind at the battles' doorstep. We will go in together,' Shari signed.

Yessna snarled again. 'As you wish. Should I take your body back to your Realm when you are killed?'

'Why not? You can stuff and mount my head if you feel the need to,' Shari replied.

Yessna emitted a low growl, then signed a sequence of elaborate instructions to Shari, and added a dire warning of what would happen to her if she did not follow them. Shari signed her readiness, and they set off.

This last leg of their journey was the longest. The pair had to be quiet, stealthy, and above all, yellow. The only way to get past a uallmi was to cover yourself in their slime, which smelled like a combination canine faecal matter and three-week-old fish curry. Then, you had to move like them, in a jerky, distracted, uncoordinated manner – one with seemingly no pattern to anyone but themselves.

Years ago, Yessna had returned to Xaviour to reclaim something of hers and had to get past these foul-smelling insects to do so. She was glad that her months of observation were coming in helpful again.

The two women made it past the outer layers and were almost through to the innermost sanctums of the hoard when they were shaken off their feet. Luckily, the rest of the uallmi were as well and didn't notice the two intruders. Yessna shot a look at Shari, and when she saw the Altoriae was all right, she once more began their erratic movements.

As they reached the innermost caves, they heard a girl whimpering. Shari ground her teeth together and tried desperately to think of something else. Yessna looked at her, and she nodded. She was more than ready to go in and give Anriluka a few more holes to breathe from.

Suddenly, a scream echoed off the cave walls.

Yessna motioned to Shari. Now was the perfect time to strike. One after the other, they slipped through the tight tunnel and into the mammoth cave, Shari going left and Yessna going right.

Shari saw why Anika was screaming. As she watched, Anriluka tore a strip of flesh off the girl's ribcage with the sucker attached to the end of her two-metre tongue. To add insult to an already horrendous injury, the U'tan was merely doing it for the fun of hearing her scream, and not to gain any sort of nourishment. The strip attached to her sucker came free with a wet, squelching sound. Anriluka twisted her hideous tongue and sent the flesh flying into an already considerable pile.

"Cry, you wretched creature! I cannot wait to see what you do when the salt in your pathetic tears stings your open wounds!"

Shari and Yessna glanced at each other one last time. They'd seen enough.

Yessna crept to the first pillar on the right, while Shari edged her way around the rough cave wall on the left. Anriluka had Anika lashed to a column by another, smaller entrance to the cave. In front of Anika's almost unrecognisable body was a pile of shredded flesh.

Staring in horror, Shari turned to face the wall for a second. She looked at the rough grey rock and raised her hand to feel the texture.

Her eyes locked on the small pockmarks, tiny defects in the otherwise solid structure, and she was able to shut her compassion off. Turning back, she studied the scene in a detached manner, noting the position of the pillars and how far away Anriluka stood from them.

There was a moment – a fraction of a heartbeat – where Shari paused.

Anriluka was a vicious, cunning creature. There was a good chance Shari would not be bringing Anika back to Ronah. She could feel a chunk of her very soul rebelling at the thought, but in the back of her mind, a memory of Jonathan's voice played out. 'Sometimes you will have to decide who will live and who will not. You must always – always! – choose the lives of the many over the lives of a few.'

Another scale clinked into existence in the wall around her heart. This was another one of those damnable times when she may just have to decide. The unenviable fate of a spoilt, selfish, spiteful girl or the lives of every being on Lissae. Despite being Anika's favourite target since they were toddlers, Shari would much prefer not to have to choose at all.

As the beating of her heart caught her attention, so did Yessna's subtle signal.

Together, Yessna and Shari broke out from their hiding spots. Yessna held one arm out straight, fist pointed at Anriluka, and ran her other paw down her outstretched arm, sending a veritable hailstorm of needle-sharp fur shooting towards the unsuspecting U'tan. Anriluka looked up in horror as the wickedly sharp fur slid deep into her exposed feeding tentacle.

The outraged shriek echoed through the cavern, causing Yessna and Shari to flinch. Anriluka was horrified to find her meticulously crafted plans were all blown into an unreachable Realm. The Altoriae worked *alone*. They had never deigned to fight alongside anyone other than their Guardian. This being threatened to throw centuries of planning out of order.

Shari rolled forwards, hands diving into the pile of discarded flesh. Her fingers slid and squished through the mound until she felt something hard. Shining a feral grin, Shari wrenched her hand free, only to see it was a tooth. Composure almost lost, she plunged her hand back in. Something hard struck her fingers. Once more, she withdrew her hand. This time, she had found the jewel.

Hearing a slight scuffing of a booted foot across the stony ground, Anriluka's eyes opened impossibly wide at the sight of Lissae's Altoriae pulling back a slingshot. Time once more seemed to slow down as the red jewel left the sling shot and sped across the cavern.

Despite her injured tentacles, Anriluka, in a burst of energy, started to move out of the impending path of the jewel which would bring about her end. Yessna hissed in displeasure and, with a shockingly loud *crack*, the U'tan was pulled back into the road of the jewel by the Ferah's extended, whip-like tail. It hit with a soft slurp, and a strange look crossed over Anriluka's face before she imploded into a squishy grey mist.

Bone tired, elated and triumphant, Yessna and Shari staggered back to the portal. Held up between them, bleeding and barely conscious, was Anika. The girl continued to moan, and as Shari and Yessna tried to keep a steady pace going, it seemed like it was becoming harder and harder to go on. Yessna, with her free hand, signed that Xaviour was capable of slowing down their progress. Shari set her jaw and trudged on; a trail of blood became the only sign of their passing.

After what seemed like a lifetime, they arrived at the xarit. Yessna signalled they should all go through together. Nodding, Shari took a step forward, and as her atoms swirled through the xarit, she felt the incredible strain being lifted off her soul. She was free! Her Innarn back up to full strength, she swung into action as soon as they reappeared on Karara. Without waiting to step free of the xarit, she shifted them all back to Ronah, briefly greeting her Realm on the way in.

She didn't know what she was expecting when they arrived back, but she knew it was not Jonathan's long face, nor Mitch's pale one.

CHAPTER TWENTY-NINE

5 days left

Jonathan looked at Mitch in amazement. "Are you sure?"

"Positive," Mitch said. "I checked, her death fits the modus operandi in the Handbook, plus her mum and dad saw it happen."

Hanging his head, Jonathan sighed. Becky Ribeck, only thirteen-years-old, yet another victim in Anriluka's unbearably long list. "Better get the Guild together. Make sure no one goes out by themselves." Jonathan paused. He felt his connection with Shari kick in. "Shari will be back soon, so..."

Before he could finish the sentence, Shari and Yessna appeared in his lounge room with an oozing being between them.

"What's wrong?" Shari asked. Yessna lifted Anika and placed her on the couch she had lain on not so long ago.

"Becky Ribeck is dead. Anriluka killed her."

"You can mourn later. This creature needs help," Yessna announced, waving their concerns away.

Shari knelt beside the couch and raised her hands above Anika's chest. A gooey string of the uallmi slime dripped down her palm. Before it could reach Anika's prone form, Shari hastily cleaned herself and Yessna with a quick burst of Innarn. Settled and free from the uallmi's eye-watering stench, a fine green mist seeped out of her hands and surrounded the unconscious girl's body. Slowly, muscles reformed, skin grew back, and Anika's face took on a more peaceful appearance.

Apparently satisfied Anika was healed, the green mist dissipated, and Shari removed her hands.

The effect was immediate and ear shattering.

Anika screamed as her body convulsed before their eyes. All of Shari's healing was undone, and the girl started bleeding anew as the regrown skin slipped away from her flesh.

Yessna, horrified, looked at the girl by her side. "What is happening?"

Confused, Shari once more laid her hands above Anika's chest. Once more, the green mist seeped from her hands and surrounded the girl's agony-wracked form. As before, muscles reformed, skin grew back, and Anika's face took on a more peaceful appearance. But this time, Shari did not remove her hands.

Yessna sensed a lightening quick exchange between Altoriae and Guardian, and he nodded. Placing one hand on Shari's shoulder, and the other on the top of the unconscious girl's head, they disappeared, hopefully to get the bleeding girl some help.

Yessna blinked. Apparently, her help was no longer required. "This is for the healer," Yessna said, stepping towards Mitch, and handing him the hilt of a short sword that he really didn't want to know where she had pulled it from. "Make sure she gets it."

The yellow blade looked sharper than her claws and just as lethal. The hilt was a dark blue, and of no metal Mitch had seen before.

He nodded. "I'll make sure she gets it. The Altoriae Guild thanks you for your help."

The Ferah nodded stiffly back at him and turned to Sam. "The U'sala will be waiting for me," she said. "We need to recover from your kin's latest attack. Can you suggest a new healer?"

"Jeran undoubtedly knows of one. Send my kin into the Realms of Hell for me. If Jonathan were here, no doubt he would thank you for all of your help," he replied. Placing his hands together, fingertip to palm, he gave her a short bow. "Fight well, live free."

Surprised he knew the traditional farewell of the U'sala, Yessna gave him a curt nod and replied, "We shall see each other in Immosa, if not before."

Sam nodded and watched as the Ferah shifted back to the U'sala. Feeling Mitch's eyes on him, he turned to regard the boy. An almost infinitesimally small pocket of the boy's mind showed his dissatisfaction with something. Sam decided he didn't really care what the hatchling was not happy with, but he still deserved a warning.

"You'd better fix your problem. If you cannot look at your life and be completely happy, you'll be next."

Clearly startled, eyes wide with shock, Mitch asked, "Next for what?"

Raising an eyebrow, Sam turned away from the boy and muttered something.

"Wha...?" Mitch asked again and lost his balance as Ronah shook underneath them. The dawning look of horror on his face said it all.

Anriluka had struck again.

Sam just hoped the hatchling understood the warning.

Mitch, Samuel and Jonathan all arrived at the Stuart-McMullin residence at the same time. Jonathan looked at them and murmured, "Shari's already inside. She dropped Anika off at the Healers and shifted straight in."

They heard the psychic grief before the physical and knew there was nothing they could do.

Kym McMullin had crossed into the Spirit Realm.

"I don't understand this!" Shari raged, pacing up and down in Jonathan's study. "I used the slingshot! I got the red jewel. I... oh..."

The others watched in dismay as her face fell.

"I hate that sound," Mitch muttered, "It always feels so... resigned."

"What's the matter?" Jonathan asked.

"Until an Altoriae, find a Thorne red jewel, and free the curse, from the shining blood, of Anriluka. There's the problem. There was no blood. She just disappeared in a grey mist."

"Maybe," Mitch murmured, swiping a hand across his eyes, "maybe the jewel you had wasn't the right one..." he trailed off, tears leaking out the corners of his eyes. Kym and her family were close friends of Mitch's family.

Shari stared at her friend. The other occupants in the room could almost see the cogs grinding in her head. "There's only one person who will know."

"Now really Shari, I cannot allow you in!" Holli Doonavan sighed in exasperation. "You know how wearing healing is, and we've had to take shifts at healing Anika until the solution is mixed up."

"Solution?" Tania asked.

"Yes, Anika is going to have a solution put on her wounds to encourage her body to heal by itself. Innarn healing doesn't work, so we'll just have to wait."

The Guild could see how frustrating the wait was to the healer, who could usually fix someone up in quite literally the beat of a heart. To have an invalid in the Healing Centre wasn't something she was accustomed to it.

"Can you at least ask her who gave her the necklace?"

"Fine, fine. But you can all wait here," Holli said. '*No peeking, Miss Dawn!*' she added to Shari.

'*I would never!*' Shari replied, and hastily removed herself from Holli's mind. Healers could always feel a piggy-backer, but she hoped Holli would be too distracted to notice.

After a few minutes, Holli returned, and she said, "It was her great grandfather, Edward Thorne."

"Thanks, Holli, you've helped heaps," Shari said. The Healer blinked when she saw the crowded room had emptied.

"I will never get used to Shari being able to shift," she muttered, and then went to check on her other patients.

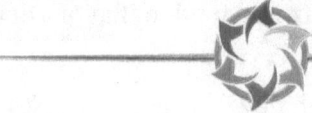

Shari and the Guild reappeared outside of number one Short Street. "I had better do this alone," Shari muttered. The rest of the Guild grumbled, but she continued, "I need you guys to go back to the store and figure out a watch roster. We have to inform the town and make sure no one goes to sleep alone. I'll talk to Edward. The Thornes are honour-bound to help us with this."

Mitch and Tania nodded.

"Call me when you're done," Jonathan said. She could feel him pressing against her inner thoughts, and she smiled. She could tell he was worried about her, and she sent a reassuring shaft of thought at him.

Mitch put his hand out to stop Shari. "Before we split up again, I have something for you. Yessna left it, and asked me to make sure you get it," he said, handing her the handle as Yessna had done to him.

Shari eyed the deep-blue metal of the hilt for a moment, curious. The blade was yellow and seemed to draw light into it, rather than reflect it. She took the short sword from Mitch and tested the weight, unsurprised to find it was perfectly balanced. She'd have to check later with Jonathan what it was made out of, but the blade itself would be a valued addition to her arsenal.

Mitch looked at her, and she nodded. They didn't have to talk, mentally or verbally — they'd trained together too long for that. Shari knew he'd help Jonathan with the watch, and she knew he'd be there if she needed his help for anything else.

"What about me?" Tania asked. The others had left, and the two girls were standing alone in the dark. Tania shivered as a light wind swept past her. Although Mr. Thorne's garden was lit up, the night felt eerie, knowing a being that equated in her mind to that of a demon... oh, Gods... a *demon* was on the loose.

"I need you to calm Ronah down. This... this isn't meant to happen. Dark Entities aren't supposed to be able to come to Lissae, let alone Ronah. And the Island's had to let go of two souls today. She'll need reassurance. If you can get her calm enough, try and see if you can find out where Anriluka is hiding."

Shari sensed the hesitance and resentment in Tania's mind. "I'm not trying to get rid of you. Keeping Ronah calm is going to be a hard job — and a vital one. Ronah's more than just a chunk of dirt. Our whole lives are tied up with this Island. You don't know what a relief it is to have someone who can talk to Ronah on such a deep level. Ronah is my friend. Has been since I was young, but I can't fight on her ground and keep her calm at the same time."

When her newest member of the Guild smiled, Shari knew she'd struck just the right note. Sometimes, people didn't realise there was a whole lot more to being Altoriae than just slicing and dicing.

Tania gave a small smile and shifted to Ronah's caves. Shari could feel the slight tremors of anxiety the Island had been sending out slowly calming, and she felt like she could take a deep breath without it getting trapped in her throat for the first time since Anika's disappearance.

Walking down the path to the Thornes door, it opened before she could raise her hand to knock.

"Welcome, Shari. I was wondering when you'd get here." As Edward Thorne ushered her inside his warm, cosy house, she got goose bumps. Immediately, she realised she was about to hear something she really wouldn't like.

Edward and Harmony were two of her favourite people on Ronah. Edward guided her into living room, which was cosy and full of family memorabilia. Shari's eyes were drawn to a picture of Anika. She wondered how she was doing now.

Harmony, a sprightly eighty-six-year-old, was sitting in front of a loom, creating another masterpiece. Edward, she realised, was only four years Harmony's senior, and none of the spring had gone out of his step either.

"I'm sorry, I can't chat. I guess you know why I'm here," Shari said as she sat down.

"Yes. We are aware of why you've come to visit, and it's not for the carrot stew." Edward tried for levity, but couldn't help sighing as he lowered himself into his favourite recliner, looking old for the first time Shari could remember. "The pendant Anika wore was a fake."

Unsurprised that he knew, Shari merely raised an eyebrow, inviting him to continue.

"We had always suspected," Harmony said, her work at the loom never stopping, "our great granddaughter was just as fake as the pendant we gave her. A true Innarnian would have been able to feel the vibration of the real pendant. Sadly, she did not notice the difference between the genuine and the fake when we showed her the pendants. She just chose the bigger one." Eyes full of tears, she paused her work. There was a heavy bitterness over the whole incident that Harmony had been hiding for a long time.

"If Anika chose the fake, where's the real pendant now?" Shari asked.

Edward looked at his wife, and she gave a slight nod and left the room. "Do you know the story of the pendant?" he asked.

Shari shook her head. "I only know my test requires it."

Edward gave a small smile. "It's a rather beautiful tale, actually. One member of the Thorne family has carried the pendant since Kay'imi first gave it to Eminlith, her Guardian. Eminlith married the first Thorne who arrived on Ronah, Timony. He was so enthralled with Eminlith that he vowed to Kay'imi that the Thorne family would forever protect the Altoriae and her Guardian, and presented her a ruby, which Kay'imi set into the pendant and gave to Eminlith.

"To this day, we keep Timony's promise. And yet, over time, it has been added to. We have sworn to also protect the people of Ronah, and Ronah itself. The ruby pendant is a symbol of all our love, care and protection. Of all the Thornes who have ever sacrificed their lives to save any who we defend. This is why you can use the pendant to destroy Anriluka. It will protect our Realm and our Island as surely as we have protected the Altoriae for all this time."

Harmony had returned sometime during Edward's story. She stood in the gateway, tears glistening in her eyes and the pendant gleaming in her hand.

"Aim true," she said to Shari as she gave the jewel to her.

Shari bound the jewel to a crossbow bolt tightly, and the ruby seemed to glow more brightly as the Island rocked once again. *'Will the Thornes once more join in the battle?'* Shari sent to them. As the Elders of the Thorne Clan, it was their right to agree or refuse her request.

'The Thorne Clan is always at your service,' Edward sent to her, smiling and flexing the hand she'd healed for him.

Shari nodded and shifted back to Jonathan's bookstore, waiting until she was alone before she let the tears trail down her face.

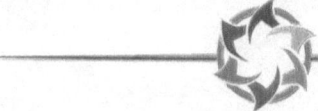

Two-year-old Eric Shansky no longer rested in his bed, safe at home with his parents and siblings. His new home was quite a bit different. He could sense the sadness and grief felt by the town, but the little spirit didn't know why. He just knew he was a bit colder than normal.

CHAPTER THIRTY

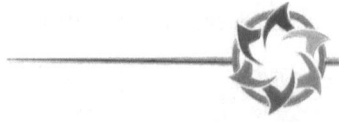

4 days left

Shari swore she could feel her heart breaking. Eric Shansky had been the sweetest little boy on the Island. He, like most children his age, had never been afraid of her differences. He'd always sought her out, and even when she'd pulled long days at school and even longer nights protecting Lissae, he'd never failed to make her smile.

Now he was gone.

Anriluka had stripped him away from his parents, his family, his friends and Ronah. A dark cloud gathered in her thoughts, and Jonathan, who was watching her brood in the relative safety of his lounge room, watched mournfully as miniature lightning bolts flashed above her head.

Shari turned her gaze on him, and said in a voice which did little to mask the violence lurking in her eyes, "I need you to put out a call."

Jonathan felt his eyebrows climb. Was Shari going to voluntarily ask for help?

She nodded. "We need to set up a meeting with the Mayor. We're going to get Anriluka out of our Realm."

Dawn saw the Altoriae Guild staring into the waves crashing into the cliff face below them from the highest point on Ronah. Shari, standing closest to the edge of the cliff, was the first to see the townsfolk looking up at them. She did not move. Not to wipe away her tears nor to straighten her armour. She felt sick to her stomach knowing three people had died and she hadn't officially been the Altoriae for even a week yet. It was her job to protect these people, and it looked like she was failing miserably.

'Don't dwell on it, Shari. You'll have a lifetime to go over mistakes you believe you could have prevented. Now it's time to fight,' Jonathan sent to her. He could feel her fragile mind and knew she would deal with her anguish better while holding a blade or two.

Shari sniffed and drew her shoulders back. Straightening her armour, she said, "Anriluka has taken too many of our loved ones from us. It's time she left Lissae and never returned!"

For such an intense, heartfelt announcement, it was met with little noise, but great strength of mind.

Samuel, in his seabird form, watched the Altoriae Guild disappear. He really wouldn't want to be Anriluka at the moment.

'Thinking of me, lover?' a velvety voice purred in his mind.

'Not for aeons,' he replied.

'Your loss. Care on telling me what the brat is up to?'

'Not even for all the pixie brains in the Realms.' His eyebrows rose at some of the curses she started throwing at him. 'Now now, play nice, and I'll give you a little tip.'

'What can you tell me?'

'I'd get out of here and never come back if I were you. That little brat is a lot stronger and smarter than you give her credit for.'

'She doesn't scare me. Besides, the smarter they are, the tastier their brains. Why haven't you gone after her yet?'

'I bide my time, and I live. And if you don't bide yours...'

'I have bided my time! I've waited for centuries to torture the cestoray slime vattar who kept me prisoner in my own Realm! And nothing is going to stop me from eating the little hanotqe's brains as soon as I get the chance to!'

'Go for it. I'm not stupid enough to stand in your way.'

Suddenly her tone changed back to the dripping velvet that he so hated. 'Do you know your Elders are looking for you?'

'They know where I am.'

'You play a dangerous game, lover.'

'So do you, Anriluka. Happy hunting.'

'And to you,' the dripping velvet voice sent back.

The sound left a sour taste in his mouth he hadn't expected.

As he wheeled through the sky, looking for a place to land where he could change back without being seen, he found himself rather unsurprised when Ronah once again rocked underfoot.

Anriluka had claimed her next victim.

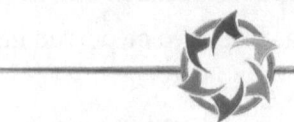

"When will this end?" Claire McMullin sobbed. She had come to visit her daughter at the stables where she worked, and she found her asleep.

She'd seen the expression of horror twisting her daughters face just as Ronah shook, and she knew Reanna, her youngest daughter, had been the latest victim.

Shari and the Guild had ported in to find Mrs. McMullin holding her daughter's body. Tania tried to comfort Claire, as Mitch and Jonathan tried to gently pry her away from her daughter.

"My little girl. My baby!" Suddenly, she spun around and looked straight at Shari, her blue eyes brimming with tears. "You have to stop this. Don't let that creature take someone else's baby."

Shari nodded. She found herself unable to speak, as a large lump of tears stuck in her throat. Reanna could be counted amongst the few townsfolk who had not teased, tormented or taken pity on her when they thought she was a Blank, and the stables were a place Shari knew she was always welcome.

This creature... this demented being... was slowly killing off the people Shari protected. She wanted to ensure it wouldn't get the chance to take another soul.

"Get Alan," Shari said, her jaw set. Jonathan and the others exchanged a glance. They would not want to be Anriluka right now. "We have to talk."

Alan Pratt stood in the centre of the Town Square with Ronah's inhabitants all around him. A furious Shari Dawn, Innarn crackling all around her, commanded the attention of everyone there. There was no need to call for quiet, as no one gave voice to their thoughts, despite the seven-hundred-odd people who stood in the square.

For the sake of the Blanks and the newcomers to Ronah, Alan spoke out loud, as well as sending his message.

"Last night, Jonathan Buan contacted all of you, letting you know not to be alone, to take shifts at sleeping and to only sleep lightly. Well, now that's not quite enough. Too many lives have been lost, and it is time we made our Altoriae's job easier. We must take care not to sleep! This is when the U'tan will strike – and she delights in doing so. Shari and her Guild are attempting to neutralise this threat as quickly as possible, but for now, we must not sleep. Anriluka has often come to torment us here, and the inhabitants of Ronah have had to do this before. It must be done!"

The square was eerily quiet. For the Hollingsworth Family, it felt weird. Town meetings were usually raucous, and this one was as silent as a... Tania shuddered at the thought. Quiet murmurs were starting, building into an audible babble. It seemed the Innarnian's had been discussing things amongst themselves while the few Blanks stood by, occasionally nudging their companions to fill them in on what was happening.

Finally, it looked like a decision had been made.

"Those who cannot avoid sleep – like the very young – will go to the hospital and be put under the care of the Healers while being watched by the Thorne clan. The Healers have a way of inciting a dream state where everyone is part of the same dream, which will make it far easier for the Thorne clan to watch over them, rather than having to hop from one dream to another," the Mayor announced. "Those who can do without sleep are to make regular checks of the Island and report any strange sightings directly to the Altoriae or her Guardian. Blanks seem to be safe from this creature. They will be able to sleep as normal, but just in case, an Innarnian should watch over them."

Liza Hollingsworth shuddered at the foreign thought of her new family being attacked in their sleep. Thank the Gods they were all immune to this thing. She saw Tania turn and look at her.

"I can watch over you and the others," Tania said.

The noise the crowd was now making seemed to fade to an irritating background buzz. "What do you mean, Tania?"

"I'm an Innarnian. Seems like I take after Grandpa after all," she replied with a half-smile.

Liza smiled, and although she tried desperately to hide it, she could tell her daughter could feel the fear coursing through her body.

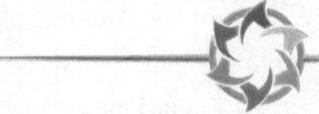

The Healers announced earlier they'd managed to cure Anika. It seemed like the girl had decided the town meeting was a perfect place to make an announcement to her friends. Anika appeared to be back in top shape after her ordeal. Shari tried to sneak past the group without being noticed but paused when she heard what Anika was saying.

"Yeah, that horrible creature stripped me of my powers," Anika forlornly announced. "I'm a... a Blank now." She cast her eyes down, staring at the pointy tip of her shoe, allowing her hair to fall forward and hide her face.

"No way! I didn't realise Anriluka could do that!" Maeve gaped at her, tongue ring flashing in the falling light.

Elizabeth looked over at Shari as well. "Is it true?" she asked quietly. A hush fell over the crowd as they waited expectantly for her answer.

Shari locked eyes with Anika. Here was the perfect opportunity to pay Anika back for all the spiteful things she had endured at her hands. There was probably no better time than now to announce to the Realm that Anika had always been a Blank, and would always be one. "Anriluka had some pretty unusual powers. What she did to Anika..." Shari paused, and the other girl's eyes widening in fear. "What she did to Anika was pretty horrible. I wouldn't want to experience that."

Anika closed her eyes for a moment, and Shari knew it was likely to be all the thanks she got.

As Elizabeth and the others turned back to Anika to console her, Shari slipped away from the group.

"That was a big thing you just did," Jonathan said.

Shari nodded. "I'm not just about saving lives, you know," she muttered. "These are my people after all, and so far I'm doing a lousy job of protecting them, but that's going to stop now."

"And now you know how some of the rumours about the Altoriae started."

"Oh! I hadn't thought about that!" Shari mused over what else could have come to pass because the Altoriae or her Guardian had agreed with something to help someone else feel better.

"Shari! Shari! We've found her! Anriluka is back on Rataeo!"

Shari concentrated and felt a familiar tingling sensation overcome her body. Her soul sat above her flesh for a moment, before she blinked – and was elsewhere. Jonathan's fury at her racing off washed over her, but she shrugged it off, needing to see this nightmarish creature again.

Anriluka lifted her heads. She sensed a Grey one in her Realm. Her cavernous mouth stretched open in a deafening chorus. How dare someone enter her Realm without her permission!

Furious, she lashed out, only to find nothing and no one there. Where had they gone? She lashed out again, her tentacles going in every which direction to make sure she had missed nothing. Whoever had disturbed her was going to pay!

Jonathan scowled down at Shari. He just managed to catch her prone body after she Soul shifted out.

'*I taught you better than that!*' he sent to her as he helped her sit up. He could tell his scalding had really gotten to her. He felt her drop her shields to him, and he saw the misery, guilt and anguish she felt coursing through their bond. Something had to be done to help Shari. At this point, he had no idea what form that something should be.

CHAPTER THIRTY-ONE

3 days left

The sting of desperation lashed against Shari's soul. Anriluka knew she just had to wait and Lissae would be open to her. Shari, on the other hand, had a limited time to track down a crafty, dangerous, starving U'tan who had absolutely no intention of being caught.

"Jonathan, what do we do now?"

Jonathan noticed his young charge seemed desperate and dispirited. She had never had a public failure before, nor had she lost so many of those she'd sworn to protect to one creature. She was beginning to take it personally, which, Jonathan had to admit, was somewhat hard to take any other way.

The curse had been created centuries ago just to test Shari's mettle as an Altoriae. But by taking it personally, it would affect the performance of her duties. Shari had to learn how to separate her emotions from her work. He just hoped he could give her the right guidance to help her do so. Otherwise, the forecast for their Realm was rather grim.

He watched her, along with the rest of the Guild, as she paced up and down, wearing a groove into his lounge room rug. "We wait until she moves. Trying to get to her on her home turf will be impossible."

"Maybe we should set some bait." Mitch wiggled his eyebrows and tipped his head towards Jon.

"Can we use Samuel?" Shari grinned.

Jonathan sighed. "I don't think so." The mention of his friend brought a frown to his face. Just what was Sam up to? Although he trusted Samuel more than most of his race, and he knew of his mixed heritage, Jonathan was still wary of him, especially since he'd caught the conversation between Samuel and Anriluka. But the problem of what to do with Samuel would have wait until this current disaster was out of the way.

"Then who should we use?" Shari pouted.

Jonathan looked at her and raised an eyebrow. "Do you know someone who is more than capable of defending themselves if things go wrong?"

The grin returning to Shari's features, she said, "I know just who we can use as bait!"

"Why are you looking at me like that?" Jonathan asked, edging away from her without realising it. Shari had the gleam in her eye that said it was best to get out of her way. Looking at the others, he realised they'd figured something out while he'd been lost in thought. Rather than finding himself at the mercy of a bunch of teenagers, Jonathan rose and mumbled something about refreshments before making his way towards the door.

Before he had even managed to face the door, a mud wall appeared, blocking off the door and his only escape from the room. He was hit by a tangle of vines that wrapped around his legs and pulled him gently to the ground.

As he hit the floor, he managed to broadcast, '*Why me?*'

Fuming, Jonathan looked at Shari through gauze-covered eyes as she helped him onto the couch. As he became horizontal, he said, "This was not what I had in mind!"

Shari, with the help of the rest of the Guild, had convinced him he was the best bait. They couldn't use Shari as Anriluka knew she wasn't weak, whereas he remained an unknown factor.

Sighing, he acknowledged they were right. He couldn't help but feel nervous. Anriluka had claimed more lives on Lissae than any other creature, including those of Sam's race. Suddenly, his nervousness turned into sheer terror. Despite the mild weather, his teeth began to chatter, and he started to shake uncontrollably.

With the little bit of his mind which wasn't frozen with fear, he sent to Shari, '*Ronah knows.*'

Both Jonathan and Mitch felt the flicker of impatience that crossed Shari's mind. Fear had no place in her world. Turning to Tania, she said, "I think it's time for you to have a talk with Ronah now."

Nodding, Tania said, "I know. It's more mind over matter than anything, right?" Her lips quirked up in an uneasy half-smile before she disappeared, shifting back into Ronah's caves.

Shari gave a tiny smile, and watched, relieved, as Jonathan's shaking subsided. "Time for you to dream," she said.

A panicked look in his eyes, Jonathan said, "Shari, wait, I..." he paused mid-sentence and ended with a snore. Shari and Mitch looked at each other and laughed anxiously. It sounded high-pitched and forced to Shari as she lay down on the floor next to the couch.

"Let's do this," she said grimly. She looked at Mitch, who nodded solemnly.

The last she saw before she succumbed to the darkness of dreams was Mitch fiercely working on the wards around Jonathan's house.

Shari waited in the dark, not moving, not breathing. People often forgot that in dreams, anything went. She waited for Mitch's signal. Once she got that, she had to be by Jonathan's side instantly. She felt the Thornes ruby in her palm and resisted the urge to turn it over and over in her hand. The heat it gave off was helping to keep her centred, but she was impatient. It felt like she'd been waiting a millennium.

Eventually, the call came, and Shari projected herself into Jonathan's dream world. She found herself standing by a stream. Confused for a moment, she stood and studied it. Where was he? Hearing a hoarse cry from behind her, she took off at a run. After a short distance, she found him standing in the middle of a field. He was being attacked on all sides by creatures Shari had never seen before.

Dull rust-brown in colour, their bodies were no bigger than a grapefruit, but they had at least ten spindly limbs. Each limb had a wicked scythe-like hook on it, and they were using the hooks to attack Jonathan, rending great slashes into his clothes. By the tiny amount of blood staining the corner of only a few of the tears, the hooks weren't as useful as they appeared. Although he was managing to fend off most of the creatures, there were so many it would be just a matter of time before they overwhelmed him.

Concentrating, Shari blasted them away in one powerful thrust.

'You thought you could trap me! Slime-filled cedore! You have no hope of stopping me now! I'm stronger than you believe!'

She couldn't believe how potent Anriluka sounded. Her words thrummed around Shari's head. Struggling to stand, she made a desperate lunge and grabbed hold of Jon. She dragged them both backwards, shifting them out of the dream world and to safety. When she opened her eyes again, she found herself once more in Jonathan's lounge room.

Looking up at Mitch, she opened her mind to him, allowing him to see what had happened. Shari fell back to the floor, exhausted. That was her last-ditch effort. She didn't know what else she could do. Dropping her head and closing her eyes so he couldn't see her expression, she felt tears of rage forming behind her eyelids. This being was attacking her Realm. Her home. Why was she so difficult to catch?

Because she had the memories of several Altoriaes before her, who had failed to catch the canny U'tan. Looking up at Jon, she realised he'd helped her come to that conclusion.

Somehow, she had to suppress the memories she carried around with her for so long. This wasn't going to be easy. But, she reminded herself with a shrug, as Jonathan often said, *anything worth fighting for is rarely easy.*

She had to beat this Dark being. Once and for all.

CHAPTER THIRTY-TWO

2 days left

Turning to trudge down the hall towards her office at the Sanatorium, Holli Doonavan unsuccessfully stifled a yawn. After such a long day of making sure everyone was too busy to sleep, she really wanted to crawl into her comfortable bed and snuggle underneath the warm blankets.

Rubbing her tired eyes, she slumped down in her seat. Closing her eyes for a minute couldn't hurt, right? Before she had time to fully complete the thought, she was asleep.

Three blocks away, Shari's head snapped up. After their failed attempt at using Jonathan as bait, they'd decided to wait until one of the townsfolk fell asleep on their own – just as Holli had done.

'Let's *move!*' Shari commanded, and Jonathan gave the signal for Shari, Mitch and Tania to project their souls before sending a call out to Sam.

'Keep an eye on us, *will you?*' he asked.

He could see Sam's smirk as he replied, 'And why should you trust me to only keep an eye on you?' Unspoken was the idea that he'd be more likely to keep a claw on them instead.

In a rare display of temper, Jonathan snarled at him, 'If you don't get it yet, you semaed's backside, then you're unlikely to understand it anytime soon!' Seeing the mentally raised eyebrow Samuel sent him, Jonathan snarled again before placing himself in the Realm of Dreams.

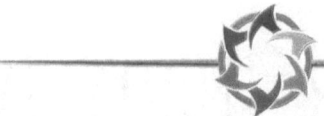

Holli's dream world was abstract. To Shari, it seemed much more like the stuff dreams were made of than Jonathan's had been. After being in more dream worlds than she could remember, she was still surprised at the things some people's subconscious came up with. No matter what they thought up, she watched over them to make sure only dream creatures were there, and not the ones who could actually hurt them.

She motioned in Veti Cant to Jonathan that they should spread out. Jonathan translated to the others. They had decided before they went in that Shari should try as much as possible to limit her exposure here, which meant she couldn't talk or send to anyone.

Mitch stepped next to Shari. She was surprised to see he didn't appear to be scared. To her left, Jonathan stood stock still, eyeing the haphazard blue cliff which would cut him off from the others. Looking right, past a building that looked like someone had taken an eraser to part of it, she could see Tania and Mitch. Mitch looked strained, and Tania... Shari couldn't get any sort of reading on what she was feeling.

Facing forward again, Shari could sense the shadowy forms of the higher level Innarnian of the Thorne Clan all around them. Nodding, she moved forward, the others keeping pace with her.

For Tania, a newcomer to Ronah, she couldn't intellectualise the idea that a dream could be dangerous. Everything she'd been taught told her otherwise. How many times had her mother said to her, *don't worry, it's only a dream*? And now she was finding out you really did have to worry. As she looked through the window of another half-finished building, she saw the woman they were looking for. She was bent over a desk, studying something intently.

Raising her eyes, she met Jonathan's gaze through the windows. Shari and Mitch noticed where their partners were looking at the same time. Shari hung back a moment. Something was wrong. Who *studied* in their dreams? She could feel the Thornes converging on their position. Something really struck her as wrong. Mentally probing inside the building, Shari realised she could feel no life force, despite being able to she could see Holli quite clearly.

'*Everybody stop!*' She signed frantically.

Terrance Thorne looked at her pityingly. "Don't worry," he said consolingly as he patted her arm, "We'll get her for you."

Furious, she brushed his hand away. The feeling that something wasn't right was growing with every person who drew closer to the sight.

It dawned on Shari. Every Innarnian who drew closer to the building was having a bit of energy syphoned off them and into a vast pool. She'd used a similar tactic so many times before. Once the energy pool had reached a certain level, it exploded, levelling anything and flattening anyone in the area.

Glancing around frantically, Shari could almost hear the energy in the air humming. If she didn't do something now, everyone here would be flatter than Mitch's dad's pancakes.

Apologising wordlessly to Holli, Shari abruptly pushed everyone out of the dream. They were thrust from the dream world and back into their bodies so fast that, upon arrival, everyone clutched their heads, most already well within the agonising grasp of a migraine.

Shari, the only one left in the dream world, harnessed the energy pool and sent soothing, healing waves to those she sent back. She noted Holli was safely awake and back in Ronah, just as an energy thrust struck her, catching her off guard and dropping her to her knees.

Anriluka's form shimmered into being directly in front of Shari. A tentacle lashed out at her. Swiftly, she rolled backwards, landing on her feet in a crouch. In her right hand, a long curved sword appeared, on her left arm, her black glove morphed into existence, blades already out. Without conscious thought, she used her Innarn to energise both weapons with Light power. As a Dark being, Light power was more effective on Anriluka than any poison the Realms could concoct.

Another tentacle lashed out at her. Slashing down with her sword, she succeeded in cutting the tip off. Letting a blood-curdling warble out, Anriluka began a lightning fast attack, lashing out with numerous tentacles at once while releasing devastating blasts of raw energy at the same time.

While Shari fended off each new wave of attack, she wondered if this was all part of Anriluka's plan. As the U'tan sent another wave of energy at her, Shari reached out and collected it, putting it with the other blasts the Dark creature had sent her way. Each time a blast landed, Shari would grunt and stagger a little, trying to make the U'tan think she was weakening. It seemed to be working. Another three blasts and she'd have collected enough energy to summon her crossbow and slam the ruby right into the slimy creature's heart.

Another blast hit Shari, who somersaulted backwards in mid-air, landing just in front of the blue cliff face.

Tentacles came at her from all sides. She sliced down with her glove and blocked with her sword. Jabbing forwards with the glove, her 'claws' ripped through the slimy flesh of Anriluka's primary tentacle and out the other side.

Time seemed to slow down as Shari drew her hand down, creating two long oozing wounds in the tentacle. As Shari brought the sword around to cut the wounded tentacle off, Anriluka gave another deafening cry and disappeared.

Sliding back down the cliff face and resting on her haunches, Shari knew she'd been lucky. Anriluka had fared better in battle than she thought she would. Although she knew Anriluka was more of a planner than a fighter, she was adept at striking with her tentacles to inflict the most pain. Having time to think, Shari began to feel exactly where the slimy creature had landed a few shots. As painful as they were, she knew the U'tan was far worse off.

Feeling all the energy she had collected humming around her, she gathered some of it and healed her wounds, using the excess to push into Lissae's wards.

As Holli's dream world began to fade, Shari pushed her consciousness back to Ronah to let the others know what happened, frustrated at her lack of success.

CHAPTER THIRTY-THREE

S hari awoke to a town filled with pandemonium. The sending channels were all taken up. It seemed the entire population wanted to know what was going on, and when one person didn't know, they'd ask another and another until every Sender on Ronah was sending to someone else.

On a separate level, Shari noted that the Hollingsworth household seemed to be the only one not affected by the turbulent Innarn racing around the Island. Then she saw Tania's older stepbrother, Alistair, appeared to be having a hard time. Gently, without probing, Shari found that he, like his Father and brother, had extraordinarily strong natural Innarn shields. It just happened Alistair's were taking a beating from the Innarn everyone was letting loose.

Rapidly, his shields began to break down. He fell from his seat at the kitchen table, clutching his head and screaming for the noise to stop. As the rest of his family looked at him in astonishment, Shari placed temporary shields around his fragile mind.

As the other members of the Island became aware of a new Innarnian in their midst, the conversation came to a standstill. Grabbing as many channels as she could, and placing the equivalent of Innarn earmuffs on Alistair, Shari broadcasted, '*See what you've done!*'

Innarn was meant to be tested gently, under controlled circumstances, so a reaction like Alistair's would not happen. After such an event, it was entirely possible he would burn out, or he would be too scared to use his powers and would throw up unconscious shields so powerful that nothing could break through them. Of course, in rare cases, it could increase his natural Innarn exponentially. It would be a while before they could tell what happened in Alistair's case, but whichever way the pendulum would swing, Shari was deeply ashamed of how the residents of Ronah were acting.

Knowing the Hollingsworth's had not yet been tested on Ronah, even in the extenuating circumstances, their reaction was still a bitter pill for Shari to swallow.

'*See what you've done,*' she broadcasted again, this time at a more reasonable level. Shame and disappointment coloured her words, and she could see people all over the Island hanging their heads in shame, their eyes downcast as they apologised wordlessly. With a hint of irony, which Shari didn't let show, she noticed Anika was in her room, brushing her hair, completely oblivious to what was happening. '*Town meeting. Now. Make sure everyone who needs to be there is. This is not something I'm going to repeat.*'

Shifting into the Town Square, Shari noted the Elders of the Clans were the first to arrive. She gave each one a solemn nod as they took up their positions on the outskirts of the square, making sure all of their clan members were accounted for. As the last of the townsfolk staggered into the Town Square, Shari stood a bit straighter.

"Thank you for attending so quickly," Shari said. "Please remember there should be *no* excessive uses of Innarn until the Hollingsworth's have been tested, which won't happen until after Anriluka has been defeated."

"And when will that be?" one of the Silverstone's asked.

"In a little over a day," Shari answered. Voices swelled in the square until there was nothing but noise.

Shari held a hand up for silence. "I am grateful for all of your support in the quest to remove Anriluka from Lissae. We have laid traps for Anriluka, but she is, after all, one of the U'tan. She has escaped so far, but I'm not done yet. There is, as I said, a little over a day left. I'm asking for you to be a little more patient."

"Be patient while our children die?" a voice called out, choking on a sob.

Bowing her head, Shari found she was at a loss for words. Taking in a deep breath, she said, "If I could change what happened, I would. Anriluka has had centuries to plan her attacks on Lissae, but it doesn't matter, because I plan on stopping her. When she's gone, I will mourn your losses with you."

"Together, our fallen will be remembered," the crowd murmured back the traditional saying when someone had fallen in battle.

There were a few quiet sobs, but Shari stood strong, the sting of tears behind her eyes hidden from the crowd.

"What can we do?" someone called out from the sea of faces before her.

"Be ready to heed my call," Shari replied.

Voices rose and fell as the townsfolk talked over what she'd said, and for the first time since she had announced she was the Altoriae, she felt positive vibes from the townsfolk after a town meeting. Glowing in triumph, a small part of her couldn't help but wonder what Anriluka was doing now.

Anriluka hissed as the healer began regrowing another one of her tentacle tips. The little hanotqe they called Altoriae had fought well. She had underestimated her opponent, something she'd not done for centuries. Something she was not planning to do again anytime soon.

But now, the next phase of her plan was easy, if not boring.

She would wait.

It wasn't the most exciting thing she'd done, but she had the luxury of time, whereas that cestoray maiden did not. Soon, she would be able to feast, and even the *hanotqe* wouldn't be able to stop her.

As soon as the healer had finished regrowing the last tentacle, Anriluka lashed out at her. Although the healer had tried as hard as she could, growing back tentacles or limbs hurt. And no one hurt Anriluka and lived to tell the tale. Not healers and most defiantly not the Altoriae.

1 day left

Alistair opened his eyes to see his stepsister leaning over him, pulling faces.

"Tania!"

Giving him the same mock-horrified look, she mimicked back at him, "Alistair!"

Grinning, he tried to sit up in bed. Tania held a hand out, holding him down. "Stay there."

329

"What? Why?" He brushed her hand away and sat up straighter. Immediately, he regretted not taking Tania's advice. Groaning, he sank back against the pillows, his head aching. "What's going on?" he asked weakly.

"Your head is mush."

He looked at her drolly. "You're kidding." Tania raised an eyebrow and looked straight at him. "You're not kidding?"

"Nope. You're a certified mush-man."

He made a face at her, and she laughed.

"Oh, alright. The residents here were a bit worked up after our expedition into a dream world. They were yelling and talking to each other through Innarn, and it was too much for you." As she talked, Tania reached to the bowl of fruit sitting beside her stepbrother's bed in the healing ward. Grabbing a bunch of grapes, she picked a large one off before continuing. "Apparently, Jordan, Chris and you all have these incredibly strong Innarn shields. They keep the rest of the world out, but last night was too much for you and..." placing the grape in the palm of one hand, she brought her other hand down on it hard, spraying grape juice everywhere. ". . . your amazing natural shield got mushed-ded."

"You have such an amazing way of describing things," he said drily as he wiped the grape juice off his face.

With a mock curtsy, Tania rose off the bed. "Why thank you. Now I have to go and get Jordan and Mum. They'll want to know you're up."

"Tania?" Alistair called as she reached the door.

"Yes?" she asked, turning back to face him.

"Why won't you call him Dad?" Watching in amazement as his usually cheerful sibling's face darkened with an emotion he couldn't place; Alistair felt a stirring of fear and hatred he knew was not his own.

Her face took on a neutral expression again, leaving Alistair to wonder if he'd imagined it all. "I wouldn't want to taint him with that brush," she murmured.

Alistair closed his eyes in confusion. Taint him with what brush? When he opened his eyes again, it was to an empty room. It seemed that beneath Tania's clowning, carefree exterior, there lay a world of hurt he couldn't imagine.

CHAPTER THIRTY-FOUR

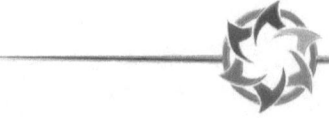

16 hours left

Boot heels ground into the rug as Shari paced the room.

Mourning the loss of his new rug, Jonathan wondered if he should order another, or maybe he should ask Ronah for tiled floors? Surely it would be harder to wear through than wood. *Although*, he thought with a shrug, *this is Shari we're talking about. Maybe I need ziom tiles.*

Shooting him a venomous look, she said, "I heard that."

Grinning sheepishly, he shrugged again. Even though he was worried his rug wouldn't survive their current disaster, he felt more concerned about what they were going to do.

The whole Guild had agreed that Anriluka was likely to strike back after Shari's defeat of her. But so far no one had seen so much as a tentacle tip. Their last day was drawing to a close. In less than sixteen hours, Ronah would be at the mercy of Anriluka, and there would be nothing the Guild or anyone else could do about it.

Sam was lounging in a seat, one leg carelessly thrown over an arm, the other foot planted firmly on the floor, looking completely relaxed. Jonathan, however, knew differently. He could see Sam was intently studying Shari. He knew his Dark friend wanted to say something, but the other man kept his mouth closed and persisted in pretending to read a book.

After watching Shari pace up and down for another half hour, Jonathan was feeling dizzy. He got up, gruffly announcing he was going to get a drink. He received a grunt from Shari and a nod from Sam.

"Not the most talkative of companions," he muttered to himself as he left the room.

Shari completed another circuit before wandering over to Sam's chair. "You wanted to say something?" she asked tightly. Her relaxed posture belied the tension in her voice.

Hearing the strain in her voice, Sam discovered an emotion he hadn't felt before. He couldn't quite label it, and to be honest, wasn't sure he wanted to. But he could empathise with her current condition. Giving up his pretence of reading, he tossed the book to one side and rose smoothly out of the chair.

Grasping her shoulders, he looked down into her eyes. She didn't flinch. She met his eyes without fear. Sam wondered if she'd do that if she knew who he really was.

"Out with it," she said hoarsely.

It appeared she was oblivious to the effect she had on him. And he had to be too, he realised. There was no way in *any* Realm that he, of all beings, could get involved with an Altoriae in any other way than annihilating her. "Why don't you just speed up time? It'll make the waiting go away."

For a moment, Shari looked at him as if he'd lost his mind. Then he felt her breathe in deeply, becoming energised with something other than stress again. "Sam, you're a genius!" Standing on tiptoe, she wrapped her arms around him in a brief embrace.

Standing stock still, Sam found he had no idea what to do. From another world, Sam heard a glass shatter in the doorway. He didn't care that Jonathan had walked in and seen Shari holding him. He didn't even care of his pledge a few seconds ago not to get involved with the Altoriae. All he could think of was the sweet feeling of her arms encircling him.

Shari pulled away and saw Jonathan staring at them, his face pale. "Sam's just figured it out!"

"I have?" he said, sounding dazed.

"Get the Elders together. We need to meet at the centre of the Island!"

"Where's that?" Sam asked.

"The Castle!" Shari called over her shoulder on the way to the door.

Sam and Jonathan were left staring at each other. For a long moment, neither man moved. Jonathan had never ever felt like punching someone more than right at that very instant. He knew exactly who Sam was and what he was capable of doing, and he didn't want him any closer to Shari than he had to be.

Sam was barely aware of Jonathan's presence. He was still lingering in the warm thought of Shari's hold. Therefore, he was blissfully unaware when Jonathan walked up and gave into his urge and knocked him out cold.

"We'll talk about this later," Jonathan muttered, leaving his 'friend' prone on the floor.

The Castle stood in the centre of the Island. Traditionally, it had been home to the Altoriae, her Guardian, and their respective families, but in the last fifty years or so, it had become home to the Island's young bachelors, and had become known as Castle Bachelor.

The Castle itself was a feat of Innarn ingenuity. The base of it was made by a huge volcanic crater which had ceased its activity on Kay'imi's command. This left incredible natural catacombs beneath the Castle that were mostly used for storage or the occasional prison cell.

Merged with the top of the crater was a wall of plasma, with a doorknocker which boomed every time it was used. Windows of clear air dotted the structure, and those inside could choose to darken or lighten them at will. A bereni tree grew at the heart of the castle, making not only a secure place for the Altoriae to train, but a solid structure should the outer walls fail. The branches and leaves of the tree made up the majority of the rest of the castle, except for the top, which sprouted turrets of flame, and the floor of the second floor, which was made of blue-green water.

The Great Hall was on the lower level of the Castle, and stepping inside for the first time felt an awful lot like coming home to Shari, despite the plan she was preparing to deliver to the Elders. She had to take a moment to get her thoughts together.

A few minutes later she found the Elders of the clans looking at her expectantly as she strode towards them, entering through the doors of the Grand Hall of Castle Bachelor.

As Alan Pratt squeezed into the room, he looked at her, and she sent him a radiant smile.

"We've figured out how to get Anriluka to attack early," Shari noted now she had the full attention of the crowd. "We need to make her think she's not attacking before her time is up." She paused, expectantly.

Confused whispers spread around the room.

Impatience flaring in her eyes, Shari continued, "We have to create a localised time rift. One where it seems like time speeds up on Ronah."

The Elders started muttering again, and Shari noted, to her relief, that there was a lot of nodding going on.

Someone called out, "Why?" Searching for the voice, she picked out Malcolm Hudson.

"We thought that after her latest defeat, Anriluka," at her name, a ripple coursed through the room. Ignoring it, Shari continued, "would attack again as soon as possible. But it appears she's biding her time. Perhaps she's having trouble getting a healer, who knows. Something I do know is we now have just over fifteen hours before there isn't anything able to stop her. If we speed up time, just a bit, it'll make her think that she can attack and she'll be safe. But we'll be ready for her."

"How will a localised time rift help? Won't she be keeping her own time?"

"She's injured and impatient. We know she's been watching Ronah, and hopefully, she'll think she misjudged the time difference enough that she'll attack early," Shari replied.

"That's a lot of things to base off hope," Elder Silverstone sneered.

"Hope can be just as powerful as Innarn, if you use it right," Shari replied.

The Elders talked some more amongst themselves before Malcolm spoke up again. "What do you need us to do?"

Answering without hesitating, Shari said, "I need you to create the Time Rift. I need to be ready to strike as soon as she lands on the Island. She may do her hiding thing again, so I need you to do this as soon as possible. Jonathan is a Time Master," she added, smiling at her Guardian. "If you lend your Innarn to him, he'll be able to create the rift, and I'll still be able to fight."

"Shouldn't we warn the others?" Kaciee Doonavan asked.

Shaking his head, Jonathan answered, "No. Unfortunately, we need their terror to be real. It's a stronger lure than even Anriluka could resist. Just ask them to gather in one spot. That should be enough."

More muttering and nodding ensued. Shari was impatient. If they didn't do this soon, there wouldn't be any point.

Jonathan made his way through the crowd. "I've asked as many people as I can to gather together. It should be an offering Anriluka can't refuse."

"And one I'm never going to let her have," Shari said. Jonathan saw the steely glint in her eyes and gulped, glad he was on her side. "Let's stop this monster!" she cried out.

The others in the room echoed her call.

Shari shifted herself to the front of the shop. For everyone else on the Island, time would seem to run at normal speed, but for Shari and the others, it would seem as if time had just jumped forward. She could feel the time rift building, taking place, and...

Bang!

It was almost sunrise.

CHAPTER THIRTY-FIVE

2 hours left

P ale, dappled sunlight fell on Shari and Jonathan as they stood under the trees, talking in low voices. "She'll go for the crowd, Shari. Trust me on this."

"I trust you, Jonathan, I do. But something isn't right about this. Something just feels... off."

Exasperated, Jonathan clenched his teeth, took a breath, and tried to reason with his charge again. "It's textbook perfect, Shari. You *know* that!"

"Shh!" A few of the townsfolk were beginning to look over at them, and Shari did not feel like any extra attention right now. "She's going to be somewhere else. If I could just figure out where," Shari muttered.

Her eyes wandered over the crowd. Quite a few people were still in their nightclothes, despite the order not to sleep. Young children were curled up on their parent's laps or in their arms. More than one person rubbed their arms briskly, trying to keep warm in the pre-dawn chill.

Searching further, Shari found Edward and the other Elders hidden amongst the bushes which lined the path back to the town. Mitch should be closer to the highest point of the Island. Tania was with Ronah in the caves, ready to calm the Island if need be. Sam waited at Jonathan's house, ready for their call.

Shari and Jonathan, standing just up the hill from the crowd, were meant to be there to protect them. Shari couldn't remember ever feeling so vulnerable, standing out in the open the way she was now, on edge, wanting to do something, *anything*. She almost couldn't wait for Anriluka to show her slimy purple tentacles.

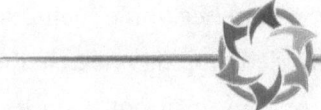

Seeing the sunrise brought tears to his eyes. Another day had come, another day playing second fiddle to his mentor. He scanned the horizon, looking out over Ronah's sea shelf. He was standing on the higher side of the Island, one of his favourite spots on all of Ronah. It was still as lush and green as the rest of the Island, but it peaked into a cliff which looked over the shelf on the 'back' of the Island.

He sat down, his back against a rock which seemed to be made to cradle someone perfectly as they overlooked the view. Twisting a stem of a long piece of grass, he stared straight at the sun as it rose. This was the best moment of his day. A time between times when he was no longer Mitchel, Apprentice to the Guardian of the Altoriae, son of Daniel and January Hoffman, brother to Kris, Jana, Lyndal and Krya Hoffman. He could just be himself, Mitch. Just him.

Deep in thought, Mitch failed to see the sleek shape rise between the sun and him. An astral projection, it cast no shadow. Only the lines of its form visible. But then it began to change.

Mitch felt Ronah's protest, her cry clear and loud in his mind. He, like the rest of her inhabitants, could feel her screaming in protest. They could feel Lissae's agony through her. Someone was coming who should not be allowed entry, but because of the curse, she would be allowed in. Mitch swore. There were always damnable loopholes!

He went to stand, turning back towards the mass of Ronah as he did so. Concentrating hard on blocking out Ronah's agony, he almost didn't hear the loud breathing of a hideous beast behind him. Almost didn't feel the slithering, slimy tentacles wrapping around his ankle, and then he wished he couldn't feel anything at all.

Anriluka was more than happy to grant the boy his wish. Four slimy tentacles gripped four disgustingly dry, withering limbs. She shuddered. Growing up in the acidic slime pits of her home realm, she found bipedal humans hideous. She had once tried dipping one in her home pit, but the slime had eaten away at the human until not even its bleached white bones remained. Her primary tentacles gripped the human's skin, and Anriluka held on, allowing her feeder tentacles to unfurl, and she started to feast on the fresh meal of flesh.

Mitch no longer cared. He struggled to free his thoughts from the agony he was going through. He could dimly, in a faraway place, feel the beast stripping the flesh off his bones. But that was not the thought he wanted to hold onto. He tried to take a deep breath, but he just drew more blood into his lungs. He dispassionately listened as he gurgled. Separating his mind from his body, Mitch knew he still had work to do.

A quick send to Shari, letting her know where Anriluka was. He sent longer goodbyes to his family and Jon, hiding the pain he was going through from them. As Anriluka pulled the last of the flesh from his back, Mitch caught Tania's mind and held it.

Gently, he mentally nudged her shoulder. 'Hey you, need a favour.'

'Hold on Mitch, we're a bit flat out right now... Shari and Jonathan are almost ready, just hang on a bit longer!'

'*I can't. I need you to look out for Shari for me. She's bad at that. I...*' Mitch didn't mean for it to happen. He didn't count on the tentacle being shoved into his brain and wriggled around, and he certainly didn't count on Anriluka making jelly out of his shields. He hadn't counted on Tania trying to probe his mind at the very same instance.

He felt her drop to her knees as his agony overwhelmed her. '*I'm so sorry. I wish...*' he broke the connection between them, not wanting her to suffer anymore.

Anriluka growled her triumph as she finished scooping the human's brain out of its eye socket. Brains were always one of the most delicate parts of this pathetic race. Just as she held its prize in her primary tentacle, she felt a stinging sensation near her midsection. She looked down in time to see the flesh of the creature she'd just stripped falling out of a hole which wasn't meant to be there.

She looked up and saw a crowd of humans on the rise. One was poised, ready to fight; another stood slightly in front, her long hair swirling in the wind.

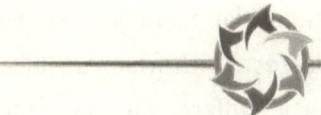

The Island began to shudder. Shari looked at Jonathan. If Ronah were human, she would have said the Island was shaking in fear.

"Oh Gods," she exclaimed, her eyes widening as she received Mitch's warning, '*Anriluka is here!*' She couldn't help it, she knew she was broadcasting. She could feel her adrenaline kicking in. She knew she would only get one shot at this and she had to make it count.

"Get everyone together... no. No! Mitch!" In a flash, she was gone. She felt Jonathan and what seemed like the rest of the town lock on to her. They appeared right behind her in the forest. Cursing as she ran up the hill, she never expected the sight that greeted her at the top.

She watched as Anriluka pulled Mitch's brain out of his eye socket. She didn't stop to think about what had happened to his eye. She bought her crossbow around and took aim.

Emotions had no place here, she reminded herself.

Time slowed as her hands steadied and she knew her aim was true. She squeezed the trigger, and the bolt flew at the U'tan. She lowered the crossbow as the bolt hit home and watched as the flesh of her friend fell out of the wound. She saw Mitch's body hit the ground behind Anriluka as the U'tan exploded. Even as the purple gunk covered her from head to toe, she didn't take her eyes off what was left of Mitch.

Shari stood rooted to the spot while the rest of the town cheered around her. She found herself unable to look away from where Mitch had fallen, even though Ronah had shifted him to his gravesite already. She had lost so many people already. How many more of her dearest friends would be put at risk during her reign as Altoriae?

As people brushed chunks off their clothes and slime out of their eyes, Jonathan wiped a hand across his face. As the muck came free of his eyes, Jonathan saw the whole Island had been slimed. Shari had very publicly passed her first official test as Altoriae. Anriluka, U'tan demon of Rataeo, left the Realms with little fanfare, but lots of mess.

> And free the cure
> From the shining (life force – blood?)
> Of Anriluka

The threat was over.

Blinking, Shari looked around. It seemed the townsfolk had carried the celebration into the centre of town. She could barely believe that her test was done. How was it possible that after the ten longest days of her life, she could finally claim the title of Altoriae, and no one could deny it any longer?

From out of the forest, a voice called, "Shall we join them?" Jonathan stepped forward, and Shari nodded. She took one last look at the place Mitch fell and then turned back to Jonathan.

"Let's go," she said, her voice thick with unshed tears.

Once again, she was deep inside Ronah's caves. Ronah was nervously chattering away when, completely unexpectedly, Mitch reached out to her. Just as she pushed to find out why he was asking her to watch over Shari, the Island let out a resonating wail.

Linked to the Ronah, and combined with Mitch, Tania felt the stabbing pain in her brain before her connection with Mitch just... disappeared.

Ronah's wail shook her right down to her bones. She could feel the Islands pain and did what she could to help. When she had talked the Island into a calmer place, Tania raised a hand to her face to find tears streaming down her cheeks.

Mitch was dead.

'*Anriluka is dead too,*' Tania sent, trying to console Ronah. It had little effect on the Island and even less on Tania, who was still kneeling on the ground with no sign of the tears stopping. Mitch was becoming her friend. One of the few friends she had. And now, in the blink of an eye and the whip of a tentacle, his life was over.

Unexpectedly, she felt the others on the Island who were suffering, and the other Shifting Islands all comforting one another. It did not relieve the sadness, but it lessened as it was shared. Tania saw images of Mitch growing up flashing behind her closed eyes. She could see how happy he'd been in life, could see that he'd done what he'd needed to and now he needed to be somewhere else.

She would miss him, the boy who'd almost been her friend, but she had a strange feeling, almost like a warm shiver slipping over her skin. They would see Mitch again. She was certain of it.

CHAPTER THIRTY-SIX

he townsfolk wanted to celebrate her victory. They'd set out long
tables in the Town Square which were laden with all sorts of mouth-
watering food. Shari was seated on a dais, along with Jonathan,
Tania, the Mayor and the Elders. Everyone was talking and laughing,
relieved the nightmare had ended.

It was just as Shari lifted her fork to take the first bite from her
victory lunch that she saw it out of the corner of her eye. A small section
of the purple goo off to her left started twitching. Then it shimmered,
purple turning silver and then yellow, mauve and blue before it
shuddered and expanded.

Mouth unattractively agape, she snapped her head around to get a
better view of the now waist-height blue goo. It grew arms, and a head
and from the semi-globulous form, shoulders appeared. It continued to
grow, and an agonised scream came from the blue mouth.

Forks clattered against plates and glasses smashed unheeded onto
the cobblestones of the main street as people whipped around to see the

source of the scream. The goo changed colour again, and Shari found herself standing in front of the morphing form with no memory of how she got there. Knees slightly bent, blade and glove at the ready, she waited for the now tanned goo to solidify.

Ignoring the scream from the being before her and the terror and confusion from those behind her, she managed to count to thirty before the goo shimmered again and then solidified into the form she was least expecting.

"Mitch?" she whispered.

"Shari, you don't have much time. Shield everyone! They're coming!" Mitch babbled frantically.

"You're back?" Shari asked, hand reaching out but stopping just short of touching him, she got the sense she was missing something important.

"Yes, but so is everything else Anriluka ever ingested." Mitch's hazel eyes locked with Shari's green ones. "The Realm is in danger, Shari. Some of the things she has eaten..." He shuddered. His hands reached out to grip her upper arms. "Get the kids out of here, quick. Anywhere that isn't covered in Anriluka's insides. They're coming, Shari."

Shari faintly remembered Sam's warning to make sure she killed Anriluka in an enclosed space. Suddenly it made sense. Before she could say anything else, Mitch's eyes went almost comically wide and his mouth opened in a silent, agonised yell. Someone on Shari's right screamed, and the sound broke through the confusion clouding her mind. She looked down and saw the tip of a pincer protruding out of Mitch's chest cavity.

'So much for dying at a ripe old age.' He gave a pained, lopsided smile.

Sniffing back tears, Shari sent back, 'Only the good die young, Mitch.'

A moment before the claws snicked apart, Mitch broke the connection between their minds. He'd learned his lesson once before.

Watching her friend fall for the second time in a handful of hours, Shari narrowed her eyes. Someone was going to pay.

The claw pulled out of Mitch while it was still wide open. Forcing herself to keep her eyes on the pincer, Shari almost snarled when the thud of her again late friend hit the ground. But she kept her eyes up, and what she saw behind Mitch was enough to make her pale. She gathered everyone under the age of fifteen together in her mind and shoved them roughly towards the Castle with a side note to the oldest to take care of the rest.

She shielded who she could at the same time as she drove her blade viciously into the skull of the sedolic, a green scaly dog-like animal with two large pincers at its front. It snarled at Shari as the light left its eyes, and around thirty of its pack-mates growled as it sank to the ground. She felt someone at her back and let out a relieved breath to find Jonathan guarding her.

As the sedolic pack began to close in on her, she could hear horrified cries rise all around her. The sedolics appeared to be Anriluka's favoured foods, as Ronah was reporting masses of the creatures from all over the Island.

Ronah sent a frantic call to Jonathan, asking for help clearing the Cliffside. He shifted out immediately.

Reaching out to Tania, Shari shifted her to Jonathan, even as she ripped what passed for a throat out of a sedolic's rear end. As she shifted some of the older townsfolk to watch over the children at the castle, she felt another power join hers.

She turned to see a stunning man with raven-black hair and flashing blue eyes. His eyes met hers, and then slipped away as he gave her a cocky grin before his sword shot out, striking just above her right shoulder, and when he drew it back, a ribcage of a sedolic was on it.

Non-pulsed, Shari shrugged and turned again, just as the man behind her sent, '*Watch the skies!*'

Instinctively, Shari ducked, and a small pterosaur-like creature flew overhead. The prehistoric bird bled blue when the warrior raised his sword and split its guts open.

As his sword fell, he laughed. "Adeon! It's good to be home again!"

'*Home?*' Shari asked as they moved back to back, her blade and his sword flashing in tandem, driving the sedolics into the growing piles of their dead kin.

"Ronah! There's nowhere else in the Realms like her!" he grunted as he strove to split open another diving pterosaur.

As a single finger flicked up, resulting in a rush of air that kept her eyes free from the blood and gore, she sent. '*Who are you?*'

"Muran."

Despite only seeing it once before, she could picture the cocky grin gracing his face. Even with the near constant wave of combatants, Shari found it easy to fight with Muran. They fought without words, only the snick of their blades on bone, the gnashing of teeth and the sizzling of cooking sedolic flesh marring their silence. Muran sent out one last burst of flames from his palm and turned to smile at her.

'*Shari, you're needed!*' Jonathan sent, sounding just this side of desperate.

Shari nodded to Muran in thanks and moved to shift to the cliffs, but in the last instant, he grabbed hold of her arm before she went, tagging along for the ride. She had no time to chastise him; the battle before them was in full swing.

Jonathan and Tania were standing back to back. Tania was using Ronah herself to fight by raising huge dirt waves and crashing them down upon the hordes around them as if she'd been doing it her whole life and not just a matter of days.

Jonathan was fighting more fiercely than Shari had ever seen before. He was taking on the deadlier creatures, sending out jets of high-pressure water at some Xanter troops to extinguish the flames they were trying to throw his way, while his other hand sent burning balls of magma to prevent the poisonous claws of the pteradiles from reaching the group. Tania aided him by pushing massive updrafts which ensured most of the burning reptilian birds fell into the sea rather than on their heads. In spite of bearing scratches and nursing minor wounds and the occasional scorch mark, the remainder of the Altoriae Guild seemed to be coping well.

Until the fulni arrived.

The last herd of fulni had been mysteriously wiped out over two-hundred years ago, but as they came charging up the hill, Shari couldn't help but think *mystery solved*. Although she was glad to have figured it out, she could have done without the evidence right in front of her.

The fulni charged through the masses of sedolics, ripping and tearing with their fearsome jaws. It appeared they were ravenous. Jonathan, Shari and the others froze, stunned at what they saw. Then the wind changed, and the fulni realised there was more prey to be had. As one, the fifty-strong herd raised their heads to look at the humans on the cliff top.

They charged.

'Their tails! That's their weak spot. They'll bleed out in seven seconds. Go for the base!' Muran frantically sent.

As quick as lightning, they were at the top of the hill and before Jonathan and the others in the space of two blinks. Shari had never been more thankful that shifting only took a second. She arrived amid the pack, removing the tails of two as they passed by her.

Muran, with his longer sword, managed to get three tails before Jonathan cottoned on to their half-baked plan. He shifted Tania farther inland a bare moment before the whiskers of the first fulni reached her, before shifting himself to Shari's left and removed two tails with his daggers before slashing a third with a well-placed crossbow bolt. Five more ended up with bolts in their rears before he had to reload.

The injured ones were slowing now, and when the first two dropped, the fulni crowded around their fallen to feast on their flesh, and Shari could remove another six tails alongside Muran.

Jonathan took out nine more tails before his crossbow jammed on the tenth and final bolt of his reload. Swearing silently, he struggled to remove the stuck bolt. Shari looked up from her last tail severing at his swearing and saw a fulni charge at him as he wrenched the bolt free. It was too close to Jon. Even if she shifted, there was not enough time to stop it. As she slashed out with her blade to remove another tail, she found herself unable to tear her eyes away from the impending demise of her mentor.

Sam gritted his teeth. This was not the first time, nor would it be the last that his ears rang with horrified screams of innocent victims.

Jonathan was wrong. He wasn't hiding. He was engaging in self-preservation. His current form was much more susceptible to injuries than his customary one.

Without warning, the CVS flickered to life, showing him the arrival of the fulni from the sea. His jaw fell open as Shari, and the man with her, began decimating the herd, slashing their tails. He felt a fury he'd long held dormant rear as the iridescent white blood of the fulni began to spill onto the ground.

Screw self-preservation. He'd lived enough already.

Time seemed to slow as Shari felt her blade drop to her side, waiting for the fatal bite to end Jon's life. The fulni had its head turned, salivating jaws spread wide, ready to tear her Guardian in two, when a golden shape shifted in, and a garbled yell sounded, starting behind her and ending in front of her.

Blinking in confusing, Shari couldn't fathom what happened. She looked around in mild confusion, but there was no time to waste. Others needed her, and she could not mourn nor wonder where her Guardian, Muran and the last dozen fulni had gone.

'*Altoriae, there's another U'tan! How do we kill it? It...*' the gurgling sound which punctuated the end of Nicolette Zephyr's frantic send did not bode well.

'*Don't kill the U'tan!*' Shari sent anxiously. She shifted, broadcasting the same message again, only to arrive at Nicolette's side to see Terrance Thorne shoving a broadsword through the primary feeding tentacle of the U'tan and withdraw it, triumphantly lifting it to show the shrivelled nut that served as the U'tan heart. The creature exploded, spraying more purple goo over the town.

"You fool!" Shari snarled at Terrance. "Are you incapable of following orders in general, or is it just mine you have a problem with? Never mind. I'll deal with you later." Shari shifted him roughly into one of the holding cells below the castle.

'*If anyone else locates another U'tan, notify me immediately! If it is killed, I will Banish the killer from the Islands!*' Shari broadcasted. Then she set about clearing more of the sedolics from Ronah.

There seemed to be fewer pteradiles left now, but Shari still found herself glancing at the skies with every third swing or stab of her blade into a sedolic. There were only two left in her vicinity, which she disposed of quickly and was about to leave when she heard a branch snap over to her side. She whirled, only to see Eric Shansky standing in his pyjamas, sucking on his thumb.

"Eric!" she cried, stunned.

"'Lo Ree." He smiled shyly around his thumb.

"Come here, Eric, come to Ree," she said, crouching down and beckoning with one hand while she scanned the area, blade still at the ready.

"Piky," Eric said, pointing at the hand she'd gestured to him with.

Her mind drew a blank for a moment, and she looked behind her, half expecting a pike-bearing troll. There was nothing. Then it clicked. "Ah, want to see the spikies, Eric?" she asked, twisting her wrist so they gleamed in the fading sunlight. *Kids liked shiny things, right?* She thought desperately.

He shook his head solemnly. "Piky bad."

Trying not to swear, she banished her glove, despite the vulnerable feeling it gave her. "Look, spiky gone now. C'mere Eric," she pleaded.

A crashing sounded behind Shari. Something was breaking down the bush to get to her, but she dared not take her eyes off the two-year-old. She dared not use Innarn either, as she had no idea what effect it would have on someone who had returned from Anriluka's intestines.

Eric took a hesitant step towards her, then another, before he pumped his little legs as fast as he could. The crashing behind her got louder and louder. He wasn't going to make it. She started running towards him, arms outstretched, shoving her blade into the sheath strapped to her belt.

He leaped into her arms just as she felt fetid breath hit the back of her neck. She had no choice now but use Innarn. She shifted as claws raked down her arm.

352

Acting quickly, she passed Eric into the arms of one of the older girls in the bottom of the castle before she shifted back to the forest, appearing behind the minotaur who's claw marks still stung her arm. A sword appeared in her hand and she clenched her fingers around the hilt tightly.

"You picked the wrong person to mess with," Shari snarled as she drew her sword back.

"No!" the minotaur cried. "I meant no harm! I wish to go home," he said as he fell to his knees.

"Where is your home?" she asked, sword still held high, prepared to strike.

"Canak-Maku."

"Fine," Shari shifted the minotaur before he could say another word. '*Altoriae! U'tan!*'

Shifting again, this time back to the Town Square, some small part of her noted that her victory lunch was still laid out, but she shifted her gaze the U'tan in the middle of it all, tentacles waving madly.

"Who are you?" it sneered at her.

"I am the last thing you will see on this Realm." Shari grinned ferally as she sent a thrust of power at it and succeeded in knocking it over. Before it could recover, Shari sent it back to Rataeo.

A great cheer rose, just as Shari received another send. '*Altoriae! U'tan!*'

No time to celebrate, Shari gathered some of Ronah's power to supplement her own, then shifted to the site of the latest call, and found herself outside the museum. Another U'tan, this one smaller than the others, was busy flaying the flesh off... someone. They were unrecognisable. A quivering mess of oozing flesh.

Shari had seen so many horrifying sights today that she barely flinched. She shoved a clear icicle through two of the U'tan's tentacles, pinning it together. She snarled, something she seemed to be doing a lot of lately, as she sent the latest U'tan back to Rataeo.

Slumping to the ground beside the goop which used to be a person, Shari wondered who it had been. She checked for any sign of life but found none. A lone tear slid down her cheek unchecked before she gathered herself and shifted back into the fray.

The battlefield seemed eerily quiet to Shari. Was it because, for the first time ever, she was fighting a major battle on her home Realm and Lissae sought to aid her by ceasing the cries of the dead and dying before they reached her ears? Or was it because of years of the same sorts of battles she'd become so accustomed to such cries they no longer warranted her notice?

As she slammed her blade into the chest of another sedolic, she found herself sincerely hoping for the former. The latter left a bad taste in her mouth which she could not seem to shake.

Thirteen hours later saw Shari standing in the Town Square again. She had sent the last – and by Ronah's reports, the final – U'tan back to its home Realm.

The cheer that went up this time was muted. The people around her were tired and had been running on adrenaline for most of the battle. Shari began quietly moving around the square, stopping to say a few words to each group. The townsfolk seemed to be more accepting of her now they had fought alongside her. She sent out Nadine, Shelley, Jonas and Iain Ribeck to scout around the Island and see if they'd missed anything. As she moved through the crowd, she kept an eye out for any of her Guild.

Parents started drifting over towards the castle, hoping for the all clear. Shari moved towards Andrew and Louise Shansky, who were holding each other and looking towards the other parents with tears in their eyes.

"You may want to go over there," Shari said gently. She felt them reel back at her perceived insensitivity. Before they could comment, she continued in a rush of breath. "I found Eric in the forest while I was dealing with a sedolic pack. He's fine, though. Not a scratch on hm. He's waiting for you at the castle with the other kids."

They looked at her with shock, apparently too stunned to speak.

"Go, find him," she urged gently.

They rose shakily from the ground, clutching at each other. Shari stepped to the side, and they stumbled past her in a staggering run, heading flat out for the castle. Others moved out of the frantic couple's way, allowing Shari to finally see her parents near the far side of the fountain. Her mother was nursing her arm, looking pale and tired. Her father was slumped against her, asleep. As she drew closer, she could see the blood staining her mum's shirtsleeve, and sent out a pulse of green light which wrapped around her wounded arm, emitting a soft glow before it faded into her skin. Her mum looked up, astonished, and Shari grinned.

"Good to see you!"

"Shari! You're alright! I am so glad to see you!" she said, and nudged her dad awake and they stood, the three of them holding each other tightly.

"Have you seen Jonathan?" her mum asked.

Shari's face shuttered and became unreadable. "Not since the fulni were charging at him. Last time I checked, he wasn't on Ronah anymore."

A voice from behind her said, "Check again."

Shari whirled to see Jonathan behind her, looking dirty and grungy, but more rested than she'd ever seen him before. *'Jonathan!'* she cried mentally, and ran to him, hugging him tightly. *'Where in Na'reh's name did you go?'* she demanded as she stepped back.

'I will tell you, Shari, but now is not the time. Is Ronah clear?'

'I have some scouts out checking, but so far so good. Where is Muran?'

Jonathan's eyes lowered, and Shari felt her gut clench. She didn't need to hear his response. Turning away, she blinked back tears just as her scouts came back, Jonas holding his stomach with a blood-covered hand. Shari rushed to his side, healing him before they met in the middle of the square.

Nadine, Shelley and Iain Ribeck grinned at the stunned look on his face and told the others how a stray sedolic had tried to rend Jonas in two, but they'd managed to drag him back and slay the beast right at the end of their sweep. As far as they could tell, the sedolic was the last thing left of Anriluka's past meals. Shari finally allowed herself to smile. For the moment, at least, it was over.

The parents rushed to get their children from the castle, and Shari realised she had to inform the Elders of Terrance's failure to follow her orders before the others found him.

'Elder Thorne, one of your kin, Terrance Thorne, failed twice to obey a direct order from me during combat. I shall leave it to you to see to his punishment. I do not expect it to happen again.'

'Altoriae, I understand and will take appropriate action. I will inform you of the outcome after I have spoken to the others who were involved... Shari, I am glad you are safe.'

Smiling again, Shari sent back, 'I am happy you are safe too, Edward. I have more work to do before I can rest. I bid thee well, friend.'

'I bid thee well.'

Catching sight of the Mayor, Shari excused herself from her Guild to talk to him. "Mayor Pratt, can I have a word?"

"Always, Shari... err, excuse me, Altoriae." He wiped a weary hand over a dirty brow. "It has been a long day, and I know more than once I've fought alongside you, but I still can't wrap my head around you being the Altoriae."

"No doubt it will take all of Ronah a while to adjust," she said, quirking her lips. Privately, she wondered if some would ever change their thinking of her, but she said nothing of it. "Mayor, we have suffered losses today, and they need to be recorded and put to rest. Once we retire for the night, Ronah will wash the Island clean, and tomorrow we can hold the grieving ceremony. Could you inform the Elders for me?"

"Of course, Altoriae. How bad do you think our losses are?" he frowned. Clearly, he did not like to think of it any more than she did.

"It is hard to say. Last time Anriluka was here, she devoured so many of our people, and now some of them are back. Others were lost again, and some of the current residents were lost as well. However many losses it is, Mayor, it is too many."

"Yet without you, none of us would be here at all, Shari. Even as I wish you did not have the burden of saving Lissae on your shoulders, after seeing what you can do..." he shook his head. "I am *glad*, Shari Dawn, that *you* are our Altoriae."

A glow lit inside her chest. So, this was what it felt like to be appreciated by others. She murmured her thanks and headed back to her Guild. It was time to head home.

CHAPTER THIRTY-SEVEN

S tanding on Ronah's shoreline bare-footed, just a whisper away from
lapping water, Edward Thorne and Sampson Silverstone read the
list of the departed. For Shari, it seemed to never end. She didn't let
a single bit of moisture slip from her eyes – she had cried herself out on
Jonathan's shoulder last night at her sanctuary. As the two Elders read
down the list, she noted that Muran's name had been excluded; she cut
her eyes to Jonathan and saw him nod sadly.

Muran Curtis, the sixth Altoriae, had died to save Jonathan. He'd
shifted in front of him before Shari could and had taken the bite the fulni
had intended to end Jonathan's life. The second time around, he'd not
even lasted a whole day on his home Realm, but then, many of the fallen
had been in his position too.

The Elders had finally come to the end of their exhaustive list. Robes
of purple were straightened nervously as every resident on the Island
stepped forward into the water, members of the families of the fallen
standing, backs straight in front of the others. Everyone cast their eyes

out to sea, where the spirits of the fallen were floating, just above the water. More than one person had to brush away tears as an unfelt wave swept through their silvery relative.

"And so, we bid farewell to those we have lost. Our fondest memories of you will stay with us forever," Nathan Collins, dressed in his formal silver-grey robes as High Cleric of Ronah, said. Standing to his right was Simone Thorne, the other High Cleric of Ronah. Neil Thorne and Holly Collins, both Clerics, stood next to Simone. The families of the departed stood to Nathan's left, up to their knees in water.

All the Clerics intoned together, "Our souls shall remember your souls, and once more will we meet again, somewhere in the Realms." They moved so each of the Priests were facing one of the four winds. The spirits of the departed souls weaved around the Clerics, who each raised a wooden ceremonial fan to propel the souls to their next life and their next destiny.

Samuel turned and was surprised to see the smiles on people's faces. They seemed happier now, knowing the souls of the dead had gone on to better things. Jonathan, who appeared to be avoiding him for some reason, approached him now.

"You ah... you didn't have to come."

"I know. I wanted to see what it was like," Sam said flippantly. He felt the anger rear in his friend's mind. To lessen it, he added, "It will be tough for you, to replace Mitch as your apprentice."

Jonathan bowed his head. "It will be."

"Do you have anyone in mind?" Sam asked.

"Not yet. There are many... factors to consider." Jonathan paused for a moment, stuffing his hands in his pockets as if he didn't know what to do with them. "Has Ronah talked to you?"

"To me? No. I dare say the Island has been busy..." He paused, seeing the look on his friend's face. He had been going to add in a biting comment but figured Jonathan had just about had enough. He didn't particularly want his *friend* to knock him out cold again.

"Yes. Yes, Ronah has been busy. She wants to start on your house."

"My what?" Sam asked, rocking back on his heels. A few people turned to look at them, but he didn't notice.

"Your house. You know, your dwelling, home, residence, abode."

"Yes, thank you, I know what a house is," Sam replied, his cheeks flushing with badly disguised anger. Sometimes Jonathan could be too glib. Sam found he had to watch his reactions more and more on this Realm. "But I never asked for one."

"You asked Shari to help you settle down on Ronah. So, she did. A rezem is being grown for you. Ronah has to ask you a few questions and then it should be ready in a few weeks. It would be sooner, but the testing for the Hollingsworths needs to be done, and the houses for the Returned need to be started too."

"Eager to kick me out?" he asked casually, although he was given away by the tense set of his shoulders as he waited for Jonathan's answer.

"No. I like you where I can see you," Jonathan said laughing. Samuel almost flinched at the cold note he saw in Jonathan's eyes, though. It seemed his only friend didn't trust that much after all.

Shari sat alone in her room, staring at the wall. The faces of the fallen kept swirling around in her thoughts. She brought each one close, one at a time, kissed them gently on the cheek and bade them farewell. Over the course of her life, she had lost so many people that she had to find some way of coping with the loss.

A knock on the door startled her out of her thoughts.

"Yes?"

It opened a fraction, and her father peered through the crack. "Can I come in?"

"Sure."

He entered quietly, his feet making no sound at all. "Shari."

She looked at him properly and was startled to see how pale he appeared. "Dad, sit down!" she said, jumping up and grabbing him by the arm. She guided him over to a seat, ignoring his protests.

"I'm all right, Shari. I'm fine. Just a little shaken."

"What's happened?" she asked.

"It's your Grandfather. He isn't well." He lowered his eyes to his clenched hands. "He's dying."

"What? Granddad's dying?"

"The Healers think so. You and I are meant to go to Rakemyst as soon as possible."

"But I'm not meant to leave the Island," Shari said automatically. Both Jonathan and her parents had drilled it into her so frequently that it came out more by route than any real desire Shari felt.

A half-smile appeared on Calem's face. "Glad to see you listen to us sometimes."

Shari smiled too. "I always listen, I just don't always apply it."

"I'm meant to take you, my eldest, my only child."

"I know, but Dad, I don't even have my wings yet."

"Well." Looking rather resigned to the fact, Calem rose. "If you have no objections, I guess I'll send your apologies."

"Probably for the best," Shari said, her half-hearted smile falling.

'If I may, you may wish to hold off on your trip. Rakemyst has requested that we join up so she can check on me,' Ronah sent to them.

"Really?" Calem asked, surprised. Excitement quickly took over his thoughts, and he kissed Shari on the head as he left to track Arilla down to tell her the news.

The Islands hadn't met up since before Shari was born, so their plan to converge now was a bit of a shock. After Anriluka's campaign, Ronah had suffered quite a bit. No doubt Rakemyst would want to check up on her. The Islands coming together would be a reason to celebrate. For Shari, it would likely mean pulling double duty to ensure the Realm stayed safe.

Chuckling, albeit a bit watery, Shari rose and crossed to the window. It was surprising how suddenly things seemed normal again.

CHAPTER THIRTY-EIGHT

Enclosed in his lounge room, the fire crackling merrily behind the grate to keep out the darkness beyond the windows. Samuel looked at home, as sprawled out as he was in Jonathan's favourite chair.

"Why did you do it?" Jonathan asked.

"Do what?" Sam asked lazily as he lifted his eyes from his book.

"Save me."

Samuel had admitted he had shifted to the cliffs moments before the fulni had charged at Jonathan. He'd seen Shari and the other man, and had used a power akin to shifting to drag Muran in front of Jonathan, so the old Altoriae had been bitten in half, not the current Guardian. Once Samuel knew Jonathan was safe, he gathered him and the remaining fulni and shifted them all into Ronah's caves. He'd threatened Jonathan with disembowelment until the Guardian had allowed Samuel to leave, taking the fulni with him. Before Samuel left, he weaved a Sleeper's Heal over Jonathan, ensuring the Guardian would be well-rested when he returned to the fight.

Unfortunately, it had taken him longer than expected to get the fulni filled and settled, so he was only able to wake the Guardian after the majority of the fighting had finished. Clearly, he did not intend to allow the person who guaranteed his meal ticket to expire. Jonathan found that he was thankful he wasn't on his friend's menu, really.

"It wasn't so much to save you as to save the fulni. I could not be responsible for such a becoming creature to embrace extinction for the second time," Sam drawled. As if the subject was closed, he returned to his book.

Jonathan sighed as he sat down. After Sam had returned from his rescue mission, some careful probing had revealed that apparently, Sam couldn't remember being knocked out. Of course, Jonathan valued his life too much to ask and was not going to bring it up again.

Still, as they sat together, reading their books in his living room, Jonathan couldn't help but feel there was more tension between the two of them than there had been before.

Sam looked up at him, catching his eye and startling him. "You don't mind, do you?"

"Mind what?"

"Shari... she was just excited, that's all."

Jonathan couldn't get a lock on what Sam was feeling, let alone thinking. He was locked down so tight he made Lissae's security look shabby. "I don't mind. I just don't want it to happen again," he answered truthfully.

Sam gave him a long, searching look. "Well, I don't mind if it does happen again." He seemed to be watching Jonathan's reaction a little too closely. Jonathan couldn't tell if Sam was stirring or just seeing how his outrageous comment was taken.

Deciding the best policy was not to say anything at all, Jonathan clenched his jaw and grunted. He was not going to get into an argument about something which wasn't going to happen. Ever again. Raising his book to signal the conversation had finished, he stared at it blankly for a time. When he sensed Sam's gaze had stopped boring holes in the book, he forced himself to concentrate on the page in front of him.

'Never shall some believe the sights I have seen, the deeds I have performed. Please, young ones, do not misunderstand an old, tired warrior's words. My life has not been filled with danger and intrigue as some may claim, but of tedious chores and annoying disturbances to clear up.

During my time as Altoriae, I have endured many attempts by various different entities – both Dark and Light – to infiltrate Lissae. So many attempts, too many to keep track of, but one stands out in my mind...

There's a race of extraordinarily dark creatures which inhabit the darkest of Realms. I hope you, dear one, never meet them. They are – and forgive me, I know your training goes against this, but – they are evil. They thrive in chaos. Sunlight hurts their most inner being. They feast on the souls of others, and as they devour these souls, they cause an unbelievable amount of pain, almost as if they are tearing chunks out of your flesh. How do I know this? They tried to consume Lissae. These creatures are called Q'Aralide.

There is an especially nasty one. He (well, I assume it's a 'he') is golden in colour. He is the priest who led the attack on Lissae. From what I have been able to ascertain, he is only part Q'Aralide – the other part I am not sure, except that it is humanoid, which is how he managed to get into our Realm...'

Jonathan froze and looked up from his reading. Had Sam been here before? He looked over and met his friend's glittering eyes, lit by the last, dying embers of the hearth fire.

"Discover anything interesting?" Sam asked, idly flicking through a book from the store.

Jonathan snapped the old Altoriae's diary shut. "No, nothing remotely interesting." He could not take his eyes off the... the man he thought he knew. "Nothing exciting at all," he muttered again.

"Well, I'm off to bed," Sam said, putting his borrowed book to one side.

Nodding, Jonathan said, "I've got a few more things to do," his gaze not leaving Sam's. Sam raised an eyebrow, but nodded and left the room.

After he'd left, Jonathan leant back in the chair, and hastily flicked through the diary until he had found the entry he had been reading.

'Nothing would surprise me as to the lengths this one would go to, to return to our fair Realm.'

Once again, Jonathan wondered if he had done the right thing. He had a nagging suspicion he would find out soon enough.

GLOSSARY

Active – A term used to describe when a person's Innarn manifested and they became aware of it.

Adeon – The God of the Element Fire and husband of Ke'ra.

Akoren – One of the sentient Shifting Islands on Lissae. Originally home to Lissae's Deities, now it is inhabited by a few, select representatives of the races that came from the other Shifting Islands.

Altoriae – Protector of the Realm of Lissae. Traditionally a female role, although there has been one male Altoriae. Previous Altoriaes have included Kay'imi, Muran Curtis and Jali Thorne, Fiona MacAde. Forces of nature cannot kill me. They must swear to uphold the seven duties of the Altoriae. They are: 1. Protecting the Realm; 2. Protecting Ronah and its residents; 3. Calling Ronah's residents to arms in times of need; 4. Teaching Ronah's residents; 5. Maintaining peace on Ronah; 6. Ensuring that Ronah's young remember their Elders pledges to the Altoriae; 7. Maintaining the Altoriae's Handbook for the use of future Altoriaes.

Ahana – A lone Innarnian Ahana archer is credited with the death of Kay'imi. The Ahana are from a Light Realm, but not much more is known about them.

Amaer – A Grey desert Realm. Dry, desolate and rocky, the landscape has been altered by the Kemmae.

Anriluka – A U'tan from Rataeo who is older than Lissae's calendar and the being Shari must stop if she is to prove that she is the Altoriae. She has almost devoured Ronah's entire population before Muran Curtis' Guardian banished her back to her home Realm.

Azmine's Ridge – A place on Mid Canak which is close the entry to Lissae.

Bereni trees – Trees that are grown to be used as buildings. The size and design of the tree can be controlled by an Innarnian or by one of the sentient Islands.

Blank – A person who can't use Innarn.

Boon – Something that is granted for a completed task or heroic deed.

Buta sprouts – A small, round root vegetable that tastes like ten-day old socks.

Canak–Maku – A Grey Realm that is home to the Minotaurs.

Cantash – One of the sentient Shifting Islands on Lissae. He is home to the Daen's.

Castle Bachelor – The centre point of Ronah and the traditional home of the Altoriae, the Guardian and their respective families. The base of it was made up by a huge volcanic crater, one that had ceased its activity on Kay'imi's command. This left incredible natural catacombs beneath the Castle that were mostly used for storage or the occasional prison cell. Merged with the top of the crater was a wall of plasma, with a doorknocker that boomed every time it was used. Windows of clear Air dotted the structure, and those inside could choose to darken or lighten them at will. A bereni tree grew at the heart of the castle, making not only a secure place for the Altoriae to train, but a solid structure should the outer walls fail. The branches and leaves of the tree made up the majority of the rest of the castle, except for the top, which sprouted turrets of flame, and the floor of the second floor, which was made of blue-green water.

Clans – Family lines.

Crystals – Hold energy which is turned into electricity. Often installed in clusters to gain more power and last longer. Different coloured Crystals do different things. White Crystals are used for communication. Black Crystals gather power and Orange Crystals connect currents to create fences. Crystal necklaces are given to young children and Blanks for them to manipulate the Crystals.

Camor – a large, quadrupedal species, with a hump on its back and short, thick legs. Camor flesh is prized in the Dark Realms, and is considered a delicacy in some of the Grey Realms. Thick skin protects its sides and back. Although it is said to make one of the saddest calls in all the Realms when dying, only certain races can hear the noise due to the pitch.

Coqi – A Dark Realm that makes your fears come true.

Crystal Video Screen – Or CVS, is similar to Earth's televisions.

Crystal See and Speak Communications – Or CS&SC, also called Crystal Send. Similar to Earth's video telephones.

Curses – Several curses are common on Lissae, including: Adeon's fire; By the Life of Lissae; Ke'ra's Flash; Zoemer's Rocks; Rasshnae's Floods; Vebnah's Breath; Na'reh's Ghosts. Other curses from the Realms include: ketarr; dathae; tu'zar; tongue of a Ne'fora; whales ass; basalt chewing hemmit loving buzzard; cestoray; slime vattar; hanotqe; slime filled cedore.

Guardian – The rank for the person who is in charge of training and caring for the Altoriae, and for Lissae. In cases of emergency, the Mayor and Elders defer to the Guardian.

Daen – A short, fierce and loyal race with amazing control over the Fire Element.

Da'mar – A humanoid race with lizard-like features who resides in the caves under Lissae. They lived by a warrior code that is difficult for other races to understand.

Deities – Lissae has six Deities who are said to have lived on the Shifting Island of Akoren. See: Adeon, Ke'ra, Na'reh, Rasshnae, Vebnah and Zoemer for more details.

Duties – Ronah's residents must swear to uphold five duties. The five duties are: 1. Protect the Altoriae at all costs; 2. Assist the Altoriae in any way she asks; 3. Answer an Altoriae's call without hesitation; 4. Ensure a safe place for the Altoriae to train; 5. Help to maintain peace amongst Ronah's residents to the best of your abilities.

Elders – Those who have, through age and experience, managed to survive the Realms long enough to guide their people. They also act as advisors to the Mayor.

Elements – Lissae has seven main elements that Innarnian can manipulate: earth, air, fire, water, plasma, spirit and technology.

Eminlith – Guardian to Kay'imi. She married the first Thorne, Timony, who arrived on Ronah. Eminilith's ruby pendant has been passed down the Thorne Clan for generations.

Eni – Malicious shape-shifters, able to permanently assume the form of influential figures to summon others of their kind to possess the subjects they have gained. Seriously Dark beings, the Eni are not often seen out of the Dark Realms. The Eni mentally 'piggyback' their prey before assuming their form.

Ferah – Humanoid beings with cat-like features, including fur, tail, whiskers and claws.

Fiona MacAde – The twelfth Altoriae. She took up the title in 3981 at ten years of age.

Frito – Small, bird-like animal with wings similar to a dragonfly. They live their lives in the air, only returning to the ground to lay their eggs or die.

Fulni – An animal similar to Earth's buffalo, but carnivorous and with two heads. The last fulni herd went extinct over two-hundred years ago. Their tails are attached to a major artery, and if the tail is removed, they will bleed out in seven seconds.

Ginorti – One of the sentient Shifting Islands on Lissae. He is home to the Satyrs.

Hanotqe – a short, squat being who's large skull holds a significant amount of fat, and very little brain.

Hantra – Earth spirits summoned by the Wisara. Unable to be controlled or stopped by the Shifting Islands as they were given bodies made out of the earth. They are slow moving and persistent, their only goal to do what the summoner has told them to. The only way to kill a Hantra is to remove both arms before decapitating it. Raising the Hantra is taboo on any of the Shifting Islands.

Hekkor Mafae – A book about Dark Ones that Jonathan is very uncomfortable in having on Lissae.

I bid thee well – A traditional phrase when two or more people separate ways.

Ilutri – Winged humanoids from Lissae. They are usually found on Rakemyst and are high level Innarnian. They include some of the finest archers on the Realm.

Immosa – The final resting place for the souls of Warriors who left Lissae.

Innarn – Predominately Elemental magic which is present in all Realms to varying strengths. Innarn is split into three main groups: Dark, Grey and Light. Each variant of Innarn has its own specialties. See Elements for more information. There are also other disciplines of Innarn, including Animal, Crystal, Mental, Realm and Time.

Innarnian – A person who can use Innarn.

Jali Thorne – The tenth Altoriae. She held the title for three years.

Karara – A Realm that contains a xarit that leads to Xaviour.

Kay'imi – The first Altoriae. She lived until she was 1217 years old when she was killed by a lone Ahana archer.

Ke'ra – God of the Element Plasma and husband of Adeon.

Kemmae – Originally from Bantaris, they are a race of malicious mischief-makers who delight in moulding the earth of the Realm they inhabit to make it inhospitable to others. They are crab-like in appearance, standing between two and four inches tall and between six and eight inches across; their pincers have a toxic coating which eats away at the flesh of humanoids.

Korvie – A humanoid race from the Dark Realms who primarily uses Water Innarn.

Lissae – A Grey, sentient Realm who is defended by the Altoriae. Comprised of six continents, seven sentient Shifting Islands and multiple fixed islands, she is home to ten races. She is said to be a Mother Realm. There are two moons in her orbit.

Lissaen – A person who lives on Lissae.

Lore teller – An oral storyteller who passes on information from previous generations. They are held in high regard by the general population and are thought to be unable to lie.

Mafay – Light Realm that is home to fire-breathing dragons.

Metsari – A small reptilian animal from Rataeo that spits poison to protect their territory. They also have a very eerie call, which sounds like a cross between a high-pitched whistle and a wolf howling. They usually live in packs of ten or more. There is a sacred area on Rataeo where the largest grouping of Metsari lives, called Planomest. The only way to avoid the Metsari is to not touch the ground. When they feel vibrations through their bodies, they spit poison. The only cure for their poison is to lick it off.

Mid Canak – A Grey Realm which is next to Lissae.

Minotaur – Bull-headed bipedal beings, minotaurs live on the Realm of Canak–Maku. Generally a peaceful race, unless they are away from home, and then they will fight to get back.

Muran Curtis – The sixth Altoriae and the only male to date. He was killed by Anriluka.

Na'reh – Goddess of the Element Spirit and wife of Vebnah.

Ne'fora – Generally considered amongst the most wise and venerable races of the Realms, the Ne'fora stick to telepathic communication, as the instant they open their mouths, unintelligible screaming comes out.

Neharn – A desert Grey Realm with two suns.

Neutral Realm – A Realm where Innarn is impossible.

Nine Hells – The name given to a particularly nasty set of nine Realms.

Palon – Native to Lissae, the palon is a small, six-legged creature descended from wolves. They have soft fur and long tongues, with a preferred diet of insects.

Patrol – Any Innarnian resident over fifteen is required to help the Guardian and the Altoriae patrol the Realms to watch for any possible threats.

Piggyback – Mentally piggybacking is something that telepathic Innarnians can do. It is a way of gathering information and listening to conversations. It can be stopped by strong mental shields.

Planomest – A sacred area on Rataeo that is used for rites and rituals. It has a labyrinth of tunnels and caves, and is home to a large group of Metsari.

Pteradiles – Reptilian birds with poisonous claws. A favoured snack of the U'tan.

Q'Aralide – A vicious Dark race who wielded spirit, earth, plasma and air Innarn. Approximately thirty feet tall, their social status depends more on their colour and abilities than anything else. Quite apart from their Innarnian, their breath is something to watch out for, as it can strip the flesh and the life from someone in just one exhale.

Rakemyst – One of the sentient Shifting Islands on Lissae. She is home to the Ilutri.

Rasshnae – Goddess of the Element Water and wife of Zoemer.

Rassu – People who claim to be Innarnian, but who use trap doors, sleight of hand and tricks to reproduce the effects of what a real Innarnian can do.

Rataeo – A virtually uninhabited Dark Ice Realm, with a time speed double Lissae's. It is home to the U'tan*. Most of the animals are relatively harmless, except for the Metsari* (*see entry for more details).

Realms – Planets which inhabit various parts of the multiverse on three main levels, Dark, Grey and Light. Although there can be many sub-levels and a mix of Dark and Grey, or Grey and Light within the same level. Dark Realms are places with little to no natural sunlight. Most lights in these Realms are made by Innarn. Grey Realms are places with a similar amount of light to Lissae and Earth's equator. Light realms are places where there is an abundance of natural light.

Rezem – A building built out of a mound of earth. The size and design of the mound can be controlled by an Innarnian or by one of the Sentient Islands.

Ridden Hall – The school on Ronah.

Ronah – One of the sentient Shifting Islands on Lissae. She is home to a variety of races and the traditional home of the Altoriae. Traditionally, Ronah selects a being to be her spokesperson. Ronah is one of the six gateways to the Realms. Ronah also has duties to the Altoriae, which are: 1. Ensuring a safe place for the Altoriae to live; 2. Ensuring a safe place for the Altoriae to train; 3. Maintaining peace amongst the residents to the best of her abilities; 4. Training the Altoriae if asked; 5. Guiding and guarding the Altoriae when no Guardian is available.

Rutenberry – The frosted dark-purple skin of the rutenberry hides the chocolate-like fruit inside. It can be eaten raw, although the skin can be bitter. Skinned, mashed and cooked, it can be added into cakes, biscuits and other sweets, including drinks.

Satyrs – A humanoid race with legs and tail similar to a horse from Lissae. They are usually found on Ginorti. They include some of the finest crack troops on the Realm.

Sedolic – Green, scaly dog-like animals with two large pincers at its front that are a favoured food of the U'tan.

Semaed – a dull, grey skinned, quadrupedal creature who has the ability to pass through narrow spaces, thanks to their thin frame.

Send/Sent – The word used for telepathic communication.

Sennet – A board game that originated with the Egyptian people of the Realm of Earth, and a favourite game of Elder Thorn of Ronah.

Sephina silk – Collected from silk worms that feast on the Darfionious Oak tree, which is only found in the Sephina Ranges. It is the warmest, softest, strongest fabric on Lissae, and there's just something about it that makes it immune to Fire and Water Innarn.

Shifting – The Innarn art of mental teleportation from one space to another.

Shifting Islands – The name for the group of Islands that travel around Lissae's seas, seemingly on a whim. They are sentient beings who care for the residents who make them their home. See Akoren, Cantash, Ginorti, Vannali, Rakemyst, Ronah and Talhan.

Shem'ar – Shem'ar are small dragon-like creatures, no bigger than a large dog and about as intelligent as canines. Kept most often as familiars, guard creatures, messengers and family pets, shem'ar have soft, furry hides that come in almost any colour. Although incapable of Innarn or talking, owners of the shem'ar could communicate telepathically with the creatures, some of whom understand more than others.

Solfruit – Palm-sized fruit with crisp blue skin and a creamy coloured, crunchy flesh. Native to the Shifting Islands of Lissae.

Soola – A green leafy vegetable that can be eaten raw or cooked with butter, salt and herbs. Its musty taste can be improved by adding salt and a sprinkle of Innarn.

Spirit Realm – A Realm that is found alongside Lissae, where the spirit or souls of the deceased go when their physical bodies are no longer needed.

Talhan – One of the sentient Shifting Islands on Lissae, and the only one to start with an all-human population. He now accepts immigrants from all races on Lissae.

Toulana – A green vine with thin leaves, and lots of tendrils which react to vibrations in the air and on the ground. Toulana is often planted to keep pests and birds away from the rest of the garden. The vine can distinguish between a positive presence and can become friendly.

Tu'zar - A cute, fluffy bipedal species, descended from apes, the Tu'zar generally inhabit the jungles of the Dark Realms. Their dark fur helps them to blend into the shadows. The most common marking is a 'mask' across their eyes.

U'sala – A group of beings from all over the Realms who have banded together to protect the Realms from creatures who wished to change them for their own benefit. Currently led by Jeran Metasta Voutar, and his second in command is Yessna. The numbers of the U'sala varied because of the high turnover rate.

U'tan – A race of extraordinarily powerful strategists who reside on Rataeo.

Uallmi – An insect whose noise can burst humanoid ear drums. They spit acid if anything other than their own kind gets too close to them.

They live in a cave on Xaviour. One of the ways to tell if the uallmi are close is yellow slime. The best way to get past the uallmi is to cover yourself in their slime and move the same way they do.

Vannali – One of the sentient Shifting Islands on Lissae. She is home to the Weavers.

Vebnah – Goddess of the Element Air and wife of Na'reh.

Vennph – A particularly Dark Realm that was home to the Wikkur and the Eni.

Veti Cant – Or Cant, is a sign language that uses hands and facial expressions to communicate. It is often helpful when overcoming language barriers. There are variations for beings with more limbs, but the essentials of the Cant remained the same.

Vitampit – Small insects who travel in large swarms and deliver irritating, poisonous bites. Once a target is identified through a hive-mind, the swarm will seek out the target, intent only on draining all of the blood from their victim.

Wards – Innarn shields designed to protect specific areas.

Weavers – A strong Innarnian race from Lissae. They reside on Vannali and usually keep to themselves. They are regarded as one of the oldest races and are often considered mythical beings as they rarely leave Vannali or allow visitors.

Wikkur – A race of tripedal Dark beings, both cunning and savage.

Wisara – Wisara are primarily ocean-dwelling beings whose bodies – although humanoid – look like the tangled roots of lotus flowers. Their 'hair' is the leaves of the lotus, and the flowers act as adornments. Wisara can change form to a more traditional humanoid shape and inhabit land areas in either form. They move around as gypsies and trade between the continents and Islands of Lissae by walking the ocean beds. They are the perfect oversea (or in this case, undersea) merchants, as storms have little to no effect on them. Custom dictates that the Wisara are offered fish and bread and other items to restock their larder by the towns they visit. As payment, the Wisara would tell the Tales of Lore. Only the Eldest of the Wisara is given the title of 'Lore Keeper', although anyone could tell one of the tales.

Xanter – A humanoid race from the Dark Realms which uses Fire Innarn.

Xarits – Special portals which enable travel to and from neighbouring Realms. There are only a handful of Realms that have xarits leading to them. Only one side of the xarit is a Realm where Innarn is possible, the other side is completely neutral.

Xaviour – A neutral Grey Realm where the preferred type of warning system is insects.

Yettara – A Dark Realm that resides in perpetual darkness and is one of the few Realms that have a black sky. Its time speed is five times slower than Lissae's. It is sentient and feeds off any creature from the Light or Grey Realms who come to visit. Only the strongest creatures from the lighter Realms can survive. Any magic from a creature of the Light or Grey Realms that is performed there will be unlikely to succeed in doing anything but draining the being further. The prolonged stay of creatures from the Light or Grey Realms on Yettara is guaranteed to end in death.

Zhahyeem – An expression meaning, 'be calm'.

Ziom – The hardest metal in the Realms, found on Lissae. Used for the creation of housing frames, precious jewellery and weapons.

Zoemer – God of the Element Earth and husband of Rasshnae.

ACKNOWLEDGEMENTS

This book is dedicated to my fabulous beta readers. Cyrus, who eagerly volunteered to read countless drafts and keeps coming back for more. Lisa, the most awesome plot-hole spotter ever, your encouragement means the world. Jodie Lane, who gave me fantastic advice and was so eager to read my book, which is such a thrill after reading her books – seriously, check them out! Romany, spelling/grammar nitpicker extraordinaire who found words I'd skipped over dozens of times. Kathy, who told me I could write and was the first adult to encourage my geeky side.

I can't forget Eanna Roberts, my wonderful editor from Penmanship Editing, who agreed to polish my words into something amazing, and was incredibly patient with me. Thank you to Desanka for picking up the stubborn typos. And to Vanesa Garkova who created the stunning cover.

Kudos must, of course, go out to my family. Jess, the only other person who read the first draft in full – If I could, I would give you a shem'ar for Christmas, but the book will have to do. Danny, for letting me run ideas past him all the time and debating on how things work – you've made Lissae a better place for all the time you've played Devil's Advocate. Corin, for the concept of the elements, and Savannah for helping me find the time to finish writing the book and being my biggest fan. My parents, for being wonderfully supportive of my dream. My mum, who found all of the mistakes everyone else had missed.

But the biggest thanks of all must go to you, the reader! Keep on reading and exploring new Realms between the pages of a book.

ABOUT THE AUTHOR

R. Lennard is the Australian author of the young adult fantasy series *Lissae*. She is an avid fantasy and sci-fi reader, and in her spare time, she works as a librarian. She enjoys learning about ancient civilisations, cosplaying and endless cups of tea. Residing on the beautiful Sunshine Coast in Queensland, Australia, Rebecca enjoys the natural beauty of both the beach and the bush, finding hidden writing spots as a makeshift office.

Having completed a Bachelor's in Librarianship and Corporate Information Studies, Rebecca found that she was longing to go back to writing fiction, and finally completed her first novel at the end of her degree.

After more to read? *The Eni Inside* is a short story prelude to the Lissae series included in the 3rd Australian Pen anthology, *The Evil Inside Us.*

The Headmaster of Ridden Hall, Lawrence Anderson, went out on patrol, but never returned. Instead, a being bent on taking over Lissae came back in his place.

Full of stories about dark secrets, you'll want to join the masses and buy your copy of *The Evil Inside Us* now!

Available at: www.lissae.com/short-stories

When evil walks, there must be a Guardian to save them all...

After his father was killed protecting the Realm, Jon Buan became just another street rat. Now, Jon must face the same menacing darkness as his father. Following the guidance of his strict mentor, Jon discovers his magic is stronger than he ever thought, but will he be strong enough to protect the whole Realm?

Will Jonathan survive the deadly Realms, or will he be forever changed?

If you like fierce heroes, pulse-pounding action, and unique magical worlds, then you'll love R. Lennard's page-turning introduction to the *Lissae* series.

Buy *Guardian* to bend the elements to your will today!

Available at: www.lissae.com/short-stories

Arrows fired. Broken wings. Will Shari survive when Lissae is invaded?

Shari Dawn, Altoriae of Lissae, has more questions than answers. She still hasn't discovered what sort of being crossed over, there's a mysterious race using arrows that can suck the Innarn right out of a being who are bent on taking over Rakemyst, and she has no idea why.

Add in Elders clamouring for a new Guardian's Apprentice, Returned struggling to cope, and Shifting Islands coming together for the first time in decades. Shari finds she is having difficulty adjusting to the events happening around her.

If you like fierce heroines, pulse-pounding action, and unique magical worlds, then you'll love *Rakemyst*.

Keep up to date with the *Lissae* series, and receive exclusive extras by signing up to the newsletter at: www.lissae.com/welcome

www.ingramcontent.com/pod-product-compliance
Lightning Source LLC
Chambersburg PA
CBHW030339120726
47901CB00007B/1846